Ghosts of Boyfriends Past

Carly Alexander

KENSINGTON PUBLISHING CORP.
http://www.kensingtonbooks.com

Acknowledgments

Many thanks to the people who helped with my research: to Judy Blundell for leading me up the hills of San Francisco, to Maureen Hartley for the insiders' guide to Britain, to Ailsa Winroth and her "Mum" for the grand Edinburgh tour, to Susan Noonan for the enlightening tours of the Walters Art Museum, to the retailers of New York City for those inspiring Christmas displays.

Special thanks to Julie Abbott, coffee guru and able reader, and to my editor, John Scognamiglio, for keeping me on track while letting me run wild.

Prologue

Rockefeller Center
December 8, 2003, 5 P.M.

Y ou can't beat New York City at Christmastime.
Passing through the smoke of chestnuts roasting on a vendor's cart, I dropped a dollar into the bucket of a street-corner Santa and continued down Forty-ninth Street.

The Santa tugged his beard. "Merry Christmas."

"Merry Christmas," I said, feeling a swell of holiday spirit. I loved Christmas, really, I did, but at the risk of sounding desperate, I was getting a little skittish at the thought of spending this one alone, sans boyfriend and marriageable prospect. At thirty-one you do not want to be without prospects. You want to be planning your wedding, registering at Tiffany's and Bloomingdale's, and picking out quaint houses in the suburbs with cozy dormered bedrooms ideal for nurseries. And somehow, Christmastime points all that up, making you feel like you have a drab, pathetic little life if you don't have a sweetheart to help you put up your tree.

I paused as the huge Rockefeller Plaza opened up before me—the line of silver flags flapping in the wind, the bright egg-sized lights on the tree, and the clusters of tourists posing for photos. How the hell would I find Sugar and Leo in this mess? Leo should have been the first one here since he worked right above Rockefeller Plaza, but he was probably peering out of an office window trying to think of a way to avoid this crowd scene.

I flipped open my cell phone, speed-dialed Sugar, and got her voice mail; she was probably in the dead zone of the subway. "I'm here," I said. "You were right, the Plaza is a zoo. Meet me at the bar in Morrell's." Feeling very Double-Oh-Sevenish, I tucked my tiny phone away and dodged the flashing camera focused on a group of women—about two dozen of them, all blond. I moved past them, wondering if the blond connection was just accidental or if it was some sort of club. Blondes from Billings? You never know.

Rockefeller Center is always crowded, with tourists mugging for the morning shows that are broadcast from studios inside the street-level windows, but this time of year, the place is really hopping. People come from near and far to pay homage to the mecca of Christmastime, the giant tree. Fifth Avenue gets more clogged than ever with out-of-towners in limos and SUVs doing drive-bys, and the Plaza itself teems with pedestrians, like ants swarming a cake crumb. On weekends, you have to bob and weave and push past puffy coats to get near the tree.

But it's worth it. Come December, New Yorkers grow a little nicer. Not that they're giving it away, but I have seen doors held open at Bloomie's on more than one occasion. And once, in the theater district, just as the shows let out, some guy let me have his cab. I swear to God. And it was starting to rain, too. A cab in the rain is worth its weight in gold. It's truly the miracle of Christmas. Everyone gets a little warm and fuzzy, and I admit I'm the first one to get misty eyed. Or maybe it's because I can mark each Christmas by the guy I was seeing that year.

Passing by the window of Teuscher Chocolates, I paused to let my eyes feast on the display in the window: a pyramid of tiny boxes, each one wrapped with foiled ribbon and festooned with red bells, tiny pinecones painted gold, or Christmas angels with ethereal blue wings. Love those little boxes! For my money, Godiva is the best chocolate, but these boxes are so damned cute!

Sean used to buy them for me. One year he sent me a different box for each of the twelve days of Christmas. I pinned them up in my cubby at the museum, which made the other girls in the office insanely jealous. "Your boyfriend is so romantic!" Nicole used to sigh. Of course, I didn't tell the chicks that despite his fabulous taste in gifts, Sean was a little on the cold side. Distracted. Workaholic.

When I broke up with him, he barely blinked. I wanted to think that he was covering his emotions, but maybe there was nothing to cover. You know that saying: "Lights on upstairs but nobody home"? I'm afraid that was Sean Keenan. Bright and handsome on the outside, dim and emotionally blank within. At the time, I thought he was exactly what I wanted. I mean, when a guy isn't emotionally blank, he's loaded with baggage or angst or strong opinions, and let's face it, all of those things are way too hard to live with. But Sean outlived his usefulness last January when we went skiing together in Vermont and I decided to end our trip early because of total boredom. I couldn't face one more snuggle by the lodge fireplace with Mr. Emotional Vacancy. Big yawn.

Besides, the mountains drive me crazy after a while. Way too rural. Nope, give me this blessed, smelly city any day. And speaking of smelly, I was standing on the corner at Forty-ninth, waiting to cross over to Morrell's, and the grate of a sewer was dangerously close. Wincing, I started to step away. It wouldn't do to lose one of the metallic heels of my strappy new Chanels in a city sewer. As I moved, the grate seemed to move, too. I gasped as a fat rodent poked his head up, ready to emerge.

Right there on the crowded sidewalk of Rockefeller Center at Christmas!

Do city rats have balls, or what? I stumbled back quickly, shuffling my feet to scare him off. Why is it that, in a city full of people, when you encounter a rodent you feel so utterly alone? No one else noticed as the rat's whiskered nose twitched in annoyance, as if I'd disturbed him.

"Get in there!" I ordered, stamping my Chanels. A man turned to study me cautiously, obviously wondering if I'd just escaped from Bellevue.

"There's a rat!" I said, pointing.

The man looked at the grate, then shrugged as the vermin crawled back inside. I guess he considered rats unremarkable, but that did it for me. Deciding not to wait for the light, I crossed between cars and ducked into the candlelit opulence of my favorite wine bar.

I pushed past the heavy velvet drape, my mouth watering for a buttery glass of chardonnay. Damn, it was crowded in here, too. No seats at the bar, and people were two bodies thick. I moved as elegantly as possible toward the back, hoping to claim a little pocket of space. There was a slight break in the area by the phone, and as I cozied up to a wall and unbuttoned my coat, I tried to decide which wine to begin with.

That's when I noticed him—Mr. Middle-age, and I say that with the knowledge that statisticians claim that middle age begins at forty-five. At thirty-one, I figure I still have a few good years before total panic sets in. Anyway, Mr. Middle-age caught me in his sights and tried to woo me with his reptilian manner. The not-so-subtle lift of the eyebrow, the cagey smile. His smarmy expression reminded me of the rodent I'd met on the other side of the street. Was he wearing a rug or had he simply oversprayed? I didn't want to look too long to find out, since looking at him would only encourage him. Don't get me wrong, I like men, really I do, but I was in no mood to fend off Austin Powers III.

Damn, I would have to leave. I pretended not to see his big smile as I buttoned up and pushed toward the door, all the while wondering who in the bar had allowed admittance to this lounge lizard. Morrell's had always been a safe haven, one of those places that you could walk into alone and not feel like a piece of meat. I made a mental note to call my friend Lisa, who waitresses there, as I stepped out into the cold air and wondered about an alternate meeting place.

"Madison!"

Leo walked toward me with his usual sullen expression. Not that he doesn't wear it well. Tall and thin, with a perfectly shaped shaved head and green eyes that always seem to be focused off in the distance, Leo wears his discontent like fashionable ennui.

Sugar bobbed along beside him, her dark hair sculpted in wisps around her chocolate face. With that hairdo, she resembled a Christmas elf, albeit a rather tall one. Sugar had legs up to her neck, one of those coltish shapes that seemed to be improving now that she'd hit her thirties.

"I'm freaking out here!" Sugar exclaimed. "Did you see who just walked by in that fabulous patchwork duster? It was Steve Tyler!"

"No, it wasn't," Leo said through clenched teeth. "That was Steven Cojocaru, fashion guru. He does spots on the *Today* show, and their studio is just across the street."

"Steven Cojocaru? I love his red-carpet reviews," I said.

Sugar pressed her hands to her cheeks. "Shit! I am so bad at star-spotting! One of these days I'm going to totally flub it on a show." Sugar was a radio deejay on a very hot show— *Mornings with Cream and Sugar*—and while she possessed a knack for yack, she often mismatched names and faces. "I'll call Matt Damon, Matthew Perry, or Matt Lauer, or something."

"And who can keep those Olsen twins straight?" Leo said. "Ashley . . . Mary-Kate . . . I think they switch off just to confuse us."

Sugar reached toward the wine bar with one arm and clasped her neck with the other. "I'm parched. I figured you'd be deep into a cocktail by now."

"It's crowded," I said. "And the clientele isn't very promising tonight. Too many rugs and tanning-booth victims."

Laughing, Sugar peered in the window. "Phooey! I was so in the mood."

"This is insane," Leo said. "I can't believe you talked me into coming out here when I can see this whole mess from my office. Well, from my boss's office. But really, all these people converged on this concrete square of land to eyeball an electrified dead tree."

"You're a big, fat liar and you know it," Sugar said, rolling her eyes. "You're just as excited about this as any old fella here." Sugar is from the South, and though she's been in New York for more than ten years, she loves to lapse into Southern belle mode. "Why, I swear," she went on, "I see a blush of color on your cheeks!"

"From the cold." Leo took a fleece hat out of his pocket and tugged it on. "I'm freezing my chimichangas off here. If we're not going into Morrell's, let's go ice skating."

"You're cold and you want to hit the ice?" Sugar questioned him. "What's that about?"

"I look down from the office every day and see the rink. It seems like such a fun thing to do, but I never can bring myself past the onslaught of tourists."

"I wouldn't mind skating," I said as we made our way toward the skating rink. "It's been a long time since I was skating here. Three or four years ago, with Henry."

Henry—that was a relationship that didn't end well. He'd wanted to get married and be settled, while I'd wanted him to visit an Ear, Nose and Throat specialist and figure out how to stop that snoring. I lost so much sleep while I was with Henry, and it wasn't because we were having sex all night.

"Whatever happened to Hank?" Sugar asked.

"Last I heard he was married and living in Brooklyn, attending Baby Gymboree classes with his infant daughter," I said. "I guess he found a woman who could sleep through the rumbling tides of his snoring."

"Maybe he found a woman who also snores," Sugar said. "Duets."

I nodded. "Sounds like a new musical. See *Duets—A Love Snore* at the Vivian Beaumont Theater!"

"Jealous?" Leo asked. "You, too, could be living in the outer boroughs with a husband and baby."

"It's not exactly jealousy," I said. "More like regret."

"Get out!" Sugar nudged my arm. "You're too young to have regrets."

"I just . . ." I hesitated, not wanting to get into it.

"Oh, you can't stop now," Leo prodded. "You can't just dangle the bait and reel it in."

"Really," Sugar insisted. "Throw us some chum, honey!" Spoken as the true Southern girl who used to go shrimping on her daddy's boat.

"Chum . . . now there's a savory image," I said, wondering if that man in the leather jacket was Rick Granger, my adorable cameraman. "Oh, wow, is that Rick?" I grabbed Leo's coat sleeve. "He used to work for NBC right here at Rock Center. Do you think?"

The leather jacket turned, revealing a sloping face with a rather large nose. Not Rick.

"Have you gone mad, girl?" Leo said.

"Maybe," I admitted. "See, that's the problem. Lately I've been haunted by my old boyfriends. Every time I turn around, some Christmas memory pops into my head. Skating with Henry. Shopping at Bendel's with Philippe. Desserts with Logan at Serendipity . . ."

"How do you remember all those men?" Sugar asked. "I mean, I'd remember an old flame if I ran into him. At least, I hope I would. But I don't revisit the relationship every time I pass a street corner where we kissed."

"Really," Leo chimed in. "Do you have a directory of dates, Madison? A list on your computer?"

"I can't help it." I grabbed the lapels of Leo's coat and launched into a fit of drama. "These men are haunting me, I tell you! I'm being visited by ghosts of boyfriends past!"

"Easy, Ebeneeza," Leo said, eyeing me suspiciously. "Is this just another ploy to get us to watch your old tapes of *A Christmas Carol* and *It's a Wonderful Life*?"

"Actually, I have them both on DVD now," I said. "But don't try to sidetrack. It's creepy. Thirty-one years of dating, and what do I have to show for it?"

"Let's hope you had some fun doing it," Sugar said.

"Wait." Leo frowned at me. "You were dating since birth?"

I shrugged. "I was an early starter."

"We're missing the point here, people," Sugar insisted. "Dating isn't about putting in time or getting practice. It's about having fun with another person. You know—being in the moment?"

"But now, when I try to be in the moment, I realize that I'm alone. I've spent my whole life worrying about making each Christmas special, with someone special, and for what? So that they can all come back to haunt me? Because this year, since I don't have anyone for the first December in a long, long time, I have to admit, I'm quaking in my boots. Christmas alone." I crossed my arms, shivering.

"You don't have to be alone. You've got us, honey lamb!" Sugar reached over to give me a hug. "Tell her, Leo."

"Yes, of course." Leo patted my shoulder. "Your dysfunctional urban family will always be here for you, supporting you in our bass-ackward way. Doesn't Sugar continually fix you up with guys? I'm sure she can bring you a date for your tree-trimming party. And doesn't Jenna give us all psychotherapy for free? Am I not going to sneak away from work to help you deliver all those toys so that you can keep your job?"

The toys—I'd almost forgotten. "That reminds me. I need you tomorrow. We've got to pick up, like, a thousand bears from FAO Schwarz and deliver them to Roosevelt Hospital."

Leo had agreed to help me deliver toys for a charity drive I'd organized at work. It was one of those things that had sounded good when I'd started it, but somehow it had blossomed into a Christmas nightmare.

Sugar eyed Leo. "She sucked you into that?"

"She caught me in a moment of weakness." He glanced down at the rink. "Are we going to skate or what? I skipped the gym this morning and I could use the exercise, but . . ." His eyes narrowed. "You're not hearing a word I'm saying, are you?"

I looked at him over Sugar's shoulder. "It's just that I'm a little busy feeling sorry for myself here."

"Well, while you two finish the pity party, I'm going down to check out the price of skate rentals," Leo said, disappearing down the stairs.

I pulled away from Sugar and pressed my leather-gloved hands to my face, trying to pull myself together. "Am I a big baby, or what?"

"No! Not at all," Sugar insisted. "We just did a segment on the show about how so many people take an emotional dip during the holidays." As a morning deejay, Sugar has learned an abundance of self-help psychology. "Expectations are high," she went on, "and all the advertising and books and movies make us feel like we should all be having happy, candy-coated Christmases, though in reality we all encounter our fair share of holiday hurdles."

"It's not just Christmas," I admitted. "It's where I am in life. Over thirty. Unmarried. Not even dating. My ovaries are going to dry up like prunes if I don't do something soon."

"Maddy, please, one problem at a time. Much as I love you, I am so not into talking about ovaries."

"I can't help it." I tightened the plaid Pendleton scarf around my neck. "It bothers me."

Sugar linked her arm through mine. "We have fun, don't we? Really, sweetums, being single can be a hoot sometimes."

I nodded in spite of myself.

"You know, my mama used to tell me this: When the elephants are stampeding, ignore the monkeys throwing coconuts."

"And that's supposed to make me feel better?" I squeaked. Sometimes Sugar spoke in Southern hieroglyphs.

Sugar smiled, her perfectly capped teeth gleaming against her gorgeous brown skin. "Honey, you are obsessing on the monkeys."

"You think I'm being silly." Down on the ice, Leo was already skating, surprisingly well. He bent low and swung his arms like a speed skater. "I mean, lots of people have worse problems than being without a guy for Christmas."

Sugar nodded. "Mmm. I have to say, much as I love a good man, I never quite saw them as Christmas ornaments. But it's about more than that. You're upset because you want a lasting relationship—God knows why."

"Do you think so?" I had my doubts. When I examined the relationships I'd had over the last few Christmases, there wasn't much substance under the trappings. "Oh, God." I pressed a warm hand to one frozen cheek. "Am I a Christmas slut?"

Sugar folded her arms. "You know I never use that 'S' word. There're too many people walking around without a clue about how sex is supposed to be an integral part of our lives. Did you know that sexual activity is quite good for the cardiovascular system?"

I frowned at the sexual image . . . another Sugar tactic. When losing an argument, she changed the topic. But to be fair to myself, relationships weren't all about sex for me, and I didn't always have a boyfriend at Christmastime. There were those horrible years in college when I'd suffered a terrible dry spell. I'd leaped from San Francisco society to the cool underground at Columbia University, and for some reason New York boys didn't know what to make of me.

I was a dateless wonder that first year after graduation

when I headed home to San Francisco. Lucky for me, the Christmas elves worked their magic and changed my fortunes.

Looking down on the skating rink, I was reminded of the ornament Leo had given me as a gift that year. It was a tiny snow globe of Rockefeller Center, the rectangular buildings surrounding the skating rink and the majestic tree, similar to the scene before me.

That was the Christmas when Leo and I had bonded. Yes, that was a fabulous Christmas.

Part One

I'll Be Home for Christmas

San Francisco, 1993

1

As our plane touched down in San Francisco, I nudged my bud Leo. He was tuned into his Walkman, tuned out from the roar of the reverse thrust engines, probably trying to escape the fact that he was headed off for a family vacation with his straight friend.

I leaned closer and pulled one earphone away from his ear to see what he was listening to. The low groan of the singer from Crash Test Dummies told me it was the "Mmm Song."

"Cut it out, nosey," Leo said, slapping my hand away.

"You know, before we get back we have to make a decision on the roommate thing."

"I've already decided," Leo said. "We'll run an ad while we're gone and start interviewing when you get back in January."

"Has anyone ever told you that you're a control freak?"

"No. Never. Shut up and restore your tray table to its upright position."

"But what about Sugar?" I said. "I thought we were going to talk about how she might fit in." Sugar was one of my best friends, and it just so happened that she needed a place while

Leo and I were looking to fill the third bedroom of our new apartment.

"Ebony's answer to Scarlett O'Hara?" Leo frowned. "Not sure I can stand all that Southern charm dripping over the kitchen counter."

"Sugar is my friend."

"That's your right, but I don't have to live with her."

We'll see about that, I thought, letting the subject drop. One thing about Leo, you don't want him to dig his heels in on something. He can be so stubborn. I'd have to give him time, and it wouldn't hurt to soften his resolve with a little of the traditional Greenwood Christmas cheer. "This is going to be a blast," I said. "My mom really knows how to do Christmas."

"Stop, you're scaring me." He adjusted the earphones and closed his eyes. "Not to burst your bubble, Madison, but has anyone ever told you there is no Santa Claus? No elves to fill your stocking? And since we'll be in San Francisco, there will be no snow for Christmas, thank God."

"Do you get off on being a deconstructionalist?" I asked him, wowing him with what I'd learned in Philosophy 201, one of the few things I'd learned in that class. I wasn't the best student Columbia had ever enrolled, and now I could thank my lucky stars that school days were behind me.

"Bah humbug."

"Go on, be a Scrooge," I said. "Mom and I will win you over."

"Just don't ask me to do midnight mass," he said. "And promise me you won't even put me in the same room with that wretched fruitcake."

I wasn't sure if the fruitcake referred to my mother, the Christmas Freak, or the actual candied cake, but either way, I wasn't going to push him. I had worked hard to get Leo here, and I figured it was best to just let him settle in and enjoy. He'd spent the last month mooning over his old boyfriend, Jordan, who had stuck with Leo through college only to leave him on graduation day for an older man with a fabulous job and a big apartment on Riverside Drive. That's the thing about men; they're always quick to trade you in for a flashier model, and that's something a woman does so rarely. A girl hangs on to her guy through thick and thin, defending him when his boss disses him and when his buds argue with him and when his mother keeps buying him those tight Fruit-of-the-Loom grundies he used to wear in junior high. Damn it, we go to the mat for our men, and for what? So that they can use us as a stepping stone to the next gorgeous woman? Don't get me started!

Okay, maybe I was in a semi-rant because I'd been suffering a dry spell. Ever since I'd started at Columbia my luck with men had gone bad. I kept telling myself it was New York guys, with their dark hair and dry humor and self-absorption, bumping past you on the street without an apology and flipping open their *New York Times* in a restaurant without caring who they offended. Rude boys. Back in California I'd encountered guys who were lacking in the manners department, but none who offended with such a brazen sense of entitlement.

Maybe that's why I fell for Hugh Paddington. Yes, *the* Hugh Paddington, legendary poet and Editor-at-Large for *Skyscraper* magazine. I've been working there as an assistant editor since I finished my course work, and although it is probably the coolest magazine to ever hit the east coast, my job is distinctly uncool. Photocopying, answering phones, redirecting calls to our subscription service. Occasionally an editor will throw me a bone and give me some fact checking. Big whoop.

It's a totally stupid job, and the biggest irony of all is that it's considered to be a plum position for journalism students. I mean, you need an Ivy League degree or a reference from a big shot (both of which I had) to get this job. And for what? For Drucie-the-giant from production to tell you that you're a slow reader and you missed a syntax error?

But don't get me started on the hierarchy of suppression in publishing. Even though I'd majored in humanities, it was totally the wrong job for me. I mean, I didn't even graduate with my class because I couldn't finish writing the goddamned senior thesis, that fierce, festering editorial canker that oozed new errors and became riddled with warty queries every time I handed it in to my advisor. But don't get me started on the sore spot of my overdue thesis, which I'd finally turned in two weeks ago. Writing that thing nearly killed me, and yet somehow I was working for a magazine, being groomed for a position as an editor/writer. How could I have landed in such an ill-suited position?

Parents. Robin and Dr. G. were going to make sure their little darling lapped up all their juicy connections. Thousands of miles away, and still they meddled. Thank God for my friends. Like Leo.

Anyway, I'd spent the past month bugging Leo about coming home with me. "You can't be alone for Christmas!" I had insisted over and over again. "That would be so wrong! Come back to San Francisco with me. My parents have a huge house we can knock around in, and it's a fabulous city."

He just kept making noises about how he couldn't imagine Christmas without Jordan, and how he couldn't face his bossy dysfunctional mother, and how the turkey special at the diner would be just fine. Pulllease! I wasn't about to let him play the martyr. I finally got Leo to commit at my company Christmas party. Leo was my escort that night since I needed a date so that I didn't look incredibly hopeless, and I needed a date to ward off Hugh, who was still making noises about getting together even though I kept assuring him that we had no chemistry.

The party was held at Top of the Sixes, a posh bar at 666 Fifth Avenue, and Christmas spirit was flowing nearly as fast as the champagne, courtesy of *Skyscraper* magazine, my employer. It was the only way I could currently afford coldies at a place like this, being twenty-one, working for slave wages, and in the process of finishing my senior thesis. Did I mention how relieved I was to be through with school?

Anyway, Leo and I stood by the windows, having a Nick and Nora moment as we gazed out at the handsome buildings that filled the majestic grid, finally giving way to the trees and browning grass of Central Park. Leo looked totally suave in his dark jacket and red silk tie. I knew the other girls from the office were salivating over him, if they weren't picking up on the undercurrent of gayness. Leo is tall and lean, with thoughtful green eyes that make you want to swell up and spill your life story to him.

"Have you decided what you're doing for the holidays?" I asked him.

"I will carefully avoid all familial events, and certainly drink heavily."

"I think you should go with me," I prodded.

"I think you should have another martini, darling."

"I'm having a whiskey sour," I said.

"A beginner's drink," he said. "Leave out the lemonade, take two aspirin, and call me in the morning."

"Don't try to change the subject. I'm not backing off, Leo. Not until you promise to spend Christmas with my parents and me."

"I don't do parents well," Leo said. "They always have issues. They either want to undo my body piercings or marry me off to their daughters."

"My parents aren't like that," I insisted, hoping it was true. Well, I knew that my mother wasn't that way, and my father, a surgeon, always spent so much time at the hospital that he wouldn't be a factor. "Oh, come with me, Leo. We'll have a blast! We'll bake cookies and have lots of coldies in cool West Coast bars. You can't spend the holidays moping about Jordan."

"I'm not moping," he insisted sternly. "I'm having the time of my life, darling."

I noticed the way his brow creased, which always happened when he was lying. We'd been together all through college, and we knew each other well. He was my best friend, especially since we didn't have to deal with issues of sex or competition. "Just say yes," I prodded.

"You just don't get it, Dr. Ruth. I want to be alone, to wallow in self-pity, to rent videos of pathetic old movies. Cry in my microwave popcorn. This is my Christmas of mourning."

"Oh, pulllease. Jordan isn't dead. He's probably peering through opera glasses in a box at the Met with his big daddy, even as we speak."

Leo winced. "You are ruthless."

I nodded. "Totally ruthless. I have to confirm my flight reservations tomorrow, and you know what? I'm going to book you a seat."

He smiled at me. "You are not."

"Dare me?"

He lifted the little sword of olives out of his glass. "Like that would stop you."

"Good. Consider it done, then." I lifted my whiskey sour in a toast. "Here's to a great Christmas in San Fran."

"I hate you," he said, toasting me back.

"You so do not!" I said joyously, realizing that people were admiring us—and why not? We really were a striking couple, silhouetted by the glass windows and darkening sky. And who was watching? The girls from copywriting? The gang from layout? My boss, Ms. Macy Gramble, the beautiful bottle-blonde pasted together by Valium and bountiful compliments of gentleman callers?

Or Hugh. Where was he, anyway? I shot a glance over at the bar and located him in a cloud of people. Hugh could be a total pip at a party. He was the quintessential storyteller, and he knew tons of celebrities and prestigious writers. That was the good Hugh, the Hugh I would have loved to be with tonight, posing as his arm candy.

Yes, I wasn't beyond selling myself short to be in his entourage. When you're with Hugh, celebrities come up to you and talk to you as if you really matter. And then you become a celebrity by association.

Hell's bells, I even thought I was going to get a promotion out of him. I mean, he sort of alluded to it. "You have much to learn if you want to get ahead in this business," he used to say. Other times, he would look at me and sigh. "I see I have my work cut out with you, Madison. Youth is a gift wasted on the young." I know it sounds schoolmarmish, but Hugh has a way of delivering lines like a Shakespearean actor. Witty, funny, self-deprecating . . . Hugh Paddington is the man you want to be with.

Until the lights are out.

That's when I was reminded, in most graphic details, that I was dating a man who is, like, forty years older than I am. I mean, I'm twenty-one and he's like . . . I don't even know, but his body sags in places you can't even imagine, and despite all his whimsical talk and charisma, he has zero magic under the sheets.

"I can tell you're thinking about him," Leo said. "Is he here? Where? Tell me."

I raised my head and cocked an eyebrow at the bar, trying to appear regal. "He's at the bar with his posse."

Leo gracefully sipped his martini as he eyed the party crowd. "Tweedy blazer and bow tie? You know, he could be my type."

"No, no, the one in the dark suit. Dark suit, silver hair."

"Très petit." Leo seemed perplexed. "How could such a little man cause you such major concern?"

"Just promise me you won't let me out of your sight tonight," I said. "No matter how many coldies I consume."

"Sure thing. Which reminds me, we need a refill." He took my glass, still staring toward the bar. "But refresh my memory, how bad was the sex? I mean, you'd think that with that much life experience, the guy should know a few tricks."

"The sex was lacking," I said, trying to sum up without

having to revisit the whole, ugly affair. "He . . . I don't know if the sex was really the problem. He's so damned persuasive, he had a way of making me go for it. Plus he helped me with a pitch. He backed me up in front of everyone in the editorial meeting."

"And you thought a round of nookie would pay him back for his editorial services?"

"I hate you," I told Leo. "And him. Why am I looking at him?" I turned away from the bar.

Leo lifted his drink, assessing Hugh over my shoulder. "He's not so bad."

I lowered my voice. "But his body is so old. Once you've seen a flabby ass puddling like vanilla pudding on your office desk, you're happy to do a few extra minutes on the Stairmaster."

"Okay, then, why don't I get those drinks." He headed toward the bar, turning back to me to murmur, "That's enough to put me off pudding for a long time."

Leo's exit left me thinking of the one person I was trying to banish from my mind. I'm still trying to forget that first night, when he took me out to dinner and invited me in for coffee at his apartment. He had poured two glasses of brandy, which I hate, and told me to follow him as he led the way into the bedroom. Hugh isn't a bad kisser, and before I could say "Oh, you old perv!" my shirt was unbuttoned and I'd tugged off my camisole. "You're so beautiful," he told me as he ran a hand over my bare shoulder and down, down over my breasts. He stroked my chest and tummy, which wasn't an uncomfortable sensation, but then he plucked at my nipples, causing me to let out a yelp.

"What the hell are you doing?" I said.

"We're going to make love," he said into my cheek, and I could smell the brandy on his breath. I wanted to tell him that, yes, I knew we were going to have sex. What was I, an idiot? I mean, two people half-naked in a bed . . . You do the math. But that nipple tweaking just about iced me over.

"I'm not into S and M," I said.

"Such a clever girl," he said, kissing my neck. "Too bright for your own good. Don't you see that I'm trying to turn you on?"

And it was almost working. I felt a little tug of desire as his fingers slid down between my legs. The man seemed to know his way around a vagina, at least. He slid his hand in my panties and drummed a little beat down there. I know it sounds weird, but it was sort of ticklish and exciting at the same time.

Yes, it was working. I could feel myself warming to him. I pressed myself into his hand, wanting more. How long had it been since I'd had sex? This was only the second time in New York, and . . . Oh, damn! He pulled his hand away.

"Hey, I was liking that," I said.

But he was already positioning himself on top of me, trying to fit his thing in with all the finesse of a carpenter lining up a bolt.

And then he was pumping away, in and out, breathing heavy, making me wonder if his heart was going to burst. Which was never a worry while I was going at it with any other boyfriend.

That was when I knew it was over, before it had ever really started. As Hugh nailed me in his musty bed, I stared at the ceiling and found myself wondering when he'd had it painted last. Which is not a good thing to be doing when you're supposed to be rising to the big O.

After that, I somehow repeated my mistake a handful of times, which is typical of me since I'm always looking on the bright side and telling myself things weren't as bad as they seemed (and usually I am *so* wrong). Besides, I didn't know how to turn down someone so overwhelmingly engaging. So I went to dinner with him again, and we ended up back at his place with me hoping that the sex would go better the second time. (Again, *so* wrong!)

So even though I knew there was no future for us, I kept

getting sucked in when Hugh would support my pitch in an editorial meeting, or take me along on a power lunch with a famous author, or offer to read my thesis. For a while we settled into this sort of business relationship in which I'd be his cute office pal and he'd be my mentor, which was fine with me, until sex came into play. Once, while I was in his office going over some queries, he closed his door and slipped off his shoes and told me he couldn't live without me. Can you believe it? This guy was a charmer, I'll give him that.

"You're kidding," I told him.

"My dear, you are the essence of springtime in the autumn of my life," he said.

"Really?" I smiled nervously. I was flattered, even though I knew it was a crock. But I didn't have the nerve to call Hugh on his embellishment—I never did. The student does not question the master.

That afternoon in the office, I have to admit, I wanted to do it with him. The danger of someone coming in was sort of a turn-on for me, and as I lifted my skirt and pulled my panties aside, I wondered again if a relationship between Hugh and me could work out. I mean, I wanted to be one of the planets in Hugh's orbit. Ever since the day he first defended my pitch in an editorial meeting, everyone had looked at me with a little more respect, a little bit of awe. Besides, men never really bothered much with me in my years at Columbia, and now, here I was, Hugh's girl, the rising young ingenue at *Skyscraper*.

I wanted to be wanted by someone important. I wanted to ride on the wave of his vast reputation.

But I also wanted a guy who could heat me up and make me shriek with delight, and on that level Hugh could not deliver. Christ, you'd think that after such a long dry spell I'd be happy to have any guy touching me. But Hugh was fast and methodical with his sexual ministrations, and no amount of skill was going to gloss over the fact that his body repulsed me. Yes, my dreams of being Hugh's girl faded that afternoon as I watched him tuck his wrinkly, pink thing into his pants.

Okay, so I let it happen once more one night at the office when I was working late fact checking a story, and Hugh sauntered in with a glass of sherry for me. I sipped the sherry but gave him a shrug when he said something about us working late together. I didn't meet his eyes, but I didn't stop him when he ran his hand up under my skirt and dipped into the waistband of my tights.

That one I really regretted, mostly because I do not usually have sex with someone if there's no potential for a relationship. With me, as with most girls, so much of the euphoria of a relationship is wrapped up in the emotional appeal of a person. It's about wanting to connect with the guy, wanting a deeper, more intimate connection than a kiss.

I knew it wasn't there for Hugh and me. Why didn't I stop him?

The next day, when copy about date rape landed on my desk, I spent a good half hour feeling sorry for myself. I hadn't wanted it, and he'd pressured me, and I just felt lousy about it. But by the time I'd marked up the copy, I'd made a few resolutions: I was not going to use sex to get a promotion at work, and I was not going to sleep with Hugh Paddington again.

Which may be a long way to go to explain why it was so important that Leo accompany me to that party and protect me from the lascivious Hugh, who, by the way, breezed past us and said a bright, genuine hello, then headed off with Sebastian Lavor, the magazine's publisher. And all the time my heart was beating like a rabbit because I wanted to be noticed by Hugh but I didn't want to be snagged by him, which doesn't really make any sense at all when you think about it.

In any case, it was at that party that Leo agreed to join me for Christmas, and now, looking over at Leo, I suffered a pang of anxiety, worrying that he would be disappointed. I mean, I always loved San Francisco at Christmastime, but what if my enthusiasm didn't rub off on my skeptical friend?

The flight attendant was making the perfunctory announcements about staying in your seat, blah-blah-blah, but people were already up and rooting through the overhead compartments. Leo handed me my leather jacket and carry-on bag, which I slung over my shoulder.

"This is going to be the best Christmas ever," I told him.

With a deadpan expression, he said: " 'God bless us, every one.' "

2

"I'm glad you two are here in time to help me decorate the tree," my mother said. "I've baked the cookies but held off so you can help me with the icing, which is so time-intensive. And before I forget, I've signed you up for tonight's lamplight tour of Pacific Heights." Did I mention that my mother is a Christmas freak?

"Sounds good." I couldn't help but smile as I snuggled into the backseat. Home for Christmas. What's not to like?

Leo reached up to ping the jingle bells hanging from the rearview mirror of Mom's BMW, but ended up slapping the dashboard as Mom swung wide on the freeway. Leo had seemed pleased when I'd given up the front seat, but I'm no fool. Nineteen years of watching my mother's car eat up asphalt had cured me of wanting a front-row seat.

"You'll never guess who I ran into at the symphony last week," Mom said, flashing a look at me in the rearview mirror.

"Uh . . . no, who?"

"Just Mr. Brophy from the high school. He's still the principal, and he wants you to come to the school to speak to the students about publishing."

"Mom, I'm just an assistant editor."

"At one of the hottest magazines on the East Coast!" Mom said, beaming with pride. "I told him you would squeeze it in before you head back in January. You are staying on for awhile, aren't you?"

"Sure," I said. "Leo needs to head back after Christmas, but I'll be here." The *Skycraper* offices were closed until the second week of January, and I was taking some vacation time. I'd been looking forward to holing up at home, eating for free, and heading out for a few shopping sprees with Mom's credit cards in my pocket. My father is an incurable cheapskate, but Mom has figured out ways to overcome that. She just says Dad was born with a silver spoon in his mouth and he worries that if he opens up too much, he might drop it.

As the graceful San Francisco skyline rose before us, Mom chattered on about plans for our family's traditional Christmas Eve bash. She was working closely with the caterer, she was making all her own desserts this year, she had melted wax into tiny molds in the shape of pine trees, she had acquired eclectic decorations from far and wide to trim the old Victorian house. "Gold, silver, lavender, and white," she was saying. "Those are my colors. I'm keeping it simple this year, and quite tasteful." The BMW's tires screeched as she pulled into the driveway of the tall, twisting gingerbread house I called home.

Mom got out, slammed the door, and popped the trunk. "Oh, geez," she said, checking her watch. "You two had better toss your things inside and wash up. You don't want to be late for the lamplight tour." She slung one of Leo's totes over her shoulder, then hiked up the stairs to the house.

When Mom was out of sight, Leo turned to me. "Is she always this bossy?"

I felt myself bristling. "What do you mean? The lamplight tour is fantastic. She just doesn't want us to miss it."

"And the party details . . . white and silver? It sounds like she's planning a wedding."

"Ha! Fat chance of that, especially with all the action I've seen lately."

"You're right," Leo said as he lugged his suitcase up the steps. "Maybe it's good that she has a party-planning outlet. You're not getting to the altar anytime soon."

"All right, already! Do you have to pour salt on the wound?"

Leo just laughed and bumped his suitcase onto the porch.

As I stepped into the old house, a magnificent building painted lavender with dark purple trim, I walked into a swirl of old feelings and memories: the soapy smell of the marble floors in the front vestibule, the laughing gingerbread trim along the rising staircase, the cozy, round turret room where I'd lost my virginity one weekend when my parents had been away at a medical conference. I had to resist the urge to drop everything in the hall and plotz on the couch with a bowl of ramen noodles and the remote in hand.

But Mom would have none of that.

"Better take those bags right upstairs," she said with all the flexibility of a drill sergeant. "You'll want to freshen up and head out. The tour starts at Pacific and Van Ness, and it includes a few of the grand old mansions. I hear the Wedding Houses are strung with Christmas lights."

"Wedding Houses?" Leo shook his head.

"Oh, I'm sure you've seen photos of them," Mom answered with a dismissive wave. "They're really quite famous."

I began to wonder if Leo was right; was Mom a bitch? I'd never really questioned her authority, and we'd seemed to get along just fine.

"You're in your old room, Madison," she called after me. "Leo can have the guest room. Sadie already cleaned up there, but let me know if she missed anything. And there are extra towels in the linen cupboard. Use the yellow. The red ones run."

"And you think *I'm* controlling," Leo said at the top of the stairs.

"Shut up and get your rear in gear," I said. "Mom doesn't tolerate tardiness."

"And you think this family is free of issues?" He nodded smugly, heading down the hall with his bag.

Best friend or not, he was beginning to get on my nerves. "Leo, promise me you are not going to spend this entire trip analyzing my family."

Leo paused at two tall doors and tugged one open. It was the linen closet. "Where the hell am I supposed to go, anyway?"

"End of the hall," I told him.

He closed the door and grinned. "Sorry. I promise, I won't peek into any more of your closets. Wouldn't want any family skeletons popping out."

You gotta hand it to Leo, he does have a way of getting under your skin.

"Well, that was a fabulous tour," Leo said as we climbed one of those incredible staircases cut into a hill. "So informative," he said, beginning to puff with exertion. "Quaint. Christmasy. Remind me to wear my jingle-bell earrings tomorrow."

"You know, I'm beginning to enjoy your Christmas defiance," I said, trudging up behind him. "You're like the Joan Rivers of Christmas. Can we talk about mistletoe? Why in the world would I want an excuse to kiss my Uncle Harry? The man has goiters the size of"—I was running out of breath—"of . . . Santa's . . . sled."

When I reached the top, Leo was leaning against the rail, laughing between jagged breaths. "I *love* Joan! Am I really that sarcastic? No, I'm not!" He pinged my shoulder.

"Did you have to make that snide comment about the tour guide's costume?"

"Did you see how he was dressed? I thought he meant to be a Christmas elf."

"The theme was Victorian Christmas," I defended. "And we were lucky to get inside the Whittier Mansion. It's rarely open to tourists."

"Well, you can't tell me that they wore green velvet lapels in Victorian times."

"You'd be surprised," I said. Growing up in San Francisco, I'd been immersed in Victorian-influenced architecture and pieces; you get to the point where you don't question excesses.

We headed down Geary Street to a bar that had always been a popular grad student hangout when I was in high school. Dartmouth Castle was probably still as tacky as ever, but they served excellent brews, and I knew Leo would like the dartboards. It's something that I had learned about men from my father when he taught me to play billiards: Men don't like to talk face-to-face. You're always better off sitting side by side, pretending to watch television or shop or even watch a ball game. When men have a place to focus their attention, they are much more relaxed conversationalists.

Inside, we ordered two pints of Anchor Steam and waited our turn at the dartboard. Leo took a long sip of beer, then sighed. "Heaven. Why can't they brew a decent beer in New York?"

"It's the water," I said, lifting my glass. "Way too clean." I took a sip. The cranberry flavoring was noticeable, but I sort of liked it. Somehow, it mingled well with the Jackson 5 version of "Santa Claus Is Coming to Town" playing in the bar.

Leo unwrapped his hand-knitted muffler and twisted his stool to lean against the bar. "Don't look now. Sailor at five o'clock."

I turned around to gape, and Leo hissed. "I told you not to look!"

"Like that's going to stop me," I said, checking out the worthy sight: a handsome boy in his crisp Navy uniform, smooth and white as a vanilla milkshake. That is, the uniform was white; his skin was more the color of peach flesh.

He was bobbing behind two dart players, commenting on the game.

"What did I tell you?" Leo beamed. "Hunk, or what?"

"He's a cutie, all right," I said, "but not my type. I don't go for soldiers. Unless they're dancing in the *Nutcracker*."

Leo's face scrunched in disapproval. "He's not a soldier; he's a sailor. Don't you know your armed forces?"

I didn't argue. I was too busy eyeing Vanilla Milkshake, sure that I knew him. Not that I know *any* military types. That whole military program puts me off, from the advocacy of violence to the blind compliance to authority. Which is why I have always been attracted to the rebel type, the bad boys with shades and leather jackets and unregistered motorbikes.

As I was staring, Vanilla Boy looked over, and suddenly I was caught. I sort of rolled my eyes, as if I had no control over them. When I looked back at him, he was cruising right at me.

"He's coming over!" Leo hissed in a loud whisper. "He's waving, like he knows you."

"I think he does," I said, checking out his nameplate. *Wilkinson.*

As Vanilla smiled in my direction, it hit me. "Ohmigod! Ryan?"

"Madison?" Ryan nodded. "How are you?" From up close his uniform looked even crisper. Crispy, crunchy, and smooth.

Leo eyed us suspiciously, trying to decipher how we were connected.

"This is Ryan Wilkinson. We used to be . . . I don't know. What were we, Ryan?" Did I sound idiotic or what? I'd tried to avoid saying that we'd been a couple for awhile in high school, until it all ended badly. My fault—totally.

Ryan's smile seemed confident. "We used to go out."

Leo seemed impressed. "You dated a sailor?" he said to me. "How unexpectedly patriotic of you."

"We were in high school," I said. "Ryan had a lot more

hair back then. I mean . . . it was longer!" I was really stepping in it today. But while Leo would have freaked if I pointed out prematurely thinning hair, Ryan didn't seem to mind. He took off his cap and ran a hand over his buzz cut.

"Bristly." He grinned. "The girls love it." He bowed his head. "Wanna try?"

I waved him off, but Leo reached out and delicately grazed the edge.

"Oooh!" Leo almost giggled. "That would tickle."

I had to smile. Despite the uniform, this Ryan was looser than I remembered him being. This was not the guy who asked permission to kiss me, the guy who was afraid of pulling his zipper down in front of me. I wasn't sure I liked the new Ryan, but then, I was never too crazy about the old one, either. "So the Navy's made you cocky," I said.

Ryan blinked. "Me? No, ma'am."

My mouth dropped open. "Are you ma'aming me? Oh, please! I'm way too young for that." I wanted to add: And I've seen you with your pants down, bud! But I didn't think Ryan would have appreciated it.

"No offense, Maddy." Ryan tucked his hat under his arm. "It's second nature now."

Maddy . . . Only my parents called me that these days. Amazing how a nickname can reduce your age and thrust you back into another era of your life—an awkward era for me. Feeling a little uneasy, I lifted my pint and took a long sip. Somewhere in the back of my mind I had known that Ryan was in the military. I must have heard it from one of my old high school friends, because two years ago, when we huddled in someone's dorm room on campus watching bombs streak through the night sky of Baghdad on CNN, I had worried aloud that Ryan might be caught in the crossfire until someone pointed out to me that the military didn't pluck college kids out of their academies to serve in war. At least, not since World War II, but what did I know? I was a registered Democrat who had donated money to Greenpeace.

"What luck," Leo said. "A class reunion. Now all we need is the quarterback of the football team and the head cheer-leader."

I ignored him and tried to finish up the small talk with Ryan. The glow of seeing an old acquaintance was quickly wearing off, giving way to the old feelings that had made me break up with Ryan. He could be so pedantic and cloying . . . so literal. A perfect military automaton. "So . . . Ryan, are you stationed here, or just home on a visit?"

"I'm here on a holiday furlough. Usually I'm on a ship—the *Ticonderoga,* out of San Diego. I've got to report back on the twenty-sixth."

"So you'll be here for the annual Greenwood Christmas bash," Leo chimed in. "I'm sure you're invited. Madison's mom is just throwing a few things together. A casual, drop-in black-tie thing." He turned to me, adding, "I forgot—is it BYOB?"

"I think Mom has the drinks covered," I said, reminding myself to give Leo a major noogie on the back of his thin-ning head the next time we were alone. Bad enough that he was inviting Ryan to the Christmas party. Did he have to make fun of Mom, too?

Ryan's eyes were on me, as intense as ever, and I remem-bered a time back in high school when I'd asked him to stop staring. He had swallowed hard, tearfully, I think, and said something incredibly cornball like: "I'm just so much in love with you, it hurts." Ugh! That had been the beginning of the end. I may not have been the most worldly teenager in Nob Hill, or Snob Hill, as my friends and I liked to demean the place, but I knew enough to run from raw emotion when I saw it.

"I think I'd like that," Ryan said, all over me.

I had to take a swig of beer to protect myself from his total adulation. The guy was just too intense. When I'd chugged enough to make my toes relax, I took a breath and nodded at Ryan. "You're always welcome," I said. "It's on Christmas Eve. Anytime after seven."

"Great," he said. At least, I think that was the word he used. His eyes transmitted a different message: Love me! Save me! Validate me!

I turned back to the bar and took a deep breath, hoping Ryan would take it as a sign of dismissal. But Leo undermined me, engaging Ryan in conversation. Leo teased Ryan that I must have been a real pain in the ass back in high school. Behind me, Ryan defended me vehemently, telling Leo that I was so beautiful. So beautiful? Who even says that anymore? And didn't Ryan know that feminists didn't want to be defined by their physical appearance?

"Hey, look at that! It's our turn," I said when a dartboard opened up. I moved away from Ryan, then turned back, to make sure he knew this was the end of our conversation. "You take care now, okay?"

He stepped forward, extended his hand, and pulled me close.

Oh, no! The kiss!

I turned my head so that he pecked the outer rim of my cheek, just in front of my ear. "I'll see you on Christmas Eve," he said.

"Okay, then . . ." I scooted toward the dartboard, trusting Leo to follow.

"Oh my God, he is so cute!" Leo exclaimed under his breath when we were a safe distance away from Ryan.

"Don't get your bloomers all twisted," I said, taking a practice shot. "Ryan is all facade. Underneath, there's just a lot of cloying air."

"I like pretty facades," Leo insisted. "I can be very superficial, you know."

"Bullshit. Besides, last time I checked, Ryan didn't like boys."

Leo tapped the tail of a dart against his chin and looked

back toward Ryan. "Such a pity. If I can't have him, the least you can do is scarf him up so that I can enjoy him vicariously. The man is an Adonis in ivory."

I dared a look back at Ryan, who was now sitting on a barstool. Straight back, broad shoulders, tight butt. "Yeah, the Navy filled him out nicely," I admitted. "And that costume . . . Vanilla *GQ*. But I'm not interested. He represents everything I'm not."

Leo smiled. "For Vanilla, I'd be tempted to compromise. But tell me everything—dish the dirt. Did you at least have some fun together before you split? Was it a bad breakup?"

"The breakup was awkward," I admitted. "My doing. Ryan was so intense in high school, so serious. When it came time to send out college applications, I had my sights set on Columbia or the University of Chicago. But Ryan was totally focused on getting into the Naval Academy at Annapolis. That floored me. I was seventeen years old, in the throes of a rebellion against my parents, dying to get away to an alternate lifestyle in college, and Ryan wanted to pledge to Old Glory and sign his life away to Uncle Sam."

"A man with principles," Leo said. "How refreshing."

"Not for me. I found it stifling. He was diametrically opposed to everything I believed in. Once I realized that I had to end the relationship, I couldn't wait to shake him loose."

Leo threw a practice dart and narrowed his eyes. "But that was then, this is now and . . . wow! You must admit the boy grew up beautifully."

I sighed. "Leo, he's a Republican! In the service! Can you see me as a military wife? Living on base and crocheting quilts for the officer's club bazaar while my man is out at sea in some undisclosed location—"

"Shades of *An Officer and a Gentleman*." Leo pursed his lips. "Oh, if I close my eyes I can almost imagine Richard Gere coming through that door. He would sweep me into his arms, whisk me out of this honky-tonk bar and—"

"Leo, stop it now."

He swatted the air in my direction. "Don't stop me, I'm on a roll. He'd be wearing his dress whites, and I'd be looking forlorn in . . . let's see, maybe washed-out jeans and a distressed muscle shirt. We'd—"

"Leo, you've never worn a muscle shirt in your life," I said, leaning close to my friend. "And if you don't snap out of the fantasy and start throwing darts, you're going to lose your turn."

"Oh." He blinked and faced the dartboard. "Did I go off there?"

"A little."

He shrugged, unwrapping a link from his muffler. "Well, if I'm sounding pushy it's only because your love life is drier than the Sahara. I mean, did you *ever* fuck anyone in college?"

"I did!" I insisted. "And how about you?"

"Please! Can we not go there?" He pressed a hand to his chest, and one of the darts popped through his sweater. "Ouch!" He rubbed his chest. "Here I haven't mentioned Jordan all day, and you have to throw salt on the wound."

"Sorry," I said, "but I thought you, of all people, would understand that I've been holding out for a relationship with an emotional component."

With a stern grimace, Leo took aim and released the dart. It hit the board with a satisfying *thwack,* landing left of center.

"Oh, man, I thought you had a bull's-eye," I said.

Leo nodded sadly. "So did I."

I slid an arm around his shoulder and gave him a hug. "Hey, at least you found someone, even if it was just for awhile. 'Better to have loved and lost,' right?"

He tilted his head. "Stop with the Hallmark one-oh-one and get me another coldie."

I patted his shoulder. "There will be other men in your life, Leo. Gorgeous, smart men, just like you."

For a second his satirical mask slipped away, and I saw a

flicker of genuine concern in his eyes. "Thanks, sis," he said. "But don't think kind words will distract me. It's your turn to buy the beers."

"I'm on it," I said, digging into my coat pocket for loose bills. As I ordered the drinks, I felt a flicker of pride. The fact that I didn't just fall into Ryan's arms was a sign of my personal growth. Yes, I'd been going through a dry spell, but I'd stood my ground, confident and sure, willing to wait until I met the guy who could be Mr. Yang to my Yin.

Oh, who was I kidding? Right now I'd be willing to take a chance with Mr. Half-a-Yang if he had the right rap.

3

"I never thought I would spend the holidays hoisting pebbles," Leo said. He let out a grunt as we lifted the last bag of gold glass beads into the trunk of Dad's Mercedes. Mom had arranged for us to pick up the beads and votive candleholders from a wholesale supplier that she'd gotten through her florist. The task had sounded simple when she'd described it that morning. Who knew that the glass beads would come in twenty-pound sacks, and that she required nearly twenty cartons of candles to be sure that the downstairs of the house would glow with golden light?

"They're not pebbles," I said. "They're glass beads."

"And the backseat of the car is full of cardboard cartons." Leo brushed off his hands. "If this is what we have to go through for candles, I'd hate to see what we're doing for food. Maybe she'll ask us to woo a bull to roast on an open spit? Or maybe we need to go down to the bay and wrangle an octopus for fresh squid."

I slammed the trunk closed. "The food is catered."

"Thank God."

"By one of the toniest caterers in San Francisco. Kasami Catering. I used to have such a crush on the owner's son."

"If he's anything like your other ex-boyfriend, Ryan, let me at him!" Leo teased.

"Oh, Greg Kasami was not a boyfriend," I admitted as we climbed into the Mercedes. "He was the elusive one, the untamable boy every girl wanted to tame." I thought of how I'd gotten close to him one night—my arms around his waist, my legs straddled behind his on his minibike. I was only fourteen then, and I think he was barely sixteen—certainly not old enough to be driving on the streets—but no one questioned his mastery of the bike as it screamed up hills and buzzed around curved streets.

That day . . . It had seemed sort of magical that Greg had spotted me in the crowd, let alone taken the time to offer me a ride. I'd been on my way home on an electric bus that rode off the wires and stalled, dumping all the passengers at a bus stop in North Beach. For some reason I wasn't with my friends, and I couldn't reach Mom on the phone to pick me up. So I ended up milling around, listening in on other peoples' plans to get home.

And there came Greg, a blast of blue jeans and black leather and gleaming white helmet. His bike shrieked as he rolled up beside me on the sidewalk and flicked his visor up. "Want a ride?" he'd asked, as if it were a daily occurrence. In seconds I was climbing on behind him, tucking my hair into my sweater, holding on to the smooth leather around his waist. How I wanted that ride to stretch on down an infinite road! I think I was lost in a fantasy of being Greg's girl when he pulled up in front of my house.

"Okay, this is it," he announced, as if he were a tour guide or a train conductor.

I held on for a moment, unable to let go. I remember inviting him in, trying to stretch out the moment. But he'd just pried my fingers off and nodded toward the steep walkway leading up to the house.

I stepped off, and with a roar, he was gone.

"Every high school has one of those," Leo said. "The bad boy we love to hate." He checked his watch, then stretched back as much as the seat would allow with dozens of crates behind him. "Home, James," he said. "I've got someplace to be this afternoon."

"Your Aunt Sophie?" I knew that Leo had been trying to get in touch with a distant relative who lived in Berkeley.

He nodded. "She's not really an aunt, but she feels closer than my father's real sisters." Boxes shifted as we pushed up a hill. "God, I hope her new husband isn't a jerk." He reached over to grab a box as it slid back over the console. "What exactly are these candles and rocks for?"

"Mom will show us. She always has great decorating ideas."

"Something to look forward to," he muttered. "I hope Martha Stewart is willing to put off arts and crafts class until another day."

"You are such a snob," I told him.

He crossed his legs and let out a contented sigh. "I try. I really try."

At the house, Leo and I propped open the side door and started loading our candleholder cargo into the mudroom. We had almost emptied the trunk when the kitchen door swung open and Mom peered out, lifting her reading glasses to her red hair.

"There you are!" she said. "Good, good! Come into the kitchen as soon as you're finished. We're having a tasting, and I'd love your opinion." The door swung closed behind her as Leo dropped a heavy bag onto the tiles.

"A few savory scraps for the slave laborers?" he said.

I laughed. "You must have been a holy terror for Nancy and Jack." I lined up a stack of boxes, then took the keys from my pocket. "Why don't you go on in. Let me just close up the car, and I'll join you."

Leo smoothed the lapel of his leather jacket. "Am I dressed for a tasting?"

"Get your ass inside," I muttered, running down the path.

By the time I got into the kitchen, Leo had undergone a major attitude adjustment. He sat at the kitchen table opposite Mom, loosely clutching a glass of white wine.

"Definitely with the sauce on the side," he said as he and Mom nibbled cute little dumplings with chopsticks. "For some discerning palates, it might overpower the buttery essence of the lobster."

Gentle cooking smells warmed the kitchen. "Smells delicious," I said.

Mom gestured grandly toward the stove. "Madison, you remember Greg Kasami, don't you?"

As I swung toward the open refrigerator, I had to make a conscious effort to keep my mouth closed. Greg Kasami was here, in my parents' kitchen! What would the girls on the cheerleading squad say?

Oh, grow up, I told myself as I pushed a strand of hair out of my eyes. *You're finished with high school and college. Thank God!*

The large stainless steel door swung closed, and a gorgeous man materialized. Shiny, jet-black hair. Smooth Asian face. Enormous smile. And his body . . . so tall and lean and graceful, like every girl's fantasy of a ninja warrior.

I swallowed hard. Was this the rebel boy who had infuriated his father by driving that Kawasaki all over town?

"You were in school at the same time, weren't you?" Mom asked, stabbing another dumpling.

"We were," Greg said, dazzling me with his huge smile. Then he was all business again, crossing to the stovetop to stir a sauce.

Trying to ignore the shiver of excitement, I washed my hands then joined Mom and Leo at the table.

"Try this last lobster dumpling," Mom ordered, dabbing

at her apricot lips with a napkin. "I'm going to watch Greg stir the pot."

Leo and I let our eyes follow her. Somehow, we all were mesmerized watching Greg stir the pot, his fingers strong and slender, his shoulders straight and regal. You'd think the three of us were watching Yo-Yo Ma perform a solo.

Leo kicked me under the table and mouthed: *He's gorgeous!*

Trying to ignore the hormones bombarding my blood, I kicked him back and mouthed: *He's mine!*

He crossed his arms. *I saw him first.*

I swallowed the last of the dumplings and smiled. *He likes girls.*

"Darn," Leo said aloud, checking his watch. "I'd better go get changed. Auntie Sophie waits for no one."

"We'll save some of the sake for you," Greg said.

"Sounds great." Leo pushed away from the table and went over to the stove to check out the simmering sauces.

"Wait till they taste the spinach baskets filled with sea scallops," Mom said, closing her eyes. "They are glorious."

"But they don't keep well," Greg pointed out. "Maybe we should do them another time, since you said you had an appointment, too?"

Mom glanced up at the kitchen clock and pressed a hand to her cheek. "That's right! I'm supposed to meet Emily at the club. Then I've got to pick up Dr. Greenwood at the airport." For as long as I can remember Mom has called my father Dr. Greenwood, as if she were a secretary booking his surgeries.

"Mom, if you want, I can get Dad at the airport," I volunteered.

"But then I'd have to cancel Emily, too, and I can't do that to her." She turned to Greg with a pout on her face. "I am so sorry! I truly thought we'd have more time for this today."

"It's not a problem," Greg said, flashing her that sunny

smile. "I'll stop by another time before your party. But someone needs to taste the beef burgundy. It's almost ready."

All eyes turned to me.

"Sure, I'll check it out," I offered, wondering why my throat was suddenly so dry. I went to the fridge to grab a bottle of water.

Leo edged in beside me to grab his own bottle. "Enjoy the beef," he told me with a cagey look.

Slamming the fridge shut, I tried to hide my grin as Leo disappeared up the back stairs. How had I landed in this situation, playing hostess to Greg? It seemed ludicrous that I was suddenly the recipient of Greg's culinary ministrations when just a few months ago I was picking through the vat of scrambled eggs at the school dining hall. Even more bizarre that I'd have the rest of the afternoon alone in the house with the Tall, Dark and Dangerous Bad Boy of high school. The possibilities made my limbs tingle; and yet, considering my lack of appeal for men over the past few years, I wasn't expecting much.

Mom gave Greg a few more instructions, then headed up the back stairs to change, leaving me to feel awkward with Greg Kasami in command of my parents' kitchen. A white dishtowel was tucked into a belt loop of his black jeans, and his black mock turtleneck looked spotless, despite the fact that he had been cooking and was now slicing carrots into perfect julienne strips.

"I brought along a nice Cab that you may want to serve with the beef," Greg said, darting me a glance without lifting his head. "That bottle of B and V. Why don't you open it?"

"Sure." Now this was something I could do, I thought as I drilled into the bottle cork. A wine connoisseur, my father had trained me to open bottles and sniff corks when I was in junior high. I splashed some into a glass, then paused. What was the etiquette here? Should I offer some to Greg, or was it against the caterer's code of honor to drink on the job?

"Would you like a glass?" I asked.

"Absolutely," he said. "Wine is a wonderful taste enhancer for many foods."

I nodded, pouring a second glass. When I brought it over to the stove, he was stirring the browned beef into the delicate sauce. "I hate to cook," I admitted as I handed him the wineglass. "Is it a drag to cook for a living? I mean, it seems to me you would either want to eat all the profits, or else you'd begin to hate food."

"I love a well-cooked meal." He held the glass under his nose and took a deep breath, then sipped. Then he sighed deeply, and I felt a twinge of jealousy at the way he could shut out everything and savor the wine.

When he opened his eyes, I was still staring at him, but he didn't seem to mind. He faced me head-on, his face a mask of beauty, his obsidian eyes a window to some dark, exquisite world. "Is it a drag to work on a magazine for a living?" he asked.

I took a sip of cabernet and smiled. "Only when I'm working—which is most of the time. Publishing seems more glamorous than it is. Most of my job involves fixing jams in the copy machine and slugging—checking to see that typos are fixed."

"And is it satisfying?" he asked as he dumped fat rice noodles into a pot of boiling water. The water seemed to flare for a second as Greg worked his magic over it.

I let out a breath, a little unnerved that Greg was able to zero in on my fledgling career within five minutes of our reunion. "Hardly ever." I leaned against the counter, watching as he folded in mushrooms. "That would be nice," I mused, "a job that brings satisfaction."

"It's a necessity," he said. "You need to find work that fulfills you, Madison."

At the moment my mind was on a totally different type of fulfillment as my eyes went over Greg's broad shoulders and down his back. His butt was smooth and flat, but from the fit of his jeans there was definitely a round rise of flesh to grab on to. My body was warming to him—or maybe it was the wine. Either way, I couldn't deny the glimmer of heat that permeated my body, making everything warm and fuzzy, like a photo in soft focus. I wanted to move closer to him, to feel him brush against me, but I didn't have the nerve.

Oh, get your mind out of the gutter, I told myself. *He's here to do a job, not to jump your bones!*

But there was no denying Greg's attraction. I wondered if he'd ever gotten married. I wanted to ask, but of course, I chickened out. "How long have you been working with your father?"

"A little over four years. I went to Berkeley for two years, but it seemed like a waste of time, since I knew I'd end up in the family business."

"Really? You were so sure of that?"

"I always knew I belonged in a kitchen." Greg scooped up a dollop of beef burgundy and cupped his hand around the spoon to blow on it. "And I think Dad has been grooming me for the family business since I was old enough to hold a chopstick. We always got along well."

Even when you were tearing through the hills of San Francisco on a minibike? I wondered. How was it that Greg's life was so beautifully ordered, with all the aesthetics of a Japanese tea garden, while mine seemed to bump along a road full of potholes?

"Try this," he said, extending the spoon toward my lips. The gesture seemed intimate, especially since he'd blown on it. As I parted my lips and leaned forward to taste, I felt like a budding sex goddess, partaking of Greg's nectar.

It was ambrosia. I closed my eyes to savor the sauce laden with wine and garlic and rich flavorings I couldn't identify. "Delicious." When I opened my eyes, Greg had already turned back to the stove. He dished up two plates of noodles and beef and motioned me over to the table, where we sat opposite each other.

Under the Tiffany lamp, we ate at the kitchen table like an

old married couple. The food was to-die-for, but I still felt like I hadn't cracked Greg's shell. The untamable bad boy of high school was as elusive as ever.

I decided to take a shot. "I have to admit, I'm a little surprised," I said. "That you take cooking so seriously . . . that you're so into the family business. You were such a rebel in high school."

"You mean the motorcycle? Yeah, I was a punk back then." He grinned. "How could you stand me?"

I rolled my eyes dramatically. "It was difficult. But then again, we weren't best friends or anything."

"Not like you and Ryan Wilkinson."

"Ryan?" I scrunched up my nose. Enough with Ryan already! Was my life's reputation tainted by that cling-on? I could just imagine my biography: *Despite her accomplishments and their global impact, Madison was always pegged as Ryan Wilkinson's girlfriend.*

"You guys were tight."

"For about a month," I lied. "Anyway, that's way behind me. I'm a free agent now." I figured it didn't hurt to advertise.

"Me, too." He took a long sip of wine, but his dark eyes stayed on me.

Did he know that those words had started my heart hammering in my chest? Hard to believe that Greg was still single, but I wasn't about to question my good fortune.

With the ice broken between us, we ate and drank wine and talked about classmates. Greg wasn't really friendly with anyone, but he seemed to know the whereabouts of kids who had stayed in the Bay Area.

"James Min is going for a master's at Berkeley," he said as he sipped a second glass of wine. "Something like folklore—or is it philosophy? Anyway, I was teasing him that it's a master's of bullshit."

We both laughed. "Sounds like James," I said.

"And Sara Vega." He paused. "She's had some hard times.

I don't see her much, but she moved to the Midwest for a while."

"To Kansas," I said, having heard about Sara from my best buds. "For nine months."

He blinked. "So it's true?"

"I heard she put the baby up for adoption, but then the father showed up and demanded custody. Her parents have disowned her, and now she's living with a brother in Seattle."

Greg shook his head. "It's sad. She had a lot going for her."

"But her parents were always lunatics," I said. "She's way better off living hundreds of miles away from them. Weird how we know such personal details about some of our classmates."

I scooted my chair back. "That was delicious, thanks."

"It's all part of the package," he teased. At least, I think he was joking.

I took our plates to the sink and started rinsing. Greg went to the stove and turned on another burner.

"Don't tell me you've got another course planned," I said.

"Dessert, of course." He spooned a glob of something into a saucepan and stirred.

I turned back to the dishes, enjoying the presence of Greg in our kitchen. While I rinsed, he dished up two small bowls of vanilla ice cream, then poured a thick sauce on top. I dried my hands and smiled. "Hot fudge sundaes."

"Not quite. This sauce comes from a secret family recipe. It contains an ancient Japanese ingredient that's known to be a love potion."

"An aphrodisiac?" I stabbed at the sauce with a spoon, then lifted it to his lips. "You taste first and we'll see if it works on you," I said, amazed at my brazenness.

Greg parted his lips and I slipped the spoon in. "Mmm," he groaned, sucking on the spoon. "Better than sex."

"We'll see about that," I said, taking a taste of the rich, dark chocolate swirled with melting ice cream. I closed my eyes and sighed. "Not better than sex, but close. Damn close."

"I see the secret herb is working."

"You're full of shit," I said. "I know chocolate when I taste it. Though it's been known to be an aphrodisiac for some people."

With a laugh, he pushed the bowl to the back of Mom's granite counter and lifted me into the space he'd cleared. It happened so quickly, I was still reeling when he pressed against my knees and ran his hands over the denim of my skirt. "Do you feel it?"

I wasn't sure if he was talking about the aphrodisiac effect or the incredible chemistry between us, but I definitely felt something. I nodded, reaching out to his shoulders. So broad and warm beneath my hands.

Greg parted my legs and pressed against me until his body was against mine, his lips on mine. I let him kiss me, softly first, then with urgency. As I ran my tongue over his smooth teeth, he dug his hands under my skirt, up my thighs, to my hips. Swiftly, he grabbed my panties and pulled as I wriggled back and forth. He dropped them to the floor and began to explore along my inner thighs, up, up, until I gasped with longing.

He ended a kiss and left me sitting on the counter while he pulled over a low kitchen chair. For a second I didn't get it, but then when he sat down and I noticed that his head was just at counter level, his face just inches from my knees . . . I think it made me moist all over again.

I sucked in my breath as he gently parted my legs and buried his face in my skirt. I gasped when he licked me, but he seemed to find the right spots quickly, bringing my body to the edge of a frenzy.

My head rolled back and my eyes closed as he stroked and sucked, smoothly and steadily, sending shivers of sensation radiating through my body. I felt primed and ready, so ready to find pleasure with him. I was a tense knot of desire, and then suddenly, I was rocking with him, howling out loud as sweet sensation shot through my body.

Greg held me close as I waited for my heart to stop pounding so wildly.

"Oy," I whispered. "I haven't felt that good in a long time."

He leaned back to look at me, then ground his hips against my pelvis. I could feel his erection, and that excited me all over again.

"What do you think?" he said, rubbing my thigh. "Should we try another course?"

I smiled as a new wave of lust licked through me. "Tell me you're not charging my mother by the hour, and I'll eat all night," I teased.

He grinned. "You are a bad, bad girl."

"Coming from the bad boy of Nob Hill High, that's quite a compliment."

From that day on, I decided, I would have a new respect for cooking . . . and my feelings about the family kitchen would never be quite the same. Yes, there was something to be said for eating in.

4

The next day, I waited until Leo and I were firmly ensconced at a table at Enrico's, one of my favorite tapas brunch spots, before I sprang my news on him.

"No, no way!" His eyes were lit with amazement. "I'm aghast . . . and a little impressed."

"Well, thanks," I said, slicing off a piece of salmon bruschetta. "I'm a little shocked myself. The guy barely gave me the time of day in high school, but everyone was so insecure and evil then." I stirred the celery stick in my Bloody Mary. "He's not married. Man, I wonder if . . . no. I can't go there."

"Dreaming of white picket fences and two point five kids?"

I shook my head. "That would be stupid, wouldn't it? I mean, Greg is not relationship material. I should think of him as a conquest."

Leo stabbed a fat fried oyster. "A notch on that cute little French provincial bed that your mother hand stenciled?"

"Why the hell not? Men do it all the time."

"I wouldn't dream of forcing monogamous morality on you," Leo said, dishing up a smashed olive concoction. "So, Julia Child, do you think you'll be dining with him again?"

"I sure hope so. God, it's going to be so awkward if he doesn't want to see me again, with him setting up for the Christmas party." I smacked my forehead. "Oh, I didn't think of that! I'll be so embarrassed if he wants to cut it off."

"Before you go cutting out a big scarlet 'A,' " Leo began, "remember that you're outta here in January, anyway, and there's no reason for him to cut it off, if you two shellacked the kitchen counters all night. Hell, I'm surprised he didn't show up for breakfast."

"I wonder if he'll call," I said. "Or maybe I should call him?"

Leo shook his head. "Give it a few hours. Besides, you promised to take me shopping this afternoon. *Christmas* shopping, although I'm not sure what that means. Will we be buying mistletoe and pine boughs? Fat red ribbon and Santa hats?"

"I was hoping to find a gift for my mother. I love getting her the perfect gift, but she's always such a challenge."

"Tell me about it," Leo said, dropping crushed olive onto a crust of bread. "Buying a gift for Robin is like saying a prayer for the Pope—we're talking major overload."

"But Mom really appreciates a thoughtful gift," I said defensively. "For Dad, I usually just pick up some cologne or a bottle of brandy. He's so cheap himself, he always tells me to save my money, but Mom is different."

"Aunt Sophie gave me my Christmas gift last night," Leo said, unwrapping the gold chenille muffler around his neck and flinging it back. "Do you like?"

"I love! It's so you."

Leo chewed rapidly, nodding. "I think my mother tipped her off, but who the hell cares? When the label says Neiman Marcus, my little heart just goes ka-ching!"

I laughed, choking on a piece of bread. "Please," I coughed. "You're going to make me snort up an oyster."

"Now there's an attractive image," Leo mused. "Hold on

to your lunch, Sally. We've got some major shopping to do. Neither of us has attire for the illustrious Robin Greenwood Red Carpet Christmas Party. I say we'd better scope out some of the couture collections, then head down to Marshalls to find the appropriate knock-offs."

"Oh, please, let there be something on the clearance rack at Saks," I prayed. "Besides, aren't you just going to rent a tux?"

It was Leo's turn to choke. His eyes bulged as he tried to blink away the dreadful thought. "Does Michael Jackson rent a tux? Did Rock Hudson dress like an overgrown penguin? I see my work is cut out with you, Pygmalia. We'd better finish eating and get shopping."

Pressing a napkin to my mouth, I tried to run the schedule for the next few days through my mind. Shopping for gifts, shopping for wardrobe, tree trimming, cookie decorating. Leo and I had tickets to the *Nutcracker,* and amid all those activities I knew Greg would be a fixture at the house. In fact, Mom had mentioned he would be stopping by this afternoon. Would he want to see me? Did he like me? Just thinking of him made hormones wiggle through my blood.

Trying to tamp down my adolescent worries, I took another sip of my Bloody Mary and glanced at the twinkling white lights on Enrico's blue and silver tree. I was going to have myself a sexy little Christmas, indeed.

After brunch we strolled through North Beach, peeking into a few boutiques while Leo expressed uncertainty over the attitude he wanted his clothes to express on Christmas Eve.

"I'm not so into emoting through attire," I said, shoving my hands into the pockets of my well-worn jeans.

"Well, that's obvious," Leo muttered, guiding me toward a vintage shop that I'd been in once or twice before. Rarities was a North Beach institution, but I'd always found the help there a little pushy, and I'd never been charmed at the prospect of wearing someone else's castoffs.

Just inside the door, Leo was immediately drawn to a rack with colorful jackets and vests—a profusion of sparkling beads and bright, flouncy feathers. He whipped off his jacket, and a tiny woman dwarfed by dark hair was suddenly there to hold it while Leo slipped on a patchwork jacket with gold fur lapels.

"Don't you love it?" Leo crooned, smoothing his knuckles through the fur. "The gold matches my highlights."

"It's glorious!" the mound of black hair raved.

Personally, I thought the gold fur was a bit too close to Leo's highlights, blending so well that the fur was a continuum of gold swirling around his shoulders. But I knew he would never stick with his first pick, so I kept my mouth shut and smiled.

As I expected, Leo quickly moved on to a beaded vest in Christmasy red and black. Although it made him look like a matador, the salesclerk, who'd introduced herself as Angelique, praised it as "Marvelous!"

I faded into the back of the store as Leo made his way through the sales rack, eliciting bountiful compliments from the dark, vapid Angelique. Sinking into the shadows, I tried on a vest covered with rich emerald-green sequins, but it smelled musty and felt grimy, so I browsed through a pile of sweaters, pretending to be interested while Leo modeled "glorious" fashions for Angelique.

Eventually he came to the back of the store with two pairs of slacks. "I'm going to try these on," he said as Angelique swished open a dressing room curtain, then retreated tactfully to the back of the store.

"Don't you love this place?" Leo exclaimed as he ducked into the booth and closed the curtain. "I've just died and gone to heaven."

"Actually, I've always felt preyed upon here." I lowered my voice to whisper, "The sales staff is a little intimidating."

"Not Angelique!" Leo called out merrily. "She's a regular gal pal! Doesn't she remind you of Cher?"

"More like Morticia Addams."

The curtain opened, and a pair of pants emerged in a hand. "These will never do. Be a mensch and tell Angelique I want to try the faux snakeskin slacks."

"Blech, but okay." Reluctantly I took the pants to the sales counter, where Angelique was ringing up a purchase for a tall, dark-haired man in a ponytail. When I approached the counter they both turned to me. The man squinted, studying my face.

"Wolfie?" I asked, recognizing the stately browridge over jet-black eyes.

He smiled. "It's just Wolf now, but hey, how's it going?" He reached out and shook my hand in that brisk European manner that Wolfie could never completely wipe away. He had spent his early years in Portugal, where his parents were some sort of European royalty. For some weird reason, when Wolf turned twelve his parents had wanted him to be educated and raised as a "normal" child in the States, so they had shipped him here to live with an uncle and attend public school. In the way that misfits find each other, we'd become friends in high school, but I hadn't run into him since I'd left for college.

"I'm still in New York," I said. "Working in magazine publishing and hating it. What are you up to?"

"I'm still here, quite happily. My parents pulled me back to Portugal after high school, but I hated the whole scene there . . . and here I am, back in San Fran." His eyes lifted as something beyond me caught his attention.

"Madison," Leo said from behind me, "who is this hipper version of Antonio Banderas?"

Without turning to look, I smelled interest. "My friend

from high school, Wolf Tarouca," I said, stepping back to include Leo. "And this is my college bud, Leo Vespucci. We came from New York for Christmas."

"A pleasure." Wolf stepped toward Leo, again with the polite handshake.

As they faced each other, the spark between them was palpable. *Ka-ching!*

"So you live in New York?" Wolf was asking Leo—not me, not his old high school buddy—but the man he'd just met. "I get over there from time to time. I'm from Portugal originally, but I've been trying to make San Francisco my home. I love it here."

"I do, too," Leo said, letting the lie slip out so softly, I almost believed him for a second.

I was going to add something about how it was so great to run into Wolfie, but I could see that I was suddenly not part of the conversation, not really. I was an electron circling on the periphery of the atomic lovefest.

These guys were smitten with each other.

It couldn't have happened to two nicer people, but I have to admit, my toes curled in my boots as jealousy reared its ugly head. Why couldn't I fall into unconditional, mutual love? Oh, I'd had quite a lustfest yesterday with Greg, but that was different. We didn't see stars or experience an emotional connection on the level of colliding planets.

"Is that yours?" Leo asked as Wolf picked up a jacket wrapped in plastic.

Wolf nodded, lifting the plastic to give us a peek at a maroon brocade smoking jacket—very chic, very retro. "I was just picking it up," Wolf said. "They altered the cuffs for me."

"Glorious," Angelique bellowed. "Simply marvelous, isn't it?"

"Now why couldn't I find something like that?" Leo posed the question to Angelique.

The female Cousin It shrugged beneath her mane of hair. "You will. Give it time."

I wanted to chime in that I needed a fabulous Christmas ensemble, too, but that would imply that I'd buy something from Angelique, and I was fairly sure we did not share the same sense of the *"Marvelous!"*

"Madison, it's so good to see you," Wolf said, suddenly turning his attention back to me. "We should have drinks some time."

"Oh, yes! Let's do that," Leo said, sounding like a character from a Noel Coward play.

"We'll have to fit it in before you leave," Wolf said. "How long are you here?"

"I have to head back after Christmas," Leo answered.

"Then there's no time at all," Wolf said, checking his watch. "What are you guys doing right now?"

My head ping-ponged back and forth as they volleyed information and quickly decided that we would abort our shopping mission and head off for coldies immediately. Suddenly Rarities and Transylvanian Angelique and the musty collection of marvelous vintage clothes were behind us as we piled into Wolf's BMW convertible and decided it would be insanely funny to put the top down. Wolf steered with one hand and worked the shift with the other while he held a cell phone pressed to his ear to tell someone at the office he would be delayed a bit.

From my spot in the backseat, I was duly impressed. A guy with a cool car in the city, a cell phone, and a job where he could call in and blow them off for awhile. It made me wonder what the hell I had been doing wasting my time in college for four years. We decided to check out a new bar in the Cannery—always a great place to eyeball tourists—then laughed our way over hills and into bursts of rolling fog. I had forgotten the low, damp clouds of cool mist so distinctive to San Francisco. By the time we got there, my hair was suffering major frizz, but I decided not to obsess with taming it since I was with two gay men who clearly had eyes only for each other.

Over the first round of margaritas, Wolfie gave Leo the *TV Guide* synopsis of his life.

"My parents are royalty. I'm next in line to the throne in Portugal; however, I find it difficult to tolerate the confines of the lifestyle." The light left Wolf's dark eyes as he stared down at the table. "The endless duties and ceremonies, the constant scrutiny, the formality of the simplest daily events—"

"Holy shit," Leo gasped in awe. "You're like bonny Prince Charles. I didn't think that sort of thing went on anymore, outside England and Monaco."

"It goes on," Wolf assured him. "However, instead of ruling the country, we rule protocol. Much time is spent fundraising and establishing protocol, and then there's all that hogwash about setting an example. It's all very boring, really."

Leo snapped a tortilla chip in half and turned to me. "I can't believe you never told me any of this."

I shrugged. "Wolf is a friend. The royalty stuff never figured into it for me. In high school, he was just like every other kid."

"Of course he was." Leo gritted his teeth. "I'm being a cad. Sorry, Wolf. Just starstruck, I guess. I've never been in the presence of royalty before."

"Well, don't worry," I said. "You don't have to bow or anything. Wolf is just a regular guy—with an exquisite sense of style, of course."

"That's one of the reasons I like it here." Wolf lifted his glass and leaned back to take in the view of the crisp, blue bay. "Few people know who I am. Those who do, don't really care. It's so liberating. I could never obtain this level of freedom in Portugal." He took a sip of his drink, then smiled. "I love my family, but when I visualize where I'd like to be in five or ten years, I know I belong here."

Leo slapped two fingers against the table. "Then dammit, this is where you need to stay."

"I wish it were that simple," Wolf said. "As the oldest son, I'm supposed to carry on the family tradition and act like a prince—the future king. But I'm trying to talk my father into passing the throne to my younger brother. The role is a far better fit for Jorge, and he wants it. He's got a Portuguese girlfriend from a very fine family, and he enjoys the celebrity. Jorge belongs there." He swiped at the drops of condensation on his glass, then looked up at Leo. "How about you? Where do you belong in this world?" he asked earnestly. "Where would you like to be in five or ten years?"

Leo let out a sigh. "Your Highness, if I had the answer to that one, then I'd be king of the world."

As we settled into the third round of coldies, I realized the sky over the bay was deepening to a cobalt blue. Red and white Christmas lights strung over boats at the bottom of the hill flickered on with the gathering dusk. Dusk . . . It was getting late, and Greg was going to stop by the house. What time? My margarita-soaked brain wasn't all too clear on the details anymore, but I knew I had to go.

I stood up and raked my hair off my face, as if a fresh-combed look would sober me up. "I need to head home. There's that appointment with the caterer," I said, speaking in code to Leo. "And remember, we're trimming the tree tonight."

"Right." Leo leaned back in his chair, obviously not ready to part company with Wolf just yet.

"Look, I'll take the cable car home from here. We'll meet up at the house later."

As Leo nodded, Wolf reassured me that he'd drop Leo off at the house. He even remembered where my parents live. "That's so nice," I said, digging in my bag for cash to cover my part of the tab.

"No, no, I got it," Wolf insisted. "I feel like I owe you a favor, since your father took excellent care of my dad when he was here."

This was news to me. "He did?"

"Didn't he tell you? My father was visiting when he experienced some chest pains. Your father saw him immediately and stayed at his side until everything checked out. Turns out it was some kind of muscular thing, but your dad was very reassuring."

"Good," I said, wondering why my father hadn't mentioned it. Then again, my father was not the best communicator in the world. A fine doctor, an excellent cardiologist, but a bumbling father. Long ago I had resigned myself to the fact that although my father loved me, he was seriously lacking in parenting skills. Dad was a quick learner, but if it wasn't published in a medical journal or included in the curriculum at med school, it wasn't worthy of Dr. Greenwood's attention.

As I made my way down the hill to the streetcar through a mist of margaritas and San Francisco fog, I wondered if Dad would turn up for the tree trimming tonight. It was a family tradition, but Dad had missed it a few times due to scheduling conflicts. I thought of the quick greeting he'd given me last night before he'd headed off to read in bed. I'd teased him about getting grayer, but otherwise, he was still the same old Dr. Greenwood, energetic, confident, and very much removed from his family. It was a wonder that my mother had managed to deal with being second-string to his career all these years. No wonder she buried herself in meticulous decorating details and endless lunches and teas with friends like Emily and Camille.

A strange worry about my father niggled at me until I burst into the house and found my mother sitting on the floor in front of the parlor fireplace. The wide marble foyer was dwarfed by a huge tree that had been delivered yesterday, its branches now relaxed and ready to bear ornaments. A fuzzy warmth from the fire suffused the room, and Mom's cheeks were nearly apple-red with a glow that I could only attribute to the joy of Christmas.

"How was your shopping, sweetie?" she asked, skillfully wielding her hot glue gun around a red velvet ball and pressing gold beaded string into place.

"Fun but fruitless," I admitted. "We ran into Wolfie Tarouca, and Leo is still hanging out with him. What are you making?"

"Ornaments to auction at the hospital charity ball. How is Wolfie? How is his father doing?"

"Fine." I slid out of my leather jacket and dropped onto the couch. "Why didn't you tell me about his dad being treated by our Dr. Greenwood?"

"Oh, didn't you know?" Mom shrugged. "You know your father. I only found out when his secretary mentioned it by accident."

I picked up a string of blue sequins and wrapped them around my index finger. "Mom, do you ever wonder about Dad? I mean, you've done a great job of getting around the fact that he hates to spend a buck. But what about the fact that he's so distant and . . . I don't know. Sort of aloof?"

Mom nodded. "Oh, I used to wonder. I used to chastise him and complain about it. We had many an argument about his blind commitment to his work . . . and his lack of commitment to family."

"And whatever happened?"

"Nothing, really," Mom said, tapping a bead into place on the ornament.

"Did he ever promise to put family first?" I couldn't believe such a corny sentiment was coming from my mouth, but somehow it seemed important.

Mom glanced up at me, her gray eyes sympathetic. "He always said his family was a priority. But then he also contends that being a surgeon is a calling. He used to ask me what was more important, saving a person's life, or attending one of your dance recitals."

"No way! That is such an unfair question!" I tossed the blue string onto the table.

Mom just nodded.

"Wow. You've put up with a lot of crap from him."

"Watch your language, dear," Mom said as the doorbell rang. "That must be Greg."

"I'll get it." I jumped up, suddenly worried that my hair was totally out of control with no time to fix it. I paused in the marble vestibule to peek in the gilded mirror. The wind and moisture had definitely taken their toll, but I didn't really mind the thick, wild texture of the brown hair around my face. I did a quick finger comb, then opened the door.

"Hey, Madison." Greg was a *GQ* portrait in black against blue sky.

My heart skipped a little beat as he stepped in, hooked a finger through a belt loop of my jeans, and pulled me toward him. I sucked in a breath, so conscious of his soft, sweet cologne as he brushed his cheek against mine. "I want you," he whispered.

I reached up to touch his black silk shirt, dying to shout "Take me now!" or something much cooler-sounding, but Greg was already moving inside, his silk shirt slipping from my grasp as he called out a greeting to my mother. Damn! How the hell was I going to get in his boxers with Mom around?

Still, as I followed him into the parlor I felt reassured by his Neanderthal greeting. Greg wanted me! He liked me! Perhaps I'd broken the jinx that had kept desirable men at bay for the past four years.

Mom and Greg were deep into conversation regarding the logistics of feeding a hundred guests with ease.

"I think the china stored in the basement pantry will cover it," Mom said. "Of course, it needs to run through the dishwasher, and since there are a few different patterns we'll need to sort it by room. I wouldn't want to serve olives on Lenox beside a Royal Doulton platter of crudités."

"Absolutely," Greg assured her. "I can inventory the china now, and I'll even get started with washing it."

Mom was nodding sagely. "There's a new dishwasher downstairs, and you're welcome to use the KitchenAid up here, if you need it."

Yes, yes, it's all true. Mom is a huge collector of crystal and china, and our basement has been renovated to include a separate apartment which my parents could rent out, if they could stand to have strangers living in their home. I know it all sounds excessive and decadent, but since Mom judiciously collected her precious china over the years in various trips to places like Czechoslovakia (when it was called that) and Dresden, it had always struck me as a practical hobby. Especially since she used the good stuff every day, serving orange juice in Waterford glasses and cereal in lovely Mikasa bowls.

"Terrific," Greg said, turning to me. "Why don't you show me around downstairs, Madison? We can let Mom get back to her work here."

He called her Mom! My throat tightened at the fabulous possibilities of what might be. What if I hooked up with Greg Kasami, one of the most eligible bachelors of San Francisco? Ha! I could just imagine the looks on the faces of all those in-girls from high school. I would invite every single one to our wedding . . . every cheerleader, every unblemished blonde.

"Give a holler if there's anything you can't find," Mom said, ducking her head to reload her glue gun.

I blinked back my surprise, wondering if it could be this easy to steal some time alone with Greg. Trying to play the role of the good daughter, I led him down the back stairs to the basement that my parents had renovated when I was a kid. The term "basement" didn't do that part of the house justice, as the back half of the floor had full-sized windows and a door that opened to Mom's well-tended English-style garden, now in its dormant phase, but decorated with white lights over the trellis and fat outdoor bulbs in the trees.

Flicking on the light in the downstairs kitchen, I spread my arms wide to indicate the built-in cabinets. "Here it is, the Greenwood family fortune invested in crystal and china."

Greg shot me a curious look. "I never knew you had such a wicked sense of humor."

"How could you know?" I said as he opened cabinets and began to take inventory. How could he know that the quivering girl on the back of his bike was a multitalented vixen, eager to indulge his every whim? Although I'd definitely been more into romance than sex, I probably would have slept with him that day when he gave me a ride home . . . if only he hadn't pried my fingers off his leather jacket with such precision.

"Let's wash these first," Greg said, taking down a stack of Royal Doulton dinner plates, white plates with a grandiose blue and gold crest in the center. While he counted the Lenox and the Mikasa, I gingerly loaded dinner plates into the dishwasher, adjusting the top rack so that there was plenty of room for the spinning arm to clear the china. When the dishwasher was full, I poured powdered soap in, then closed and locked it.

"What next, boss?" I asked, thinking how well we work together.

The noise of churning water rose as the dishwasher started running. Greg closed a cabinet and stepped up to me, planting his feet on either side of mine. "Next, we take off all your clothes."

I laughed as he pulled up my sweater and slid his hands in. I was wearing a teddy underneath, and his palms moved smoothly over the silk, over my rib cage, up to cup my breasts. How I loved to be touched by Greg! But I had to be careful; Mom was right upstairs.

"Okay," I said, letting my hips grind against his. "So I get naked. Then what do we do when Mom comes down to check on us?"

He groaned as I rubbed against him. "She's not coming down," he said. "Unless you like the danger of that . . . the thrill of danger, that we could be caught with our pants down? Some people find danger to be an aphrodisiac."

When Greg touched me that way, I didn't need an aphrodisiac. "I don't need the danger," I said, pulling his silk shirt out of his pants. "But I do need this." I pressed one hand over the bulge in his black jeans, and he groaned again. He leaned down to kiss me, and I felt so close to him, as if we were breathing the same breath, moaning in our throats with the same licks of passion.

He broke the kiss and quickly unzipped my jeans. "We need to find a place," he whispered as he yanked down my jeans, unsnapped the crotch of the silk teddy, and pressed his fingers into me. "Behind a door, in a closet . . . someplace where we'll have a moment's warning. Where can we go?" he asked.

I moaned. How could I think when my body was off in a sexual wonderland? "The den," I managed to murmur. I pulled up my pants and stumbled into the small den, the room planned as my father's study until we realized he never used it. I pulled Greg along with me, releasing his hand to flick on the gas fireplace. He closed and locked the door behind us, then came to me in the firelit darkness and took me gently into his arms.

We kissed again, tugging at each other's jeans until we could kick them off. Then we were on the floor, kissing and rolling over the Persian rug until Greg growled and pinned me beneath him. I was so wet with wanting him that Greg slid into me easily, but he started with shallow strokes, so teasing and gentle that I had to cry out for more.

"Yes!" I gasped when he plunged in.

In the next room, the dishwasher made a shooshing noise

as water surged in. Feeling freed by the camouflaging noise, I let myself spiral into the maddening pleasure Greg evoked.

Oh, I could see myself doing this in five years . . . ten years . . . thirty. Yes, I could do this indefinitely.

5

"Oh come, oh come, Immanuel," sang the choir on Mom's Canadian Brass CD. It was one of my Christmas favorites, and I made sure we played it at least once each year while trimming the tree. Mom had bought fresh pine boughs to hang from the Victorian arches in the parlor, and the scent of pine mingled with the waves of orange and cinnamon coming from the cups of warm wassail that Mom had heated on the kitchen stove. When Wolf stopped by to drop off Leo we had talked Wolf into joining us, too, and now he was poised at the top of the ladder, fastening ornaments to the highest spot while Leo and I dug into boxes of tissue for Victorian-style ornaments, our theme for this year. That meant we had to set aside all the other ornaments—the family keepsakes, the cutesy things I'd made in grade school, the Mickey Mouse–shaped disco balls.

"The Victorian ornaments will work well with your subdued color scheme," Leo told Mom. "Where in the world did you get those candle-shaped lights?"

Mom snickered as she wove green florist's wire through a pine branch. "I ordered them from Tokyo last June. I had seen them at Madeline Canby's New Year's bash last year, but when I learned what she paid for them at the Christmas Boutique on Union Square—" Mom pressed a hand to her chest, feigning a heart attack. "I realized I had to go directly to the manufacturer."

Leo was nodding so vehemently with approval, I pinged his shoulder. This was the guy who had been calling my mother Martha Stewart just days ago.

"Ouch," he said, plucking an ornate lavender and silver glass bulb from my hand and handing it up to Wolf.

The night was sweet, and I was acutely aware of being in the moment, so comfortable here at home with Mom, the Christmas maven, so tickled to have my two good friends Leo and Wolf here to play with, so exhilarated with hope about my future with Greg. It was one of those few times in which I was happy and also aware of that happiness even as it embraced me—a poignant, giddy moment.

"Shh!" I grabbed Leo's sleeve. "This song is so exquisitely beautiful, I could cry."

Leo frowned. "Doesn't sound familiar. What's it called?"

"I don't know, something French."

"D'ou viens-tu, bergere," Wolf answered in melodic French.

"You speak Portugese and French, too?" Leo blinked in obvious approval.

"And Spanish," Wolf said modestly. "But you, too, would be multilingual if you were born in Europe."

"So modest," I said, looking up at Wolf. "Isn't he just the perfect guy?"

"You don't have to sell me," Leo said, tossing aside crumbled tissue papers.

I was so tickled that they were falling for each other! I wanted to dance around the room and hug them both, then give Mom a squeeze for good measure, but I had to remind myself that Wolf and Leo were new to Christmas with the Greenwoods, and I didn't want to frighten them and send them off shrieking from my shameless display of emotion.

"Where is Dr. Greenwood this evening?" Leo asked as he handed a velvet angel up to Wolf.

"That's right," I said. "Dad usually takes off so that he can decorate the tree with us."

"He's on call," Mom explained.

She didn't seem ruffled, but it sounded like a lame excuse to me. "I thought that meant he was supposed to keep his pager on in case of an emergency."

Mom kept winding wire around the evergreen branch. "A few years ago he decided that his spare time was better spent at the hospital, where you can always find an emergency."

"I don't know, Mom," I teased. "Sounds suspicious to me. Are you sure Dad isn't having a fling with some nurse?"

I was joking, but the words seemed to take Mom by surprise. "Hell, no," she said. "No such luck." I stared at her. What was that all about?

Mom turned away from me and focused her attention on Wolf and Leo. "Guys, promise me you'll never go into medicine."

Wolf shook his head. "I'm a programmer. Computers are my forte. People are too complicated."

"I'm in television," Leo answered. "Talent development for DBC Network."

"Really?" Wolf brightened. "How interesting. Do you have dealings with celebrities?"

"Rarely," Leo said, obviously not willing to admit that he was answering phones for the Director of Talent Development. Being a good friend, I let it slide and pulled out some pearlized beads for the tree. "But I run into celebs all the time at Rock Center," Leo went on. "That's where our studios and offices are located."

"Now that sounds exciting," Wolf admitted as he descended the ladder. He cradled a cup of spiced wassail and sat on the velvet sofa. "I'll bet you know some great places there."

"You should come," I said.

"We're getting a new apartment," Leo added. "A converted loft in Tribeca."

"Which we need to fill with roommates as soon as we get back," I prodded Leo.

He waved me off. "Come stay with us, Wolf. You're welcome anytime. You'll love New York."

While Mom went into the kitchen to take a call, the three of us collapsed on the furniture to sip our drinks and stare up at the half-decorated tree. The CD changed, and jazz strains from the Vince Guaraldi Trio's *Charlie Brown Christmas* made me smile. "'It's a sad tree,'" I said.

"'It's not a bad little tree,'" Leo chimed in. "'All it needs is a little love.'"

"That was so cool, the way those cartoon kids would wave their arms over the scrawny tree and turn it into a Christmas masterpiece," Wolf said.

"Hey, it could happen," I said. "Anything could happen at Christmas."

"Thank you, Linus," Leo said. "The only person I know who could stretch a one-day holiday into a month-long event."

"Oh, that's Madison," Wolfie said quietly. "She was always that way, upbeat and hopeful. Looking for the silver lining in the cloud that was dumping on you."

"Wolfie! You make me sound like a frosted flake," I said.

"No, not at all." He reached across and squeezed my hand. "You were a good friend during a very difficult time for me."

"What was the worst year of high school for you?" Leo asked.

Wolf snickered. "All of it. I spent those years trying to be someone I wasn't, trying to make my family happy."

Trying to be straight, I recalled. Wolf had made a dutiful effort to conform, but the kids who knew him well had been able to see how that struggle tortured him.

"How did you two get to be friends?" Leo asked.

I leaned back and let my head loll toward Wolf. "We were friends by default at first, weren't we? When Mr. O'Dell made us lab partners?"

"And you looked so cute in those goggles," Wolf teased.

I sighed. "The best part about high school is that it is now over. I would never want to relive those years."

"But we had some fun, didn't we?" Wolf asked.

"How about the senior prom?" I nudged Wolf. "When you smuggled that bottle of champagne inside your big, black umbrella?"

He nudged me back. "What about you, with that silver flask in your tiny beaded bag?"

Leo's jaw dropped. "I can't believe you two went to the prom together. Don't tell me you rented one of those tacky tuxedos."

"We did it all!" I insisted. "From the tacky tux to the rented limo and the orchid wrist corsage. And I'll have you know, I have fond memories of my senior prom."

Wolf was smiling. "God, I hated those years. But you were a good friend, Madison. You always dealt with me honestly. Other girls tried to manipulate me, back me into a corner." He rubbed his eyes for a second. "Brrr!"

"So when did you come out?" Leo asked.

"Graduation day. I wore cowboy boots and a pink tutu under my gown."

"Needless to say, his parents were not pleased or impressed," I added.

"Ah, yes." Leo nodded sagely. "Parents often have trouble dealing with the pink tutu."

"Especially when the shoes clash," I said.

"They thought my sexual identity was a result of spending my high school years in San Francisco. As if it were that simple. But they blamed themselves, then tried to reform me. Obviously, a gay man is hardly a fruitful heir to the throne."

Leo took a sip of his drink, then frowned. "And Edward the Eighth thought he had problems when he met Wally Simpson."

"You're way too young to know about Edward and Wallace," Wolf said.

Leo shrugged. "I'm a hopeless Anglophile. I'm so upset that Di has left Charles. Do you think they can work it out? Prince Chuck can be such a cad. Have you ever met them?"

Just then Mom breezed back in and stopped to gaze up at the tree. "It's really coming along," she said cheerfully.

I nudged Leo with my foot. "That means: Back to work!"

As we returned to our posts, sorting and hunting and stringing and hanging, I stepped back from the towering tree and let my eyes go fuzzy. It was a trick I'd started as a child, a way to soft-focus on the tree as I tried to capture the romantic image in my head. Of course, I always had the Carpenters' *Merry Christmas, Darling* playing in the background as I ventured off into my Christmas fantasy.

This year, the object of the song was Greg. I knew he was working tonight; after our romp in the basement, he had mentioned a catering gig at the Art Institute. With his holiday schedule, I realized that we would be spending many nights apart.

But here I was, gazing up at my Christmas tree and thinking of him and of our future together.

Was he thinking of me as he arranged swirls of California roll on trays and dished up tender filets of salmon muniere? Was he planning to make me a part of his private Christmas celebration?

Somehow, I doubted it. With his cool demeanor and calculating manner, Greg seemed to operate on a different emotional level, his feelings buried miles beneath those dark brown eyes. I bit my lip, wondering how to gain access to that well-hidden territory. Oh, why hadn't I paid more attention to *Men Are from Mars, Women Are from Venus* when the galleys circulated at work? Weighing heavily upon me was the memory of Greg, the bad boy, and Madison, the dull, brown-haired honors student. I couldn't let those old roles rise again! I had come so far since high school.

Visions of my New York life taunted me, complete with Drucie from copyediting yelling at me for being late, and Hugh sneaking into my office with glasses of sherry. Then there was my boss, Ms. Macy Gramble, who barely noticed me on a Valium-induced good day. On a bad day, she mistook me for a doormat. Okay, maybe I wasn't the most assertive person in the world, but I was going to hold my own in this relationship with Greg. It was obvious that the guy liked me. All I needed to do was parlay his feelings into something deeper.

Of course, I didn't have a clue how to do that, but I was determined to give it the old A-plus try.

Although I worried that Greg refrained from articulating his emotions, I was reassured by the way he demonstrated his attraction to me so many times—and in so many delicious ways—over the days that followed. One afternoon while Mom was off with her new best friend Emily, I sneaked Greg up to my old room and we put a real notch in the old French Provincial bedpost. One night when the weather wasn't too chilly, we sneaked out to Mom's garden and made love under the blanket of stars, being extra careful to swallow our moans and cries so that we wouldn't alarm the neighbors. Although Greg and I maintained casual conversation about the party details, I wasn't able to swing the topic over to the subject of our relationship. Somehow, it was difficult to segue from "Do you like the lavender lace tablecloths?" to "So where do you see us in two years?"

But today I was determined to get some answers. The sex was great fun, but I'd seen enough of the developing relationship between Leo and Wolf—who were already planning a summer trip to Portugal—to know that Greg was dodging intimacy.

That day, after Mom made a final decision on the tablecloths (ivory with a gold lace overlay) I rode with Greg in his van to the linen supplier. I sort of enjoyed commanding the passenger seat, pretending to be Greg's sidekick as he headed down 101 to the supply house in Bernal Heights. *Bad Boys,* that theme song from the TV docudrama *Cops* was playing on the radio, and Greg tapped out the beat on the steering wheel, as if he actually enjoyed it.

"So," I said, realizing I was going to just have to take the dive. "How does your family celebrate Christmas? Any Kasami family traditions I should know about?"

"Holidays are sort of a nonissue with us. My dad's been in the catering business since I was, like, four. I don't remember having a single Christmas dinner with my family. Certainly not on Christmas Day."

"But you must do something," I prodded, hoping for an invitation to join in, even if it was just an eggnog party or a simple gift exchange on the twenty-sixth.

"Not really."

"Do you at least exchange gifts?" I asked. "What about your sisters and their kids? Don't you pick up a few things for the nieces and nephews? I'd be happy to help you shop." There! I'd wedged my nails into the crack.

"My sisters usually take care of that stuff. What do I know about buying for kids? She picks up what they want and I give her the money. It's easier that way."

Thwarted, I turned toward the window as the lyric spilled out: "Whatcha gonna do when they come for you?"

"I hope they have enough gold lace overlays," Greg said.

"Maybe I should have called ahead. This time of year, everyone is stretched by holiday entertaining."

How could he dwell on mundane details when our first Christmas together was crumbling before my eyes. "So what are you doing on Christmas?" I asked blatantly. "I mean, I know you've got our party on Christmas Eve, but—"

"Actually, I have two parties Christmas Eve. Yours and the Collins party on Russian Hill."

Call me wimpy, but my heart sank a little to learn that we didn't have an exclusive on Greg for Christmas Eve. "Oh. Bummer."

"Hey!" He reached over and rubbed the back of my hand. "Don't sound so betrayed. I'm not sleeping with any of the Collins daughters."

"That's a relief," I tried to joke.

"Yeah. Especially since they're, like in their sixties."

I laughed, turning my hand to give Greg's a squeeze. What was I worried about? The chemistry between us was undeniable.

"I hope you don't mind a minor detour," he said, taking the exit for John McLaren Park. "I know a very private little drive, surrounded by trees. I used to come here on my bike and do yoga in the woods, back when I had spare time."

I wanted to tease him, but the image of Greg meditating in the woods appealed to me in a Zen sort of way. "Feeling the need to meditate today?"

"Definitely, and I figured we'd better make a stop before we load up." He pulled the van onto a grassy lip off the side of the road and turned to me. "You know the old adage: Never meditate with a van full of linens." He grinned at me, then headed into the back of the van.

"Don't think I've ever heard that one," I said, following him. The van was clean, the floor covered with smooth industrial carpeting. The small windows in the back were dark enough to keep anyone from looking in. Which would prohibit them from seeing Greg strip off his clothes, which he was doing at the moment in a relaxed, almost teasing manner.

"Do you always meditate naked?" I asked, folding my arms as I hunched there.

"Always." He tossed his boxers onto his black jeans, then knelt before me. His body was so perfect, lean and strong, his shoulders a beautiful square, his chest hairless and rippled with subtle muscles. I must have been gaping, but I'd never seen him totally naked in this glorious light.

"You're staring." He latched onto my belt buckle and pulled me down so that I was kneeling opposite him.

"You're gorgeous," I answered, running my hands over his shoulders and down his chest. It was imminently clear that Greg wanted me right here and now, but I wasn't ready to abandon my mission. "And you know I'm crazy about you. But I have to know if this is about more than sex."

"Is anything ever so black-and-white?" he said. He pulled my sweater off over my head, then dug his hands under the waistband of my jeans to cup my butt. My body was betraying me, warming to his touch. My hard nipples pressed through my bra into his chest, wanting him, wanting more of him. "How could this be only about sex?" He moved his hands around to undo my belt buckle and split open the zipper of my jeans. I closed my eyes and sucked in my breath when he shoved a hand in my panties.

He had me by the short and curlies, as they used to say in high school. But I couldn't relent now. I couldn't.

"I have to know, Greg," I whispered with my eyes closed. "What are we about?"

"So far we've done just fine without drawing any diagrams."

"Really, Greg. I need to know. Does love enter into this?"

"What do you think?"

Damn, he was making this so difficult. "I think . . . I think, yes, I may be falling in love with you."

He thrust his hand deeper, and for a second I felt as if my entire body hinged on his answer.

"Then let me love you," he whispered, kissing my ear. "Let me love you."

Bingo! That was all I needed to hear.

6

"There is nothing relaxing about a relaxing Christmas with the Greenwoods," Leo said as we sat at the big dining room table, assembling the votive candles according to Mom's specs. Leo's job was to place white votive candles into the glass holders, then sprinkle in clear amber glass beads. Then it was my turn to finish each candle off with a fat gold lamé bow. "Really," Leo went on. "Next year, remind me to book a cruise or a quiet trip to Disney World."

"You're having a great time, and you know it," I said confidently. "Is it my fault you stay out late every night with Wolfie-poo?" Leo and Wolf had been making nightly pilgrimages to local bars. Sometimes I joined them, when I wasn't pretending to take care of some catering task with Greg. Aside from that, I'd had dinner once with Mom, but her calendar was so loaded with engagements with her friends that she was rarely around in the evenings. And, of course, Dad was seldom at home. Usually he rolled in from the hospital around ten-thirty and planted himself in the small parlor, where he would stay up until eleven and watch the late news before heading up to bed. Hard to believe he was a prestigious cardiac surgeon. Honestly, he reminded me of a hamster in a Habittrail, going from feeding to sleeping to running on the wheel with unwavering regularity.

"Let me remind you," Leo said, "I stay out late every night at home, too. But I didn't count on having to get out of bed each morning for crafts seminars. Hot-gluing cranberries to foam balls. Dressing muslin angels in eyelet and organza. Sewing white mittens out of felt—"

"Oh, did you see how the mittens turned out?" I pointed to the main staircase, where Mom had hung the finished garland along the banister. "Mom added gold ribbons to the mittens, then strung them into a garland. She used fresh pine branches and faux ivy with white on the tips. It came together so beautifully."

"Can we turn off the craft channel for just a few minutes?" Leo griped.

"Just as soon as you finish your job there, and don't scrimp on the beads." Above our heads, a wreath adorned with gold snowflakes and dripping glass beads hung from the chandelier. It was the day before Christmas Eve, and every corner of the house had been festooned with some type of ornament, display, or garland. The decorations only added to the building momentum of the holiday, which seemed to be cresting along with my intense relationship with Greg.

"You're awfully chipper for a girl who's spending her Christmas with Mumsy and Daddy," Leo teased.

Tightening a gold bow, I smiled. "You're looking at a woman in love."

Leo gasped mockingly. "No! No way! You haven't actually used the 'L' word, have you?"

I nodded. "I am in love with one of San Francisco's most eligible bachelors." I hugged myself. "Hell's bells, I'm in love, Leo!"

"No! It can't be!" Leo was shaking his head. "What are you going to do? Holy Christ, do I need to find someone to take your share in the apartment?"

"I don't think we'll do anything so radical right away," I said. "Yes, I fantasize about staying here and making cute little babies with Greg. But not right away. I mean, we haven't really discussed the details."

"Hold on to your hat, Hester Prim. Are you sure that you and Greg are on the same page?"

"Sure," I lied. "We've talked about our feelings."

"And about commitment? And marriage? And bicoastal living arrangements? And the pros and cons of marrying into another culture?"

Sometimes a good friend could be a total pain in the ass. "No, we didn't go that far," I admitted. "But we have a great time together, and we have discussed our feelings."

Leo was still shaking his head.

"He told me he loved me." Sort of, but it wouldn't hurt to edit a few things out. "Leo, you know how guys are. They can give you a complete rundown of last week's Forty-niners game, but when it comes to detailing their feelings and plans, they choke."

"Especially when they don't *have* any plans," Leo said.

"Nuh-ugh!"

"Uh-huh." Now he was nodding like a bobble head.

I turned away from him and focused on tying yet another perfect bow.

"Don't ignore me, because I'm not going away. Look, Madison, if I'm all wrong and you and Greg end up living in a cute little Victorian in Pacific Heights, I'll be thrilled for you. Ecstatic. But what if I'm right, honey? I'm just telling you to protect yourself. Beware of gorgeous men bearing orgasms."

When I winced at him, he shrugged. "Hey, it's always worked for me."

"But it's not true of Wolf," I pointed out.

"True, Wolf is a rare exception. The boy is an angel. It's his family I need to be wary of."

"Are they coming for Christmas?"

"No, but Wolf is flying to Portugal to be with them for New Year's. We'll actually be leaving San Francisco on the same day, so we'll share a ride to the airport."

I nodded. "Okay, why don't I feel compelled to warn you about Wolf? To ask you if you've done a background check and grilled him over his intentions."

Leo let out a deep belly laugh. "Because you've known him since high school and you can attest that he's a great guy." Leo took a deep breath, puffing himself up proudly. "You must admit, you couldn't have hooked up two nicer people."

"Don't be so smug," I said. "Wolf is great, but I'm still not sure about you."

"Oh, shut up and finish up with those bows! We've got that matinee of the *Nutcracker*, and I told Wolf we'd meet him for dinner."

"Don't forget about my dress," I said. "You promised to hit the Union Square stores with me before the performance. I'm outta time, partner. Tomorrow is the big day."

"Calm down, Cinderella. Your fairy godmother will conjure some magic for you." He let out a mock sigh. "The things I do for friends."

Every year, I looked forward to seeing the *Nutcracker* ballet, the classic story of a young girl who defends her sorry-looking Christmas gift, only to have it come alive, join her in a battle against a group of inflated rats, then turn into a gorgeous prince who dances her off to the Land of Sweets. It's a darned good Christmas story—at least the first act—and the familiar music is an incredible source of comfort. I have occasionally wondered what kind of opium Tchaikovsky was smoking when he drummed up that story, especially the weak second and third acts, which seem to be fluffy excuses for dancers to leap on stage and perform a series of pas de deux. And then there is the six-headed king of rats—definitely a villain born of drug-induced hallucinations.

All the more reason to love the *Nutcracker*. I rarely missed it.

I'm not sure that Leo shared my enthusiasm, but he did manage to wake up when I nudged him somewhere around the beginning of Act Three.

Afterward, over a round of drinks at Top of the Mark, I looked out at the jeweled lights of the city and let the alcohol roll over my tongue. "Wouldn't it be wild if you and Wolf ended up living here in San Francisco?" I said. "Maybe Greg and I could get a place near you guys."

"Ach!" Leo held his drink as if he were one with the glass. "Don't go off on one of those dangerous fantasies with me as the godfather of your kids. I will not be your labor coach, and I don't change diapers."

"I'm just saying it could be nice. All of us together here."

"Pullleeze, don't jinx things for Wolf and me. I really like him," he said in a mousy voice. "Besides, I like living in New York. I like our new apartment. That is, if you don't get yourself married off before we can move in."

"I don't think things will happen that fast," I said. "But I meant to tell you, I just talked to Sugar yesterday. I told her you were softening on the roommate issue."

"You what?" His handsome face stretched in a scowl. "You big, fat liar."

"But I don't understand what the problem is. So Sugar is a little bit out there. She's a kind, honest person, who won't swipe your valuables, won't leave dirty dishes in the sink, and she will not dance around with your underwear on her head while you're not home."

"I should hope not!"

"So you are softening?"

Leo tossed back the last of his Tom Collins and lifted a brow. "Buy me another drink and I'll think about it."

While I was at the bar, Wolf appeared, looking retro in a black turtleneck and plaid blazer. Plaid. On anyone else it would have looked like a rejected kilt, but somehow Wolf managed to pull it off.

"Madison." He approached and kissed me on both cheeks. Somewhere between our reunion and his sleeping with my best friend we'd moved from casual handshakes to European kisses.

"Nice threads. You are too cool, Wolf." I patted the lapel of his blazer. "So what are you drinking, you big beautiful man?"

He touched the paneled bar and told the bartender "Dubonnay rocks."

"See? You are the only person I know who drinks cool drinks like that. You know, people in L.A. would pay you to loan them your sense of style."

"Ironic, isn't it? The very thing that made me the butt of jokes in high school now makes me the flavor of the week."

"Don't let it get you down," I said. "I'm still the butt of jokes."

"How was the ballet?" Wolf asked as we joined Leo at our table by the window.

"Fabulous," Leo said. "Any excuse to watch buff men prance around in tights is fine by me."

"Oh, please, tell me you did not spend the entire performance staring at crotches," I said.

"Musculature," Leo said, lifting his tall glass in a toast. "Here's to tight, well-toned musculature."

I pinged him on the shoulder. "You're too young to be a pervert."

"Tell me you didn't look?" Leo said.

"That's beside the point," I said, straightening my skirt. "But let's bring Wolf up to speed. We finished our Christmas shopping and wrapped the remainder of the gifts this morning. You should see them under the tree—it looks like a spread from *Family Circle*."

Leo laughed. "It really does! A few weeks ago I would have found that highly disturbing, but now it brings me great tidings of comfort and joy." He plucked the lemon skin garnish from his glass. "Robin has won me over. Call me anal, but I've come to appreciate her whole-hog approach to Christmas."

"Well, she's got little gifties for both of you under the tree," I said, "so I hope you're planning to stop by on Christmas, Wolf."

"Absolutely. And I'd like to be adopted by Robin, too. Do you think there's room in her heart for two gay sons?"

Leo slid an arm over Wolf's shoulders. "I'll run your proposal by the boss," he said.

"But wait!" I held up my arms. "Let's not forget the most important event of the day." I turned to Wolf. "I have been to the mother ship! I scoured Neiman and combed Marcus. I searched Macy's and Saks. And at last, in a tiny boutique off Union Square, I found it!"

Wolf rolled his eyes, as if someone in the periphery was going to cue him in. "Oh, dear. Is this the point at which I'm supposed to guess what 'it' is?"

"I found the perfect ensemble for tomorrow night," I explained.

"With my help," Leo added.

"Really?" Now Wolf perked up. "What's it like?"

"I don't want to jinx it by talking about it," I said, thinking of the fine lines and textures of my gown. "But I will say, it's one of the best things I've seen by our good friends Dolce & Gabbana."

Wolf whistled. "Isn't that a bit steep? I thought you said you were still on a college budget."

"It's one of Mom's gifts to me. Whenever I'm home, she lets me go wild with the credit cards." It was a treat I tried not to take advantage of too much, but I think Mom enjoyed seeing me spend, especially since she'd worked so hard to find a way to circumvent Dad's cheapness.

"I tried to talk her into a gorgeous Oscar sheath," Leo interjected, "but she didn't like the bare shoulders."

"Why not?" Wolf asked. "Your shoulders are fine. Not at all like those brawny girls on the swim team."

"It wasn't the style, it was the color," I said. "That baby blue just doesn't work for me, and it ties into one of my lifetime rules: Never wear blue eyeshadow. Never."

"Isn't that a little extreme?" Wolf said.

"If God had intended our skin to be blue, he wouldn't have made it the color of bruises," I said. "Besides, pale blue on a brunette is so tacky."

"What about Emma Thompson at the Oscars?" Leo pointed out. "She was heaven, wasn't she? That sparkling blue bodice and the silky wrap. Her gown was by an obscure designer. Caroline Charles, I think."

"Emma looked stunning on the red carpet," Wolf agreed. "But her gown was a darker blue. A peacock blue, I'd say."

"You guys need to remember that Emma Thompson has a lot more gold in her hair than I do. Actually, she's sort of a taffy blonde, anyway."

"When are you going to abandon the boring brown?" Leo asked. "Brunette is so dead. Go red, or even blonde. Do something radical."

I touched the ends of my long hair and twisted it around my fingers. "But I don't want to put chemicals in my hair. At least, not until it turns gray."

"I think Madison's hair fits her personality," Wolf said. "Many European women actually dye their hair darker. It's elegant."

But Leo shook his head in disapproval.

"What about Sandra Bullock?" I asked. "Or . . . or . . ." Damn it if I couldn't think of another famous brunette younger than Elizabeth Taylor.

Leo lifted his glass. "I rest my case."

"Well, I am not going radical for Christmas," I said

firmly. "And I trust you two won't show up with shaved heads or flaming red Mohawks."

Leo lifted a hand to his schoolboy do—a short, straight cut, parted to the side and held in place by a miracle gel that seemed to plasticize as it styled. Not that it looked bad, but it took Leo forever to shape, volumize, and tame his hair. "Honestly, I don't have much left to flame," he said, "unless we're talking up in smoke."

It was one of Leo's sore spots, and I thought it was brave of him to draw attention to it.

Wolf twirled his glass, as if searching for something. "Funny, how we all long to be something we're not." He gestured toward his dark hair, pulled back in a thick ponytail. "As a kid I was excruciatingly embarrassed about having so much hair. Hair all over my body, like a bear." He shook his head. "If only we could transform ourselves."

Leo grinned. "Honey, that's the job of plastic surgeons."

"But I mean from the inside," Wolf said.

"Ohmigosh, Wolf! That is so what Christmas is about."

"Again, in English, please," Leo prodded me.

"Isn't Christmas about transformation?" I said, riding a wave of inspiration. "About making our world a little nicer? Being a bit kinder to people?"

They looked at me with a mixture of thoughtfulness and confusion.

"That's an encouraging thought," Wolf said.

Leo lifted his glass and laughed. "Oh, man, you two got it bad!"

Christmas Eve dawned gray and overcast, but we were so busy preparing for the party that we barely noticed the climate beyond the front door. There were tables to move, tablecloths to press, candles and centerpieces to set out just so. Of course, Leo lipped off a running editorial on the torture of preparing for a Greenwood Christmas Party, but I could tell he was loving it.

"Leo," Mom said as we popped open canisters of the cookies we had decorated. "I leave you in charge of getting these goodies onto trays in a decorative manner."

"Robin, you are a slave driver!" he teased. "But the colored sugars will look elegant surrounded by these powdered-sugar puffs, don't you agree?"

Except for a bout of rebellion in high school, I had always enjoyed pitching in on Mom's parties, working in the shadow of her precision, creativity, and dogged determination. Mom's secret to successful entertaining had always been to do the work in advance so that she'd have time to enjoy the party. So as we ran up and down the stairs, ironed out creases, and stacked glassware, I had to admit, I was having a good time already.

"God, I love Christmas," I muttered to Leo as we smoothed a lace overlay atop the dining room table.

"Yes, yes, but do you think that's straight?" He squinted at the table, folding his arms.

"You know," I told him, "if things dry up for you at the network, you could always become a consultant."

"Shut up and pull your side down two inches!" he barked.

As Leo stacked china on the dining room credenza, I wandered into the front foyer to gaze up at our Victorian tree. A pile of wrapped gifts flanked the base of the tree in a festive display of velvet bows and satin ribbons that would rival Macy's window.

"I love this day," I called to Leo. "Every Christmas Eve, the air is so thick with the scent of expectation. I've always felt that excitement when the gift boxes are stacked up with their shiny foil paper and fat bows. You just want to rip them all open immediately."

"I see you ogling the presents," Leo called. "No fair peeking."

I picked up a package wrapped in pale lavender paper. Before I checked the tag I knew it was for me, since Mom had always played up to the fact that I loved purple. "Hmm." I gave it a shake and heard something rattle inside. What could it be?

"Do you know what Robin got for me?" Leo asked. "I can't stand the suspense!"

"But if you know, then there's no surprise on Christmas morning," I said, fingering the white velvet bow on my gift. "You know, once when I was a kid, I did sneak a peek. One afternoon while Mom was out, I managed to neatly unwrap and rewrap every package with my name on it. I was like, ten or something, and there were some great gifts that year—I remember a Walkman and a really cool leather jacket. But when Christmas came around, I was so disappointed. There was no surprise. I had burst my own bubble."

"And let that be a lesson to you, Peeping Thomasina," Leo warned.

"Oh, I learned my lesson," I said, shaking the lavender package again.

"Put that down before I'm forced to call the gift police!" Leo called.

With a laugh, I dropped the present back onto the pile. Tomorrow would be soon enough.

With all the nervous jitters of a prom queen, I descended the stairs to a festive houseful of guests, their voices rising over the harmonic song of the carolers Mom had hired to fill the front foyer with Christmas cheer. Dressed in red and black Victorian gowns, the singers nodded cheerfully as I passed by on my way to the kitchen—always the heart of a party. I figured Mom would have a few last-minute chores for me to take care of, especially since Greg wouldn't be here until later. He needed to attend to the Collins party first, but his people were top-notch caterers.

When I pushed open the kitchen door, I saw that Greg

had employed a legion of servers. In fact, they stacked, sorted, and rinsed with such command, I felt like an intruder in a hostile camp.

"You look lovely, princess," Dad said, handing me a cup of warm spiced cider.

"Thanks, Daddy." The childish word sort of slipped out, and I hoped no one noticed as he kissed me on the cheek.

"That's a pretty dress," he said.

And it cost a heck of a lot more than you'd like to spend, I thought, smiling. Thank God Mom handled the credit card bills now. Upstairs I'd had the panicked realization that my beautiful black sheath with its beaded red jacket was too prissy, too Barbie doll. I'd been tempted to cut a slit in the side, but had compromised by letting my hair hang around my shoulders instead of the twist I usually wrapped it in for formal occasions.

"When you get a chance, there are a few docs outside I'd like you to meet," Dad said. "Most of the new surgical residents are here." With that, he pushed past me, making his way to the parlor.

"Great! I'll catch up with you in a minute." Lest you think that Dad was trying to hook me up with a doctor, that was simply his way of saying that he wanted to show me off, his offspring, to the guys at work. Because, if you haven't noticed, for Dad, it's all about work.

I looked around the kitchen for my mother, but didn't see her in the small army of white-shirted workers. After a long hit of cider, I ducked a tray of scallops and bacon to pop into the dining room. Wolf and Leo were there, positioned in front of Mom's display of gold votive candles, which cast an angelic glow from the built-in shelves. The backlighting provided a dramatic mood for my two friends, who seemed to be enjoying each other's company, as usual.

"You would love my sister," Wolf was saying. "She's very goth, very dramatic. My parents thought boarding school would tone her down, but her spirit is unquenchable."

"Speaking of unquenchable." I dangled my empty cup in the air. "I need another drink. Wow, that cider goes down easily."

"Pace yourself, sweetie," Leo said. "You've got all night to get your drunken groove on."

"I forgot how these parties always make me nervous at first. I'm supposed to go and meet the new fleet of doctors on Dad's rotation."

"Ooh, men in white," Leo cooed. "Mind if I tag along?"

"I dare you," I teased, ducking into the next room. I knew Leo was afraid of doctors and needles and all things medical, ever since he'd had an AIDS scare a few years ago. Navigating the crowded dining room, I thought back to that rocky time. The catch in Leo's voice when he asked me to come along to the clinic. The knot of fear in my throat as he shared some of the details about his one-night stand with an "oustandingly gorgeous" guy who later admitted to working as a prostitute in the meat-packing district. Horrors unfolded upon horrors when Leo noticed a dark spot growing on the side of his face. As we waited for the test results, I prayed for a second chance. *Please don't take my friend because of one mistake. Please, please.*

If there is a God, he heard me that day. The clinic worker emerged with a smile. Leo got his "do over." A second chance. How rare is that?

Tucking that memory away, I crossed the front foyer and nearly bumped into Mom's friend Emily, who was handing her cape to the woman designated as coat taker. She patted her swept-back hairdo, though the gesture was unnecessary, as Emily's hairdresser must have dumped enough gel to lube a truck.

"Madison!" She spread her arms wide and gave me air kisses. "It's been so long, dear. How is your mother? Actually, where is your mother?"

"I'm sure she's around here somewhere," I said. "But you should be the best barometer of how she is, with all the time you spend together." Mom had tea or lunch or sherry with Emily nearly every afternoon.

"Oh, no, dear, not anymore. Didn't she tell you? I have a job now," Emily announced proudly, her perfectly lined lips parting in a reserved smile. "I'm treasurer of the Ryder Foundation, and the job has taken me off the luncheon circuit."

What? My radar went wild, blipping and shrieking, but I managed to plaster on a neutral smile as Emily went on about her new position. Okay, so Mom had been lying about her outings with Emily. That meant my mother was spending scads of time doing . . . what? A job search of her own?

I tended to doubt that Mom was trying to get back into the workforce. But the obvious alternative seemed so film noir . . . so unlikely. Robin Greenwood lived by the rules; the woman could be the cover girl for *Good Wife* magazine.

Tell me I'm in denial. Call me Queen Denial the First. If I was dragging my heels, it was for good reason.

It is just no fun to realize your mother is cheating on your father.

7

In the parlor, I found my father holding court with a group of men near the bar. I recognized two of the men: Dad's longtime associates from the hospital, his colleagues Dr. Feinstein and Dr. Meuller. As Dad spoke, the men nodded thoughtfully, as if listening to a complicated diagnosis. It struck me how the three surgeons had acquired such similar appearances over the years—three pink-skinned white guys with white hair. It was actually sort of creepy, watching the Stepford Doctors conference in our parlor, knowing my own father was one of them.

I was still a little shaken from getting wind of Mom's scandal, but I'd swiped another glass of hot cider, and the rum in the mix softened the edges of Mom's crime. I figured it was best to do the obligatory meet-and-greet with Dad; then I'd be totally free when Greg arrived.

"Merry Christmas, everyone," I said, waving to Dad's crew.

"You remember Dr. Meuller and Dr. Feinstein, don't you?" Dad asked, pulling me into the circle.

"Of course," I lied. *Which one are you?* I wondered as I kissed the taller man with the glasses. Feinstein . . . because Feinstein can't see so fine. And Meuller was always shorter and heavier, like a mule. Don't ask.

"Madison's had quite a year," Dad announced proudly. "Graduated Columbia, then found a job working for *Skyscraper* magazine. She's got an office on the twenty-third floor."

Actually, it was a cubicle, but since the docs weren't going to fact-check Dad's story, I figured I'd let it slide.

"Good for you," Dr. Meuller boomed.

"Do you know Tina Brown?" Dr. Feinstein asked.

"No, actually, she's at another magazine," I said.

"But Madison works with Hugh Paddington," Dad added proudly. "Tell them, honey."

"Tell them, what, Dad?" That I'd been in Hugh's pants and lived to tell the tale? I swallowed hard. This was going worse than I'd expected.

"She's taken meetings with Paddington," Dad bragged.

Why was I surprised that Dad was spreading exaggerated tales of my success? He'd always had trouble dealing with my lack of ambition.

"Is that right?" Dr. Meuller nodded.

"Oh, sure," I said. "Hugh is a fixture at *Skyscraper*." And probably older than some of the fixtures in the building. I wanted to say it, but Dad gazed at me with such hope in his eyes, I took the leap. "When I've had dinner with him, you'd be surprised at all the people who stop by the table to say hello." The last statement was a stretch, but I felt confident that I'd casually upped my cachet (and Hugh's) in one clever name-drop.

Just then a short man with dark hair leaned into the group and made some comment that elicited laughter from Drs. Meuller and Farsighted. Dad chuckled and clapped the man on the shoulder.

"Dr. Mehta, I'd like you to meet my daughter," Dad said. I shook hands with Dr. Mehta, whose dark eyes sparkled with mirth.

"You are the daughter who is a famous publisher in New York!" Dr. Mehta said, waving toward someone behind me.

"I would like that you should meet my wife, Zara. She is a very gifted storyteller."

"I'd love to meet her," I said, "but I'm not actually a publisher. I work for a magazine. *Skyscraper* magazine."

"Zara! Come now. There is someone here who would like to talk about your story!"

A shy, dark-haired woman joined us, bowing before me. "I am so happy to meet you!" she said.

"Tell her," Dr. Mehta prodded. "Tell her your story."

I felt my facial muscles tense as sweet little Zara tried to speak over the men. I couldn't hear her, but I could relate. It reminded me of every story-pitch meeting at *Skyscraper*.

Beside me, my father and the other doctors slipped into a conversation about the performance of the Dow this week. Dr. Meuller joked about mixing up one of the financial indexes with his handicap, which they all found incredibly funny. Then, while Zara and Dr. Mehta tried to pitch a sad book about a child who walks the earth in search of a clean water well, Dad reeled in a few other new residents and flew their names by so quickly, all I could do was nod and shake hands.

By the time Leo appeared in the parlor, I was pinned to the Oriental rug like a butterfly on a board. "Help . . . help . . ." I transmitted desperate brain waves.

The picture of etiquette, Leo came to us, excused himself, and announced that I was needed in the garden.

"Oh, excuse me." I bowed before Zara, then quickly backed away from the group.

"You looked like you needed saving," he muttered. "Besides, people have started dancing downstairs and Wolf wants to see if you've improved since the prom."

"God bless you," I said under my breath as we quickly escaped the room. I needed to find Greg and let him hold me. I wanted to cry all over his solid, hunky shoulder, but so far I hadn't seen him, so I'd have to dump on Leo instead. I grabbed Leo's arm and swung him into the corner at the bottom of the staircase. Buffered by the big Christmas tree, we'd have a modicum of privacy in this sea of happy faces. "I am in the middle of a semi freak-out," I confessed, "and the last thing I need is a bunch of strangers barking in my ear."

"Oh, no, Tiny Tim. You can't freak out on Christmas Eve!"

"Wouldn't you wig if you found out your mother was having an affair?"

Leo's face stretched in an overblown gasp of shock. "No!"

"Yes. At least, I'm pretty sure." I told him about Emily's new job. "And do you remember the other night, when I joked that Dad was having an affair? It really hit Mom, even though she insisted it wasn't true. But maybe she thought I was on to her, which I totally wasn't. I actually believed she was spending all that time with her gal pals. I mean, since my father had no time for a home life, I figured she needed *something*."

"Well, I'd say she found that something." Leo pursed his lips. "And I'll bet his name is Clay Webster."

"What? Why? How do you know? Have you seen her writing his name in her diary?"

"Hardly." Leo grinned. "But she introduced Clay to Wolf and me, and I sensed that Robin really, really liked him. I'd say they've been doing the horizontal mambo."

"Eeeuuw." I winced. "Could we not go there?"

"Just trying to lighten things up a bit, because I think you're taking this all too seriously. Think about it, Madison. Is it really so awful?"

I yanked him closer and whispered between my teeth, "She's cheating on my father."

"Yes, but didn't Dr. G. abandon Robin years ago? Maybe there wasn't another woman, but some people use their work as a mistress. Your father has neglected your mother, and you, for a long time. Why is it wrong for your mother to want a companion?"

I rolled my eyes. "Okay, okay, maybe I'm overreacting. I just need a little time to absorb."

"You do that. But at the moment we've got to navigate out of this quaint little corner and get our asses downstairs. Wolf is waiting."

I took a deep breath chock-full of cinnamon and orange and spices and fresh pine, then faced the crowd. Now that most of the guests had arrived, the house was brimming with people—an attractive crowd of men in suits and women in velvets and satins and shimmering jewels. As Leo and I excused our way through the dining room, I recognized a few expensive gowns I'd seen on the untouchable racks—one black Channel, and a fabulous Hermes that would have looked a hell of a lot better on me than on Mrs. Ripole. *And by the time I get into the income bracket to buy that gown, I'll probably be sagging just as much as Mrs. Ripole.* Sometimes irony just bites you in the sagging ass that way.

Downstairs, the mood of the party was more mellow. The doors to the garden were propped open, and couples were dancing to a jazz version of "Have Yourself a Merry Little Christmas."

Someone handed me a drink, and I took a sip. Mmm, a bourbon sour. I took a long drink. When I came up for air, Leo was snapping his fingers in front of my face. He removed the glass from my hand and whisked me onto the impromptu dance floor.

"Wolf is dancing with Robin," he said, "so I guess I'm stuck with you."

I took a deep breath. The room was fuzzy, but Leo's face was in perfect focus. "You look so . . . so happy."

"Oh, please, don't jinx it," he said.

The bourbon had begun to work its magic, nipping away at my anxiety. Suddenly, my gown had increased in beauty. I felt happy my mother had found someone. I had fallen in love with Greg Kasami. I realized I was so fucking lucky to have my two best friends here to celebrate Christmas. I leaned forward to hug Leo. "I'm so glad you came here for Christmas."

He patted my back, a little embarrassed by my display. "What, are you drunk?"

"Hell, no," I said, stumbling as Leo led me into a turn.

"Now, dip!" he hissed.

I leaned back and let my head tip. I scanned the upside-down room for my mother, but all I saw were two sparkling blobs of gown.

As soon as I was upright, a woman rushed forward and got in my face. "Hi! How are you?" she asked in a hoarse, smoker's voice.

I blinked. Her face was definitely familiar, but I couldn't place her. As I made a mental voyage over her sloping nose, olive skin, bottled black hair in a petite beehive do, I wished she'd cue me in. Was she a neighbor or a former teacher? A distant aunt or a member of Mom's book club? "Merry Christmas," I said, feeling lame.

She nodded. "I think your boyfriend is here," she said, shooting a look over my shoulder.

"Oh, finally," I said, feeling my spirits lift. I turned to find Greg, but he wasn't there. Instead, Ryan stood watching me, decked out in his uniform like a crisp vanilla milkshake. He waved and smiled. "Oh, no." I turned back to the nameless female party guest. "He's not my boyfriend. Where is my boyfriend?"

But the mystery woman didn't care. She was busy pouring on the charm as Ryan joined us. She shook hands and introduced herself as Sandra. "I'm so glad to see you here," she told Ryan. "I want you to know, I for one appreciate everything you guys are doing for this country. God bless America."

"Thank you," Ryan said so politely I thought he was going to click his heels together and salute Sergeant Sandra.

"Where are you assigned, young man?" she asked, pointing to his name tag. "Mr. Wilkinson? I think I remember you from years ago."

"I'm on the *Ticonderoga*," Ryan answered. "As for our next mission, I'm really not at liberty to say."

"Say no more." She held up her hands, and I flashed to an image of the same woman holding up her hands, trying to get us to stop talking.

Sandra Sonnenberg, the high school librarian. What the hell was she doing here? Mom must have really stretched the guest list this year.

"I completely understand when it's a matter of national security," Mrs. Sonnenberg went on. "And I do remember you, young man. You two were quite a couple."

Past tense . . . way past! I wanted to say. Her sentiments made me want to squirm. Not that I didn't appreciate our Armed Forces. The problem was Ryan. The mere sight of him made me bristle, sending me back to those old days when he'd been such a gawky goofball. Not that I'd been so experienced either, but some of the things he had said! "I love you so much, it hurts," he used to mope. Raw, untempered emotion . . . It was such a turnoff!

"Would you like to dance?" Ryan asked me.

"I . . ." I was totally unprepared for this. "You know what? I need to run upstairs for a minute," I lied. "But . . . why don't you two dance?" I pried Ryan's hand from mine and hooked it onto the librarian's arm. "The music is so perfect down here, isn't it? Really puts you in a Christmas mood."

"Oh, that would be charming," Sandra said, giving Ryan no choice. A true officer and a gentleman, he tucked one arm behind her and gestured toward the dance floor with his right hand.

Phew! I picked up a cocktail napkin and pressed it to my brow. Where the hell was my *real* boyfriend?

A hand touched my arm. Mom. She was smiling, but a

rueful expression darkened her eyes. "Honey, are you okay?"

I wanted to tell her that at the moment I felt like a displaced character in *The Crying Game,* but I didn't think Mom had seen the flick. "I'm just having a merry little Christmas," I said. "Or, at least, I'm trying."

Mom tilted her head sympathetically. "Leo told me that you know and you're upset." I had to give Mom credit, she sure knew how to cut through the crap. "I'm so sorry, honey. Would you like to meet Clay?"

"I . . ." My mouth opened and closed like a bubbling fish. *No!* my mind shrieked. "Yes," I answered.

Mom linked her arm through mine and guided me toward the door. "He's out in the garden, and he was hoping to meet you. He's heard so much about you."

I'm going to hate him, I thought as we stepped into the night air. The chill ran through my body, icing over my disposition. I wasn't going to like this sleazoid, this homewrecker, this intruder.

We stepped under the rose trellis to the old-fashioned bench. Wolf sat there, talking to a man leaning against the stucco wall. Silver hair, dark sports jacket, head lowered, intent on Wolf's words.

"Sorry to interrupt," Mom said, "but I know you wanted to meet Madison."

Clay straightened, swinging his attention toward us.

"This is Clay Webster," Mom said. "He's a psychologist for the Board of Ed. We met while I was working on the literacy program in one of the local schools."

Clay shook my hand, staring directly into my eyes. On some people, that level of intensity could be unnerving, but coming from Clay it felt like warm, genuine interest.

"A school psychologist," I said. "So you're one of the guys who tries to figure out why good kids go bad?"

"I'm afraid it's not quite so comprehensive," he said. "Mostly we try to keep students on track so that they don't drop out of school, and we need to make sure they're getting all the support the city is obliged to offer."

Wolf asked him about the city's dropout rate, and the conversation went on from there. Clay mentioned the problems school-aged children faced, adding that he had a son in fourth grade whom he didn't envy. It struck me that this was a man who cared about kids, a man who probably worked hard as a child advocate. After I had gotten the grilling from Dad's friends, Clay Webster was not at all what I expected. While most of the men his age were closed down to input, Clay's quiet presence said that he was open, ready to listen, willing to wait for an answer.

Okay, I didn't hate him, though I wasn't sure that would make the situation any easier.

Clay was talking about the literacy program Mom was involved in when Leo came over and nudged me. "Your boyfriend is here."

"Please, tell me you're not talking about Ryan."

Leo wrinkled his nose. "Greg is upstairs supervising the main courses. The chicken smells divine. And Greg asked for you." He turned to Wolf and Clay. "Anyone hungry? They're setting out the main courses now."

"Sounds great," Clay said.

With that, the three men moved toward the door. Following them, I had to wonder at the absurdity of it all. My two best gay friends were going upstairs to dine with my mother's secret lover, while my old high school boyfriend was downstairs dancing with the school librarian. It sounded like a British spoof.

Upstairs, my heart did a little flip when I caught sight of Greg looking *GQ* gorgeous in his classic tuxedo. The jacket accentuated his broad shoulders and narrow waist, and from his spot at the dining room entrance he seemed to rule the buffet table like an ancient emperor.

Although I didn't want to undermine his professionalism

by kissing him in public, I couldn't help but scurry over to him.

"Hey, you," I said, smiling up at him.

The look he gave me just about melted my panties. There was nothing quite so wonderful as being the center of Greg's universe. "Merry Christmas, Madison."

Warmed by his presence, I glanced over the buffet queue and smiled. Why was I beating myself up over the tiny events of the evening? Greg was here, and I was going to spend the rest of the evening with him. My honey. My guy. One of San Francisco's most desirable bachelors.

Santa had been generous to me this year, and here I'd been moping about a few family dysfunctions. Lifting a glass of champagne to my lips, I saw the holly-strewn path to glory with sudden clarity. This was going to be the best Christmas of my life.

8

After the main course was served, Greg was free to step away from his role as the chief of catering police and join the party a little more. He didn't want to dance, but he enjoyed taking me on a culinary tour of some of the side dishes he'd prepared for us. On one end of the kitchen table, he set out two dishes dotted with foods, including sweet, light, shrimp dumplings; tiny new potatoes stuffed with caviar and sour cream; sauteed scallops in baskets of crisp-fried spinach; lobster ravioli; candied carrots with walnuts; and delicate asparagus turnovers.

"This sure beats the deviled eggs and honey-baked ham Mom served last year," I teased.

Greg's eyes opened wide in horror until he realized I was joking. "You nearly stopped my heart."

I savored a shrimp dumpling, then smiled. "Although past menus weren't quite so mundane, they never came close to the fabulous eats you prepared."

"Thanks." He flipped his chair around, then straddled it to face me. "I love to see you eat . . . enjoying the fruits of my labor."

A little glob of sour cream squirted onto my knuckles,

and Greg took my hand and sucked it off. The sensual gesture reminded me of the many times and ways we'd managed to make love in this house over the past week or so. I'd become very comfortable with the way Greg's body fit into mine . . . not so comfortable telling him I didn't want to go there, which was really my plan for tonight. Maybe it was crazy, but I wanted to remember our first Christmas as a time when we enjoyed each other's company. The thing was, I was planning a happily-ever-after with Greg, and I didn't want the foundation to be built on sex.

"And that's my speciality," I teased. "Madison knuckles topped with a dollop of sour cream."

"Mmm." He turned my hand and kissed the pulse point of my inner wrist. "Very delicious. I'd like to taste more of Madison."

I frowned. "Right. A little poke in the pantry, and then you head off to the Collinses, leaving me here to face Santa alone."

"No," he said flatly. "It doesn't have to be that way. Do you think it's all about sex with me?"

"No," I defended, "but you've got to admit, we haven't done a whole lot of other extracurricular activities. We've never caught a movie together, or gone out for drinks or dinner."

Greg squeezed my hand. "That's because this is my busy season, with parties every day, sometimes two. You know that, don't you?"

"Sure," I said, though I was glad to hear him imply that I was more than a fuck buddy.

"Okay, why don't we do something special tonight?" he said.

Some special time together on Christmas night? I wanted to kick off my Jimmy Choos and do a happy dance on the kitchen table, but I let Greg explain.

"If you'll come to the Collins party and help me finish up

there, I'll take you for a little midnight cruise. My parents have a boat in the Marina District, and I've made a tradition of taking it out on Christmas Eve. It'd be just the two of us."

"You want to go out on the water on Christmas Eve." I spoke as if I were weighing the statement carefully. In truth, I was trying to read between the lines and figure out his true motive for getting me out in the bay alone on his family boat. The fact that it was the family boat—and that by boarding I would be stepping off the pier onto Kasami family property—was not wasted on me. I so wanted to be in! "I'm warning you, I don't sail."

"We'll just be motoring tonight, but it's going to be gorgeous out there. There was a new moon last night," Greg said. "That means no moonlight, and when you get away from the shore there's less light pollution. The sky just opens wide . . . way wide. You'll see."

Honestly, it wasn't my idea of a cozy outing, but it was so Greg. Meditating in the woods, sailing in winter . . . If I was going to be drawn to a guy with a Zen spirit, I would have to be careful not to clip his wings.

At the Collins's party, I helped Greg by passing trays of tiny dessert pastries and cordials—everything from Cherry Herring to fifty-year-old brandy. Judging from the way the guests laughed so loudly and teetered as they walked, I didn't think they needed a whole lot more alcohol to keep the party hardy, but Greg told me that Mrs. Collins had insisted on a floating Viennese hour—whatever the hell that meant.

So I found myself in Greg's van, wearing his leather jacket over my gown and sipping sake from a Thermos.

By the time we got to the Marina District I was floating along on a gentle sake cloud. Not that I was wasted or anything, but the warmth of the wine suffused my body like a gentle blush, from my toes right on up to the top of my brows. I was laughing—about nothing, really—as Greg took my hand and led me down the path toward the docks. My Jimmy Choos didn't quite like the gravel walkway, but they clicked along sweetly once we reached the weathered wooden platforms.

"It's a gorgeous night," Greg said, adjusting some ropes. "Perfect for stargazing."

"Well, this will prove that it's not all about sex," I said. "Because there's no way we'll be able to get naked in this wind."

"I told you it's not all about sex," he said. "Besides, there's always the cabin."

I stamped my foot on the deck in a mock temper tantrum, but Greg didn't seem to notice as he worked the boat closer to the dock, then reached over to help me on. I sort of hopped into the air, and Greg caught me, making me feel like a Broadway dancer jumping into her partner's arms. That made me laugh again, and I couldn't stop giggling as Greg rolled up a blue tarp and moved about, getting the boat ready to motor out.

I sat on a bench, wondering why I felt so giddy. Maybe it was the sake. Maybe it was all the trappings of the occasion, with San Francisco swathed in twinkling Christmas lights and my good friends falling in love. Even my parents seemed to connect on some level tonight.

And Greg. Despite his tendency to put me off he'd managed to find a few minutes to be alone with me on Christmas Eve. Was this going to be it—the magical interlude in which we made the big decision and began to chart our lives together?

I don't know why the prospect of so much happiness put me in a hysterical frenzy, but I just couldn't contain myself.

"Okay, Giggles. Why don't you give me a hand here, and we'll be off."

I followed Greg's instructions, listening as he told me

some of the rules of sailing, that we wouldn't be using the sails tonight, that we had to stay right of the red markers, keep out of the shipping channel, etc. More information than I could really process, but I let it billow around me like the wind that lifted the chiffon overskirt of my gown.

"Are we crazy for being out here tonight?" I asked.

His eyes glimmered as he shot me a look. "Are you cold?"

I shoved my hands into the pockets of his leather jacket and shook my head.

"Then this makes perfect sense." Greg stood at the wheel, steering with one hand as if it were second nature to him.

As we cruised out and I got a hit of engine fumes and salt water, it reminded me of how I used to get seasick. It had been so long since I'd been on a boat, but now the gentle motion didn't bother me at all. As he guided the boat to a cove and dropped anchor, I stared out at the dark water, leaning on the fiberglass surface of the boat. The notion of the bay at night had seemed romantic, but in truth it was dark and vacant—an expansive void. Why was Greg drawn to these bleak, distant places?

"Why the hell would you want to come out here?" I said aloud.

"Wow, you really are a party pooper," he said from the cabin.

"It's just cold as hell out here, and pitch black, too. Get your hot bod out here and warm me up."

He emerged with a tray of goodies that fit right onto the little shelf on the bench. Dried cranberries and dusted almonds and a small wedge of brie.

"Impressive," I said, "but I'm a little dry."

He beamed, ducked back into the cabin and returned with a bottle of champagne. "I thought we could salvage some of the night for ourselves."

"That is so sweet." I popped a cranberry into my mouth

and kissed him on the lips. Had he listened when I'd asked about celebrating the holidays together? Yes, he must have.

Greg kissed me back, then drew a line along my jawbone with one finger. "Did you notice the stars?" he whispered. "They're amazing from out here."

I glanced up at the sky, a white-on-black scattering of varied diamonds. "It is beautiful. I imagine you've got all the constellations charted."

"I can pick out a few," he said. "You always start with the North Star. And I'm sure if you paid attention in Girl Scouts, you could find the Big Dipper."

"I was a terrible Girl Scout," I said. "And in college, we were supposed to take this class at Hayden Planetarium, but I couldn't be bothered, so I just took it pass-fail and used somebody else's notes."

"Not a stargazer. So I guess I won't be astounding you with my astronomical expertise."

"Can't we just talk?" I said, trying to guide him to the important question.

He turned to me and slid a hand inside the leather jacket. "So you want to talk, do you?" His fingers found the bodice of my dress, dipping inside to tease one nipple. I sucked in a breath as he pushed the bodice down to cup my breast.

As always, his touch evoked a sexual thrill, but tonight I didn't want sex to get in the way . . . not when our future was about to be launched.

"Look, Greg—" I pulled away and adjusted my bra. "I really don't want to make love tonight."

"Really." He tipped his head back. "And you're not into astronomy, so I'm not going to bore you with all that. Okay, then, what are you up for?"

"Talk. Can't we just talk?"

"About what?"

His tone was so genuine, but the question hung there awkwardly.

I wanted to smack my forehead, realizing I'd totally miscalculated this evening. Disappointment seeped through me, chasing away the last of the warmth evoked by the sake. There was no surprise engagement ring hidden in the bowl of dried cranberries. "About us. Our future."

It was Greg's turn to be disappointed. "And what might that be?" he asked crisply.

"Well . . . together, I think. I mean, wouldn't that be good?" I didn't mean to sound whiny and pleading. Maybe I just felt that way when faced with Greg's lack of relationship savvy.

Remember, he's really not good at making an emotional connection, I told myself. I needed to be the assertive one. I needed to take him by the hand.

"We're together now, right?" He shifted away from me. "You know, this is just so typical. What the hell else do you want from me?"

"I'd like to know that we'll be together again tomorrow," I said.

"It's possible," he said.

"And the day after that . . . and after that."

"You're the one who's leaving. You're flying back to New York in January."

"But I don't have to." *Not if we have some sort of commitment,* I thought.

Of course, I wouldn't dare say the "C" word—not even to a man who loved me. I was crazy about Greg, but I wasn't stupid.

"What's that supposed to mean?" he said in a pissy voice.

"It means that, that I don't have to go back, Greg. Not if there's a reason to stay." I hated having to spell this out, but someone had to do it. "Dammit, would you just give me a reason not to go back to New York?"

"And what would that be?" he flipped back at me. "Because, much as I like you, I barely know you, Madison. And you don't know me. You barely know anything about me."

"But that's changing," I insisted. "We're getting closer by the minute."

He swung around and scowled at me. "Now you're scaring me."

That was when I realized I must have been giving off the scent of happily-ever-after, a musk that obviously offended Greg. He sat up straight and folded his arms. Although I wasn't multilingual, I could read "Fuck off!" in the international code of body language.

"Greg, where do you see us going?" I asked, desperately trying to give voice to the question that hung in the air between us.

"Back to the marina," he said, his eyes silver with fury.

And before I could argue, he was preparing the boat to move. As he started the engine I turned back toward the water and clutched the seat cushion in a near fetal position, trying to ignore the voice ringing in my head. *He doesn't love me. He doesn't love me.*

How could that be true? All the right signals had been there, hadn't they?

The boat rocked and bounced as Greg piloted toward home. Despite the cold night, my palms sweated and my face felt warm. As I dug my fingers into the seat cushion I realized we were moving at the whim of the currents and waves in the dark bay. It tossed us along its glassy black surface, jogging and bobbing, a tiny fleck in the huge black abyss. I sucked in a breath, trying to go with the motion— the rocking motion of the bay, the eddying swirls from the Pacific, the subtle, steady spinning of the planet.

Leaning into the boat, I could feel the Earth spinning, tilting on its axis, moving through space in its path around the sun. Beyond that, I imagined our solar system thrumming within the gigantic arena of space, a huge, buzzing diorama within a larger theater. No one could stop the inevitable motion. No one. It was foolish to even consider the notion.

But fool that I was, I would have tried. If I could stop the spinning planet and turn back time, I would have done something—anything—differently with Greg. Somehow, someway, I would have made him love me.

How I wished I could have made him love me.

9

The next day, Christmas Day, my hangover was amplified by depression.

I'd been dumped on Christmas Eve! Or maybe it had happened on Christmas, since my brain had been so fuzzy with champagne and sake and spiced cider, I'd lost track of time. It was almost too awful to talk about. Fortunately, Leo had a knack for reading between the lines. By the time he had polished off half a tray of Mom's sticky buns, he had guessed most of the tragic details of my evening.

Unable to eat—more from the hangover than the depression, since depression makes me want to consume massive quantities of yum-yums—I hugged a coffee mug covered with dancing Santas in one hand and picked candied pecans off the buns with the other. The dining room was surprisingly tidy, considering the scores of friends and neighbors who had feasted here last night.

"I can't believe how it happened," I said. "I felt the earth move."

Leo's brows shot up. "Nothing wrong with that, as Carole King can attest. But I take it that happened before you broke up?"

"Not that old euphemism. I was actually clinging to the

boat, feeling the earth spin through space." I scratched the back of my head and yawned. "That's the last time I'll mix sake and champagne and spiced cider."

"And bourbon sours and martinis," Leo added.

"No! I wasn't drinking those, was I?"

"When we were dancing out back in the garden? Don't worry, I'm sure you sweated most of the alcohol away."

"No one can sweat that much." I winced. Maybe it was a good thing that Christmas only came once a year.

"Good morning! Merry Christmas." Mom appeared fully dressed in jeans and a hand-knit sweater with a snowflake pattern around the neck.

"Merry Christmas, Mom," I said quietly. I admit, I felt a little pang of daughterly love as she leaned over the table, straightened a sprig of holly in the centerpiece, then trouped off to the kitchen for coffee. Mom must have been so lonely knocking around in this big, empty house. I really was glad she had found someone, and from my brief conversation with Clay I agreed with her choice, but I couldn't ignore the throbbing voice of my conscience that worried about Dad suddenly realizing that his wife had mentally checked out long ago. I didn't want my father to feel abandoned.

Ugh! I had come home for a cozy Christmas and had opened a can of wormy issues instead.

I pressed my hands to my cheeks. "I want to go home."

Leo eyed me over his Rudolph mug. "You are home, Dorothy."

"No," I hissed, glancing over my shoulder to make sure Mom didn't hear. "Back to New York. To our new place."

"Why don't you use my ticket and I'll stay," Leo tossed off. "I could use another two weeks with Wolf."

I opened my eyes wide, considering the prospect. In two days, I could be back in New York, squeezing into crowded subway cars and dodging the smoke of hot pretzel carts. "You're on."

"Just kidding." Leo winced. "You know I'm out of vacation time. And since Vilma is out for two full weeks, there's going to be a ton of administrative catch-up, especially on the soaps." Vilma was Leo's boss, and she seemed to be responsible for every aspect of the network's three daytime dramas—at least, that was what she tried to make people believe. From what I'd witnessed, over the past few months Leo had become her entire backbone, doing everything but taking lunches for her. He sat in on meetings, kept her calendar, made her decisions, and pretty much ran the damned office.

"When is Vilma going to promote you?" I asked.

"I've only been there since July. But my six-month review comes up next month."

"I say you dig your nails in and squeeze out every penny you can. Vilma and those temperamental producers would be lost without you."

"Do you think?" Leo scratched his chin. "Christ, I'd love a promotion, but I don't think Vilma will let go of me just yet. Who else would order her flowers and yell at the dry cleaner?"

"Are you two talking shop on Christmas morning?" Mom asked, mug in hand. "Boy, times really have changed. Years ago you used to drag your father and me out of bed at the crack of dawn. Now, you're lingering over coffee while there's a mountain of gifts inside waiting to be unwrapped."

"You're right. We're too complacent, aren't we?" I stood up and stretched. "There must be some way to strike a balance between ripping the gifts open and totally ignoring them."

"I wasn't ignoring," Leo insisted, "I was politely waiting for all to rise."

"That's right," I said, turning toward the grandfather clock. "Shouldn't we wait for Dad to come down?"

"Oh, your father left for the hospital hours ago," Mom said. "Didn't he mention it last night? He agreed to take over a shift so Dr. Feinstein could spend Christmas morning in Sausalito with his grandchildren."

"That rat!" I huffed. "It's not like I'm here every day, and Dr. Feinstein can see his Sausalito family anytime."

"Honey, you're preaching to the choir," Mom said. "But I learned long ago not to let our happiness ride on your father's actions." She carried her mug in to survey the gifts under the tree. We managed to extract the gifts for the three of us and toted them into the small parlor, which was a lot cozier than the very grand marble-tiled living room.

First, I opened my gift from Leo—a tiny snow-globe ornament depicting Rockefeller Center, where he worked. "This is so great! Next year, I'm going to have a tree-trimming party back in New York."

"I used to do that in my first apartment, fresh out of Stanford," Mom said. "It's a great way to meet guys."

"This is so exciting," Leo said, pulling off a velvet bow. "My mother hasn't bothered to wrap a gift for me since I was ten."

"You poor dear," Mom said, watching expectantly as Leo tore the paper off an odd-shaped carton. The shiny, waxed cardboard was shaped like a Chinese take-out container.

"How kitschy!" Leo opened the flaps and pulled out a waxy-looking dumpling. "It's bath soaps!" he said, holding up the soap dumpling. "I love it! This is just the thing for our new apartment. Did Madison tell you I'm getting my own bathroom?"

Mom smiled. "That's quite a find for a New York apartment."

Next Mom opened the box containing the creamy cashmere sweater I'd gotten her and claimed to adore it. Then I opened a box with a silk nightgown and a gift certificate to Victoria's Secret.

"Ohmigosh, I need underwear desperately. Thanks, Mom."

She nodded knowingly. "I've seen those scraps you wear coming out of the dryer. And if your mother can't replenish your underwear supply, who can?"

I put the gift certificate in a safe spot, then chased tissue paper and stray ribbon around the floor as Leo dug into another gift.

"Socks!" He held up a pair of argyles I'd given him. "And with a tag from Bendel's. Do I need to frame them, or can I wear them?"

"You have to wear them," I said. "I love expensive socks. Even when you have to wear stiff clothes for work, your cushy socks can make you feel pampered."

"Thank you," Leo said, as we shifted attention to Mom, who was opening Leo's gift.

As the decorative gift packages turned into a carnage of strewn merchandise, torn wrapping paper, empty boxes, and decapitated bows, a hollow feeling came over me. It was more than the ebbing excitement of Christmas Day.

I realized what a huge mistake I'd made with Greg. Ugh! I'd misjudged the situation in my ever hopeful Madison way. I had mistaken a fuck-fest for a meaningful relationship. I had hoped for something long term, with a house and a husband and babies.

And in the end, what had Greg said? That I didn't know him, and it was true. I had fallen in love with the image of Greg and with the romantic notion that marriage to one of San Francisco's hottest bachelors would be a *Town and Country* event.

Oh, what a major Christmas botch job.

I had committed the ultimate Christmas sin. I'd peeked into my biggest, most exquisitely wrapped package on Christmas Eve, and discovered the devastating truth.

It was empty.

That night, Mom roasted a stuffed turkey breast and I helped her make garlic mashed potatoes and string beans with almonds. Normally I hate cooking, but it wasn't fair to stick Mom with all the work, and I don't mind contributing when someone can supervise me to make sure the dishes turn out delicious. We enjoyed setting out a traditional dinner for Leo and Wolf and Dad, who was wildly appreciative, though he had to head back to the hospital to look in on a few patients afterward.

"Are you sure he's not having an affair?" I muttered to Mom as we loaded the dinner dishes in the dishwasher.

"Honey, I wish he would. I think any diversion from the cardio business would help to fill out his life, but your father is one of those single-minded workaholics."

After Dad took off, the remaining four of us played a few hands of spades at the kitchen table with a round of Irish coffees. Mom put on a Glenn Miller Orchestra Christmas CD, then curled up behind her hand of cards in her snowflake sweater, jeans, and ragwool socks. It struck me that she seemed suddenly youthful, not a liposuction alumnus, but one of those women who emerged from a magazine makeover with a new light in her eyes. Leo and Wolf seemed so comfortable in my house, I was beginning to think of them as the brothers I had longed for throughout my childhood (though when I'd fantasized, I'd imagined brothers who would bring their friends home as date material for *me*—not for each other).

"'Gone away, is the bluebird,'" Mom sang along with the CD. "'Here to stay, is the new bird. He sings a love song as we go along . . .'"

"'Walking in a winter wonderland,'" we all chimed in, then cracked up.

"Good God," Leo sputtered, "if anyone ever speaks of this evening again, I will vehemently deny my involvement."

"I won't mention it," I said. "But let me point out that you do know all the words, Leo."

"Just play a damned card," he told me.

We had some laughs and enjoyed circumventing each other's game strategies. Yes, it would have been a fun, relaxed Christmas night if it weren't for the fact that I'd been derailed by Greg the night before.

Fortunately, no one brought that up. I knew that Wolf must know all the details by now, and I suspected that Leo had shared the pertinent facts with Mom, as the two of them had become buds in the week or so of our visit. Hell's bells, they all probably knew. They were probably sitting here playing spades to cheer up poor, rejected Madison, but since no one acknowledged it I was happy to sop up their pity and enjoy the company of the three people who mattered to me most in the world. Oh, I know, it was a corny sentiment, but after all, it was Christmas night.

After a few rounds, Mom got up and gathered up the empty mugs. "I'd better change if I'm going to head over to that Christmas party," she said, putting the cups in the sink. "I could say that I'm going to Emily's house, but we all know that's a load of crap."

Wolf's eyes opened wide in amazement and glee as Leo let out a mock gasp. I was a little shocked myself, but it was a relief to see Mom back in form.

"I believe a nightcap or two at Top of the Mark is in order," Leo suggested. "What say you, warriors?"

"Sounds great," Wolf said, slipping on his leather jacket.

But I wasn't up for a night out. "You guys go," I said. "I'm beat, and AMC is doing a marathon of *It's a Wonderful Life* tonight."

"You are kidding, aren't you?" Leo pressed. "You can get that movie on tape."

"We have it on tape," Mom said.

"But it's different when it's being broadcast," I said. "You can watch it knowing that thousands of other people are watching with you. It gives you this community feeling— that you're not alone."

"Maybe we should stay," Wolf said, unzipping his jacket. But I knew he was motivated by pity for me, that he didn't share my desire to snuggle up in front of the Christmas classic.

"No, no, you guys go," I insisted. "I'll join you at the Mark if I get a second wind."

"Come on, Wolf," Leo said, tossing his muffler over one shoulder. "If I've learned anything, it's that you cannot disrupt the Greenwood women from their Christmas rituals."

"Merry Christmas!" I called after them as they headed out the side door. I turned to Mom and edged her away from the sink. "You go get ready," I insisted. "I'll take care of that stuff."

She didn't turn away from the sink and didn't look at me but kept scrubbing a clean mug with a sponge. "Are you okay with this? With my seeing Clay?"

Welcome to the world of bizarro, I thought, *a world in which your mother asks for approval and looks the other way while you're nailing the caterer in her rose garden.*

I wrapped the dishtowel around one hand and leaned against the counter. "Mom, the important thing is, are you happy?"

She let out a breath, sort of a sigh. "Yes. Yes, I am. For the first time in a long time."

"Then hold on to that," I said, feeling a little wise for my twenty-one years. But before Mom had a chance to appreciate my Yoda-esque sentiment, the doorbell rang.

"That must be Clay." Quickly, she dried her hands and dashed to the front door.

"He picks her up for a date," I said to myself. "He comes in right through the front door. Dad, you are so in another world."

"Well, this is a surprise!" I heard Mom's voice booming in that tone that said: Madison, I want you to hear me!

What now? Had Clay brought her a prom corsage? Rented a limo?

I turned toward the dining room arch to see Mom escorting a gorgeous man in white. Oh, no! It wasn't Clay at all, but Vanilla Man!

"Ryan," I said flatly, staring at his dress whites, "don't the Marines know that white is a faux pas after Labor Day?"

"Navy. I'm in the Navy," he corrected me, then he smiled that tentative smile of a kid who never quite got over the stigma of having braces. "Merry Christmas, Madison."

Oh, hit me where it hurts! I wanted to yell, looking up at the tower of white beaming beside Mom. It wasn't supposed to be Ryan; I was supposed to be here with Greg, dammit.

"Ryan, are you hungry?" Mom asked. "We've got plenty of leftover turkey."

"No, ma'am. Thank you, but I had dinner with my father and his wife," he said.

"Then coffee," Mom suggested. "And pie. We've got pumpkin pie, and apple, and pecan."

I wanted to step behind Ryan and wave the checkered flag, signaling Mom that the race was over, but she wasn't paying any attention to me. She was pulling out a chair for Ryan, opening the fridge, handing me the coffee can.

"Madison, will you make some coffee?" Mom said. "What kind of pie do you prefer? Or a little of each?"

"Some of each would be great," Ryan said, sitting at attention and placing his hat on the table. His hat. The guy couldn't even stop by without bringing his freaking general's hat.

On the way to get a coffee filter, I paused beside Ryan and looked down at him. "At ease," I said. "Apparently you've already passed inspection."

At least, he'd passed Mom's inspection, I thought. Okay, maybe it was snarky of me, but I wanted Ryan to stop being so polite and stop sucking up to Mom. Actually, I wanted him to just go away. Aside from a few teenage memories, and many of those were awkward adolescent explorations that no one ever wants to remember, Ryan and I had nothing in common. And dammit, I wanted to keep it that way.

"There you go," Mom said, placing a dinner plate of pie slices in front of him. While I hung back by the granite counter waiting for the coffee to perk, she sat down across from him, pouring on the Robin Greenwood charm that had won over my teachers and adversaries on the soccer field. "We didn't really get a chance to talk last night," she said.

Ryan nodded over a forkful of flaky pie crust. "No, ma'am, we didn't. And I didn't get a chance to thank you for the wonderful party."

"We were delighted to have you," Mom insisted. "I saw you talking with Mrs. Sonnenberg."

The old witch.

"She mentioned that you helped fund a new computer system for the library," Ryan said.

"I just organized the committee," Mom said.

As they chattered on about local biz, their words blurring to blah-blah-blahs, Mom's image paling in the glow of the vanilla god, I was haunted by one of the most awkward moments in my life. In the backseat of a car with Ryan, and I wanted to do it. I was the aggressor. But he kept saying no. No. We needed to wait. We were too young. He wanted it to be special.

So instead, hotshot that I was, I decided to give him a blow job. Ugh! How stupid was that? I didn't know what the hell I was doing. I actually leaned over him and blew air on his penis. I did! A stupid act that will haunt me till I die.

At least he didn't laugh. "I think that's just an expression—about blowing?" he'd said. "I think you're supposed to sort of rub it with your lips?"

Ugh! Even thinking about it now, I felt my face grow warm. I had to turn away and pretend to check the coffee. I'd been so naive back then, so sure that my life would be perfect if I could just squeeze my way into the cheerleader clique and get voted into the prom queen's court.

And Ryan . . . He'd been so idealistic, wanting to wait until we were older to have sex. Which had unnerved me, making me wonder if I was doing something wrong. But many times we'd come so close . . . steaming up the windows of his car, stroking each other into a frenzy in Golden Gate Park, making out between the rocks at Cliff House.

And for *what* did we wait? What the hell were we holding out for . . . permission from our parents? It was one of the reasons I'd had to move on from Ryan. Not that I was savvy, but the guy was so damned earnest, it drove me nuts.

"Maddy?" Mom said, wrenching me back to reality. "Is the coffee ready?"

"Oh, sure." I grabbed a penguin mug and poured, trying to think of a diplomatic way to get rid of Ryan as soon as he finished eating. Unfortunately, I couldn't be too blunt, and my mind was a bit too numb to conjure up a creative plan. "Here you go," I said, forcing a smile.

Mom seemed to take that as her cue to exit. "I've got to run—a party with some friends over on Russian Hill. But you two can keep each other company." Mom stood up, prompting Ryan to press a napkin to his face and rise to attention. "Oh, Ryan, you always were so polite!" Mom kissed him on the cheek, then hurried off upstairs.

I slunk down into a kitchen chair and pointed to the pie. "Finish your grub, soldier."

Sitting across from me, Ryan tilted his head to catch my eye. "Are you angry about something?"

I sighed, unnerved by the vulnerability in his blue eyes. "No, just disappointed."

"Really? I'm sorry."

"It's not your fault," I said, remembering how Ryan had always had doormat issues.

"But I'm still sorry you're disappointed."

Major doormat issues. I went over to the kitchen counter and hoisted the bottle of Bailey's Irish Cream. "Would you like to make that an Irish coffee?"

"Yes, please."

"Now you're talking." There just might be hope for you

yet, Ryan, I thought as I poured the liquor into his mug. Maybe a shot or two would loosen that stick in his ass.

An hour later, Ryan and I were ensconced in separate corners of the love seat, watching *It's a Wonderful Life*. I had hoped that the prospect of watching Jimmy Stewart disparage the value of life would scare Ryan off, but he had insisted the movie was one of his favorites.

Just my luck.

"So how is New York?" Ryan asked as George Bailey teetered on the bridge. "I've always wanted to go there. Is it as crazy as people say?"

"Crazier," I said. "And I love it."

"So you're planning to stay there?"

"Definitely," I said, though I hadn't really given the issue of locale much thought since I'd chosen to attend Columbia. Once you get a taste of New York City, it's not like you're dying to try Topeka or Cincinnati. "How about you? Where are you off to next?"

"I really can't say. I don't even know, but I have to report in tomorrow, and we'll ship out the following day."

"That must suck."

"It does."

"What else?" I asked. "What else don't you like about the Navy?"

He frowned. "It's not exactly Carnival Cruises. Life on a ship can be bleak, isolated. And it's so regimented. I'm just a cog in the big wheel."

"And I thought working at *Skyscraper* was brutal."

He snorted. "It's not always terrible. Just most of the time."

"Wow, and you seemed so into it. Back in high school, you were dying to get into the Naval Academy. Like it would make your life perfect."

"What the hell did we know back in high school?" he said casually.

"Oh, please, don't remind me," I said, warming up to him. "So there's a chink in the armor? You're not going to be a Navy man for life?"

"Please . . . I'm hoping to do five and get the hell out."

"Really?" Maybe I had judged him too harshly. I pulled my knees onto the couch and shifted toward him.

"Really. Don't you ever feel like bailing out from your job?"

"Yeah, like every day."

He squinted at me, surprised. I went on. "The real world isn't as glam as it should be. I've this boss who's a bear if she forgets to take her Valium. And I'm such a peon in the pecking order that everyone thinks they can walk all over me. I sort of hate it, but I haven't found anything else yet, and my parents think I scored a really great job. I hate to disappoint them."

"Mmm." He tugged on the hem of my pants. "Why don't you explain it to them? Your mom is pretty cool."

"Yeah, but Dad is totally out of touch. He thinks I should use *Skyscraper* as a springboard to *Town & Country* or the *New Yorker* or something. The man can't accept that his daughter was hired to count paper clips."

Ryan circled my ankle with his hand and pulled, yanking me flat on my back. "You always were a great counter," he said, leaning over to poke me in the ribs. "One, two, three—"

"Aaagh! That tickles!" I belted out a laugh.

"I still know the spots," he said, sliding his fingertips over my rib cage.

It was a fun part of hanging with Ryan—something I'd forgotten. We used to wrestle in the grass like siblings, a match that usually dissolved into a round of tickling, then . . . other things.

I squealed and flailed. "Stop!"

But his hands were relentless. "Ooh, I forgot this spot."

"No!" I gasped, rolling aside. I flopped off the couch onto the floor, dragging Ryan with me.

As soon as he landed beside me I went for his neck, wiggling my fingertips under his ears. "I remember a few ticklish spots, too!" I said victoriously.

"No!" he wailed, leaning his head down to stop the tickling. He crunched his chin over my hand and let out a howl. "Stop! Stop!"

"Ouch! You're hurting my hand!" I protested.

Suddenly, he lifted his head. "Sorry."

"Just kidding," I said, realizing that his face was barely an inch from mine. We were both breathing heavily, and I could feel the heat radiating from his body, which stretched before me, so lean and rock-solid.

"That's not fair," he said, placing a hand on my neck, tenderly. Something flickered in his blue eyes, as if he were suddenly aware of how close our bodies were. I don't think either of us had expected anything like this to happen, but now that we were here on the floor, the final outcome seemed inevitable.

I felt the familiar yearning in my abdomen. I definitely wanted to get closer, even if it wasn't going to go anywhere after today. I mean, the guy was shipping out. . . . Who knew where he'd end up? And although there was no future for Ryan and me, we did share a heartfelt past.

Locking my vision on his blue eyes, I slid a hand under the crisp hem of his white jacket. He closed his eyes when I cupped the bulge in his pants, as if he felt incredibly relieved that we could get to this point. I stroked him, realizing this was the right thing to do. Ryan deserved an unforgettable send-off from his "girl back home," even if I wasn't really his girl.

"I've missed you," he whispered.

"Shh," I said, placing his hand between my legs. I didn't

want to talk about feelings right now. "Let's just focus on this moment," I whispered. "This moment in time."

He moaned as we pressed against each other, our fingers searching for bare flesh.

Running my hands under his crisp white shirt, I felt a wicked surge of pleasure at having penetrated his dress whites. There's something about a man in a uniform . . .

10

"Ican't believe you're leaving me," I told Leo as we exited the Ansel Adams gallery at the Art Institute. "Everyone is abandoning me."

"Oh, get over it, Toots," he said as he approached a sculpture installed in the corridor. "If you want to talk abandonment issues, call Wolf. He's given me an earful in the past twenty-four hours. Besides, you wanted Ryan to leave, didn't you?"

I nodded. "But not you. San Francisco won't be the same without you."

"I'll see you next week when you get back to the Big Apple."

"Ten days," I said. "Remember? I'm taking a week of vacation." I paused in front of the rounded adobe sculpture. "What was I thinking? No one over the age of eighteen should spend more than ten days total staying in their parents' home."

Leo glanced down at the brown sculpture and pursed his lips. "Looks like a very large fava bean."

"Or an imploded embryo," I said.

He nodded. "Yes, I definitely see it." He flicked his sunglasses down from the top of his head and smiled. "Should we have lunch in the Institute café, or head elsewhere for a coldie?"

"I happen to know two cool places in the area," I said. "What are you in the mood for, a microbrewery or a tiki bar?"

Leo threw up his hands in glee. "Tiki!"

"Okay, then," I said as we stepped out in front of the Institute's outdoor fountain. "We can walk to the Fairmont from here. But promise me you won't end up dancing on the table with a coconut bra."

"Only if you'll perform a hula dance," Leo threatened.

We ended up jumping on a cable car for part of the trip, since I'd forgotten how many steep hills dotted the Nob Hill neighborhood. "How did Nob Hill get its name?" Leo asked as the car clanged on its track.

"It really was called Snob Hill, after four big swells who made pots of money building the Transcontinental Railroad. Stanford, Hopkins, Crocker, and Huntington. They poured their gold into building four fabulous mansions on the hill."

Leo nodded. "I take it this was part of your school social studies curriculum?"

"Like, every year," I admitted, signaling that it was time to jump off.

The Fairmont Hotel was one of those palatial structures that always made me feel like donning a princess gown before entering. Inside, I led Leo to the Tonga Room, which boasted tiki huts, man-made tropical rainstorms, and a floating bandstand.

Leo twirled under a puff of mist. "I love this place! What are you drinking?"

"Let's start with mai tais," I said. "Then we'll work our way up to rum punches."

The waitress let us have a table inside a tiki hut strewn with Christmas lights. When she brought our drinks in cups that resembled hollowed-out pineapples, I insisted on paying the tab.

"This one's on me. Consider it your bon voyage drink."

"That's so sweet," Leo said, adjusting the paper umbrella in his mai tai. "But you really don't have to. Or do you have an ulterior motive?" He gasped suspiciously. "Are you trying to buy my favor?"

"Of course not!" I protested. "I mean, no, not really." He narrowed his eyes at me, relentless. "Okay, okay, I just wanted to get in one last pitch for Sugar."

Leo jabbed the air with a long, decorative toothpick. "Ah ha! I knew it."

"Come on, Leo. She's been a good friend to me, and we need roommates. It's a win-win situation."

"She's a dixie-chick prima donna," he said, "and I'm not giving up the room with the private bath."

"You don't have to! Sugar is willing to share the big room with someone else."

"I'll believe that when I see it."

I took a sip from my drink, trying to think of another approach.

"But, Leo—"

"Don't 'But Leo' me. Didn't you hear what I said?"

I blinked.

"We'll give her a chance to prove herself."

"Really? Well, all right! Okay!" I swirled a fist in the air. "Woo-hoo!"

"Now who's making a scene?" Leo demanded. "And you worried about me in a coconut bra?"

I flashed him a satisfied grin. "You won't regret it. You know, we are going to have a great apartment."

"Just as long as no one tapes over my soaps, we'll be fine."

"Call me the minute you get the keys from the realtor," I told him. "And make sure the painters used the right shade of white before you give them the first month's rent. A friend of mine paid up front and then saw that the apartment was painted this hideous shade of orange. They called it 'nacho cheese,' but it was really nauseating cheese. Anyway, she had a hell of a time getting it redone by the landlord."

"I'll take care of it, don't worry," Leo said. "And if I have any problems, I'm sure Miss Sugarplum Fairy will inter-cede."

"Sugar will help you," I said, ignoring his barb. "You'll see." As we sipped our drinks, I felt myself sliding into a tiki room stupor. I was glad that things were working out back home. The apartment would be partially inhabited by the time I landed back in New York.

But I also felt a little out of sorts, stuck between two worlds. Why was I even returning to New York? Yes, there were my good friends Leo and Sugar, but I had good friends here, too. I hated my job at *Skyscraper*. I dreaded having to brush up against Hugh again. And I was sure there'd be scads of shrieking notes on my desk from Drucie complaining about missed deadlines and facts that needed to be checked.

"Madison?" Leo said brusquely. "You're looking far too serious for a young woman sucking on a coldie in a tiki bar."

"Sorry. I just had this feeling of ennui about my life."

Leo held up his hands. "Stop that, this instant, or I will rise upon this table and do the dance to summon the tiki gods."

"Don't you ever wonder if you've made the wrong choice?"

"No, never."

"If you're in the wrong place? I mean, maybe I don't be-long in New York. I definitely don't belong at *Skyscraper*."

"Then look for another job when you get back," Leo said, toasting me with his drink. "But do not throw out the entire mai tai just because one maraschino cherry has a spot on it."

I nodded sagely. "Good advice. I think I've heard it some-where before."

Leo folded up the little paper umbrella from his drink and tucked it behind his ear like a decorative flower. "And when all else fails, drink heavily."

As I watched Leo walk through the security gate at the airport, I realized how much I'd miss having him here. He was my buffer from myself, my disembodied conscience that saved me from having to face my own failings and the insecurities those failings spawned. In short, he took me from one good time to the next with just a brief, mocking nod at the issues.

God, I would miss him.

With Leo gone, I knew it was time to take care of all those things I didn't get around to while he was here. I went for a pedicure with Mom. I called two of my girlfriends from high school and found out that Rikki was living with a boyfriend in Toronto and Lizard was buried in the busy season at work (liquor sales? go figure) but that she would call me as soon as she dug herself out.

Then there was the annual father-daughter lunch. I boned up on last month's issues of the *New Yorker* so that I would have something to say when he took me to Moose's, as he had somehow gotten into his head that I was a budding literary mind. But then, over a lunch of pan-seared scallops and lobster risotto, he grilled me about books on the *New York Times* best-seller list, telling me how his reading tastes had changed from short stories to novels. *Lucky you,* I wanted to say, *at least you've got a few minutes to read each night.* Honestly, working at a magazine all day sucked up so many of my brain cells that by nighttime I was lucky I could hold a conversation at a bar, let alone read a diatribe on finding mathematics in the stars.

But could I say that to my father? And did he really care what I thought about his personal reading list?

That was what surprised me most. I sat there nodding while he reeled off his opinions, like a fifth-grader delivering book reports. It was a total waste of time, but at least the food was exquisite. As a buttery scallop melted in my mouth, I glanced off and pretended I was lunching with David Bowie or Jack Nicholson—some older guy who was still an incredible score. Then Greg would come in and see us together and—

The fantasy faded as Dad's pager went off a third time. "I really have to run, Maddy," he said, "but Mary will put this on my tab. Order dessert, if you want." He leaned over the table, kissed me on the forehead, and winked. "We'll talk later."

Oh, sure, I thought, watching him go. *We'll talk in about twenty years, when they're wheeling you out of the OR because you collapsed in some man's chest.*

I did order dessert—a rich chocolate soufflé that took thirty minutes to prepare—but I asked Mary, the owner, to give it to our waitress as a token of appreciation. In all the years that Dad, the world-renowned heart surgeon, had eaten here, he'd probably never given the woman more than a twelve-percent tip. A few weeks at home and you remember all the ways your parents embarrass you.

Struggling with feelings of displacement and the usual case of postholiday blues, I tried to bow out of the New Year's Eve cleaning of the attic. It was a ritual Mom had started when I was a teenager—a Zen way to streamline our lives and remove the extraneous possessions that weighed us down.

"Mom, at the moment, material things are not the problem. If I eat one more piece of pecan pie, I'm going to crack the marble floor at the bottom of the stairs."

She let out a laugh and rubbed my back. "Oh, honey! A few extra pounds does not a porker make. I am so glad I never had food issues with you. Those girls in your school who struggled with anorexia . . . It was such a heartbreaker, a major power struggle."

"Yes, food was never an issue with me," I teased. "I like it too much to give it up." It wasn't until college that I realized how lucky I was, not having to sweat at the gym every time I devoured a wedge of cheesecake. I probably had Mom's speedy metabolism to thank for that.

"Just help me go through a few boxes," Mom said, leading the way up the narrow stairs to the creaky attic of my childhood nightmares. "It's just too overwhelming for me to do on my own, but it will be fun if we do it together."

"You haven't seen my new method of housecleaning," I told her as she opened the door and flicked on the light. "I just throw everything away and buy new."

"And you were supposed to be the recycle generation," Mom scolded me. She waved at a dust mote and turned to the shelves built under the eaves. "You know, every year I dread this task," Mom said as she dragged a sagging box of books out from under the attic shelves and sat down in front of it. "I get hit by that energy lull after Christmas. But then when I finally dig in, I enjoy going through the stuff we've collected over the years. Old lawn ornaments and costumes. Art projects you made. Your baby pictures—"

"Oh, tell me that little fatty isn't me," I said. "I look like I'm smuggling golf balls in those cheeks!"

"You were such a sweetie," Mom said. "You still are."

"But my cheeks! You must have gotten quotes from a few plastic surgeons before you left the hospital."

"Right. We had a pediatrician tighten you up with a little liposuction."

"You know," I said, heaving out a stack of oversized books with glossy covers. "All of this stuff should just go out with the garbage collection."

Mom glared at me.

"Okay, recycle the paperbacks if you want, but it's not like we're ever going to sit and read through these things again."

"Those are your high school yearbooks," Mom pointed out. "It seems a shame to toss away so many memories."

The Warriors, 1988-89 was written in very pompous Gothic lettering. I opened the cover and the pages made a crackling sound.

And there they were—the popular girls. Some of them were cheerleaders, others just beauties so full of confidence that teachers, boys, and parents alike bent like saplings in the wind to fulfill their desires.

I quickly turned the page, wanting to find someone or something that elicited a personal connection from my senior year. My senior photo was one of those fake-oh airbrush jobs, with bare shoulders, a velvet swath, and the long, straight, untapered hair that was so popular back then. The girl who smiled up at me looked a hell of a lot more cheerful than I remembered feeling back then.

I flipped to Wolf's senior portrait. He exuded artistic misery, his dark eyes soft and sad, his hair long and pulled back in a ponytail even then.

In the centerfold was a collage of senior life, and I managed to find a shot of Wolf and myself hanging out at one of the weekend coffeehouses. We were sitting cross-legged on the floor, our heads tilted as if we were dubious about the talent of the performer, which we probably were. There was a photo of Rikki, Lizard, and me toasting each other with cups of green tea in the Japanese Tea Garden, where we'd gone for a school field trip.

"Oh, that reminds me. Mr. Brophy called from the high school," Mom said, flipping through one of the other yearbooks. "He's got you scheduled for January third at one o'clock. I told him that's fine. And you're to let him know if you need a video projector or any special visual aids."

Dread swept over me as I thought about speaking at the high school. I really had nothing to say, having spent only five months in the workforce. Besides, facing an audience of teenagers was more intimidating than tossing out an idea at the magazine's pitch meeting. "I wish you hadn't signed me up for that, Mom. Public speaking is not my thing."

"I'm sure you'll inspire a few kids to follow their dreams. Maybe encourage a few to go into magazine publishing."

"Not when I hate it."

"What?" Mom seemed shocked. "When did that happen?"

"It was never something that I wanted, Mom. Remember? Dad's New York colleague had a cousin at *Skyscraper?* I didn't even apply for the job, and before I knew it I was supposed to be the next Tina Brown or Grace Mirabella."

Mom closed the book and pressed it to her chest. "Oh, sweetie, I am sorry. I had no idea you felt that way."

"Not that I don't appreciate having a job and everything. I mean, it pays the rent, but it's so consuming that it doesn't give me a lot of time to search for a job I might like."

"And what would that be? What interests you?"

"I don't know." In college I had majored in liberal arts. I had enjoyed studying literature and art, but didn't think I was particularly gifted in either area. "I was thinking of something in television, and Leo promised to set up an interview at the network. But if and when that happens, I just don't want you and Dad to be totally disappointed that I'd ditched the whole magazine thing."

"Oh, Maddy, I hope you don't think that I'm pushing you to be something you're not." She leaned back against an old cedar chest that used to belong to my grandmother and sighed. "That is the last thing I want to do, really."

"But the way you tell your friends about my 'publishing career' . . . It's as if my job at *Skyscraper* is the only worthwhile thing about me."

"Oh, honey, no! No way!" Mom winced as if I'd wounded her. "Your father and I are proud because you are you—a bright, insightful girl with a touch of daring. You don't need to prove anything to us."

I shook my head. "It definitely feels that way with Dad."

"Yes, I know the vibe he gives off, and I don't think he can help it. Your father has certain notions about people, where they should be and what they should do, and his views are highly inflexible. I tried to soften his will for years until I realized it was no use. That battle's done for me. I've learned to work around him, subversive though it may be."

"And you found Clay," I said.

Mom nodded. "Clay has a lot to do with my liberation,

but it isn't all about him. Clay has his own demons to wrestle with. Did he tell you that he used to be a priest?"

I blinked. "He left the church for you?"

"No, not for me, though I think the fact that I'm married only compounds his guilt issues."

"That explains Clay's laid-back style," I said. "But you must have a lot of issues of your own, Mom."

"For me, it was about learning to stand on my own two feet. Stepping out of your father's shadow."

"The doctor's wife."

"That was me, for way too long. Dr. Greenwood was the center of my universe; all things revolved around him. And one day, when someone asked me what I wanted in life, I realized I couldn't answer. I was so out of touch with myself, I didn't have a dream of my own."

I thought of the years when Mom had put so much time into Dad's career, taking care of the house and me, and then pouring any extra time into hospital fund-raisers and social engagements with other doctors.

"I wasn't really living," Mom said sadly. "I existed on the periphery of life, orbiting my husband's planet."

"You were so cheerful about it," I said. "I guess I thought you were happy."

"I was so out of touch." She bit her lower lip. "But I've found myself again. I'm happy now, Maddy. Truly happy with my life. I don't want to hurt your father, but somehow I don't think it would matter much to him as long as I don't upset the order of his life."

"It's great that you figured things out," I said.

Mom leaned forward and brushed a patch of dust from the knee of my jeans. "Take my advice, sweetie. Don't ever give up your life for a man. Fall in love, find a partner, but don't sell out for him."

I nodded, understanding her on an intellectual level, but not sure I'd be able to resist selling the ranch if the right stud came along.

"Anyway," Mom went on, "I'm sorry about setting you up to speak at the high school. Do you want me to call Mr. Brophy and try to cancel?"

"No, that's okay," I said, flipping the page of the yearbook. "It won't kill me to pass on the little bit I know about magazine publishing." I laughed. "That'll take all of forty seconds. Maybe we can do a question-and-answer thing to fill the time."

"You always were a good sport."

My eyes locked on a photo of my high school English teacher, a dark-haired hunk with a full beard and penetrating brown eyes. "Mr. Minnetta," I said aloud. "All the girls had crushes on him." He was the bachelor teacher of the school, a former drama student at Yale who dabbled in Shakespearean theater in his spare time. And it didn't hurt that he drove an awesome Nissan 300ZX. *The wiener car,* Wolf had called it.

Mom looked at the open book in my lap. "Oh, yes, I remember him. Didn't he appear in a few productions in the theater district?"

I nodded. "I think he was a frustrated actor."

"He's still at the school," Mom said. "I saw him in the fall when I was working on the literacy program."

Probably married with eight kids, I thought, suddenly feeling old for my twenty-one years.

The prospect of speaking at my old high school heightened my sense of holiday depression. The only thing that might lift my spirits was a shopping trip to one of the fine department stores where my parents owned plastic. Maybe I'd feel better about appearing if I had a new Dolce & Gabbana suit and a nice pair of Steve Madden boots. That saying was true: You can't go home again.

At least, not without designer footwear.

11

The desire to lose my breakfast was surprisingly strong as I stepped through the double doors and into the hallowed halls of Snob Hill High a few days later. The current clientele was tougher and fiercer than I remembered, with guys in baggy jeans that drooped to show the waistband of their underwear, and girls sporting footwear that put my new Nine West red boots to shame. First, there was the smoking area outside the building: a cloud of escape for the new generation of freaks. Then I had to jump aside to dodge a guy chasing a girl down the hall. He caught up with her in front of the trophy case, lifted her in his arms and teased her about something until a harried man in black glasses demanded that he put the girl down.

Whoa, Mr. Brophy never would have tolerated that behavior when I was in school.

Feeling totally out of place, I tried to focus on the satisfying click of my new boots as I made my way to the office, where I told one of the office ladies I was here to see Mr. Brophy.

It turned out Mr. Brophy was not in that day—reason to panic—but Mrs. Sonnenberg, the school librarian, had been left in charge of all the arrangements. I never thought I'd be so happy to see her bland face, but she made me feel right at home with her hoarse voice and beehive hair.

"Welcome," she rasped. "I understand you're here to tell the seniors all about magazine publishing."

"I am? I am. Oh, well, yes, sort of. I mean, I've only worked at *Skyscraper* a few months, but I have a few interesting insights. At least, I hope."

"Stop apologizing and tell me, have you ever met Candice Bergen? You know . . . Murphy Brown?"

I folded my arms over my chest. "Actually, no."

"I sat two rows behind her when *La Cage* played here," she said proudly. "She had skin like butter. People always tell me we sound alike. The same vocal quality."

I squinted at her, wondering if Mrs. Sonnenberg considered the Candy sighting to be her ten minutes of fame. "I do see the resemblance," I lied.

She gave a nod of satisfaction. "Are you ready, then? We'll get you set up in the auditorium. The seniors will report there at the beginning of seventh period." She headed down the hall, and I fell into stride behind her.

"How long am I supposed to speak?"

"Forty-five minutes. That's how long seventh period is."

Forty-five minutes! I couldn't even talk to Leo that long without occasionally dropping out of focus.

The old auditorium still smelled the same—a mixture of floor wax and old cheese, though I was never sure where the cheese odor came into play. As I helped Mrs. Sonnenberg test the lonely microphone at the lonely podium on the stage, the rows of empty seats stretched before me like a vast ocean.

My breakfast coffee churned as I imagined horrible scenarios of me quivering through my little speech while chilled-out rapper types partied in the aisles. Oh, how I wanted to be on their side of the stage! I was pacing in the wings when the tone sounded to change classes. Doors pounded open and kids began to stream in, filling the back rows first. I tried to stay calm by pretending my mind had been transported to a desert spa in New Mexico as the auditorium filled and Mrs. Sonnenberg introduced me.

Suddenly, I was in front of the podium wiping my sweaty palms on my stylish new DKNY blazer. "So you're here because you want to hear about magazine publishing?" I asked with a humble smile.

"Naw!" a kid with a backwards baseball cap called from the front aisle. "We're here because you're our ticket out of seventh-period classes."

"Really? Then you can go," I said, keeping my voice level.

Students watched in amusement as the boy shook his head.

"No, really. I'm serious. Let me be your ticket out of a boring class, but don't feel like you have to stay here and be equally bored. If you have someplace else you want to be, now's your chance."

A few kids laughed as he bent down to pick up his books, then hesitated, looking over his shoulder.

"Don't worry," I said. "The other teachers won't fry you. I'm the guest lecturer. I've got the power."

Kids laughed as the boy slung his backpack over one shoulder and headed up the aisle. He did some kind of rap gesture to the back of the room and a few kids laughed, but a moment later he was gone. Time for me to get real.

"In some ways, I feel like an imposter standing here." As I spoke, I pulled the microphone out of its clip and wound it in front of the podium, walking to the edge of the stage. "Just a few years ago I was sitting where you are, wondering what the hell to do with my life." I teetered at the edge of the stage, then dropped down to sit on the edge. "As you might have guessed, I'm still wondering. But anyway, soon after I graduated from college I found myself in this entry-level position at *Skyscraper* magazine. Don't be too impressed. The magazine is very glossy, but the offices are probably smaller than your bedroom closet. They pay new kids like me dirt, and most of my day is filled with making massive photo-copies, answering phones, and running to the corner deli to get the right brand of bottled water for my boss."

I heard a few kids laugh, and I felt the power. They liked me. Maybe I should think about doing stand-up.

"Anyway, on a few rare occasions they throw me some of the upscale work." I went on to explain pitching and writing articles, setting up interviews, gathering expert quotes, and the bane of my existence, fact-checking. I figured that, since I had confessed the ugly truth about my close personal rela-tionship with the copy machine, I could at least pretend that I knew a thing or two about the editorial end of the business.

I went on, trying to paint a picture of a typical day. Then I tried to fill out the image of the staff behind the magazine, the team of editors and copywriters and copy editors and freelancers who honed each story down to its bone, then built it back up. Even though I didn't particularly care for it, the process was amazing.

When I finished my spiel, I invited the students to ask me questions. A few kids were interested in the stages a story went through prior to publication. Others wanted to know more about the exposure to celebrities.

"Have you ever met Madonna?" one girl asked.

"Can't say that I have."

"How about Michael Jackson?" someone added.

I shook my head. "That I would remember."

"Are Julia Roberts's teeth real?"

"God, I hope so."

"Did you ever meet Will Smith, the Fresh Prince?"

"The artist formerly known as Prince?"

"Aerosmith?"

"Candice Bergen?"

No, but I've met her voice double.

I held up my hands as the students started to pelt me with the names of their favorite celebs. Clearly I wasn't going to get out of here alive if I didn't do some major name-dropping. "All right, all right! I am not personal friends with the members of Aerosmith, but I did meet Steve Tyler at an MTV party. He seemed very nice. And once when I was having dinner in Tribeca, I noticed that Robert DeNiro was eating at the next table. He was wearing these big, black glasses, probably hoping that no one would recognize him, but—"

We were still dishing over celebrities when the tone signaled the end of the period. Two students had met Robin Williams in a Castro comedy club, and one kid said he'd spent last summer working as a roadie for Crash Test Dummies. A few kids came over to the stage to thank me, and I joked with them until they had to head off to their next class.

Whew! The ordeal was over, and it had gone better than I could have dreamed. I would have happy-danced across the stage, but a few stragglers still remained. Jumping off the stage, I headed out. Amazing how, after all these years, I still felt a strong desire to get out of this building. I'd just reached the rear doors when someone called my name. I turned to see a familiar, handsome face.

"Mr. Minnetta!" I gasped, trying not to sound too excited, but failing miserably. I hadn't recognized my English teacher without his dark beard and mustache. Now he sported a funky goatee that made him look like a cross between Shaggy on *Scooby-Doo* and Chris on *Northern Exposure*. He was also a little thicker in the shoulders, but it gave him a solid look—meatier, mightier shoulders to hang your hands on.

"Sounds like you're doing well, Madison," he said. He pushed the door open for me, and I stepped through. "I had high hopes for you back in English lit. You were one of my most inspired and inspiring students."

"Thanks, Mr. Minnetta," I said, feeling like a ten-year-old in black patent leather shoes.

"Please, call me Judd," he said, raking back a few pale brown curls with one hand. "I've always said once you wear that ridiculous mortar board hat, you can dispense with formalities."

My face was beginning to ache from grinning. I realized I probably looked like a googly-eyed fool, but it's startling to come face-to-face with the teacher who dominated your high school fantasies. Back in high school, none of us were absolutely sure, but we guessed that Mr. Minnetta was about six years older than us—just barely out of school himself. He had attended the University of Arizona, which had a reputation as a party school, and he had often joked about nearly failing Brewskies 101, a story that assured his place in the Freaks Hall of Fame at our school.

The man had tried to separate himself from the rest of the faculty, letting us into some of the details of his life, treating us as peers, and sharing his enjoyment of everything from the San Francisco bar scene to his racy sports car, which slowly circled the parking lot after school before revving to a higher speed as he pulled out. At one point, it was a daily ritual for Lizard, Rikki, and me: We would meet at Lizard's locker, then head out by the gym door to watch Mr. Minnetta depart for cooler, sexier regions of the Bay Area.

"I've got to hand it to you, Madison," he said, "it takes a lot of nerve to return to your old stomping grounds and admit you're not a huge success."

"I had to be honest," I answered, thinking it was a better thing to say than: *My mommy made me do it.* The second tone rang, filling me with panic that I would lose him. "I can't believe you're still here," I blurted out. "I mean, it's so great. You were one of the best teachers in this school. Probably the best."

He nodded. "I enjoy it. 'We but teach bloody instructions, which, being taught, return to plague the inventor.' "

I bit my lower lip. "That's Shakespeare, right? I feel like you're giving me a pop quiz."

" 'Tis Macbeth," he said, bowing deeply. "And you passed, milady. With honors."

"You always acted out Shakespeare's plays so beautifully in class. Are you still pursuing the acting?" I asked, wondering if I was putting my foot in my mouth again. Somehow my brain was lagging behind my hammering heart.

"I am Macbeth," he said. "Tuesday through Sunday at the Phoenix Theater, eight P.M."

"Oh, wow!" A reaction lacking in brilliance, but I was riding on adrenaline now. "I have to come see the show before I go."

"I'd like that," he said. "How about tonight?"

"Tonight? I . . ." I tried to think if I had any plans, but my entire future was a blank calender looming into infinity. "That sounds great!"

"Come backstage after the show, and I'll buy you some dinner," he said.

"Okay!" I nodded, my head bobbing like a puppet. "Okay, then. I'll see you tonight."

He gave me a quick smile, then headed down the hall in a cloud of total coolness.

As I walked out of my old high school, the shock began to set in. I had just scored a date with the hunkiest teacher of my life, who was also appearing in a play. Hell's bells. I had to call Lizard and spill the dirt, even if it was her busy season.

By the time I found my seat in the theater that night, I had lit up the phone lines with news of my dinner with Mr. Minnetta. Leo had teased that I would turn into "teacher's pet." Wolf had admitted that he'd always had a crush on Mr. Minnetta, and Sugar had told me to go for it. "Honey lamb, the girls of the world are looking to you to fulfill our fantasies. Fuck the teacher!"

Lizard had shrieked into the phone for a full two minutes. "I hate you!" she'd bellowed. "You breeze into town and scarf up the best weenie in the Bay Area! I am so jealous!" *I know,* I'd thought, *and I am totally gloating.*

The show was precise and heavy, a typical Shakespearean tragedy. I thought Mr. Minnetta—Judd—did a great job. His lines had the ring and depth of poetry even as he got across the dark story of a man who couldn't live with his mistake. After the final curtain I dashed backstage, where Judd greeted me with a sexy kiss on the lips.

My fingers dug into his satin tunic as he pulled me against him and sucked face in front of the entire cast. I quickly overcame my shock and poured a little feeling into the kiss, glad that we weren't going to do that tedious mating dance of "If you like me, then maybe I like you." It was clear that Judd liked me, and the feeling was more than mutual. If I could just get past my tiny idol-worship syndrome, things would be peachy.

After Judd removed his makeup, we hopped the cable car to a storefront on Russian Hill, a Spanish restaurant that featured more than forty different kinds of tapas. Although Zarzuela was packed, the owner managed to find a table for us, and from the way Judd teased Lucas I could tell they were old friends. The casual atmosphere and the red wine helped to dispel some of my "teacher's pet" jitters as we nibbled on garlic-flecked shrimp, slabs of cheese with paper-thin slices of serrano ham, and elegant olive chutney. And though I'd worried about making conversation, Judd filled most of the time with anecdotes about his acting career.

"People tell me I should go to L.A.," he said, contemplating the wine in his glass. "Audition for television. That's where the real money is, but for me, it's not about money. I have to be on stage. It's like breathing or eating. Acting is my means of survival."

"And you belong on stage," I said. "It was exciting to see you playing Macbeth. A real thrill."

He reached across the table and squeezed my hand. "Trying to turn me on?" he teased.

We both laughed.

"I have more sophisticated methods than that," I said.

Though at the moment, I couldn't think of what they might be. I licked my lips, thinking of that kiss back at the theater, the way his tongue slipped into my mouth so easily.

You are going to have sex with your teacher from high school, a teenage voice taunted. Something about that seemed illegal or immoral. But what could the problem be? He was probably only six or seven years older than I was. And after dealing with Greg's twentyish aloofness, I was ready to graduate to a guy with some maturity and experience.

After we left the restaurant, we were walking along Powell when Judd pulled me into his arms. "You are so beautiful in the moonlight."

I smiled up at him, feeling goose bumps rise on the back of my neck. I'd never been with a guy who spoke in poetry. "Where are you living these days?" I asked, wondering if he would take the hint.

"North Beach," he said, tilting his face until it was just an inch from mine. "I finally got a grown-up apartment. You'll have to come see it sometime."

"But not tonight?" I asked.

"Ooh, sorry, milady, but I have the day from hell with the superintendent visiting the school tomorrow." He locked his arms around my waist, pulling my hips against his. "But I'd love a rain check. Tomorrow night? That way we can both sleep in Saturday."

"Okay."

He closed his eyes and kissed me again, fast and sweet. "Mmm." He groaned, ending the kiss. "Enough of that or I'll end up getting myself sent to the principal's office."

He walked me to the cable car, his arm over my shoulders as if we'd been lovers forever. When we got to the cable car stop, he bowed low and kissed my hand. Two older Asian women at the stop stared at him blatantly, but he didn't seem to mind.

"'Good night! Good night!'" he boomed in a stage voice.

"'Parting is such sweet sorrow, that alas, I would say good night 'til it be morrow.'"

"Bye," I chirped, giving a tiny inconspicuous wave.

The women nodded at each other, then smiled at me. "Your boyfriend make a good actor!" one woman said.

"Very nice, very nice," added the other.

I smiled at them. I wanted to add that Judd didn't rush me into bed on the first date, but I wasn't sure the women would appreciate the novelty of that. So instead, I looked up at the dark sky and thought about what I would wear tomorrow night.

Time to cash in Mom's gift certificate for some new lingerie.

12

The next morning I managed to book myself at Elizabeth Arden for a total day of beauty, rationalizing that a little waxing and toning would give me a boost of confidence when it was time to drop my drawers for Judd.

I had forgotten about the searing, tearing pain of a bikini wax. "The price for beauty!" the pink-coated attendant said in her brisk Russian accent. Sadist that she was, as I glanced down at the crotch of my panties I had to admit that the woman was thorough. With these silky thighs I could abandon publishing and model underwear.

I had also forgotten that deep-cleansing facials leave your face with angry red pores screaming for the plugs that had abandoned them. Oh, well. Hopefully Judd wouldn't notice that my makeup was heavier than the pancake he used on stage.

By the time I met Judd at the theater, I was primed and conditioned from the spa, oiled and lubed from thinking about defiling my high school teacher. This was truly the stuff that adolescent girls' fantasies are made of.

Judd met me backstage with a dark look, then swept me into his arms for another dramatic kiss.

This time I laughed, nearly toppling over in my spiky heels. "If this is going to be a regular occurrence, I'm going to have to wear more practical shoes."

"I have a surprise for you," he said, guiding me out the door. "My car is parked in the garage here, and I've made reservations at Casa Madrone, that charming inn in Sausalito."

"Really? Great!" I told him, showing off my extensive vocabulary. I'd been curious about Judd's apartment, but I was secretly thrilled that he'd gone out of his way to make the evening special. He'd made reservations! He was going to spring for a room! Hell's bells, was this a grown-up relationship, or what?

As the valet appeared with Judd's car, I was relieved to see that Judd had traded in the old Z-penis-car for something more age-appropriate. This late-model Saab convertible wasn't exactly mint condition, but it was fun riding over the Golden Gate Bridge with the top down, bundled in our jackets against the chilly wind, listening to a Steely Dan tape. "I love these guys," he said. "Their songs are full of literary allusions and black humor. Did you know they got their name from the William Burroughs novel *Naked Lunch*?"

"I didn't know that," I said. Tomorrow, I'd have to run down to the library and pick it up. I didn't want Judd to discover that I'd become semiliterate since I'd left college.

I asked him about that evening's performance, and he talked about the producer of the show and the politics involved in staying in favor in San Francisco's theater community. On some level I worried that I should be reciprocating with anecdotes about my day, but I wasn't going to tell him about getting waxed and clipped at the spa. At the moment, I didn't really have a whole lot going on in the personal files, but that didn't matter to Judd, who seemed to enjoy spinning his ordinary day into extraordinary tales.

So I just leaned back and let the wind wash over me as we went under the majestic squarish spires of the Golden Gate. The tires whirred happily over the grooved bridge pavement, lending a chorus to the song in my heart. *He wants me, he wants me . . . the renegade teacher wants to be with me.*

The inn was actually a series of cottages cascading down a gentle hill. Each cottage faced the bay, explained the innkeeper, and they were connected by stepping-stones to a string of accommodations like a hot tub and sauna. There was an odd moment for me when Judd went to register.

"Yes, Mr. Minnetta," said the clerk, "your room is ready, sir."

I froze, suddenly flashing back to high school. He was Mr. Minnetta—*the* Mr. Minnetta. God, what if someone from school saw us together? I felt like the Nob Hill Lolita, corrupting this poor man to bed his young protégée.

Or was that an overreaction?

When Judd handed the clerk his credit card, I grabbed his arm and yanked him aside. "One question. How old are you, anyway?"

Judd laughed. "Old enough to know better." I shook my head. "Not buying that, eh?" he said, grinning. "Okay, I'm twenty-eight. Fast approaching the big three-oh."

"Oh."

"Is that a good oh, or an 'oh my God, he's old' oh?"

"Old? At twenty-eight? No way. I mean, you're definitely in a different place from most guys my age. But that's a good thing. I was just thinking about how those seven years made such a big difference back when I was the student and you were the teacher. But now . . ." I shrugged. "Odd, how we sort of end up on the same level."

"Speak for yourself," he said as he turned back to sign the registration. "I hate to be compared to my contemporaries who live on Chinese takeout and Three Stooges videos."

At a table looking out over the dotted lights on the shore-line and the dark bay, we sat beside each other and held hands. It was so romantic, I imagined my heart swelling up ten sizes too big, like the Grinch's. As we feasted on chicken cordon bleu with fresh string beans, Judd told me he missed home-cooked meals.

"I probably shouldn't tell you this . . . No, I shouldn't."

"What?" I fought off panic. "You're scaring me. Okay, Judd, now you have to tell me if you don't want me to run screaming down to the bay."

He sighed. "My last girlfriend was a fabulous cook. She was raised in the kitchen, she used to say. Her mother was from Greece."

I nodded, relieved. I could live with the fact that there'd been other women before me. Let's face it, if there was a void, it would confirm that Judd was seriously defective, an ax murder or a secret psychopath. I didn't mind discovering a few skeletons in his closet, as long as they weren't real decaying bones. "It's nice that you appreciated her talents," I said. "What did she do for a living?"

"She was a chef. The famous Stamata of Café Corinth."

"Don't know the place," I admitted, staring into the flickering gas flame in the stone-walled fireplace.

Judd switched the focus to me for the first time since my lecture at the school. "Do you cook?" he asked.

I shrugged. "Who doesn't? Don't we all have to eat to survive?"

From his hesitant nod, I had a feeling he was expecting more of an answer. Maybe I should have whipped out a menu of the various dishes I'd perfected. Which would have been fine, had I perfected an entree beyond ramen noodles, mac and cheese, or spinach salad with hard-boiled eggs. After all, I'd been living in college dorms, where even hot plates are illegal.

Not that I minded. That corny old joke could have been written for me. What does a spoiled brat make for dinner? Reservations!

"You know," Judd went on, "I wasn't trying to flatter you when I said you were one of my most promising students.

You had the soul of a writer. Have you pursued that, beyond fact-checking and typing your boss's memos?"

"Not really." I felt apologetic, as if I'd forgotten to turn in a term paper. "I wouldn't know where to begin."

"I can help you with that," he said. He reached into the deep pocket of his black cashmere coat and removed a slender package wrapped in green tissue paper.

"A gift? For me?" How did he know I was a Christmas nut? "That's so sweet," I said as I tore into the paper. I assumed it was a book, a slender hardcover. But the cover had no title.

"It's a blank journal," he said. "For you to start writing again. Every day, you should be writing something down—your thoughts, your dreams, your wildest ideas and fears. They're all seeds that must be nurtured."

"Oh, Judd, thank you." I pressed the journal to my chest, pleased that he thought so much of me. "Honestly, I don't think of myself as a writer. I mean, I like writing just fine, but I don't feel that incredible compulsion that most writers talk about."

"Give it some time," he said. "Put pen to paper and let your mind loosen up. Write down some ridiculous, disjointed thoughts and open the gates for the honest, profound material to flow."

I opened the book and smoothed down a crisp, lined page. "I'll do that," I said. "I'll start writing tomorrow."

"Good." His eyes never left mine as he slid his hand over my thigh under the table. "So what do you think? Should we order some dessert?"

With a sigh, I leaned my head on his shoulder. His hand was moving gently up and down—titillating, but I wanted more. "I really want to make love to you," I whispered. "Right here, right now." Can you believe me? I could barely believe myself as I placed my hand in his lap. He gasped as my palm made contact.

"How the hell are you going to get that thing to our room?" I said, my fingers closing over his fly.

"Very gingerly." He removed my hand and took a deep breath. "Okay, wicked woman, we're in cottage three. You lead the way."

Snatching up my new journal, I headed out to the lobby and threw open the door. A blast of cool air hit me, and I felt giddy as I leaped out and hopped from one stepping-stone to another. Behind me, Judd was laughing, saying something about how I had to promise not to include him in my first big novel. "Or else, make sure I'm a nice character."

I turned in the doorway of cottage three, waiting under the dim yellow bulb. "Oh, I don't think I'll be writing about us," I said. "I don't think you can print the things we're going to do tonight." Oh, why was I bragging like that? I hoped he wouldn't be disappointed.

He unlocked the door and I stepped into a warm, cozy cottage. I sank onto the bed and ran my hands over the red and tan handmade quilt, not really sure how to proceed. Should I turn down the lights and pretend I did this all the time? Or should I let him be the aggressor?

Judd closed the door behind him, went to the table by the door, and switched on his tape player. The jazzy blues of Steely Dan filled the room. His dark eyes were penetrating as he stared at me. "I have an announcement to make," he said with dramatic flair. "It's time to . . . get naked!"

He tugged off his sweater and flung it in the air, followed by his balled-up T-shirt. I laughed at first, then realized I had better get in on the action before he won the race. My sweater went flying, revealing my silky new camisole and panties. I twirled, giving Judd a chance to appreciate my lingerie before I stripped everything off and tossed it into a silky puddle on the rug. Sweeping my hair back, I lifted it in the air, then let it fall onto my shoulders.

"Oh, my land, look at you," he gasped.

I lifted my arms and spun around again, feeling a surprising lack of inhibition. Amazing, what a day of primping can do for the ego.

Judd stood opposite me, obviously happy to see me. I felt my jaw drop at the sight of his naked body, his meaty thighs and lean hips . . . so much smooth flesh.

"Let me look at you," he whispered. "You're beautiful!"

That made me feel modest. I brought my hands down and crossed them over my chest.

"No, no . . . don't do that. Come here," he said, coming forward to take my hand and pull me toward the bed. He seemed so comfortable being naked, as if he did it all the time. Maybe he did. Was I the one with the underwear hang-up, wanting to have the important parts covered while I slept?

"Relax," he whispered, covering my breasts with his hands. From the way he cupped me, massaged me, kissed me, I could see Judd was a true afficionado of breasts. "You are beautiful."

I closed my eyes and tried to enjoy the warmth rising inside me. My nipples were hard now, and I wanted him to move on to other places. I looked at him, feeling a sudden swell of willpower.

"Hey, you," I said, grabbing his shoulders and pushing him back on the bed.

He seemed surprised, but surrendered as I threw my leg up and straddled him, putting myself in the position of power. I was moist, and the feeling of him rubbing against me was exquisite.

"Madison." He threw his head back against the bed in surrender.

I moved over him, slow and steady, gasping with each little thrust. I was shocked at the pleasure, shocked at my own actions. I hadn't taken charge with a guy since . . . since the adolescent days with Ryan.

I let my hips pause over him as I took in the feeling of power and excitement.

"You are amazing," he whispered, pulling me down on top of him to kiss me.

I pressed against him, flesh on flesh, enjoying the thrill of an equal relationship.

"I can't help but think of Touchstone in *As You Like It*. 'Am I the man yet?' " he asked dramatically. " 'Doth my simple feature content you?' "

"Oh, you the man," I said. "You are definitely the man."

In the morning, Judd wanted me to come back to his apartment and spend the day with him, but I felt bad about ditching Mom. Although I'd called her from the inn to let her know I wouldn't be home, I didn't want to completely ignore her during the rest of my visit at home.

"Call me as soon as you can," Judd said as he pulled up in front of the house on Nob Hill. He threw the car into park, then leaned across and kissed me possessively. "I've got plans for the evening, which I'd love to include you in."

Inside, the house seemed quiet and empty. The tree looked bare without the packages around it. "Mom?" I called.

"Up here." Her voice came down the stairs.

I found her up in her bedroom, packing a suitcase.

My eyes popped open. "Ohmigod! Are you leaving Dad?"

"No, honey." She squeezed my arm and smiled. "Not officially. I'm going away for a week. Clay and I are going to Tahoe. The trip was his Christmas gift to me. He just sprang it on me last night, and while I'm looking forward to spending a few days without having to sneak around, I do feel a little guilty. Clay didn't realize you would be here while we were gone. I'm sorry, sweetie. I hate to abandon you."

"Oh." It took me a minute to process the whole package. "Don't feel bad," I said. "You know I can fend for myself. I've been on my own for years."

"But I won't be here to drive you to the airport," she said.

"And your last few days . . . I wish things hadn't overlapped this way."

"Mom, don't worry. I'm not leaving until next Sunday, and Judd or Wolf can drive me to the airport. I'll be fine. You just have a good time."

"I'm sure I will," she said, pausing to smile at me. "I can't get over how much you've grown up. I really am proud of you, honey. Of you, not just your accomplishments."

Realizing we were veering dangerously close to a classic mother-daughter moment, I flicked the tag on her luggage. "What's your cover for this trip, anyway?"

"Emily, of course. I'm telling your father that she's going for a skin peel, and I'm coming along for moral support."

"That is so lame. He'll really buy it?"

"He always does."

I sat on the bed and talked with her as she folded sweaters and slid shoes into shoebags. She was leaving late this afternoon, driving to the airport with Clay.

I would have to call Judd . . . This meant I could see him tonight, maybe spend the night at his place. With Mom out of the house, there was no reason to hang around. Hmm . . .

When Judd's Saab pulled into the driveway that afternoon, I ran out the door of the house, my long cashmere coat streaming behind me as I flew down the hill, my red boots clambering over the stone steps. It was one of those gorgeous San Francisco days—cool but clear, with a sapphire blue sky that allows you to see for miles.

Judd was out of the car, his arms open to me, and he seemed to hold out a promise, ready for me to snatch up like the brass ring on the old carousel at Golden Gate Park.

I jumped into his arms and he whirled me around and kissed me hard. He had the top down and "Reelin' in the Years" was playing loud, and for some reason the song sounded as hopeful and limitless as the sky above us.

In that moment, I knew it was our future—hopeful and limitless.

Judd danced me around the car, and though I knew the neighbors had to be watching, wondering if Dr. Greenwood's daughter had totally lost her mind, I didn't let myself care as I stared into his eyes, dancing and laughing.

Was it destiny or a miracle?

I wasn't sure, but for the first time in my life I had stumbled into a real, grown-up relationship. Maybe that was why I couldn't stop smiling.

13

Sunday

Okay, this is probably totally insane, and I keep telling my-self it's only because Mom isn't at the house, but I packed up a bunch of clothes and threw them into the back of Judd's Saab and now I'm in the process of unpacking at his apartment.

Just one moment of weirdness when he shoved aside a bunch of things in one closet and told me I could hang up my stuff in there. I was hanging up my long coat when I no-ticed the stuff he'd pushed back. A long rose silk nightgown. A full-length black crepe skirt with a slit up the side. A suede Liz Claiborne blazer in a beautiful shade of burnt amber. And a pair of tooled cowboy boots.

The sight of the stuff choked me up a little. "Um . . . Judd? Have you been cross-dressing on the side?"

"What?" He peeked into the closet and shrugged. "Oh, just push those to the back. I guess Stamata left a few things behind."

The old girlfriend.

Judd went to get us two beers, but I shivered, still staring into the closet. Bad enough that he'd kept some of her stuff here, but seeing the eclectic mix of styles, I had a feeling I

would like Stamata had I met her under different circumstances. I could just picture her, a dark-haired Grecian goddess
vamping in her slit skirt and cowboy boots. I shivered again.

The ghost of the ex lives on. Maybe, when Judd goes to
school tomorrow I can bag up her stuff and drop it into a
charity box. Bye, bye, Stamata.

Monday

Am writing from Backbend Café, four blocks from Judd's
place. A cute little find, with sculpted tables that resemble hu-
mans bending over backwards. Huge bulletin board that reminds me of possibilities. I can be a part-time nanny, take
massage-therapy classes, learn to make potstickers on a Wok
Wiz Tour of Chinatown. The world opens up before me . . .
life beyond my latte.

My job for the day seems to be to make us an afternoon
meal, since Judd usually eats when he gets home from school.
Not that I volunteered, but before he left at the crack of dawn
this morning he asked me what I was making. Presumptuous
bastard, but I enjoyed watching from bed as he dressed, the
blanket stretched up to my chin with one eyelid cracked open.

So anyway, I thought I'd surprise him and actually make a
great dinner. Don't think ramen noodles would really float
his boat.

Searched his kitchen and found Stamata's cookbooks.
Where the hell do you get filo dough? No way I can pull this
stuff off. Roasted lamb and moussaka? You actually peel
eggplants? Need to go home and dig out Mom's cookbooks.

Later

Couldn't find the right cookbooks at home, just books
about baking and making pastries. In a panic, raided Mom's

freezer. Found bag of taco meat. Ran to market for tomatoes, cheese, green onions, sour cream, guacamole, Coronas. This cooking thing is a lot of work.

Leo called as I was chopping onions and tomatoes, and it felt a little weird to be tracked down. "How did you get Judd's number?" I asked him.

"From Wolf, Mata Hari. Get over yourself! What the fuck are you doing there that's so secret? The painters came and the apartment is now a Pepto shade of fuschia."

"You're a big fat liar," I answered. Then we both cracked up, and I felt a little better about the fact that I'd sort of dropped my friends while I was busy falling in love with Judd.

Leo says the apartment is coming along. Sugar introduced Leo to a friend of hers—some chick studying psych at NYU. Leo says she seems cool, so I told him to go for it.

After I hung up, had a major case of the guilts. It scares me a little that I don't care who the hell they recruit, and that leads me to the difficult possibility that I might not be moving into that apartment. Can't go there yet. Leo would kill me.

Later

Judd raved about my tacos. Said Stamata never made tacos. Ha!

As he watched me chop, he sang along with Steely Dan. "'Before the fall, when they wrote it on the wall, when there wasn't even any Hollywood . . .'" A great song. Thank God Judd can act better than he can sing.

So nice to have Judd for the evening! He's usually on stage.

Went to the movies, *Crying Game* again. Makes my butt hurt. I was interested in *Lorenzo's Oil*, but Judd needs to study acting technique, thinks Stephen Rea is huge talent. Didn't get into it with him.

Drinks in the neighborhood at the Saloon, where Judd knows the bartender. Fun night until a waitress told Judd that

Stamata had been in last week. That ruined it for me. "Is she that close?" I asked Judd.

"She moved to Oakland. I don't know what she was doing here," he said defensively. Like I'm overreacting. Maybe I am; I don't know. Must run it by Wolf when I see him tomorrow; he's so judicious, he'll know what's right.

Tuesday

Supposed to have lunch with Wolf but when I called he had to cancel. He felt so bad; then I felt bad for him. "You sound so far away," he told me. "I feel like I need to reel you in."

I was sort of relieved that he cancelled. Wolf is great but he seems so much a part of my past life, and I don't know how to explain my relationship with Judd yet. I mean, is this it? Are we really shacking up? Looks that way.

Some "Mommy Squad" girls just came into the café. Grunge mommies, I think, one with a pierced tongue. Other notables: the goth lesbians who talk so loud, everyone in the place knows what they're drinking (a latte and a soy cappuccino) and why they're taking their landlady to small-claims court (a long story). There's also a lone bald man who sits at the corner table and hums while he reads. He has never said a word to me, and I like that about him.

I steal a glance at him, wondering what he's planning for dinner. The dinner issue weighs heavily upon me. I drop my head to the table (which makes it a little hard to write this, but, whatever).

Wednesday

Drizzle day. Tiny rivulets of water flickering in the air. Note: Look up rivulet to make sure it's the right word. Or is it a word at all?

Started to call Leo or Sugar or Wolf, but lost my momentum. Feel too vulnerable. Not sure what to report . . . where I stand. Can't open myself to advice when I don't have a clue what I want.

Am so tired, but I must cook a meal today. Yesterday I opted for sensational takeout—fresh sushi and salad and Ben & Jerry's ice cream from a gourmet market in North Beach. The meal was fabulous, but Judd seemed a little disappointed, tapping his chopsticks on the table so thoughtfully as he kept saying dinner was fine, really. Really. Then he asked me what I did all day. Like I was supposed to spend the day cooking his dinner.

Big sigh. I'm making him sound like a monster, when the truth is I'm probably a little edgy about being compared to Stigma, or whatever her name is.

Must make an original dinner tonight. Something that says, "I love you."

Later

Made a meatloaf for dinner. Never really liked meatloaf, but it seemed like such a cozy, domestic thing to do on a drizzly, damp day, and nothing says "I love you" like a cozy meal. It ended up tasting very beefy, probably because I used ground beef (what the hell do I know?) instead of the standard mix of three meats—veal, pork, and deer? Something like that. Still, Judd was very appreciative and seemed to enjoy his 4 P.M. meal, though he's a little obsessed with getting naked at home. Intriguing, but I like to eat dinner with more than a napkin on my lap.

Afterward we both napped, then woke up and made love. I tried to spice things up with a new position, but he told me there wasn't time, that I should save it for Monday when he didn't have to do a show.

When he left for the theater, I attacked the kitchen. Took

me forever to get meatloaf gunk off the pan; then I wondered: Was gunk there for years? My poor hands. Must get rubber gloves. *Buy rubber gloves!*

Thursday

Ugh! Woke up with Judd's alarm at six-thirty and couldn't fall back to sleep, so I decided to make the most of the day and work on my cooking skills. I showed up for this walking tour of Chinatown that I'd seen online, and the fearless leader, Shirley Fong, was a real hoot. Great tour! We visited two temples, Taoist and Buddhist. Still not sure of difference, but they were lovely. (Maybe a Buddhist blessing is just what my cooking skills need!) Tea-tasting ceremony reminded me of Japanese Tea Garden with my buds. Miss my friends. Wolf owes me a lunch.

Shirley also took us to meet a famous artist, then to an herbal shop. Amazing place with walls of drawers. Twigs and powder and grains. Bought some herbs to break writer's block, but haven't used them yet—must cook into tea.

Dim sum on the street—yummy!

Tour ended with Chef Shirley demonstrating secrets of wok cooking. Awesome! Plan to wow Judd tomorrow, as soon as I collect ingredients and purchase wok. Wonder: Did Stamata ever make potstickers? Am writing from Backbend Café. Came to soak up ambience, study character, but nobody here. Music good, though . . . Mellencamp and the Stones. Have noticed Steely Dan lyrics floating in my head while asleep at night.

Later

Ugh! Had to leave café due to small man asking intrusive questions about my writing. "Ever published? What makes you think you can write? Do you know what the average writer makes?" Where was my reclusive, humming bald man when I needed him?

Then when I got back to Judd's he was upset, wondering what happened to me, what's for dinner? At four-thirty in the afternoon. Double ugh!

Told Judd I wasn't hungry. He made himself an omelette and napped while I stewed. Woke up horny, but I was still pissed. He just left for the show, and now I feel like a total jerk. Going to movies, hoping to see *Enchanted April* again. Will even sit through *Crying Game* again if I have to. Might try to wait it out at Backbend Café until after Judd gets home.

Ugh!

Friday

Judd left this morning without a word. Sort of harsh, I think. Is he still pissed?

Will make it up to him by preparing fabulous wok dinner. Must find wok and ingredients for Shirley's potstickers. No time for café today.

Ended up seeing *Scent of a Woman* last night. Am in love with Al Pacino. Is he married? Not sure. Fantasize Al falling madly in love with me, loves me for my mind. Al has enough money for full-time housekeeper and cook. Would teach his cook how to make potstickers.

Later

Am the luckiest, most loved woman in the world.

Didn't know yesterday, but I guess that was our first fight. Making up was divine. After school Judd brought me flowers—sterling roses, pale lavender. I cried. We made love—fast and furious. I cried through half of it. Then when it was over, I told him I wanted to do it again, taking it slow. He quoted something from Shakespeare. Something from *As You Like It* about a ragged voice. "I know I cannot please you," he said. I pressed his hand between my legs and told him his touch was very pleasing. May have taught the teacher something. Interesting handiwork.

Afterward, he lounged in the kitchen naked while I cooked the hand-hacked potstickers. Kept sneaking a peek at his butt, wondering how he compares to Al Pacino. Hard to say. Never saw Al naked.

Potstickers and garlic chicken with white wine. Judd was ecstatic, says he loves having me here. Says he won't let me go back to New York. "Why don't you cancel your flight to New York? Stay and see how things develop." I almost cried again when he said that.

Can't bear to tell Mom and friends, but I'm going to stay. Judd is a wonderful guy, and I'm getting the hang of this cooking thing.

Tonight, I'll meet him after the show and we'll go for drinks since he has the daytime off tomorrow.

Need to clean up wok mess, but right now just want to wallow in bed and hug pillow that smells like Judd. First, must replace Steely Dan CD with anything else.

Saturday

Bliss! My life is bliss!

After the show last night we went to dinner with some of the cast at Mo's Grill, south of Market. Great burgers—but the best part of the evening was the way Judd treated me. Like a queen. I think he enjoyed showing me off to his friends. "She's an editor at *Skyscraper* in New York," he told one of the actors. "Better watch what you say or you'll find yourself written up in the gossip section."

Oh, right! Hate that he mentioned *Skyscraper.* Love that he's proud of me. Thorny dilemma, but at least no dishpan hands. *Still need rubber gloves!*

He told them I was staying on here, and they congratulated us as if we were getting married. That did it . . . saw myself in bridal gown. Will slip out Monday and buy copy of *Brides* magazine. Just curious.

Can't wait to spend today with him. Want to take him for coffee at Backbend, then shopping on Fillmore Street for kitchen items (remember *rubber gloves*). Suspect Stamata robbed him of spatulas and bowls when she kicked her out. Can't wait to drag him into Sue Fisher King. This place could use a comfortable chair and a good reading lamp.

Later

Disappointing day. First, Judd slept till ten and putzed around till noon. Morning vanished. Then, he wanted to drag me to a high school basketball game. I resisted, he insisted.

The school gym still smells of bad sneakers. I mentioned this and Judd started singing Steely Dan's "Bad Sneakers." Beginning to strongly dislike Steely Dan. Judd has a following of freckled girls with big hair. Very uncool girls, I think, with no visible piercings, but he seems to enjoy their admiration. Heard them talking about me in the ladies' room. They think they have a chance with him (same thing I thought in high school). Sort of pathetic.

A wasted afternoon.

He's in the shower now, getting ready for the show. Wants me to come see the show, which I don't think I can sit through. I hear enough Shakespeare from Judd's lips. Will tell him I need time to write.

Looking forward to party after the show—his friends, Linda and Harvey. Not thrilled about being arm candy again, but imagine the people at the party will be closer to my age.

At least, they won't be trying to steal Judd for a prom date.

Sunday, 2:20 A.M.

Have just arrived at the apartment alone. Judd refused to leave his fucking friends at the party, which turned out to be a celebration of the fine qualities of Stamata. Harvey and Linda were *her* friends!!!

I can't believe Judd brought me there. What the hell was he thinking?

Harvey was all: "Stamata really broke his heart. It was sad . . . so sad." Then Linda tells me: "I'm sure he's told you about Stamata? We've been so worried about Judd since she left. He was in bad shape, I tell you. But it's great that he's getting his feet wet again with you."

Getting his feet wet? What am I, a fucking puddle?!!

Judd is so fucked, and he doesn't even realize it.

Searched through the medicine cabinet for some Tylenol and what do I find? Two prescriptions with Stamata's name on it. He says it's over, but she is haunting this place.

Called Sugar to talk it out, but got her machine. Don't want to leave a message that might let her know of my growing discontent.

Everything will be better in the morning, right? Right?

9:20 A.M.

My life is shit.

Judd came home around dawn and we had drunken sex. At first I didn't mind when he kept saying that he loved me, but then it became clear that, at that point, he would have professed love for a ham sandwich if it had breasts. Besides,

with the limp noodle he was sporting, it wouldn't be long before he passed out.

Have just read this journal, which reinforced that not only
is my life shit, I can't write worth a damn. Which leaves me
without a career. Without a fucking destiny.

I would cry if I had the energy. Need to get out of here.
Go back to Mom and Dad's house? Will Dad be there?
Would rather not see him now. Don't want to see anyone.
What day is it, anyway?

Sunday . . . Sunday!

My flight was today. What time? Shit!

14

My hand trembled as I passed the ticket to the airline clerk. "You'll be traveling with us to New York today?" she asked smoothly.

"Yes," I gasped. "Yes, New York," I said, as if taking a sacred vow.

"It's too late for us to accept your baggage here," she said. "You'll have to do gateside check-in."

"No problem," I assured her. I would hold the bag in my lap if I had to . . . anything to get on the flight.

"That's flight Eighty-seven to JFK. You'll be going to gate H-Twelve," she told me, sliding a boarding pass across the counter. With quivering hand, I snatched up the ticket. "Don't worry," she said, "you have time. They're boarding now, but the gate is just down that corridor."

I nodded, picked up my bags, and ran. My garment bag banged against my side with each step, and the handle on the Neiman Marcus shopping bag of dirty clothes was starting to tear, but I pressed on, running for my life.

I was running from the image of Judd, red-faced and squinting, after I woke him up to tell him I was leaving.

"I'm going back to New York," I said. "I need to have a life."

He shook his head. "You have a beautiful life here."

"So did Stigmata. Or Stalagmite . . . whatever her name was."

"What's that supposed to mean?" He sounded cranky.

"You can read all about it in my book," I told him, gathering up my stuff in a shopping bag. I still had to cab it back to the Nob Hill house and throw everything in my suitcase to make my twelve-thirty flight.

"Madison, don't leave this way. Look at me. Talk to me."

"I have nothing to say." I turned away to open the door.

"'False face must hide what the heart doth know,'" he recited dramatically. "That's from *Macbeth.*"

"And here I thought it was from *All My Children,*" I said, pausing with my hand on the doorknob. "You need to stop using Shakespeare as a crutch. Could you come up with a few original responses once in awhile?"

Looking back now, I smiled. I had finished off with a truly brilliant line. "This Elizabethan shit is wearing thin," I'd told him. Sugar and Leo would laugh when I told them all about it, which I planned to do over many intoxicating coldies.

It wasn't until I was in my seat on the jet, buckling up, that the past few weeks flashed before me. Just weeks ago, I had strapped myself into a seat on a jet like this for a short visit home. Now, three men wiser, I was emotionally bankrupt, and probably a few pounds heavier from all the holiday treats.

But as the jet raced along the runway and tipped gently into the air, I sucked in a breath, secure in the knowledge that I was on the right path.

I was going back to New York, back to the friends who supported my insanity, back to a new apartment that would need a ton of work, back to a dead-end position I loathed, staffed with egotistical nut jobs. But hey, no one else in the office knew how to fix a jam in the copier quite the way I did.

It was a fucked-up life, but it was mine—all mine, ha, ha!—and for now, it was just what I needed.

Part Two

Blue Christmas

West 98th Street
December 8, 2003
9:10 P.M.

15

Damned cell phones! Mine had been bleeping since I'd gotten out of the subway at Ninety-sixth Street, but when I tried to retrieve the messages it kept powering off because the battery was low. And from the caller ID I could see one of the messages was from Leo's cell, though I don't know why he'd be calling me when I had just left him at Rockefeller Center. Probably wanted to announce that he'd mastered a triple salchow on the ice. I loved the convenience of cell phones, but sometimes the frustration of dealing with wrong numbers and drained batteries and rude people shouting out personal details on the bus made me question their usefulness.

At Rockefeller Center, the three of us had ended up back at Morrell's for a fabulous dinner at a table in the rear, a safe distance from Mr. Middle-aged. From where I sat, if I leaned over the bread plate I could see the bottom edge of the Christmas tree, the lower branches glimmering in the night. There's something magical about dining in view of the Rockefeller Center tree. I told Leo that we could be tiny statuettes in the snow-globe ornament he'd given me so many Christmases ago. Of course, he responded that I was full of fruitcake—or something not nearly so civilized.

While we were dining, Sugar flirted with the two men seated at the table beside us, asking them how their wine was, commenting on the buttery chardonnay on Morrell's list, asking them if she could borrow their sugar, then saying "Oops! I've got plenty of sugar—it's actually my name!"

Sometimes it's truly a disadvantage to have an extroverted, Type-A friend. And Sugar was only going to get worse when the next issue of *Playboy* hit the stands. Our very own "sugar plum" was the featured centerfold fairy for the special holiday issue. As it was, people occasionally recognized her voice from the radio; once men began to recognize her other finer points—which apparently they'd shot with her bare nipples pressed against the glass of the radio station's sound booth—Sugar's ego would know no limits.

Tonight, however, Sugar's expansive flirtations worked in my favor. One of the guys turned out to be Frank Falcone, a writer for *Newsday*. Frank was cordial, knowledgeable about wines, and interested in me, of all things. Before we left the restaurant we made plans to meet for drinks this week. I'm not going to make the mistake of inflating my expectations (because it smarts when that balloon pops). At this point, let's just say I'm encouraged by the possibilities.

After dinner, Leo tried to talk Sugar and me into a quick round on the ice, but we declined. Sugar usually passed out around nine so she could be up at five in the morning to do her radio show—a real crimp in her social life—and I secretly wanted to get home and change into my flannel jammies and watch *A Christmas Story* on TNT. Okay, if I didn't have a date, what was wrong with snuggling in with a Christmas classic? Hmm . . . I wondered if Frank had ever seen *A Christmas Story*.

I nodded at Ralph, the doorman, and took the stairs up to my third-floor co-op. I'd bought the one-bedroom in this historic, twelve-story building with the money I'd gotten when Dad passed away. I imagined he'd be happy to know I was safe and financially secure with a low-interest mortgage on, as the *Times* ad had called it, "a renovated prewar with hard-wood floors and bright southern and western exposures."

Unlocking the door, I stepped into my retreat and pressed on the light. Ahhh . . . I had to lean on the low bookshelves by the door to undo the petite buckles of my shoes—my daring black Chanel ankle-strap pumps with metal heels. They were so impractical for the cold winter months and incredibly unaffordable at seven hundred–plus smackaroos, but when I'd seen a shot of Renee Zellweger wearing them in *Harper's Bazaar*, I couldn't resist.

Barefoot, I padded over to the phone, where the answering machine was blinking furiously with five messages. A smarter, more restrained woman would have waited until after her movie to hear the messages, but I had issues with delaying gratification—especially now that my cell phone was dead. I pressed play and listened as I unbuttoned my silk blouse and dropped my trousers.

"Hello? I hope this is the right number. Madison? This is Henry."

"Huh?" I stepped out of my pants and ran to the machine.

"Henry Dombrowski, yeah, me. It's been awhile. So, hey, what have you been up to lately?"

"Certainly not dating married men," I yelled at the machine as I pressed the button to skip ahead. What was Henry doing calling me? I was going to call Leo and play Henry's message—proof that I wasn't imagining this old boyfriend thing.

The next message was another male voice. "Hey, Madison, it's Ryan. Ryan Wilkinson."

I smashed a hand onto the top of my head. Ryan! Old Navy Ryan. What the hell?

"Your mother told me I should give you a call . . . Robin. But then, I guess you know who your mom is. Anyway, I thought I'd call and—"

"Haunt me a little!" I said as I pressed down the button to skip to the next message. Was I losing it? Or was it reasonable to assume the next message was going to be an old boy-friend named Jacob Marley growling, "I wear the chains I forged in life"?

I clicked onto message number three, my mother. "Hi, sweetie! Just wanted to let you know you might be hearing from Ryan, your old high school friend."

"Ugh!" I waited with my finger poised over the button, unable to cut Mom off for fear that she had some important bit of news she was saving for the end.

"Do you remember him? Apparently he got married in the Navy, but that didn't work out for him. Anyway, he asked about you and I told him to look you up since he's living in New York now. That's where he's living. Or did I tell you that already? Oh. Anyway, that's all. Hope you're doing well. Clay and I may be coming your way after the holidays, but we'll talk as that develops. Okay. Bye, now."

And . . . cut! The next message was Leo, at last. "Why aren't you answering your cell? I'm in dire pain here! And they're taking me away to . . . what hospital?"

I gasped, my heartbeat racing to emergency mode. Leo? In a hospital? I'd be really concerned if I didn't hear his voice sounding so normal.

There was shuffling, then heavier voices, then Leo went on. "Park View Hospital! I am calling you from a stretcher." He lowered his voice. "And really, this would be an excellent attention-getting device if I didn't have real pain. Meet me at the hospital as soon as you get this."

Already I was stepping back into my pants, zipping the fly, scurrying toward my shoes, hopping around like a crazed chicken. What the hell had happened to Leo in the twenty minutes since I'd left him at Rockefeller Center?

As if Leo could read my mind, he tacked on to his mes-sage: "I fell on the ice. And don't say I told you so. Oh . . . gotta go. Come rescue me. Help!" He added in a small voice: "Help! Help!"

As I struggled with the buckles of my shoes, I chastised

myself for letting Leo go back on the ice tonight. Or maybe I should have stayed and skated with him. But I had thought the big attraction was the skate-rental guy, a harmless flirtation that Leo didn't need me around for.

Where the hell was Park View Hospital? I knew it was on the West Side, having seen a sign for it at some subway stop. Maybe the doorman would know.

Downstairs Ralph jumped up when I appeared. "Ms. Greenwood, before I forget, this came for you today," he said, handing me an oversized envelope.

"Thanks." Shoving it into my Kenneth Cole hobo bag, I told Ralph that my friend was in the hospital and I needed to get a cab immediately.

"I'm sorry to hear that," he said politely. "Let's see if I can help you flag down a ride to Park View Hospital. It's just down on Fifty-ninth Street."

With the help of his trusty whistle, Ralph plucked a yellow cab from the stream of moving traffic, and suddenly I was on my way, streaming down the avenue to rescue my fallen friend. I sank back against the seat, noticing the mail sticking out of my bag.

The stamp was unusual—overseas postage, from Scotland. I ripped it open, knowing it was my annual Christmas greeting from Andrew, the innkeeper at the Newington Inn. This year's card featured a photo of the inn, an old Victorian cottage with snow on the roof.

Flipping the card open, I saw Andrew's perfect script:

> *Remember us? Cheap and cheery!*
> *Would love to have you visit again.*
> *Regards, Andrew*

The Newington Inn was a fine place, despite my toxic memories of my time there. How long ago was it? Five years. Five years ago I'd spent Christmas in Scotland.

Well, almost . . .

Part Three

London and Environs

December 1998

16

"Hello, luv."

It was the voice I'd traveled the Atlantic for, the voice of the man I loved. I pulled the phone away from the end table and sank back under the puffy duvet of the comfortable hotel bed.

"Hello, yourself. When am I going to see you? London's just not the same without you," I teased, though I'd barely seen the city at all, having arrived at Heathrow at the crack of London's dawn, schlepped with my friends to the very grand Kensington Park Thistle Hotel, and flopped into bed to sleep the morning away. Jet lag really walloped you when you traveled east, though I was glad to have made the trip with my buds and roommates, Leo, Jenna, and Sugar—all three of whom had decided, for various reasons, that this was the year to spend Christmas abroad.

Sighing, I twirled the phone cord around my finger. "I wish you were here now." I lifted the duvet, as if searching for him. "Why aren't you here now? Get your butt over here!"

"Can't do it, luv. I've been hit with some unexpected business. A talent search for a new show we're whipping up. It's got me up here in the wilds of Scotland."

"Oh, no. No!" I squeaked, which is not a pretty sound for a twenty-six-year-old chick to make. Blame it on hoarseness from the transatlantic flight, along with major disappointment. I loved the glamorous sound of Ian's job as a producer of popular TV shows for the BBC and abroad, but more than once, that gorgeous career had been a huge obstacle to our happiness. Yes, his job was beginning to piss me off. I mean, I had a job, too, but I had managed to get time off from the gallery, despite the incredibly bitchy reaction of my boss Katherine.

"You want *what?*" she had sneered when I had mapped out the vacation time I needed.

At the time, I had wanted to tell her that I was going to London and never coming back, but in the interest of keeping my job until I had some other gainful employment, I had bitten my tongue. I think Katherine knew that I wasn't happy managing her gallery. Somehow my career move into the art world had been disappointing. I sensed that the field of fine arts was more in line with my talents than publishing had been, but, beyond gazing at a few pieces of contemporary art that struck a chord within, I had yet to find much fulfillment in my job at the Boone Gallery.

I sighed, then realized Ian was hanging on the line.

"Sorry to disappoint you, luv."

"But we had plans!" I croaked. "We were going to do London together!"

"As I remember, I was going to do *you* all over London."

"Oh, Ian, what about that fantasy at the British Museum? Squeezing your marbles by the Elgin Marbles?" Don't laugh; ever since we'd met, we had shared a fantasy of a quicky in the shadows of the ancient ruins.

"My dear Madison, I'm so sorry."

I loved the way he said my name. MOD-sin. I loved the way Ian said everything. With his mellifluous voice and sexy Scottish accent, the guy had charmed the pants off me—more than once.

Biting back disappointment, I slid a hand under the covers and glided over one round breast, teasing the nipple. "Oh, Ian. What am I going to do with you?"

"Some very naughty things, I hope, eventually."

"Ha! I'm doing them now." I slid my hand over my flat tummy, letting my nails glide over the lace waistband of my panties. "I'm in bed with just my panties on."

"No!" he gasped. "And me chatting on my mobile in this dairy burg! I'm not really in a position to drop my knickers and reciprocate."

"My breasts are pressing against this down comforter, sort of white on white. And there's a sad, empty space in the bed beside me. Where you're supposed to be."

"Oh, dear." He groaned over the phone. "You Yanks know the term blue balls?"

"I've always thought that was a myth put out there by adolescent boys who just want to get some."

"No, it's quite true. If you saw my balls at this moment in time, you'd know. They are a painful shade of blue."

I laughed. "And how would you know, standing on a village lane, unable to drop your drawers?"

"A bloke just knows these things." His voice was so humble, so earnest, I had to laugh again.

This time I sat up in bed and propped the pillows up behind me. "Okay, I'm awake now and it's just sinking in that you really are not here."

Not here after I flew all the way across the Pond to be with you, I thought, nibbling my lower lip. *Oh, Ian, don't let me down again . . . please don't.* I had come to love this man— yes, I know, I'm using the "L" word—but he had won my heart, despite his shortcomings, most of which involved the pull-and-tug demands of his beloved business. It was business that had kept him away last Christmas, and then in February when my father died of cancer. Losing Dad had been difficult, but realizing that the love of my life didn't seem to care . . . *that* had been devastating.

I squeezed my eyes shut, praying this wasn't a repeat performance.

"I'm sorry, luv," he said. "It's the drawback of the job. You know I'm not a nine-to-fiver."

A knot in my throat kept me from answering.

"Are you there?"

"Just disappointed," I admitted, wishing I didn't have these issues, wanting to put the whole trust thing behind me and move on with Ian. At the ripe age of twenty-six, I knew that you couldn't follow the advice of those glossy glam magazines and hold out for the perfect relationship. If you were looking for a guy to ace the quiz, you would be looking forever, because those surveys tried to liken human behavior to Martha Stewart's home-decorating tips. I had learned not to expect perfection, but I'd also promised myself I wouldn't settle, and Ian was the answer to my twenty-six-year-old heart that longed for fun mixed with passion, topped by the strong possibility of commitment.

"Aw, Madison, don't worry," he said. "We'll be together soon. It's just that I can't make it down to London to meet you as planned."

"Ian . . . you mean not even tonight? Or tomorrow?"

"I'll be waiting for you at the inn. Are you awake enough to remember the instructions? Tomorrow you must take the train to the Newington Inn—write it down, luv. You're to take the Bo'ness Steam Railway to Falkirk. The innkeeper will meet you there and give you a lift to the inn."

"Hold on." I scribbled down the information, still feeling put out. "You know, I come all the way across the ocean, and you can't even make the drive down to London—"

"I know, I know, I am a louse," he admitted. "But come north tomorrow and you can beat me up. Really let me have it. You know I'm into that S and M stuff."

"I'll let you have it, all right." I hugged the comforter to my bare chest, missing him. Given the reality of his job here in Britain and mine at the gallery in New York, we hadn't seen each other for three weeks now, and that was a relatively short span compared to some of our extended separations.

"I miss you, luv," he said sweetly. "What are you going to do now?"

I stretched under the covers. "Shower and get dressed. Then I'll hit the bars. Maybe I'll hook up with a nice London bloke who doesn't have to work tonight."

"You're killing me."

I smiled. "No, I'm saving that for when I see you."

"I love you, Madison."

That lump was back in my throat. You could hate a guy for letting you down, but when he's your sweetie, you forgive fast. "I love you, too," I said hoarsely.

And the killing part was that it was true. I loved Ian MacDougal. So much that I'd ditched my usual Christmas routine to come here and give the guy my holiday. It was the most grown-up, big-girl move I'd ever had to make, but then it seemed to be a time of firsts in my life. I loved a man, warts and all, and we'd already worked through a huge bump in the relationship.

I hung up the phone and slid out of bed, pulling the fluffy white duvet along with me to the window. From here, I could see the southwest corner of Kensington Gardens, a city oasis of pale green pasture regal enough to make any girl feel that London was her kingdom. And why shouldn't I be feeling awesome? I was in love. I'd met my match on the planet, and we were going to make it together, surviving all odds.

Stepping back from the drapes, I dropped the covers to the floor and did a little half-naked happy dance on the bed. This time tomorrow, I'd be with Ian, swooning and singing: "Merry Christmas, darling."

17

Although I didn't go out cruising for local blokes as I'd threatened, the night wasn't a total wash since I managed to hook up with my roommates from home. Sugar's friend Delia clued us in on a fabulous wine bar, right in our neighborhood, called Le Metro. I hooked up with my friend and roommate Jenna Chang, and we shared a cab there, all the time speculating about how long it would take Sugar to meet a man, whether he would last for more than one night, and whether or not she'd be engaged by New Year's.

"It happens every year, doesn't it?" Jenna asked. "Tell me if I'm wrong, but I think Sugar has had a fiancé every New Year's Eve, like clockwork."

"You're right," I admitted. "You're right, you're right." Jenna usually was. Those exotic brown eyes didn't miss much, and they glowed with an intelligence that was frightening at times. The child of Korean War survivors, Jenna called herself a twinkie—yellow on the outside, white in the middle. Although she was obliged to attend family gatherings and weekly church services in Queens, the rest of the time Jenna tried her damnedest to be all-American. She was an avid Yankees fan, a secret disco queen, a loyal TV viewer. Jenna was also the most logical thinker of all my friends, a quality that usually did not work in her favor, as it was impossible to make any sense of the actions and behaviors of our motley crew. Who could explain why Leo taped every soap opera on the air and kept those tapes lined up against a wall of his bedroom, sure that one day he'd find the time to view them? Or me, with my unaffordable shoe collection that choked my closet, threatened to spill out from under my bed, and bled my bank account? Or Sugar, with her take-no-prisoners attitude toward sex? While Jenna searched for meaning in a random universe, I was more likely to scratch my head and mutter, "Go figure."

"Not that I'm trying to pull a therapist thing here," Jenna went on. She always denied that she was analyzing us, which she always was, but we sort of enjoyed reaping the benefits of Jenna's years as an MSW candidate at New York University. Right now she was working her way toward what could be a lucrative private practice as a therapist by counseling patients and their families in the emergency room at Belleview Hospital. Some of her stories were gruesome, but she didn't seem fazed. Actually, Jenna was driven and motivated and altruistic; she put our decadent me generation, epitomized by Leo, Sugar, and moi, to shame.

Crossing my legs in the cab, I couldn't help but admire my chunky Steve Madden boots. They were a must for someone in my position—a much-seen, little-noticed assistant who was always on her feet in the swanky downtown gallery. As manager of the Moone Gallery, I was responsible for . . . well, all the shit that the owner Katherine Moone didn't want to deal with. Whether it meant cleaning the tiny bathroom, making cappuccinos, answering phones, hounding the bookkeeper, or wiping fingerprints off the wall, I was the one in charge, the fucking manager. The most glamorous part of my job was trying to soothe the nerves of struggling artists, who feared rejection, loathed Kathy, worried that the installation of their work was shoddy, and secretly wondered if they could have found a better gallery to show their work.

Did I mention that I hated my job?

But then, that crummy job had given me permission to buy my chunky boots. I'd been able to justify the hefty price tag with a promise that I would write the boots off on my taxes. Okay, the truth was, I loved the boots and planned to leave the damned job, anyway. It was turning out to be a dead-end position, and I had much bigger fish to fry across the Pond. I'd answered an ad for an assistant curator at the Hampstead, a small museum in London, and I'd actually received an e-mail requesting an interview. It was all set: I had an appointment with a Ms. Withers in human resources the week after Christmas. I didn't want to think about the breathtaking possibilities that might accompany that job and the move to Britain . . . *One step at a time, Mod-sin,* I told myself. *One step at a time.*

"I think it's something that should be addressed," Jenna said thoughtfully.

"What were we talking about again?" Wincing, I let my fingers close over the heel of one sexy storm-trooper boot and tried to get back into the conversation.

"Sugar's annual fiancé fixation."

"She's not really hurting anyone, is she?" I pointed out. "We all have our problems and fixations. Mine being a certain Scotsman who just stood me up for the evening."

Jenna smiled. "At least you have a real relationship with Ian. Sugar just pulls these guys out of her ass. And she's hurting herself. It's become a crutch for her, a way to avoid thinking about her life at a time of year when many people are taking inventory and reassessing."

"You are so right about that. I hate New Year's. After Christmas, it's all a major letdown." I shivered as charmingly gray, weathered buildings flashed by—a Gaugin sketch of London. Our cab stopped at a light beside one of those amusing double-decker buses that reminded me of the London of my childhood, when I would come here to shop at Harrod's with Mom and go to Madame Tussaud's wax museum with my father. Dad loved wax museums. He never got a chance to visit the new one in Manhattan.

"What are you doing for New Year's?" Jenna asked.

"I'll be with you guys, I guess. I'm hoping Ian will come to London to join us, but with his job, you never know." I didn't add that I was hoping he'd be helping me look for a flat, depending on how well my interview went at the Hampstead Museum. No one knew about my plan to move to London. I didn't want to spring it on my friends until I'd gotten confirmation—or an engagement ring—from Ian. "I don't want to lock in anything yet. I've learned to downplay the whole auld lang syne deal."

"Lots of people feel that way, Madison," Jenna said reassuringly. "But instead of looking back over the past with regret, it can also be a time to look forward. To look ahead—"

"Oh, Jenna, I am always looking ahead." I sat back against the seat and gave her a buddy nudge. "Sometimes I think I live too far in the future. I can't stop thinking about next month, next year and Ian and . . . well, mostly Ian."

"I'm just pissed that we're not going to get a chance to see him," Jenna said, squinting at me. "It sounds like you're getting serious, and we've only met him—what? Once? Twice?"

"I barely get to see him myself," I defended.

She squinched up her face. "Boy hog."

I snorted, falling back against the seat as the cab pulled up to the curb.

Jenna looked out the window, then turned back to me with a grin. "I'm sorry, our time is up for today. Next time, let's talk about your issues with Ian. The really juicy stuff."

I pretended to smack her as she fumbled with the whispery British bills and paid the driver. Then we toppled out of the boxy cab and stepped into Le Metro, a warm space crowded with the welcoming scent of roasted garlic, small bursts of conversation, and clouds of cigarette smoke.

It wasn't hard to find our girl, Sugar; I just looked to the bar, where three guys bobbed like yellow ducks at an arcade. Yup, Sugar had to be at the center of that crowd. At their periphery was a sultry redhead with gorgeous hair twisted into elaborate clip art. Flaunting a cigarette like a silver-screen star, she seemed to know all the boys.

"That must be Delia," I said, as Jenna and I let our eyes adjust to the blue, smoky light.

"Right." Jenna unsnapped her Yankees baseball jacket, letting her hair swing over her black cashmere sweater. "Looks like she's caught in Sugar's gravitational pull, along with those male planets."

"It happens," I said, making my way over to the group to find Leo huddled on a bar stool beside Sugar. "Leo?"

His fingers cradled a tequila shooter from a lineup on the bar. "Woo-hoo! You guys are late. The party has started."

"I can see that." I tucked my jacket on the back of his bar stool and picked up a shotglass from the bar. "To good friends, and to a white Christmas!" The tequila cut a swath of fire down my throat as the anonymous chorus of Sugar's males chimed in "Here, here!" and applauded.

Leo cocked a drunken eyebrow at me. "A white Christmas? Who the fuck are you, part of the Bob Hope Christmas Tour?"

"Everyone loves a white Christmas," I defended myself. Just because I wasn't home for Christmas didn't mean I'd abandoned my yuletide convictions. "It's cozy and charming . . . and George Clooney's aunt sang so fabulously in the movie."

"It doesn't snow in London!" Leo said indignantly. He turned to a guy in Sugar's magnetic field and asked, "Does it?"

I slid the empty shotglass on the bar and ordered a glass of chardonnay. "What are you doing here, anyway?" I asked Leo. "You're supposed to be in Lisbon, cavorting with Wolfie."

"My flight was cancelled. The next available seat is tomorrow morning, crack of dawn. So we decided the only way to travel is to party until four A.M., at which time I'll take the tube out to Heathrow and arrive in Wolfie's arms totally wasted. Making a fine impression on his brother, the crowned prince of Fuckenstein."

"He'll love you," I said. "Every crowned prince wants his bro to have a drunken gay lover. It's in the royal bylaws, I think." I realized I was shouting, trying to speak above the music and loud voices.

A slender, perfectly manicured hand reached out of the man-crowd and squeezed my arm. "He's not drunk," Sugar confided. "He's got a long way to go, and it's going to be up to you to keep our Leo well-sedated so that he doesn't wallow in missing-Wolfie misery."

"Hey, I'm not the girl guide tonight," I insisted. "I'm the walking wounded, too. Ian canceled on me. Doesn't that account for something?"

"You'll see him tomorrow," Leo pointed out.

"But you'll see Wolf tomorrow!" I countered.

Sugar tilted her head at me. "Sorry, honey, but the walking wounded part's been cast. You'll have to read for the loyal best friend." She looked stunning in her recently straightened and highlighted fuck-me hair worn short but teased a bit on top to give her that Diana Ross vibe. The tiny crystals dangling from her ears matched her red V-neck sweater, which probably matched her lingerie or handbag or shoes. Sugar was always totally put together. She spun her stool toward me, whipping those long legs my way. The rest of us wore jeans, but there was Sugar in her short, pleated plaid skirt with a slit up the side. All she needed was a little Peter Pan collar and a necktie to complete the fuck-the-schoolgirl fantasy.

"Can we get a table?" I asked no one in particular as one of Sugar's entourage stepped on my toe. He didn't apologize, didn't even look back, and I swore to seek him out and wreak painful vengeance if he nicked the smooth black leather of my boot.

"Oh, wait! I love this song!" Sugar jumped off her bar stool, spread her slender arms wide, and crooned: "'I believe I can fly . . . I believe I can touch the sky. I think about it every night and day, spread my wings and fly away.'"

"I believe I need another drink," Leo said. I nodded, as the rest of the crowd watched Sugar's performance, spellbound. She picked up a bottle of ale and used it as a pretend microphone, leading the crowd as they began to sway in time to the music. Ludicrous, I know, but Sugar is the kind of person who can stop traffic on Fifth Avenue with an air-guitar rendition of "We Got It Goin' On!"

"Your friend is fabulous!" some guy told Leo and me. He might have been the toe cruncher; it was hard to keep track with the tequila and wine setting in. "I'll wager you have a blast with her."

"We've never seen her before in our lives," Leo answered.

I stepped back and spotted an empty round table in a corner booth. "Let's take that one," I said, noticing Jenna was right on it, pointing it out to the waitress, who seemed agreeable.

"Perfect," Jenna called over her shoulder. She pushed past the occupied tables and slung her jacket over a chair.

Leo looked over longingly. "But it's so far from the bar, and tequila doesn't age well," he said, lifting the last full shotglass. "Oh, well." He downed it, then stumbled out of his bar stool.

"Hey, buddy, slow down," I told him. "You're moving like the poster child for AA."

Throwing his shoulders back to an erect posture, Leo smiled. "Make that triple A, and you've got a deal. I just love to travel."

18

Once the three of us settled in at the table, Delia came over and introduced herself to Jenna and me. "I've heard so much about both of you," she said, toying with a clip behind her left ear.

I toasted her with my chardonnay. "Love your hair. Does it take long?"

"It always does." Delia reset the twist of hair and clamped the clip over it. "But it's really quite wild if I don't do something to strap it down in clippies." She took the chair between Jenna and me and cast her piercing green eyes on us. "Now, which one of you is dating a local boy? No, don't tell me, let me guess." She pointed to Jenna. "You've got the look of love."

Jenna paled. "Not me. I'm still looking for Mr. Perfect."

"Although she's been dating Mister Almost-Perfect for six years now," Leo offered.

"He" was referring to Benjamin Cho, one of Jenna's high school classmates from Astoria, Queens. On paper, Benjamin was the perfect guy for Jenna. His family knew her family. He attended the same church, and had also gotten his master's in social work at NYU. He and Jenna had been study buddies, and over the years Benjamin had come to be something of a fixture in our apartment—the quiet, wise Yoda with the wicked sense of humor.

But Jenna had one problem with Benjamin: He wasn't American enough for her. Call it reverse racism or rebellion against parents or white-boy lust, but whatever the diagnosis, Jenna was determined to choose her ultimate mate from a different gene pool. That was why she didn't sleep with Benjamin (although I'd been tempted to pull him into bed a time or two. Let's face it, availability is a definite plus, and Benjamin often slept on the futon couch in our living room). As far as Jenna was concerned, they were buddies.

"Benjamin and I are just friends," Jenna insisted, rolling her eyes at Leo the way she had a hundred times before.

Delia took a cigarette from her pack and pointed it to me. "So you're the one dating the Scotsman."

Finally, I get to talk about the huge weight crushing my heart. I nodded eagerly, extending my hand. "I'm Madison, and yes, I'm the one. He was supposed to be here, but he got tied up with business."

"What does he do?" Delia asked.

"He's a producer of comedy shows for the BBC, and he's also done a few of those talent-search shows that are so popular everywhere," I said. "Like *Secret SuperStar*."

"Get out!" Delia's mouth dropped open in amazement; unfortunately, her lit cigarette dangled there, as if glued to her lip. "I love *Secret SuperStar*!"

I nodded, feeling giddy. "The British version is his show. He's really a genius at coming up with those concepts and picking the people."

Delia looked around her. "I'm sitting here with the girlfriend of the man who does *Secret SuperStar*. Unbelievable." She leaned into me and grabbed my sleeve. "Is he attractive?"

"Gorgeous," I said, trying not to gush, though I wasn't doing a very good job.

"Does he have any friends? You can give them my number," Delia said.

"Hey, get in line," Jenna teased.

Delia laughed. "It's every girl for herself in this market. I daresay you're lucky to have met a man like that, Madison. I mean, what are the chances . . . he lives here in the U.K. and you shag him in New York?" She took a thick drag on her cigarette. "Totally whack. How did you two meet?"

I smiled. How I loved telling our story!

Leo growled. "The short version."

"Killjoy," I told him, turning back to Delia. "Jenna and I were out one night—very late and very drunk. We'd gone to some museum presentation that turned out to be godawful, so we ended up at the Bull and Bear, this posh bar in the Waldorf-Astoria that neither of us can afford, but . . . What can I say? We were lit."

Leo whirled his hand around like a TV producer. "And . . . the wrap-up—"

"Anyway," I went on, trying to ignore him because the memory was so sweet, I loved to savor it. "Jenna and I were having Cosmos at the bar when Ian came in with a group of businessmen. Some from one of the big networks, a few from the U.K. All I remember is that they were intolerable. Obnoxious and full of themselves. But they paid for our drinks, and Ian sat beside me mocking them all, calling them on their bad behavior." I shook my head. "He had us laughing the whole time."

"Sounds like a charmer," Delia said.

I nodded. "So then, the bar was closing, and—"

"And so they met," Leo said, brushing his hands off. "End of story." He squinted at his watch. "Is it time for my flight yet?"

Jenna patted his shoulder. "You've got a while yet."

"And I want to hear the rest of the story," Delia said. "Then what happened? Did you sleep together that night?"

"No. Jenna and I were bad girls, but not that bad. After the Bull and Bear closed, we sort of started this pub crawl, moving on to the next place that would serve us Cosmos. One place, I swear, the glasses were big enough to bathe in."

"That was my downfall," Jenna said, "the killer Cosmos at Smith and Wollensky."

"And after all the bars closed we ended up at this private club I'd only read about, where the liquor flowed freely." I smiled, remembering that night—at least, the pieces I could remember. Somehow, Jenna and I had made it home intact and barely conscious. "The next morning, while I was still passed out, Ian called and left a message on my machine to make sure I was okay. He was flying out at noon and wanted to see me, but I was barely able to move until the following week."

Jenna pressed her fingertips to her temples. "That was the worst hangover in the history of civilization. I haven't touched a Cosmo since."

I had, but I didn't feel the need to admit that to everyone here.

"What a sweet story—you met at the Bull and Bear." Delia tilted her head and smiled dreamily. "Sort of like Beauty and the Beast."

"Oh, please," Leo said.

"And how about you, Mr. Glum?" Delia asked Leo. "Tell us how you met the love of your life."

"Yes, do tell," I prodded, folding my hands on the table.

"It was really unexpected." Leo turned away from me so that he could shower his attention on Delia. "Actually, it started in a vintage clothes boutique, but the great irony was that Yenta here was friends with both of us, and she never thought to introduce us."

Delia shot me a look. "Not a matchmaker, are you?"

I shook my head. "I don't even try anymore."

"Hey, how long has it been, Leo?" Jenna asked. "I think

you and Wolf have been long-distance lovers for as long as I've known you."

"This will be our sixth Christmas together," Leo said proudly. "Five years of long-distance phone calls and red-eye flights back from San Francisco. I highly recommend it. When you live apart, you never have time to get sick of each other. The novelty lives on."

"I don't know," I said. "I'm not sure that Ian and I would be able to survive for five years across the Pond. I want to be with him."

Leo scowled at me. "Feeling needy, are we? Anyway," Leo went on, "the first time we met . . . There he was, his back to me so I had no idea of his handsome face, but I sensed that something special was about to happen."

As he talked the waitress arrived with a tray of foods—a platter of ripe, gooey brie and crumbly Stilton cheeses with crackers and grapes, small clay bowls of French onion soup, mushroom tarts, and escargot in garlic butter. Although my mouth was watering, I shook my head at the waitress.

"We didn't order this."

"It's from your mate over there," she said, nodding toward Sugar.

"God bless you, Sugar Plum Fairy," I muttered, handing Jenna the basket of rolls.

As Leo's familiar story unfolded, Jenna and I feasted on the goodies, dipping the crusty bread into the steaming soup and cutting fat wedges of cheese. One of the guys from Sugar's group strode over with a message for Jenna, and she scooted over so he could have a seat and share the food. He introduced himself as Simon, said he was an architect, and he and Jenna made small talk while I chowed down.

Although I was glad to be with my friends, I still ached to see Ian. On the other hand, I had to remind myself how much this evening would have sucked if my friends hadn't decided to make this trip across the Pond and spend Christmas in the

U.K. Although we had come for different reasons, it seemed like kismet that we were stuck together on this first night of our trip.

Sugar had started the ball rolling by announcing that she was going to cover a bunch of holiday rock concerts in London as a guest veejay for Rock-TV. After a career plateau during which she'd been temping as a computer inputter, Sugar was thrilled to get a huge break. Somehow, we'd all been at home when she got the news, and we just went wild. Despite the super's noise warnings that we'd been trying to heed, that night our apartment rocked. Next, Jenna decided to cash in a gift her aunt had given her when she finished grad school—round trip airfare to London—and keep Sugar company. Leo had simply planned to connect to his Lisbon flight through Heathrow, and was detoured here for the night.

I'd been a little jealous to hear that my friends were going to Britain for the holidays, but I'd felt obliged to head back to San Francisco and be with Mom. After all, it was the first Christmas since my father had died.

But Mom wasn't planning to spend Christmas at home. "Clay and I have booked a week in Hawaii," Mom told me over the phone. "I thought it would be better to break tradition this year and get out of the house. Honestly, I'm not sure I have the energy to pull off all the decorating, and I guess a part of me is still in mourning. Are you terribly disappointed?" Mom asked me.

"No," I'd said as I realized that left me free to see Ian. "I'll be okay."

"Are you sure, sweetie? You're welcome to join Clay and me in the islands."

I knew her invitation was sincere, but my heart was already headed east. "No thanks, Mom. I'll be fine with my friends . . . really." As Mom repeated her apologies and went over her gift list, I turned to my computer and logged onto British Airways. Let's see . . . the six-thirty P.M. red-eye would have me arriving at six-twenty-five the next morning . . .

"Madison!" Sugar called, waving me over to the bar. I dabbed at my mouth with a napkin and extricated myself from Leo's romantic storytelling.

"Come here, honey." Sugar slid her arm over my shoulders. "This is Blake, and he wants to meet the girl who was named after a famous avenue in New York."

I cocked an eyebrow. "Oh, that's original, Sugar," I said, shaking hands with Blake. "And did you mention that your middle name is Plum?" Blake seemed surprised. "Yes, it's true," I went on. "Her real name is Sugar Plum. Isn't that sweet?"

"Sweet, indeed." Blake grinned and put his big, square head into Sugar's face. "You're so sweet, you give me tooth decay."

Sugar and I burst out laughing, and Blake raised his mug, as if he'd scored. And I'd thought New York bar chatter was inane. I grabbed Sugar's arm and whispered in her ear: "Tell me you're not going to sleep with this asshole."

She shot a glance back at him, pouting. "Why not? I think he's kind of cute."

"Cute is not the foundation for a relationship," I said, starting to feel that familiar annoyance. Sugar had a habit of picking up guys the way the ASPCA picked up strays. "Sugar, don't do this to yourself."

"Do what?" she asked innocently. "Is it the idea of having intercourse that bothers you? Because regular sex is a healthy activity that increases blood flow."

I frowned at her. "You've been doing research?"

She nodded proudly. "I've read a few articles since the last time we had this argument. Do you know that people who have more sex often live longer? Sex reduces stress and increases self-esteem."

Looking past her, I noticed that Blake had overheard this last part of her argument and was grinning like a kid on Christmas morning. He turned to say something to his buddies, and they all swung around to admire Sugar.

I sighed. "I'm just trying to look out for you, girlfriend."

"I know that, pumpkin." Sugar threw her arms out and gave me a big hug. "You're a good friend, Madison. And I'm so glad . . ." Her voice trailed off.

"What is it?" I pulled away and turned to see what had snagged her attention.

"Looks like somebody got bit by the worm in the bottle," she said.

Back in the corner, Leo was passed out, his head on the table, his arms folded underneath.

"He looks so peaceful when he's sleeping," Sugar said. "You'd never know there was a torment mired in his soul."

"That's all very poetic," I said, "but how are we getting him back to the hotel?"

Sugar winced. "Would you mind, honey lamb? I'm working on a full dance card here, and Jenna seems to be stepping out and . . . well, we know you're saving yourself for Scotland's answer to Matt Damon so . . . Would you mind terribly seeing that Leo gets home safe?"

And so I found myself cabbing it home, the windows of the taxi rolled down while Leo sang "Where Have All the Cowboys Gone?" like a drunken sailor. I found myself wishing I'd had more to drink.

He nearly fell out of the cab in front of the hotel, but I have to say, he's a nimble drunk—sort of like a rubber man. I helped him up and he flung his arm over my shoulder and let me lead him in through the lobby and to the elevator bank as he quietly sang the "Dit-dit-dit," section of the song. At last, we reached the elevator bank, and Leo fell into my arms for a big bear hug.

"You are the best friend in the world," he said, squeezing me tight. "I know you think I'm toasted, and I am, but I really mean it. You're a good, good friend."

"I love you, too, Leo," I said, staggering under his weight. "But if we don't press the elevator button, we're not going to make it upstairs."

"Oh." He straightened and cast a hand toward the elevator panel. "Okay. Whatever."

As I pressed the button I watched Leo carefully. Was he really drunk, or just a little drunk and feeling emotional? Was he too drunk to get himself to the airport in the morning? It was hard to tell.

Leo paced in front of the elevator, pausing to contemplate the fake tree lit by twinkling blue lights. "Wolf's family is going to fall in love with me." He squared his hands around his face, as if framing a portrait. "What's not to like? An alcoholic gay man with a shiny bald head?"

"You know," I said, catching him as he teetered close to the wall, "God made only a few perfect heads. The rest, he covered with hair."

"S'okay. S'okay," he said. "I'm happy with the way I look. Verra, verra happy." He was smiling at me, his face inches from mine.

I bit my lip to keep from laughing. "And if you're happy, I'm happy. 'Verra happy,'" I mimicked.

"Let's party!" The elevator doors opened and he threw up his arms and pranced inside like Madonna as the Material Girl.

I followed him in and pushed the buttons for our floors. "Are you sure you're going to make it? You've got that early morning flight."

"I'm going to party all night!" he sang, twirling around. "Woo-hoo!"

"Okay, then."

By the time the elevator reached my floor, Leo had sunk down into a heap on the floor. "Okay, you'd better come with me, bud." Somehow I managed to wrangle him out and down the hall to my room, where he stumbled in and sat on the puffy duvet of my bed.

"To be perf'kly honest? I'm not feeling so hot."

So much for the all-night party.

"Oh, no!" Leo imploded, resting his elbows and head on his knees. "No, no, no! This isn't right! I can't go to sleep. Not allowed to sleep. I'll never make my flight."

"It's okay," I said. "I'll get you up in time."

"No, you won't. You'll fall asleep just like me. And in the morning I'll be shtooped waiting another day for a . . . a flucking flight." He lifted his head and there were tears in his eyes—real tears.

I knew he was wasted, but somewhere in that land of total inebriation those tears were genuine.

"I'll get you there," I promised him. "I may need to operate your arms and legs by remote control, but I'll get you there."

"I can't missss my flight," he sobbed, turning toward the bed and lurching forward until his face was pressed into a pillow.

"Don't worry!" I insisted. "I won't fail you, bud. What time is your flight?" He didn't answer. "Leo? What time do you leave?" I crouched over him. He was already asleep. "Okay, then." I pressed a hand over the back of his shaved head, then got a blanket from the closet and tucked him in.

Time for some calculations. I found Leo's tickets in the pocket of his coat. We would need to be at Heathrow three hours early. We would also need to pick up his luggage in his room. Hmm . . . that left about two hours to sleep.

Yawning, I thought about crawling into bed beside him, but that would be way too comfy. Instead, I called the desk to leave a wake-up call, then curled into the room's only chair with my coat over me. How long had it been since I'd pulled an all-nighter? I tried to calculate as I turned on the television and flipped through the channels of Sky-TV.

I would get Leo to the airport on time. But, good friend that I was, I would hold this one over his head for a long, long time.

19

This was not at all the way I'd imagined my reunion with Ian.

Having found a seat on the train to Falkirk beside a middle-aged man who seemed dedicated to his *London Times,* I turned and caught my reflection in the window. The girl who stared back at me was scary. Her eyes were swollen like small pink onions. Her hair, suffering static electricity from her hat, seemed determined to stand up straight as if transmitting through the ceiling, and a stress zit was angrily rising on the side of her nose. Who was this pathetic candidate for a makeover?

I plunked my hat back onto my head and rubbed my face. Okay, maybe a nap on the train, then I'd be sure to lather on makeup in the restroom before we reached my destination.

The train pulled out of the station, passing through the dark of tunnels. I would stay awake to watch the scenery as we left London, then take a short nap.

The flickering light over my seat partner's newspaper was the last thing I remembered when I woke up, rocking with the motion of the train. Outside the landscape resembled a moonscape. Trees and fields and buildings were covered with snow, and flecks of white danced in the air.

I bolted upright. Where were we? My seat partner had vanished, leaving only a skeletal newspaper strewn in his wake. I had a moment of panic that I'd slept past my stop, but a woman across the aisle brought me up to speed, assuring me that I had plenty of time. I grabbed my cosmetics bag and purse and scooted up the aisle to the W.C. Although I have never been a fan of public restrooms, this one seemed cleaner than I'd expected. I soaped up my hands, splashed warm water on my face, blotted with a paper towel, and set to work.

God bless Estée Lauder! Clinique is *magnifique!*

With a newly drawn face and fluffed-up hair, I emerged from the restroom and took my seat, all too aware of the rising anticipation at seeing Ian. Settling back into my seat, I stared out at the snow-covered hills and trees, the colored lights blinking in sparse intersections, the spires of churches, the edgy profiles of rooftops clustered together. This seemed like a friendly place, a welcoming place. Would Ian and I soon be calling it our home?

We had certainly started off with a bang, more than a year and a half ago. That hangover had lasted nearly a week. I think I had just been contemplating the thought of sipping a martini once again when Ian had called me to announce that he was back in New York. He wasn't supposed to be back in New York for months, but Ian had revamped things because he couldn't wait to see me.

Meanwhile I had spent that first week since we'd met wondering if he was a dream-come-true or an obnoxious prick who got his jollies getting girls drunk. The night he called I complained bitterly to Jenna as I dressed for dinner. "I don't remember why I liked him. Wasn't he kind of loud? Was he really that cute?"

"You two had a blast together the night you met," Jenna had said. "But I can't picture his face. Was he the one with the nose ring?" I held back my scream.

When he appeared at the door—minus nose ring—I wanted to swoon in his arms. He was definitely more prince charming than girl abuser, and as we ate sushi and salmon at Sushi Taki, the spark between us was obvious. Like the *shh!* when you strike a match, that's the way the air crackled when I was with Ian.

That night I went back to his hotel for a drink, and over brandy he made a joke about showing me his room. To my surprise, I took him up on the offer and we spent the night making love in his monster king-sized bed. It was so unlike me to get physical so fast, since I'd learned after college that sex adds stress to a relationship that isn't mature. But later I rationalized that Ian and I experienced a speedy evolution; sometimes it happens when you meet your soul mate.

I thought of the precious days we'd spent together in New York during the past year and a half: jogs along the reservoir, wine tastings in Chelsea, miniature boat races in Central Park. Because of his job and his constant pursuit of an angle for a new television concept, Ian had dragged me to some highly unromantic places. We'd pretended to cruise the Nile from the cockpit of various watercraft at the Boat Show. We had joined a Syrian family's lavish feast in Brooklyn; though I don't think the grandma approved of my short skirt and ap-plique nails, she seemed to enjoy my hearty appetite for her homemade humus and meatloaf baked in a scrumptious crust. We had chatted up a man who loops his own rugs at a neighborhood flea market. Ian made me take in New York through his brassy, ballsy perspective. It was a view that I didn't always care to explore, but it was worth the trip just to be with him.

I tried to think back to the guys I had dated before Ian, but my mind drew a blank.

It was as if I didn't live or breathe before I met him.

The train went through a suburban town—there were so many more of them than I'd expected in this rural part of northern England—and the snowy parking lot of a large Sainsbury's opened up before me. Women fought the snow with their shopping carts. Others loaded groceries into their minis while their children drew pictures on the snow-covered windows of the cars.

I smiled. That could be me in five years, pushing a baby in a grocery cart, dreaming up a delicious concoction for our family dinner. Never mind that I hated cooking; I wanted to be part of the great female fantasy, dammit! I wanted to have a wedding, have a house to clean, spit out a baby, then bite off more than I could chew trying to juggle work and home.

I wanted it all, dang blast it!

I must have had a determined expression on my face, because the woman across the aisle glanced at me and bit back her smile.

"Don't be worrying. It's just a bit of snow, is all," she said.

"It's beautiful." I leaned back from the window and smiled at her. "Really puts me in the holiday spirit."

She just nodded as my stop was announced over the speaker. I gathered up my things and trundled toward the door of the slowing train.

"Falkirk!" the conductor called as we pulled into the small station.

Snowflakes tickled my face as I stepped onto the open platform and walked toward the little red station house. It was dark, definitely closed, so I walked around it to what seemed to be the main street.

There stood a sight that seemed to be plucked right out of a snow globe.

A short, stocky little man in a puffy red down jacket stood at the front of a curved wooden sleigh, stroking the horse on its flank. The horse shook its head, and a chorus of bells jingled in the falling snow. When I stepped forward, the man turned and greeted me with a warm smile.

"You must be Ms. Madison Greenwood." With his rosy cheeks and trim white beard, I'd swear the dude was Santa Claus, except that he wore a navy watchcap on his head.

Or perhaps he was just trying to stay undercover until the big day.

"That's me. Do you work for the Newington Inn?"

He came over and took my rolling suitcase from my hands. "Dearie, I am the Newington Inn. Andrew Newington, at your service."

"Thanks," I said, as he was already loading my things into the sled. "I wasn't sure you'd get the message to meet my train, but this is quite a greeting. What a beautiful sled."

"It's been in the family for generations," he said. "Too bad we only get to use it when it snows. Now if you'd be so kind as to climb in, I'll have you to the inn in no time. The missus has some warm grog waiting for you." He helped me up into the wooden seat. "I see this is your first visit. Only two things you need to know. Cheap and cheery. That's our motto. You won't find much high luxury in these parts, but we do things with a smile."

He turned from his seat to wink at me, then clucked to the horse.

"I'll remember that," I said as we slid off into the winter wonderland.

Cheap and cheery was right. The inn was a renovated Victorian cottage with cute touches and very old plumbing. Our room was charming, with whitewashed molding, diamond-patterned wallpaper, plaid quilt on the double bed, and beveled windows that overlooked "Braveheart country," as Andrew called it.

Damn, I knew I should have rented that movie.

Mrs. Newington gave me a cup of tea in the downstairs parlor, where we would be dining. The room was filled with tables with checkered tablecloths, though tea was served in a cozy sitting area with an overstuffed sofa and armchairs.

"Would you like a shot of whiskey with that?" she offered.

"Oh? No, thank you," I said, not quite ready for a cocktail. "Maybe later."

She winked, then swept off over the flagstone floor, which gleamed in the light from the huge hearth. The fire managed to warm the entire room, a welcome source of heat, as the inn itself was drafty. I sipped my tea, absorbing the fact that this was going to be a very casual vacation.

Okay, I wouldn't need my pale pink, shoulderless Atelier Versace gown.

But I had packed jeans and plenty of sweaters, and having dressed to kill for the recent stretch of parties promoting the Moone Gallery's new exhibit back in New York, it was a welcome relief to be able to kick back in a comfortable, homey old cottage.

"You know," I told Mrs. Newington as she skirted past me, "maybe I will take that shot of whiskey."

20

The whiskey did the trick, turning my muscles to warm jelly. Since Ian hadn't arrived yet, I decided to jump into the shower and revive myself from head to toe. The loo was positively icy. I stepped gingerly over the cold tiles, deciding to make it a quick shower.

An hour or so later, I was dressed in jeans and a fisherman's sweater, my hair blown out and curled gently under. It was a good hair day, with the front tips bobbing gently under my chin. I was stretched out on the bed, reading the latest Lisa Jackson novel, when there was a rattling at the door.

"Ian!" I stood up on the bed and hopped across to jump down in front of him.

"Hello, luv!" He scooped me into his arms and whirled me around. "Aren't you a lovely sight."

"You're not so bad yourself." His light brown hair fell into his boyish face, while his ice-blue eyes reminded you this guy was no boy. Ian was a sex goddess's dream come true. I liked to think of him as the Scottish version of Matt Damon, my own Good Will Hunting.

"How long have you been here? How was your trip? Did you meet the innkeeper? Seen any of the sights yet? Do you know what they're serving for dinner?" He rattled off the questions as he propped his satchel on the bed and took out his shaving kit. "Don't answer me all at once, now, as we've got plenty of time to fill in the blanks. I'm going to catch a quick shave before dinner."

I rubbed a hand over the stubble on his cheek. "Yes, you're a bit on the shaggy side."

"Wouldn't want to tear up that alabaster skin of yours," he said, leaning forward for a quick kiss, then ducking in the bathroom. "So since we're in the area, I imagine we'll have to do some of the local tourist things. A few castles, Edinburgh, and Hadrian's Fucking Wall."

"Hadrian's Fucking Wall?" I sat on the bed, watching him through the doorway as he stood at the sink, rinsing his hands in steaming water. "Is that a part of history—I mean, the fucking aspect? Or is it just a tradition instigated by the local lads?"

"If you really want to know." He switched to a pompous, high-pitched voice to explain. "Built by the Roman Emperor Hadrian around 120 A.D., this stone and turf wall marked the boundary of Roman Britain. Hadrian's goal was to prevent attacks and smuggling by the Picts and Scots."

Laughing, I fell back on the bed. "I like that voice. Have you ever considered narrating documentaries?"

He lathered shaving cream onto his face. "Amazing how a ditch with jumbled stones could warrant so much attention. There are also a few castles nearby, Stirling Castle being one of my favorites . . ."

I let his voice wash over me as I stretched back on the quilt and wallowed in the thrill of being here with Ian. Something jabbed me in the side, and I noticed that Ian's satchel had spilled open. I sat up to push his slippers and jeans back in when a flash of foil caught my eye—a small box wrapped in silver and blue foil with a blue bow.

A gift.

A small gift.

A jewelry box.

A ring box?

Holding my breath, I gently picked up the package and weighed it in my hands. Yes, it was definitely a ring box.

Joy surged through my body as Handel's "Hallelujah Chorus" exploded in my head.

It was my Christmas gift—my engagement ring.

I pressed the package to my breast, warmed by a surge of love for the man who was now critiquing local castles as he shaved in the bathroom mirror. When was he going to ask me to marry him? Would he wait until Christmas Day? I thought of the Tiffany key chain I'd gotten for Ian. It was classy, and his leather key chain was falling apart, but it was a token next to my ring.

My ring! Not wanting to spoil his surprise, I tucked the gift back into his satchel. This was definitely a moment to treasure. And I knew just how to make the most of it. Moving out of Ian's line of vision in the bathroom mirror, I pulled off my sweater and jeans. I tugged off my socks, but left on my lacy maroon bra and matching boxers. Then, feeling suave, I stepped into the doorway behind him, moving forward until my face appeared over his shoulder in the mirror.

His chin was lifted as he swiped off the last patch of shaving cream on his jaw. When he rinsed the razor, I pressed up behind him and swiped off a dab of lather from behind his ear.

"Mmm," I sniffed it, then rubbed it behind my ear like a cologne. "Smells good."

Ian cocked his head for a better look, then dropped the razor in the sink and spun around to look me up and down. "You're naked!" he gasped. "Actually, you do have your knickers on."

"Of course," I said, stealing a hand under his sweater to squeeze his amazing pecs. "Naked and shivering. It's drafty in here."

He grinned, his blue eyes stirring my soul. "I have just the thing to warm you up." He ran his hands over my smooth cotton boxers, then tucked his fingers between my legs firmly, as if implying ownership.

"I missed you," he whispered.

"Mmm." I lifted his hand and guided it under the waistband. We both groaned as his fingers slid down. "Good Lord, woman, you're damp. My sweet Scottish mum would be disgraced."

"It's a good thing she's not here." I yanked at the clasp of his trousers, eager to feel his bare skin against mine. I wanted him so much—with all my body and soul. And it was an incredible turn-on to know that I would have him now and forever.

The pace seemed frantic as we kissed and ground against each other and explored warm flesh with eager hands. Ian's lips were still locked on mine when he lifted me up to sit on the porcelain sink and opened my legs.

His fingertips circled my clitoris, teasing, watching intently as I fell helpless to the rising heat. "Very nice panties," he whispered. "Don't know why anyone would ever build them with a crotch. It makes it so difficult to do this," he said, easing himself into me.

"Ooh!" I gasped as he shoved in deeper.

"Coming already?" He leaned his forehead against mine. "I knew you missed me."

"Yes, it's great," I admitted. "But I'm not sure what's more excruciatingly vivid: the orgasm or the frozen porcelain on my butt."

"Oh, that! You pampered Yanks overheat the loos, you know." In a heartbeat, he was lifting me, holding me close so that he was still inside me, and I felt cloaked in wonder at a man who could stay hard while hoisting me in the air at the same time. I wrapped my legs around him and planted my lips on his neck to nibble the smooth flesh there as he stumbled back, out of the loo, and into the cozy bedroom. In a flurry of motion, he was sitting on the bed, and I was atop him, straddling him, wanting to hold him there forever.

"That's better," I said, writhing my hips a little.

"Mmm." He sounded so calm, but from the way his brow creased I could see I was causing him exquisite torture.

Planting my knees on the bed, I took control. I pushed him back so that he was lying on the bed. I pressed my hands against his chest, my fingers splayed over the smooth skin, down to his tight abs. Touching him, seeing his naked chest and shoulders, I felt a new surge of moisture, which I think he felt, too, as he groaned again and lifted his hips toward me in a poignant thrust.

"I did miss you," I said as I started to rock over him.

"Missed you, too," he groaned, clearly on his way to ecstasy.

I closed my eyes, riding him gently, then harder, harder. The motion was driving me wild, and I smiled, knowing this was just the beginning: the first day of my holiday with Ian, the first day of our very long, very sexy life together.

In the distance I heard the jingling of bells—sleigh bells.

"Fucking jingle bells," Ian whispered.

I laughed, writhing over him. "Andrew must be taking the sleigh out for an errand."

"Sounds like Santa Claus is coming," Ian muttered.

I sucked in my breath. "He's not the only one."

21

We lazed around in bed for about ten minutes before Ian was restless. He never was one to sit around, even in the midst of afterglow.

"Let's go for a walk in the snow," he whispered in my ear. "It was really coming down when I drove in. A winter wonderland, just like those snow globes you're so fond of."

Touched that he remembered my collection, I pulled on my clothes, switching to a thick woolen sweater over my cotton turtleneck. "Honestly, I wouldn't mind lounging in bed for awhile. Maybe till, like, noon tomorrow?"

"You always want to lounge. That's the problem with you Americans. Couch potatoes, the whole lot of you."

"Don't be jealous because we know how to relax." I pulled on a pillbox hat lined with faux fur and moved up on my tiptoes to kiss him.

"Ah, you've got it all wrong, woman. True relaxation comes after exertion."

I giggled. "I love the way you talk. Igg-ZAIR-shun. You're so sexy."

"You fancy that?" He pulled my hat down over my ears. "Well, keep listening, woman. I get sexier as the night wears on."

"We'll see about that," I said as we headed down the corridor. Since the day we'd met I'd enjoyed these mock arguments with Ian—little exchanges in which he muscled his way around me, showing off with endearing male bravado.

We went out through the main lobby, our boots clanking over the shiny flagstone floors. Mrs. Newington bustled around the cut-out reception desk, setting out candles beside the red and white poinsettias. "Dinner is almost ready," she told us. "Cook has made a lovely stuffed goose with chestnut stuffing. We'll be serving until seven, so don't be late."

"Wouldn't miss it for the world, Mrs. Newington," Ian said. He pushed the door open, and jingle bells chimed.

"It's like *Holiday Inn*," I said, thinking of the charming old movie.

"Or *Fawlty Towers*," he teased. "I keep expecting to see Basil flying out of a door."

"No, more like *Christmas in Connecticut*."

"You really are a Christmas buff, aren't you?" Ian teased as we hopped off the low porch.

"You would know that if you hadn't bailed out on me last Christmas." I jumped off the porch into the snow.

"Oh, luv, can we not go there now? It's too beautiful an evening to begin Ian-bashing."

Last Christmas had been a rough one. Dad had been sick—I didn't even realize how sick, since he didn't tell anyone about his diagnosis until the new year—and Ian had promised to fly to San Francisco with me, but had to cancel at the last minute because of business demands. The holiday season had gone off on a sour note, and I had blamed it on Ian, though it probably had more to do with the fact that my father was failing.

But Ian was right, I thought as I held out my hands to catch snowflakes. At the moment it wouldn't do any good to bring up the stumbling blocks in our past. Right now I wanted to focus on the present and future of our relationship.

Snow was still falling, though the air seemed surprisingly warm and still, as if time were suspended for this magical evening. The ground was covered with crispy, white fluff, and I ran over to a bush and tried to make a snowball to throw at him, but the snow was too dry to stick together.

"Damn! And I was going to show off my pitching arm," I said, brushing the snow off my hands.

Ian put his hands on my shoulders, sliding them down to squeeze my biceps. "Hmm. If you're nice to me I'll give you another chance to test the limits of your physical stamina later." He leaned down and kissed me, catching my lips lightly with his tongue.

In a rush of emotion, I reached up and put my arms over his shoulders. I wanted to hold him forever, afraid that if my fingers slipped away I would lose him.

He ended the kiss and pressed his smooth cheek against mine. "Now there's a bear hug. Squeeze any harder and I may need to be revived, luv."

"It's just that . . ." I wasn't sure how to say it, and before I could stop myself the raw words slipped out. "It's just that I love you so much, Ian. I don't think I've every felt this way about anyone. I love you."

Ian blinked. "I love you, too." He kissed me lightly, then took my arm and led me down the path, as if it frightened him to stop and linger in the revelation of our deepest feelings.

"Are we in a hurry to get somewhere?" I asked. "Or did I scare you back there when I brought up the 'L' word?"

"Scared me to death," he said. "Don't you know that men hate to get in touch with their feelings? From the time we're wee lads we're taught to run from emotions, fast and furious."

"Not you, Ian," I said. "You don't strike me as a man who's afraid of anything."

"Believe me, there's plenty out there that scares me."

"Such as?"

"Being destitute. You know, I grew up in a small village outside Glasgow, and back in the seventies the city was still an abyss of unemployment and economic depression. I saw my own father line up for one job after another, only to come home with nothing. All the good intentions in the world couldn't buy a man a job back then. It was no wonder he left us for the States."

"Your father went to the U.S. for work?"

He nodded. "Aye, and that was the last I saw of him, not that he could help it. He got work as a carpenter's apprentice in Boston, and sent home his check. He wanted me to join him, but Mum wouldn't hear of it, as I was yet a lad. Going on twelve years."

"What happened to your father?"

"He worked in Boston, just shy of two years; then he had some sort of attack. He died in hospital there. Someday I'm going there to look up his grave, in a city plot. It's sad when a man works hard all his life and doesn't have a few pounds for his own burial."

"It is sad," I agreed, wondering if Ian had avoided dealing with my father's death because it brought up these memories for him. Geez, I'd tried to embark on a little chat about our future together and instead Ian's rusty can of issues had popped open. Abandonment, fear of poverty . . . These were not topics that I could gloss over in favor of discussing our future. I wanted to tell Ian about my job interview at the museum in London, but at the moment it seemed wise to wait.

"Well," I said, "I have to say, you must have worked hard to overcome your circumstances. Look at your success in television! Millions of people enjoy your shows, all over the world."

He nodded. "I was lucky to get a break now and again. And we both know I am a marketing genius," he said with a wicked grin.

"Absolutely."

"And I've worked bloody hard at it," he added. "Which reminds me." He tipped his face down to me, his blue eyes earnest. "I'm going to have to take care of a spot of work on Christmas Eve. I know it sounds monstrous, but it can't be avoided."

"What?" I could feel the crankiness seeping into my own voice. "Where? All the way back in London?"

"No, not that far. I'll work out of the Edinburgh office that day. Not to worry, luv. It will be only for a few hours."

"But on Christmas Eve," I shook my head, truly beginning to despise Ian's job, despite the glamour of dating an international producer.

"Yes, it sucks, I know," Ian admitted. "Especially when it means saying goodbye to you."

As he kissed me on the forehead, I decided to let it go for now, figuring that, by the time Christmas Eve rolled around, I would be able to talk him out of going. Maybe he could phone it in for the day? I would use my powers of persuasion . . . when the time came.

Over the next few days, Ian opened up to me in small ways as we hit most of the traditional tourist sights of the Edinburgh area—the castles, the alleyways of the historic Old Town, the lovely squares and terraces of the New Town. Each morning as we went for a country walk along the quaint lanes around the inn, he would tell me something he remembered about his father. And each afternoon, the local sights opened up other memories for him.

By the time darkness fell we rarely left the inn, instead choosing to have dinner down by the inn's hearth, then retiring to the cozy sitting area where Mrs. Newington served us little glasses of scotch whiskey to keep us warm through the night. Between the scotch and the warm man in bed beside me, I was never bothered by the chilly drafts that whistled in through the windows.

As we toured the ruins of Hadrian's Wall, Ian waxed philosophical about what he would like to leave behind in the world. "Certainly not a fucking wall of ruins," he said, lifting his boot to a boulder.

After a matinee in Edinburgh, he took me to the Royal Mile for an early dinner. As we ate Singaporean satay and sipped plum wine, he told me of the summers when he had worked as a stagehand in Edinburgh's Fringe Festival, his first job in show business. Those were the salad days, when he lived in a squalid attic apartment far outside town with three other teenage boys. "I didn't know what I wanted to do with my life," he said, "but I did know that I didn't want to follow the dead-end path that my father took. If I was going to survive, I needed to take the high road."

Another afternoon we went to Glasgow for afternoon tea at the Willow Tearoom, followed by a trip to the Burrell Collection. Here, surrounded by their fine collection of medieval furniture, Impressionist paintings, and Chinese porcelain, I was truly in my element, and I was happy to see how much Ian appreciated the collection. Why is it that European men are raised to understand art, unlike their American counterparts, who seem to think that museums were built for women, school groups, and sissy artists donning berets?

As we viewed the collection, I told Ian about the fierce competition among some Impressionist artists.

"Matisse and Picasso were rivals throughout their careers," I said. "You wouldn't know of the turbulence from the tranquility of most of these paintings, but the early European Impressionists like Degas and Monet were rebels. They wanted to defy the realist style prescribed by government-sponsored exhibits. That's why you see everyday subjects, like that mother kissing a baby, or those flowers in a field. These painters turned away from the classical and romantic themes of the times, and instead tried to capture the intimacy of the commonplace world around them."

Ian nodded slowly as he absorbed the paintings. "Yes, yes, I see what you mean. This all makes so much more sense now," he said quietly.

Moving on to the Chinese porcelain exhibit, I pointed out some of the symbols on the vases and plates—the dragons, flowers, and clouds—and explained their meaning to the emperors who commissioned the pieces.

"I do believe your talents are wasted in that trendy downtown gallery you work in," Ian told me. "You're overqualified to be holding artists' hands and popping champagne corks at their bloody openings."

"I know." My heart began to beat a little faster as I realized that it was time to tell him my news. "That's why I'm looking to move elsewhere. I put in an application at the Hampstead Museum in London, and they want to see me! They're interviewing me next week."

His eyes opened wide. "You're kidding! This is wonderful news, luv." He took my hand, pulled me into his arms and nuzzled my ear with his nose. "I was wondering how we were going to work things out in the new year. I can't bear living apart from you this way."

I swooned against him, thrilled to hear him say the words. Over the next few days there would be a few more momentous words spoken, but I had to remind myself to be patient and to enjoy this moment, too. In my mind was the image of that velvet ring box, and I couldn't help but wonder what kind of engagement ring Ian had chosen for me. Was it a marquis diamond? A pear-shaped stone? A simple but elegant solitaire?

He lifted me off my feet and swung me around the gallery. "Oh, we're going to have a good time together, Madison. You must get that position in London. Use me as a reference if you like. I'll assure them that you're multitalented, indeed."

"I may just take you up on that," I said. "Just be sure you

stick with the multitalented line. Best not to slip and say multiorgasmic."

"Ooh, good point." He covered his mouth, winking. "I'll make a note of that."

22

"Calton Hill is definitely worth the climb," Ian said. "But I'll try to take it slow for you. You Yanks are lightweights when it comes to walking. When I was a lad growing up outside Glasgow, I went everywhere on foot. Running, half the time."

"I can walk," I protested. "You forget, I'm a New Yorker. We walk almost everywhere. And when you live in an apartment, you have to carry your food and drink on your back."

"I thought you had groceries delivered by that market on the corner?" he said.

Ooh, busted. "Well, sometimes. But usually I go out, hunting and gathering on my own two feet."

"And lovely feet they are," Ian teased as we hiked to the east end of Princes Street.

"Amazing that there's this untouched hill right in the middle of Edinburgh," I said.

"But barely," he said. "There was some drivel about installing an amusement park on the hill, but the locals managed to squash it. Good thing. The hill is historic, with some monuments dating from the Enlightenment. It's a true signature of Edinburgh."

"Really?" I tightened my scarf against the cold and snuggled against Ian. "Have you ever thought of doing a show based on Calton Hill? Maybe a race. Take the challenge!"

He snickered. "No, but there's an interesting graveyard up ahead that I'd love to do a piece on—at Greyfriars Kirk. It's said to be haunted by a little Skye terrier. For fourteen years that dog guarded the grave of his master. Man's best friend, indeed."

I squeezed his arm. "I like to think that a woman is a man's best friend."

"Ahh, woman, don't you know that you're a man's downfall? You have total power over us. We can't resist your charms."

I laughed. "Total power, at last," I said. "Let's see, I'll conquer Calton Hill today, the world tomorrow."

"I've no doubt you could do it," Ian said, his blue eyes twinkling, "no doubt at all."

As we rose, the city of Edinburgh fell away around us, looking pristine and sleepy under its blanket of snow. The hill wasn't too steep, but I suddenly remembered the aerobic factor of steadily climbing upwards. We were clocking in the equivalent of major points on the Stairmaster. Off to one side, on a distant hill, I recognized Edinburgh Castle, brown and formidable on its bed of dark rock. From another side of the hill Ian pointed out Holyrood, then Arthur's Seat, the Firth of Forth, and the New Town, which we'd visited a few times.

The flat, snowy hilltop was marked by a classical monument, twelve white columns that rose toward the expansive gray sky like the ruins of the Parthenon. "What's this?" I asked, venturing over to the pillars.

"It was going to be a monument to those who died in the Napoleonic Wars, but funding ran out before the builders could finish."

I went over to the monument and sat in a dry patch of its rock base. "Whew! We really earned our supper today." My thoughts clicked ahead to our cozy evening at the inn. "I've got an idea. Why don't we exchange gifts tonight? It seems silly to wait until Christmas Day, especially with you having to work on Christmas Eve."

Ian reached down and tugged my scarf playfully. "Oh, that's your logic, is it?"

"What? It makes total sense!" I insisted.

He shook his head. "I'm too smart for the likes of you, woman. And how do you even know I've brought you a gift?"

I folded my arms.

"Oh, okay, I've got something for you, luv, but don't push me." He crouched down and planted a kiss on my lips. "No reason to rush."

I leaned back and took in a deep breath of fresh air and dramatic sky. Ian was right; there was no reason to hurry. There was always tomorrow.

That night after dinner, I slid under the bed quilt and propped up my book, too exhausted to think about moving. Every muscle in my body ached a little, but it felt divine to sink into the feather mattress knowing I didn't have to do a single thing.

"Are you retiring for the night then?" Ian put his hands on his hips. "Did you in, did I?"

"You do me in every day, honey," I teased. "Sometimes more than once."

"Well, guess I'm out of luck for a snuggle."

I smiled. "Come here."

He came over to the bed and kissed my forehead. Then he kicked off his shoes and crawled under the covers, resting his head on my abdomen.

Looking down at him, I felt a tremor of emotion for this man who could be so edgy and funny and vulnerable at the same time. I raked back his hair with my fingers, tracing the neat "V" at the nape of his neck, the line of hair at his collar, the delicate shell of his ear.

He ran a hand over my lower abdomen, stroking gently, evoking a feeling of contentment.

"It's noisy in there," he remarked, turning his head to look up at me. "Let's have a listen and see what the stomach thinks of dinner."

"Ian!" I grasped his hair and gave a gentle shake. "Leave my stomach alone."

"No, wait!" he said, pressing his ear to my stomach again. "It's not the stomach at all, it's the more female regions. Ovaries and the like. I believe they're sending me a message."

I sucked in my breath. He was veering dangerously close to delicate territory.

He rubbed lower, and I felt my abdomen tighten as he approached a sensitive area. "Yes," he said, "I hear the ovaries crying out to me. Help! Help! We want to make a baby!"

"Ian." I didn't want to joke about this. "I'm on the Pill. We talked about that."

"I know." He lifted his head and faced me, but his hand still covered my abdomen, moving gently. "Have you ever thought of going off?"

"I . . . I've always been very careful," I admitted. "Getting pregnant . . . it's not the sort of mistake I want to make."

"Right, but I'm not talking about a mistake. I'm talking about the two of us making a baby. Wouldn't that be amazing?" His blue eyes were so earnest, I felt myself tearing up. "We could do it, Madison. You and I."

I felt incredibly moved and very sexy at the same time. Suddenly, the ache of my muscles was nothing compared to the ache in my groin, the need to have Ian, the desire to let him quench the cries of my shrieking ovaries. Oh, I knew that it wouldn't happen today or tomorrow, but once he proposed and our wedding was in the works . . . Well, I could go off the Pill on the next cycle and . . .

Within a few weeks, we could be trying.

We could be trying to make a baby together.

"Luv?" He rubbed my tummy vigorously. "Are you all right, there?"

"I'm fine," I said, fighting back tears.

"Don't you want to make babies with me?"

"Oh, I do. I do!" I said softly. "Honestly, I can't think of anything I'd like more."

"Phew!" He stretched out beside me, slipping his hand under my sweater. I loved the way he had come to take command over my body, as if he owned it. In a way, we were becoming a single entity, the yin and yang extension of each other. "For a minute you had me worried that you were one of those intrepid working women, too caught up in your career to want a family."

"No, that's not me," I said. "I want children. I want to have your baby."

"Mmm . . . That's music to my ears." He pushed my bra aside and bent down to suck on my nipple, making me think of how an infant would do the same. A tiny little baby with soft peach fuzz on his or her head. A baby with Ian's eyes and my wide smile.

My whole body was so heightened by all the baby talk, that every touch and stroke sent me reeling. We were going to make a baby! I wanted to shout it out from the top of Calton Hill.

We're going to make a baby!

23

"I just hate to let you go on Christmas Eve. It's so unfair." I stepped into my jeans and pulled a fisherman's sweater over my head. "What kind of business do you have on December twenty-fourth? I mean, you can't be holding a talent competition or anything."

Ian looked at me in the mirror. "Listen, luv. Do you think I'd go if I didn't have to?"

"Okay, okay." I pulled on my Prada boots and stamped my feet. "Just hurry up and get ready so you can hurry up and get back. I'm going down for coffee. Do you want a biscuit?"

"No, thanks." He pressed a hand to the towel wrapped around his waist. "Got to keep my trim figure."

"You are so incredibly corny . . . and I love you." I kissed his shoulder, swiping a dab of shaving cream onto my finger. "Love the smell of this," I said, rubbing it into my wrists.

Downstairs on the sideboard in the lobby, I noticed a few pastries with little jelly centers, certainly a Christmas Eve bonus. I swept a few onto a plate and poured two mugs of coffee. While I was doctoring mine, the bells jingled as a woman stepped in the front door. She was one of those bland, over-weight women you feel a little sorry for—a sweet, pudgy face behind shiny, flat aviator glasses, and a blob of a body tucked in an oversized tweed coat. Head down, she ambled to the desk and primly rang the bell.

I was routing around for the Scottish equivalent of Sweet and Low when she greeted Andrew. "I'm here for Mr. Mac-Dougal," she said quietly.

I swung around, sending a Danish flying off the end of the plate.

She didn't notice, but Andrew grinned at me. "Ho, there, Ms. Greenwood."

Scrambling, I rested the mugs back on the sideboard and picked up the stray tart as my ears strained to hear.

"Can you ring his room for me, then?" she asked.

"Sorry, mum, but there're no telephones in the rooms. Would you like me to fetch Mr. MacDougal? Or I can send a messenger for you?" Andrew said, nodding at me.

"No," the woman said, folding her arms. "No, I've been told not to disturb him. I'll wait until he comes down." With the quiet resolve of a lost mouse, she turned away and sat on the bench.

I forced myself to look away as my mind raced through possibilities. Who the hell could this woman be? She was way too dowdy to be a friend. And she'd been told not to disturb him.

Could this be Nina, the assistant? I shot her a quick look as I grabbed the mugs. Yes, that had to be it. Nina was here to drive to the meeting with him. Though I had to admit, I would never peg the woman as the employee of a hard-driving production company. But maybe the passive-aggressive thing worked for her. Once at the Moone Gallery, we had an employee that even Katherine was afraid to fire because she was so pathetic. Every time Katherine was about to ax her, she'd come up with some excuse. Either her boyfriend broke up with her or her apartment was robbed or she slipped on the subway stairs and sprained her ankle and appeared for work on crutches. Even the notoriously gunning, ruthless Katherine

Moone had trouble being aggressive when the target was so downtrodden.

I carried breakfast over to the window and leaned in toward Andrew. "I'll tell him she's here," I whispered, figuring it was all in keeping with the holiday spirit to keep this helpless gnome from waiting too long.

Upstairs, I had to place one of the mugs on the floor while I jiggled open the door. "Guess what?" I called, stepping in. I was about to announce Ian's visitor when I spied his travel bag open on the bed, the bow of my gift peeking out.

Was he planning to give it to me now?

I placed the breakfast things on the desk and went over to the bed, sitting beside the travel bag so that the items would spill out just a little bit more. "Ian?" I called, lifting the box wrapped in silver and blue foil. I bit my lower lip as I tested its weight. Unable to stand to wait one minute more, I waved the box at him.

"Hey, hold on, luv! You're supposed to wait until Christmas," he called, peeking out of the bathroom. He had finished shaving, and his smooth, handsome face cried out to be touched.

"But some people open their gifts on Christmas Eve," I said, bringing the gift over to him. "And it's not fair that you're leaving me all alone today, when this is supposed to be our time to go wild in the wild country."

He pulled me against him, grinding his hips against me. Even through my jeans and sweater I could feel the rise in his boxers. "Ah, woman, you drive me to distraction."

"I try." I went up on my toes and placed a careful kiss on his lips, slow at first, then more penetrating.

"Mmm . . ." Moaning, he reached behind him, took the gift from my hand, and dropped it onto the dresser. "First," he said, working the snap and zipper of my jeans, "let me open you, woman." He slid a hand into my panties.

I let out a moan, and he smiled.

"How about I get my gift," he teased, "then you get yours?"

"You drive a hard bargain," I said, shedding my clothes.

His eyes were smoky as he took me by the hand and led me into the shower.

The warm water pelting my back was heaven, only to be outdone by the sensation of Ian's fingertips on my skin as he lathered me up from head to toe. He kneaded the tenderness in my calves, then swept his fingers up to work their magic between my legs. I closed my eyes and sucked in my breath. His blue eyes were so intent on my face, watching me climax. I nearly collapsed in his arms, but he swept me up and planted a warm, wet kiss on my lips.

I stole the soap from him and massaged it over his body, loving the arch of his shoulders, squeezing his biceps, then running the soap down to his firm, round butt.

"That's about all a man can take." He took the soap from my hands and let it drop to the floor as he pressed his naked body against me and found the spot to drive it home.

I pressed my hands against the tiles so that I could thrust back, loving this man, loving the way he made me feel, loving his every breath, his every stroke. As we moved against each other, I closed my eyes and a painting from the castle floated into my head. Water sprites, dancing and splashing in the pond. Ha! That's what we were—two water sprites.

Against the shush of the water and the roar of my pulse, we both cried out.

Afterward, Ian carried me out of the bathroom and gently dropped me onto the bed quilt. He returned a moment later with two towels.

"Andrew's wife won't be liking it if we drip on the linens," he said, handing me a towel. I pressed it against my cheek, watching as he rubbed his body vigorously with the other towel. He stepped into his boxers, then caught me watching. "Staring at me again? Ah, woman, you're a vixen."

"I try." I felt totally satisfied and saturated, but I knew I wouldn't be able to contain my curiosity while Ian was away. I nodded toward the dresser. "Now . . . what about my gift?"

"You want more?" he teased. He crossed the room to bring me the present, then dropped down to kneel against the bed. "Merry Christmas, luv," he said, his blue eyes sparkling.

Suddenly, my throat was thick with emotion. He was kneeling, it was Christmas Eve, and now . . . I was opening the ring. I bit my lower lip, trying to hold back tears. "Oh, Ian, I've been waiting for this." I held the box close to my chest. "I mean, not that we've had much chance to talk about it, but I sort of saw it coming. You know I've got the interview next week and . . . well, I hope you don't think I'm spoiling your surprise, because this is probably the most romantic moment of my life."

He nodded at the gift. "Go on, open it."

It was one of those rare, poignant events, a memory I wanted to savor for the rest of my life. I didn't want to tear open the gift too quickly, and yet I longed to hear Ian say the words as he slid the ring on my finger.

"Hurry it up, woman," he said as I worked away the wrapping paper. "After all this buildup, I hope it fits."

"We'll make it fit." The silver paper fell away from a blue velvet box. Smiling at him, I turned the box to face me, then snapped it open.

A dark blue stone winked up at me.

The knot in my throat suddenly threatened to choke me. "What . . . what is this?"

"A sapphire," he said fondly. "Your birthstone. September, right?"

I shook my head, unable to hide my disappointment.

"Your birthday isn't in September?" He scowled. "How did I blow that one?"

"No, I mean, yes, it is," I said. "But, but what does this mean?"

"What do you mean? The ring? It means I love you and I wanted you to have a lovely ring for Christmas, that's all," he said innocently.

I pressed a hand to my mouth, trying to hold back tears. "Love?"

"Of course I love you, you idiot!" He sat down beside me and pulled me into a hug, but I couldn't help myself. Hot tears slid out of my eyes as my body began to shake.

"What's this?" He leaned back to study my face, then pulled me close again and patted my back. "Oh, no. No crying, please! It's not that big a deal."

"But it is," I sobbed. "It is!"

"It's only a ring, luv."

"It's not an engagement ring," I blubbered.

I felt Ian's body go stiff. "Engagement?"

"I thought we were going to get married. I thought you wanted me to stay here and be with you always. What about the babies you mentioned?"

Ian released me and sat erect on the bed. "I was speaking in the hypothetical sense, luv."

"Hypothetical? I thought you wanted me to move to London. To be closer to you." I felt my entire world slipping through my fingers, and I needed to backtrack, to hold on to reality. "Didn't you say you can't live without me? Did we or did we not talk about my moving to London? Remember my job interview?"

Ian nodded. "Of course I remember." He rose from the bed, took a shirt from the closet, and shrugged into it. "And it would be grand if you'd move to London, Madison. But, I mean, it's not like I'm *really* going to slash my wrists if you don't. I mean, 'I can't live without you' is more a figure of speech than anything else."

"Ian! You must have known what I was thinking!"

"Honestly, luv." He snapped his slacks off a hanger and stepped in. "How could I know what you were thinking? I knew you were planning to move here, and that would be great, wouldn't it?"

"Yes, but I was hoping to move here and live as your wife."

He paled. "That can't happen right now. Not marriage."

"And why not?"

"I've always seen you as being independent. It's one of the things I love about you."

"Don't try to flatter me, Ian. Why can't we get married?"

"We just can't, is all. And while I hate to end with an argument, I really must run."

I snapped the ring box closed and turned away from it, feeling utterly abandoned. "Go. We'll argue about this when you get back."

He leaned down to give me a peck on the cheek, his jacket slung over one shoulder. "Don't be mad. I'll be back as soon as I can." As he turned toward the door, I remembered the mousy lady waiting for him downstairs.

"Oh, shit! I forgot to tell you, there's a woman waiting for you downstairs, and I think it's Nina."

"No way." He seemed confused. "Nina's off in the Canary Islands having a fuck-fest with her boyfriend."

"Really?" Well, at least that fit the image of the Nina I'd spoken to on the phone. "Well, then who is she? She's waiting for you, and she didn't want to interrupt us, but—"

Ian sucked in a breath as his face turned slightly gray. "Nina," he said in a dead voice. "It must be Nina. She . . . she probably cancelled her trip."

"No!" I gasped. "It . . . it's your wife!"

24

I jumped up from the bed, holding the towel over me. "Oh my God, that's it! The woman downstairs is your wife!"

Ian shook his head, his complexion completely ashen now. "No, don't be silly. She would never come here. That is . . . if I had a wife. Which I don't." He pulled out his mobile phone and flipped it open. "See there? A message from Nina. She must have called to update me."

I didn't believe a word he was saying, and the shock of it all stung me. Denial seeped through me as I tried to find a fact to hold on to. Ian didn't have a wife. He would have told me. I would have known, all these months . . . Wouldn't he have confessed in a moment of connection? Wouldn't I have seen some clue? Why hadn't I intercepted any of her phone calls?

At first, I felt paralyzed. Then adrenaline shot through me, forcing me to take action. My hands shook as I wrapped the white towel around me. Without another thought, I snatched up the ring box from the bed and ran out the door.

"Madison!" Ian called. "Where are you . . . ? Come back here!"

The hall was very cold, but I plunged on, down the stairs, my wet hair dripping onto my shoulders. My bare feet danced over the frigid stone of the foyer and nearly skidded to a stop in front of the dowdy woman who sat waiting for Ian.

"Nina?" I murmured.

She lifted her chin, taking in my very casual bath attire. "No, dear."

My blood chilled as I gripped the jewelry box tightly. Behind me I heard the door from the stairs swing open, and I knew Ian waited there, watching. I couldn't believe I was doing this, dressed like this, but I had to know.

"Mrs. MacDougal?" I said softly.

The woman looked me in the eye and smiled. "Yes, that's me."

"Wife of Ian MacDougal?" I peeped, just to make sure she wasn't his mother.

"Why, yes." She straightened, spotting Ian behind me. "Well, hullooo, there. Surprised you, did I? Didn't want to interrupt your meeting, so I waited here. Figured we could drive to Mum's together."

I was crushed, overcome with a mixture of emotions: devastation for myself, revulsion for Ian, sympathy for this poor pigeon of a woman who was stuck with a philandering excuse for a husband.

Squeezing the box with the sapphire ring, I thrust it into Mrs. MacDougal's face. "Merry Christmas," I said. When she seemed confused, I added: "It's a gift from your husband."

"Oh." She smiled, accepting the velvet box. "Thank you very much. Though you'd better bundle up, dearie. You'll catch your death."

I turned to face Ian, who skulked back near the door. My head burned with a fury as I padded across the flagstone lobby and paused in front of Ian.

He winced. "Sorry?" He spoke softly, so that wifey couldn't

hear. "I can only imagine what you're thinking and . . . Well, Madison, before you go wild, just please let me explain. We've been married since we were kids, and well . . . look at her. I just don't have the heart to let her down flat."

He didn't have the heart . . . but he didn't mind leading me on like a heartless, lying, scheming . . .

I lifted my knee and gave him a shot in the groin.

Okay, maybe I'm not La Femme Nikita, but I did my best.

"Merry Christmas," I said, slamming through the swinging door and letting it slap back behind me. With any luck, it would smack him in the ass. "Merry fucking Christmas."

"Are you sure you won't stay on with us now?" Andrew asked me at the train station. "The trains don't run all too well on Christmas Eve. And with all the snow and all, you'll be lucky to get into London at a decent hour."

"I have to go," I said, pausing to pat his horse. "I need to be with my friends." I felt like a zombie chanting a mantra, but in my heart I knew it was true. I couldn't stay here, and well, if I had any hope of salvaging Christmas, it would be at a table with the people who loved me most.

"I understand." Andrew carried my bags to the side of the platform, then extended a hand. "I do hope you'll come back and see us again sometime. It's not every day a guest trots through our lobby in the buff. The missus will be talking for months."

"Not something I plan to do next time I visit," I said.

"Remember, cheap and cheery."

I bit my lower lip, fighting back tears. When he'd first told me those words, I'd been so happy and hopeful. I'd been a fool. "Thank you," I said, turning away from him to peer down the train tracks.

"It should be along any minute," Andrew told me.

I nodded, staring into the darkness. The train couldn't come soon enough for me.

25

Making my way through the misty streets of London on Christmas Eve, I felt like a lone woman of mystery. Independent and aloof. I knew it was a temporary disguise, a brief illusion, but for the moment, it worked for me.

As promised, Sugar had left me a key at the desk at the Kensington Park Thistle, and I dashed up to her room to stow my stuff. When I'd called to tell her I was coming back, she'd told me to get my butt back to London pronto. I could share her room until I managed to get my own. "Though I want you to know, it will definitely be cramping my style," she'd told me. "I met this fabulous guy . . ."

Upstairs, there was a note on the bed.

We're at Bunch of Grapes on Brompton Road. Glad you're back. Sorry he was a prick.

Feeling a little sick to my stomach, I checked the clock. Ten-fifteen. Maybe I should just put my pj's on and crawl under the covers. My friends were probably drinking champagne by now, riding ethereal clouds of intoxication that would sail out of earshot of my sob story. I sank onto the bed and sighed. Should I stay or should I go? The plush duvet embraced me, tempting.

But it was Christmas Eve. How pathetic would it be to curl into a fetal position and cry myself to sleep on the most magical night of the year? Again, it was still tempting.

But I couldn't let Ian ruin Christmas for me. If I caved tonight, his cruelty would cast a pall over my favorite holiday, and it would take years to shake it off.

"Enough buts," I said aloud, pulling myself off the bed. I unzipped my suitcase and changed into a goth black lace blouse to match my dark mood. With any luck, I could spend the evening hiding under this woman-of-mystery mystique. I spilled the contents of my makeup bag onto the bed. Tapping into some little-used makeup, I filled in my eyelids and painted a swirl from the edge of my lashes, fanning out to my temples. I borrowed some of Sugar's dark red lipstick and slathered it on thickly.

When I was done I stared into the mirror in wonder. "I am fucking Cleopatra," I whispered. "Either that or some odd cousin of the Addams Family."

As I grabbed my long black coat, I realized it didn't matter who I masqueraded as tonight. Just as long as I didn't have to be myself.

Bunch of Grapes was a Victorian pub in a chic, high-spirited section of Knightsbridge. When I stepped into the dark, smoky entryway, I sensed that the party had been going on around me for a long time. Sucking in a breath, I wondered if I would have to down a few pints immediately to catch up. That and a few tequila shooters. As I was unbuttoning my coat, someone emerged from behind an etched glass partition and stepped right up to me.

Sugar.

"Hey, girlfriend." Her soft brown eyes were wary, as if I were a wild horse that might bolt. "I've been watching for you. Merry Christmas Eve." She reached around me and pulled me into a hug.

Tears stung my eyes. I tried to sniff them back at first, then I just let go. I rested my head on the soft, dark cashmere of Sugar's shoulder and cried it out.

"I know," she said softly, rubbing my back between the shoulder blades. "Believe me, I know."

I sucked in a ragged breath. "I feel like such an idiot. He's married. All along, he was going home to his wife, this mousy thing who's so oblivious, I can't even hate her."

"Christ, men are such pigs."

"I feel like such an idiot."

"Why? Because he lied to you?" She leaned back slightly so that she could look in my face. "Because you trusted him? You were in love with him, Madison, and he took advantage of that. He concocted a ruse about his life because he knew you wouldn't stick around if you knew the truth, and he didn't want to lose you. It's not your fault that you believed him."

It made sense. Everything she said made total sense, but I still felt like an idiot.

"I can't believe he was such a smooth liar."

"Men are big, fat liars," she agreed.

"I'm so embarrassed. Am I that naive? Twenty-six, and I get sucked into falling in love with a married man."

Sugar dropped one hand onto my shoulder. "Honey lamb, not to diminish your pain, but, as my granny used to say, shit happens. Most of the time, the best you can hope is that you don't step in it." She shrugged. "You stepped in it, all right. And you deserve a good cry. But just not right now, okay? It's Christmas Eve and all your buds are here, and right now you need to have a good time. And look at your fabulous makeup job. A little bit of the black is running." She reached over the bar for a napkin, then dabbed gently under my eyes. "There. You're not melting anymore."

"Thanks," I said. "I mean it. Thank God you and Jenna

are here. If I had to sit on a transatlantic flight with this weight on my head, I'd totally implode."

"You know, there's another thing my granny used to say." Sugar's eyes widened, as if she'd summoned an important memory. "She used to tell me: 'Sugar Plum, everything in life can be put into one of two categories. There's the temporary category, where you can file away things that come and go. That's where you put your jobs, your homes, your men, and your bad times. Then there's the permanent category. That's the important one. That's where you put your family and friends. They're the permanent fixtures in your life. Your friends will always be there for you.' "

I smiled. "Your granny was a smart lady."

"Damn straight." She linked her arm through mine. "Come on, pumpkin. Let's get you a drink. By the way, I didn't tell anyone your news. Figured they'd enjoy the surprise."

On the other side of the etched glass screen I spotted Jenna talking, her arms flying as she told a story with her usual animation. When she spotted me, she gasped and ran over to give me a big hug.

"Madison! How great is this? You guys are in town for Christmas."

"She's here solo," Sugar explained.

"Oh. Okay," Jenna bounced back as we continued toward the bar. Something struck me as we approached the guys gathered there . . . something familiar about the bald man in the black leather jacket and the dark-haired man beside him . . .

I gasped. "Leo and Wolf?"

Leo turned on his bar stool and threw out his arms in amazement. "Is this a celestial vision that appears to intoxicated travelers on Christmas Eve, or is Madison here?"

"Madison?" Wolf came over and kissed me on both cheeks. "Or Elvira?"

"What the hell are you guys doing here?" Shock and

thrill chewed away at my pain for a moment. "You're supposed to be in Portugal. Dammit, Leo, I stayed up all night so that I could dump you on that flight. Don't tell me you missed it!"

"No, he arrived on time," Wolf said. "But we decided that the real party was here in London." He lifted his glass to me and smiled.

"Actually," Leo cut in, "Wolf and Jorge had a huge fight! I mean, Jorge was so mad he was spitting. Well, not intentionally, but when he talks he has this saliva thing going on."

"Sounds like a dysfunctional family Christmas," Jenna said.

Wolf nodded, peering at me through a lock of shiny dark hair that fell seductively over his forehead. Although Wolf had cut off his ponytail a few years ago, the guy had it going on in the hair department. "My family during holidays? Not a pretty sight," he admitted.

"The whole scene did not make for the merriest of Christmases," Leo went on, "so we dashed to the airport and jumped on a plane. Let me tell you, I felt like James Bond, boarding the plane just minutes before takeoff, and traveling with Wolf. You should see the looks on people's faces when this guy flashes his passport. It's got this gold royal seal on it, and it totally knocks the airport people on their asses."

"Ooh, I want to see it!" Sugar shouted.

"Show us!" Jenna chimed in, hopping off her bar stool.

We all gathered close to watch as Wolf reached inside his jacket.

"Whip it out, baby!" Sugar teased.

The passport was navy blue, with a gold-embossed seal stamped on the bottom. Grinning, he held it up beside his face, posing like Vanna White.

We whistled and cooed.

"Very nice," I said. "You know, Wolf, all these years we've been friends and you never whipped it out for me before."

Everyone laughed.

"I have to get drunk first," Wolf told me as he tucked the passport back into his jacket.

I laughed again. Funny how it eased the pain. For a moment there, I almost forgot about Ian.

"It's your turn, you woman of mystery," Leo said, looking at me. "The lipstick is a bit much, but I do like the goth eyes. So tell us, what brings you back to London so soon?"

I took a deep breath, looking to Sugar for support. She leaned on the bar, her hand under her chin, giving me full rein.

"Well, it's awkward," I admitted, "but the sad truth is, Ian has no dick."

"What?" Jenna shrieked. The rest of the group burst into laughter.

"Yes, I know, sad but true," I went on. "He's been swinging something around all these months, but today when I looked, it was quite a shock to see that, alas, there was nothing dangling between his legs."

"The man has no dick?" Wolf repeated, giddy with laughter.

Leo was nodding. "A dickless wonder."

"I've met a few of those," Sugar said.

"Actually, it's more common than you think," Wolf said studiously. "I used to work with a man with no dick. He had to pee sitting down."

"And I'll bet he had no brain function, either," Sugar added.

"Okay, guys, that's enough," Jenna said. "If I were a Freudian, which I'm not, I'd have to say that you all suffer from penis envy."

I swiped at the tears at the corners of my eyes. It was great to be back.

"So what really happened?" Leo asked me. "Really?"

I took a deep breath and let it roll. "I discovered that Ian was a lying slimeball with a wife stashed away." There, I'd said it.

Leo narrowed his eyes, taking it in slowly. "You were right. He has no dick."

I looked around the group, meeting each person's gaze. Jenna looked sympathetic. Wolf, stunned. Leo, a bit devastated on my behalf. Sugar seemed to be subconsciously coaching me to stay positive.

"So, I've decided that I'm putting him behind me and moving on," I said. "But it seemed important to get my butt back here so that I could spend Christmas with the people who matter most." I curled my fingers around my pint of ale. "Good people, people with dicks. My friends."

Sugar had tears in her eyes as she turned to me. "That's it. To the people with dicks! They're the ones who will be there for you when the walls come tumbling down." She held up her glass in a toast. "To us!"

We reached for our glasses and clinked them together.

"To dicks! Very stiff Richards!" Wolf laughed. "Oh, but my brother's ears must be burning."

"To dicks!" Jenna sang bravely.

"To my good friends," I said.

Leo raised his glass and crowed: "'God bless us, every one.'"

Part Four

Merry Christmas!
Well, I Guess I'll Miss
This One This Year

New York City

26

December 8, 2003

The metal heels of my Chanels clicked on the shiny floors of Park View Hospital as I raced to rescue my friend in need. Not that I could do anything to improve his medical condition, but let's face it, everyone needs an advocate when they become an admissions number in the healthcare system. I've read the stories of patients checking into hospitals and going through countless sonograms and MRIs before someone finally figured out who they were and where they needed to be. And they're the lucky ones who don't end up missing a healthy gallbladder or having the wrong lung removed because some bozo screwed up the paperwork. Trust me, I know these things; my father was a doctor! But don't get me started on the state of healthcare in the United States. . . .

I ran up to the Emergency Room desk and leaned in beside the menorah, determined to find Leo. To my surprise, the woman seated there looked me in the eye, and she knew exactly who Leo was. "Yes, he's here. Are you next of kin?"

I frowned. "About as close as you can get."

She nodded toward an area behind the desk. "You can go see him. He's in curtain three, just beyond that crash cart."

I scurried behind the counter, sideswiping a nurse in pink scrubs who seemed to be power walking through the ward. Leo lay with his leg propped up on the paper-covered bed, looking forlorn and washed out in a tacky print medical gown.

"Madison, my angel of light!" Leo called to me from the bed in curtain three.

"What happened to you?" I asked, looking him over. "Tell me you stashed your Prada shoes in a safe spot."

"My shoes! They're still at the skating rink! Oh, no, Madison, you have to promise to go and pick them up first thing in the morning."

"Don't worry," I said, patting his hand. "You need to focus on getting yourself put back together. What's the prognosis?"

Leo winced. "I don't know yet." He called out to a nurse passing his bed. "What's my prognosis?"

"We need to hear from the orthopedic surgeon," she said, pausing to check the ice pack on his knee. She turned to me. "You from Portugal? He put down someone in Portugal as his next of kin."

"No, I'm from the Upper West Side."

She shook her head. "Like this hospital is going to spring for a phone call to Portugal."

Leo shrugged. "I figured it was worth a try. Wolf should know."

"I'll call him," I said. "He's probably better off getting the news from me than from a total stranger. He'll be so upset." It was so hot in the room, I had to take my coat off. I slung it over the bed behind Leo. "So what's the story here? You really fell on the ice?"

"Oh, please." He lifted a hand over his eyes, as if he couldn't bear to look. "I am mortified. Well, I would have been if anyone had seen me go down like a broken windmill. The rink was just closing, can you believe it? My last lap."

As he spoke, a nurse wheeled a chair in and bent over it to put the brakes on. "Leo Vespucci?" she asked in a deadpan voice.

"Yes, that's me," he said. "Am I being moved to a room?"

"I'm going to take you to X ray."

"But I've already had my leg x-rayed," Leo said.

"They want another picture."

Leo sighed, grasping my hand as he eased himself off the bed onto his good leg. "Really, nurse, how long is this whole thing going to take?"

"I'm not a nurse," she said. "I'm a people mover. Move people from one ward to the other."

"Can you believe this place?" Gingerly, Leo hopped back and sat in the chair. "You come in for a broken leg, and they need a million pictures."

"Take your things," the people mover said. "Don't know where you'll end up after this."

"Exactly what I'm afraid of," Leo told me, turning to the woman. "You don't move people to the morgue, do you?"

When she didn't answer, he bit his hand.

"I'll take your stuff," I volunteered.

Leo pointed to a fat plastic bag leaning against the bed. "And promise me you won't leave me."

"I'll go call Wolfie, then I'll camp out in the waiting room," I said, walking alongside his rolling chair.

"Just don't leave me!" Leo turned in the wheelchair and stretched his hand out toward me as the people mover rolled him away.

"You're so fucking dramatic," I called.

"I know!" he called back.

I spent most of that night in the waiting room, combing through December issues of *Good Housekeeping* and *Family Circle,* which had some crafts Mom would definitely want to try this year.

For the first time ever, she was throwing the Greenwood Christmas party and I wouldn't be there. It was weird to think of her collecting ornaments and assembling decorations on her own. Or maybe Clay was helping her. I could picture it: Mom supervising while he methodically hot-glued cranberries to a Styrofoam ball or dipped pine cones in glitter. Yes, they made a great team. I was glad that Mom had found someone to fulfill her life.

I wish I had a scintilla of her luck. Having abandoned the youthful dreams of fabulously frosted wedding cakes, Vera Wang gowns, and chapels strewn with flowers and ribbons, I still wanted a man. Screw the wedding, give me someone to build a life with. My friends were still the best pick-me-up a girl could want, but when it came to a snuggle on a cold December night . . . well, I was on my own.

From the waiting room I could see the workings of the ER, with doctors and nurses and technicians and aides. One of the younger residents was a real heartthrob, with beautifully chiseled cheekbones and dark hair that fell artfully into his eyes. If Sugar were here, she'd definitely make a play for him. Me, I'd spent half my life living with a doctor; I'd given up enough to support the medical profession.

Between the visits to X ray and the wait to consult the orthopedic surgeon on call, it took us five hours to learn that Leo had a "severe sprain" and would need to rest his knee and maneuver on crutches for a while. The gorgeous young resident helped us call a cab, and we were off by three-thirty. By the time I got Leo tucked away and headed home, it was obscenely late—after four A.M. I hadn't even partied this late for years.

The front door of my building was locked, and I had to buzz the doorman to let me in. He waved, bleary-eyed, as I decided to treat myself to an elevator ride.

The door whooshed open on my floor, and as I stepped onto the diamond-patterned carpeting, the emptiness creeped me out.

The building was eerily still, with everyone sleeping.

As my Chanels moved smartly down the hall, I carefully tried to avoid looking at Mrs. Endicott's door. Apartment 302. Somehow I worried that her spirit still lingered there—and probably in the recyling room, too, where she always complained that the city should still be accepting glass. The doorman had told me a lovely young couple just closed on the place, though I hadn't seen them yet. I still thought of the apartment as belonging to Mrs. Endicott, a bold, horsey seventyish New Yorker who rode the subways and shopped at Balducci's. A cheerful woman, though she had no family, no children.

When she died last month, no one even blinked. It took a week or so for her mailbox to get clogged with junk mail and bills. When I saw the morning papers piled up at her door, I assumed she'd forgotten to stop the paper while she went to Florida. The coroner said she'd probably been dead a week by the time the doorman called the police. A whole week . . . very creepy.

Another good reason to subscribe to the daily *New York Times*.

I yawned, feeling much older than my thirty-one years. Old and all alone. What would my tombstone say?

HERE LIES MADISON
A HELL OF A LOT OF FUN
TOO BAD SHE NEVER FOUND THE RIGHT GUY

I didn't want to end up like Mrs. Endicott. No, Spirits, no! I wanted a partner in life. Companionship. Someone to do the crosswords with over coffee on a lazy Sunday morning. Someone to notice if I should slip on the stairs and lose consciousness for a few days.

Was that too much to ask? Answer me, oh Spirits!

27

December 9, 2003

After hitting the snooze button half a dozen times, I woke up with a headache, dry throat and itchy, dry eyes. Had I spent the night squeezing fun out of a worm-shaped tequila bottle, I would have deserved this look, but after a night spent aiding a friend in need? It just wasn't fair.

Of course, I was late for work, not only because I was dragging my ass, but also because I had to drag my ass over to Rockefeller Center to pick up Leo's Prada boots, and, as luck would have it, the rink didn't open until ten A.M. Why didn't I think of that? As a publicist, I'm supposed to have an overall sense of the workings of public events and institutions. Blame it on sleep deprivation. Biding my time with a huge Starbuck's venti, I waited for the rink to open, knowing Leo would never forgive me if I abandoned his boots.

Huddled at a corner table in the coffee shop, I hugged my cup and tried to relax. My boss wouldn't stress over me being late, so why was I? Besides, my work was under control. The pace as a museum publicist was far different from the demands of catering to Diva Katherine at her hipster downtown gallery. Ever since I'd joined the Taft Museum a few years ago my skin had cleared up, my cholesterol had dropped, and I was able to sleep at night without being haunted by visions of the shrill, vicious Katherine Moone getting in my face over the fact that I'd served an art critic the wrong color wine. To be honest, there wasn't a lot of day-to-day turmoil at the museum. Oh, there were deadlines and disappointments when grants were turned down, but the deadlines were generous and very often, when you didn't get a grant, the foundations told you why your project was rejected and gave you a second chance to submit your proposal.

A do over. If only we could get second chances across the board. Instant replays in which you could reshoot the scene and fix the mistake. If that were the case, I probably wouldn't be sitting here alone in a coffee shop waiting anxiously as the decade of my thirties loomed ominously.

Then again, was there any one guy I would "do over"? Who among my past boyfriends would have made a suitable spouse? A big fat zero, if you ask me.

By the time I got to the museum, I was shaking from caffeine and lack of sleep.

"We got your message," Nicole said blandly as I strolled into our modest workspace. She occupied the desk beside mine, and though she had her moments of humor and kindness, I could always count on her to compete with me for the boss's favor. "You're just in time to brew another pot of coffee."

"I feel like hell," I said, dropping Leo's boots under my desk.

My boss, Barry Fleck, poked his head out of his office, stroking his mustache. "Oh, dear. You look like hell," he commented. "Everything okay?"

"Oh, sure, if you enjoy spending the night in the hospital."

Barry gasped. "You poor thing! Tell us what happened."

As I tossed my navy Harve Bernard trench coat over the coatrack and folded my Pendleton plaid scarf, I launched into my tale of woe, reminding myself to go easy on Barry. He was such a gentle soul; even the slightest conflict ruined his day. The man definitely belonged in the arts, though probably not in the PR/education department. Halfway through my story, Nicole wandered off to seek more caffeine, but Barry listened intently.

"Poor Leo," he said. "Well, of course, you take whatever time you need to help patch him together. Everything on your desk can wait, can't it?"

I turned to my desk and perused the folders of notes, the proofs for brochures, the calendar. Across December ninth was scrawled: Teddy Bears!

"Oh, sh-sugar." I caught myself just in time; Barry didn't care for cursing in the office. I had completely forgotten about the mountain of stuffed animals Leo and I were supposed to transport from FAO Schwarz to hospitals and day care centers. Today.

"What is it?" Barry asked. "Did we miss the printer's deadline on the Book of Kings?" Barry was incessantly worried about missing deadlines, which meant paying late fees, which meant going over budget. Most times his paranoia was understandable. In these times when museum funding was shrinking, we had to stay on top of costs and deadlines for grant applications. But sometimes I imagined Barry going through the supply closet at night, counting reams of paper.

"No, no, that's all covered," I said. "It's about a toy delivery. Leo was going to help me take care of it, but now that he's out of commission, I don't know how I'm going to pull it off."

"What about Sugar?" Barry suggested. "She goes off the air at ten. Doesn't she have the afternoon off?"

I shook my head. "Although the show broadcasts in the morning, they're busy doing promos all afternoon. She told me I could use her SUV, but she's not free until the evening, and most companies close down by five."

Barry shook his head. "I'm sorry, Madison, but I just can't spare another employee. I'd help you myself, but I'm responsible for docent training for the month of December."

"I understand." I hated making decisions while Barry was watching, especially since he was a guy who sweated the details. "Listen, Bar, I'll work it out, okay?"

He placed a hand over my arm. "If it's too much for you, remember, you can decline the gifts. This program has blossomed into something beyond the museum's expectations and goals. You don't have to do it, Madison."

"I'll figure it out," I said, sitting at my desk so that Barry would go away.

"Okay, then," he said. "Give Leo my best."

"Will do." I was already turned away, logging on to my computer to get the contact info for FAO Schwarz. I had to get in touch, but what would I tell them? Should I cancel, or postpone? And who could I wrangle to help me transport toys all over town during the next two weeks—the busiest weeks of the Christmas season?

The problem was, this toy drive was my brainchild, my creation. Last year, while we were brainstorming ways to make our museum appear more kid-friendly, I'd dreamed up this campaign to have private companies donate toys that tied in with our exhibits. A costume wholesaler donated two hundred sets of plastic armor to support our medieval masterpiece exhibit. A toy maker gave us hundreds of jewelry-making kits to tie in with our "Crowns of Kings and Queens" exhibit. When schoolgroups came to visit our museum, we would pass on the gifts, and they ended up taking home something that made the museum exhibit come alive.

Well, that was the theory. The thing was, our campaign—which rolled out during the Christmas season—was so successful that other companies contacted us with contributions for the 2003 Christmas season. Big contributions, like a thousand toy bears from FAO Schwarz, twenty cases of Legos from Toys "R" Us, a hundred bicycles from a bike shop in Queens. This year, we had been offered more toys than we could store here at the museum, and quite frankly, even the most creative public relations officer, such as myself, would have trouble finding parallels between stuffed bears and the pandas painted on a few vases in our Asian Art Gallery.

The general consensus had been to say "No, thanks," to the toys we couldn't store or tie in to our educational arts program.

But that had bothered me.

I mean, was I the only one who saw the opportunity to get fabulous Christmas gifts to children who would really appreciate them?

Apparently so. But when I'd told Barry that I was going to make the transport of these donations my personal mission, he didn't stop me. The museum couldn't pay for delivery or van rentals, but Barry would allow me to use my time to move the goods from the donors to the children. With Leo's help, I could have pulled it all off, but now, as a one-woman show, I wasn't so sure.

The FAO people were lovely on the phone. So accommodating, but there was one problem. The bears were already on the loading dock, ready to go. If I didn't pick them up today, the company would have to truck them to their warehouse, as they didn't have the storage space in the New York store for a thousand bears.

I had created a Christmas monster.

"No, that's okay, I'll pick them up today," I told them. I hung up and called Sugar at the radio station. She was in a meeting, so I left a message with her assistant. "It's Madison. Tell her to call her doorman and leave me the keys to the SUV."

I was going to have to go it alone.

* * *

That night as I climbed the steps to Leo's apartment, which he'd lovingly dubbed "the garret," I wasn't sure I'd make it back down. Not that looking down at my gold Manolo Blahniks with their pert brown bows didn't give me a lift. But at the moment, I needed more lift than a three-inch heel could provide.

"I'm wiped," I said as Leo opened the door for me.

"What, trying Xanax again?"

"No, just exhausted. I did the teddy bear run on my own today, and let me tell you, those little critters are bulky. Sugar's SUV is big, but I still had to make three trips, with cute little bear faces pressed up against the glass like the damned teddy-bear parade."

Leo's mouth dropped open. "I'm so sorry I missed it. What's in the bag?"

"Dinner. You have your choice of chicken almondine or spinach quiche. I know, it's totally schizoid, but I stopped by the French deli and I couldn't decide."

"Let's split both," he said, hopping into the kitchen to get utensils. "So, you did the delivery? What about the next one? Isn't that the huge shipment you need to rent a truck for? Who's going to help you?"

"I don't know," I moaned, flopping onto his daybed and sinking back against one of the faux fur cushions. "Right now I'm too tired to think ahead." The toy-moving business was tiring, and my trek through the magnificent displays at the toy store had taken an emotional toll. Last Christmas, I'd been dating a guy who'd needed gifts for his nieces and nephews, and we'd spent hours playing with the displays of toy trains and Legos and Leapfrog computers. Kurt was a kid at heart, a quality that had seemed so endearing as we played in toy stores by day, in bed at night.

Today, while I was waiting for the paperwork at FAO Schwarz, I had ventured into the aisles of dolls and toys.

Christmas carols were playing softly, and a few toddlers stumbled past me like drunken spinning tops, bouncing from one giant stuffed animal to the next.

As I'd rounded the corner of the computer game department, I swore I spotted Kurt there, grimacing as he maneuvered the controls of a Nintendo Gamecube.

Of course, I was wrong. It was a teenage boy, probably cutting school. But Kurt had haunted me for the rest of the day. I had to remind myself that I was the one who'd wanted to end it in January. After the Christmas shopping had ended, Kurt still wanted to play with the toy displays. When I'd left him, he was trying to make it to the next level of Jet Set Video Future on his X-Box.

Chances were, he was still sitting in the same position on his living-room floor.

"You've got to get help!" Leo insisted.

"Because of the ghosts?" I asked.

"Fuck the ghosts, I'm talking about the deliveries."

"Jenna suggested that I approach one of the doormen from my building, but I don't think I have enough bribe money in my savings account. She says hi, by the way. She's coming in for my party Friday."

"She must be rather large by now," Leo said, slicing his chicken.

"She's due next month. And she promised to bring her neighbor to my party. A gorgeous bachelor." I took a large bite of quiche so I wouldn't have to elaborate on Jenna's pregnancy and the feelings of jealousy it aroused deep inside me. I sensed that Leo was aware of my struggle, especially since he changed the subject.

"I spoke to Wolf. He's decided to ditch Portugal and come here for Christmas."

"G-weat!" I mumbled over a mouthful. "Was he disappointed that you didn't feel up to making the flight to Europe?"

"Didn't sound that way. I think he'll be glad to escape from his evil brother's clutches once again. So I'm covered for Christmas . . . which brings us to you. Would you get off this ghost theme? So you've spent a few Christmases with a few different boyfriends. Don't you realize how lucky you are to have found a few good men? Honey, I've been out there, and the pickins are slim."

"Leo, did you listen to those messages on my machine? Henry . . . married Henry. And Ryan! Fucking Ryan, my adolescent albatross."

"I love it when you call him that." He grinned. "Tell me again about that Christmas when you guys did it. What were you . . . stretched out on the kitchen counter or something?"

"No, that was Greg. Ryan was on the couch of the sitting room. But you're getting off the point. Don't you think it's a little weird to hear from these guys out of the blue?"

"Not at all." He paused. "Did you call them back?"

"Of course not. You know I don't date married men—at least, never knowingly. And Ryan . . . that guy is like the kid brother who keeps trying to horn in on everything big sis tries to do. I mean, getting my number from my mother? What a suck-up! And apparently *he* was married, too. Am I the only one who hasn't found a match in all these years?" I sighed. "Fucking Ryan."

"Funny how you keep saying that. If I were a Freudian I'd have a field day with you." Leo sniffed. "I wouldn't mind seeing Ryan in that fancy uniform again."

"That was ten years ago! He's probably fat and bald by now."

"Ahem." Leo smoothed a hand over his shiny head.

"Okay, bald is beautiful, but he's probably got a belly like a beached whale."

"I'm not defending Ryan," Leo said. "It's you I worry about, Bridget Jones. When a person pushes past the thirty mark and she hasn't found a suitable mate, it's time for that person to re-evaluate her high standards."

"You've been reading *Cosmo* again." I stacked up our dinner plates and brought them into the kitchen. "Besides, maybe the person doesn't have such high standards. Maybe she just hasn't met the right mate. Did you think of that, Dr. Phil?" I stuffed the napkins into the garbage. "And it's not like I don't have anyone in my radar. Frank and I are having dinner tomorrow."

"Who the hell is Frank?"

"The reporter? Remember? We met him at Morrell's."

"Oh . . . Frank with the silver highlights? The old gray mare?" Leo slapped his hands to his face in an imitation of *The Scream*. "That guys shrieks baggage."

"Does not!"

"I'll bet he's got three kids, two in college, and still hasn't figured out where his marriage went wrong."

"And you call me a skeptic?" I protested.

"Take my advice," he said. "When Frank mentions his ex-wife—and believe me, he will—walk, do not run, to the nearest exit."

"He already admitted that he's divorced. Even has two kids." Not to mention the fact that I'd checked him out on-line. Hey, I'd learned my lesson. I was never, ever going to fall for another married man. "I can't believe you don't remember, Leo. Were you paying attention to anything that night?"

"Alas, I was exhilarated from being on the ice." He propped his knee up higher on the arm of the sofa. "Which proved to be my downfall."

"Well, I'm meeting him at Bloomingdale's." Don't ask me why I felt compelled to defend Frank so vehemently. Truly, I had no idea if he would have mileage as a friend or lover or more, but somehow I felt the need to prove that there were still a million other possibilities out there without having to lower my standards and fall back on old boyfriends who hadn't made the cut.

"Still giving that test?"

I nodded.

"You are such the Christmas maven. Would you mind

rinsing the dishes before you go? I'm supposed to stay off my feet."

I didn't mind at all, but I had to torture Leo. "No problem. But I don't wash windows, and I won't be around tomorrow night. Got a hot date with Frank."

"Right." He clicked on the television and began to sing. " 'The old gray mare, he ain't what he used to be—' "

"Oh, you're lucky I don't toss these dishes out the window."

Leo laughed, turning to *Jeopardy*. "I know you won't. They're Spode, and you gave them to me."

"Unfair."

He smiled. "Virginia, rules are made to be broken."

28

December 10, 2003

The next morning I was bound and determined to get to work on time to make up for all the hours I would be missing in toy transport, but the world seemed to be working against me. I broke a nail. My Jimmy Choos had chewing gum on the heel, and my Manolo Blahniks didn't really go with the black pants I was wearing, so I had to switch to a denim skirt and duster-length sweater. On top of that, my toaster didn't pop up and the smoke set off my smoke detector. Which brought a call from the doorman downstairs.

"Yes, yes, I know, Mrs. Warner called to complain, but there's no fire. Just my toaster."

"Good morning," Ralph the doorman said. "I was calling to let you know you have a visitor down here? A Mr. Ryan Wilkinson?"

Fucking Ryan.

"Well, don't send him up," I said as I slipped on my gold Manolo Blahniks and reached for my Burberry plaid scarf. "I'm on my way to work. Just hold him there."

"Will do."

I left the kitchen window cracked open to air out the

smoke and headed out. Riding in the elevator, I tried to tick off the toy-transport trips on my calendar. Today I was slated to pick up porcelain dolls at the Madame Priscilla Doll Factory in West Harlem. Tomorrow it was Toys "R" Us, then the bike shop in Queens . . . or was it the other way around?

Down in the lobby, I summoned my courage and refined my pitch, trying to ensnare my kind doorman Ralph in my toy distribution scheme.

"Ralph, I have a proposition for you."

He blinked at me, pushing back his cap and pointing a thumb behind him.

Leaning against the faux marble wall was a tall man in a pressed denim shirt and black cashmere coat. His posture was perfect, he had one hand tucked into the pocket of his dress pants in a very *GQ* way, and I had a feeling this was someone I would like to know. But why was Ralph twitching toward the hottie?

"Your visitor?" Ralph prompted me.

I squinted, suddenly remembering. "Ryan?" All the thrill of meeting a new man faded as I recognized the old ball and chain from high school.

"Hey, Madison . . . hi. How are you?"

"Fine," I said brightly. *I'd be better if you'd stop calling me . . . and now stalking me in my own building!*

"Your building is right on my way to work," Ryan went on. "I pass it every day, so today I just thought, what the hell, I'll stop in and see if you want to join me for breakfast."

Which just points up all of your annoying qualities: pedantic, persistent . . . As the evil thoughts simmered, I found myself questioning his attire. "What happened to your uniform?" I asked. "Is it at the cleaners?"

He glanced down at his clothes, which, I must admit, revealed impeccable fashion sense. "I got out of the Navy years ago. Didn't your mother tell you?"

If she mentioned it, I ignored her. "Oh." I didn't want to admit that I'd actually worried about him when the war broke out in Iraq—but only in a friendly way. I checked my watch. "Damn. I am so late for work." I gave Ryan a sour look. "Do you mind? I really have to run."

"No problem," he said. "I'll run with you."

Not after my head explodes, I thought as I turned back to the doorman. "Ralph, big favor. I know you have long hours here, but we've got this toy drive going at work and—"

"Sure, I'll donate," Ralph said. "Anything for the kids."

"No, I've got the toys—thousands of them. It's just that I need help transporting them around town. Time and muscle." I held up my arm, as if my mighty biceps might bop under my camel sweater. "What do you say? Can you give me a hand?"

"Sorry, Ms. Greenwood, but my wife is already screaming about the hours I put in here. Some days, the kids are in bed by the time I get home." Ralph winced. "I just can't see spending any more time away from home."

"Oh . . . okay." I tried to hide my disappointment. "Thanks, anyway. Let me know if you can think of somebody. Anyone with time on their hands, okay?"

"Will do, Ms. Greenwood."

I turned toward the door, and Ryan fell into step beside me.

You, again, I wanted to growl as we walked under the garland-covered archway, out onto the sidewalk. Thank God he didn't notice the mistletoe hanging from the arch. I told those idiots on the co-op board that it was a bad idea!

"Great day!" Ryan said. "Warm for December."

My response was something between a grunt and a hmm; I figured that an actual word might unnecessarily encourage the guy. Why is it that a sophisticated life form like *Homo sapiens,* a creature in the top level of the hierarchy, cannot sense when he is not wanted, the way a dog smells a human's fear? What a handy trait that would be.

"So isn't that a coincidence?" he said. "My office is just a few blocks from here."

"Really." *Excuse me if I don't jump for joy.*

What was it about this guy that got my goat? Without staring I let my eyes cruise his face—still smooth, with high cheekbones; his hair—longer now, spiked a little, nice and full; and his eyes—those damned gorgeous eyes. Amazing how a guy who scored bonus points in the looks category could bomb in the personal chemistry portion of the competition. But despite the physical allure, Ryan irked me.

"I think I can help you," Ryan said.

"Pardon me?"

"With the toys. I could probably help you move them."

I stopped at the edge of the sidewalk and squeezed my eyes shut. Shit. I'd just stepped right into it. When I looked again, he was still there, watching me with all the eagerness of a puppy in the park.

"It's a worthy cause, right?" he said. "And I can steal the time from work."

"Yes, I think it's worthwhile," I muttered. "Right now the only way these toys will get to the children who desire them is if I make it happen." I paused. If I accepted his help, I would have to establish ground rules. "But here's the thing. If we do this together, it's because we both want the end result." I looked him in the eye. "This is not a ploy to get us together. Because, at the risk of being brutally honest, there's no spark between us, Ryan. Nada, nothing, zippo." There, I'd said it, earning myself a place in the Super Bitch Hall of Fame.

He nodded. "I knew that."

I had to give him credit; the guy could land on his feet with aplomb.

"How soon can you start?" I asked. "I mean, you'll probably need to talk to your boss."

He shrugged. "I'm my own boss. Well, I do have a partner, but he won't have a problem with it. Let me run it by him."

My ears perked up. "A partner?" Maybe I had pegged

Ryan all wrong. Maybe he was already involved in a committed man-to-man relationship.

"In the firm."

"What exactly do you do, Ryan?"

"Building design," he answered casually. "I'm an architectural engineer. Got most of my training in the Navy. My partner would probably help with the toys, but his wife just had a baby. Todd isn't getting too much sleep."

Okay, he's got a straight business partner. Ryan was still playing the hetero game, much to my dismay. I nodded. On paper, Ryan would be quite a catch. If only I could stand to be with him for more than five minutes.

"This is my train," I said, pausing by the Ninety-sixth Street station. I reached into the pocket of my purse for a business card. "You can call me at work. Talk to your partner, and we'll see if we can work something out." *For the children,* I reminded myself. *I will make this sacrifice for the children, even if it kills me.*

When I got to the office, I managed to reschedule the doll delivery for that day, just to give myself a little breathing space. While I was on the phone, an eager voice mail came in from Ryan. Then I called Leo at the network, where he had hobbled in because he hates to miss more than a day of dirt on who's hot and who's not in his soap story lines. Although Leo wasn't a writer, he had become one of those network middle managers who dance on the fringes of the writers' teams, offering story arc ideas, stretching characters, and basically kicking the writers in the ass when they sat on a plot point for too long.

When he answered the phone, I blurted out, "Fucking Ryan."

"Excuse me?"

"He's back. He was stalking me at my apartment this morning."

"Oh, and I was hoping this was an obscene phone call." Leo paused. "So? How does he look?"

"Fabulous. I think he's been shopping at Ferragamo. I still hate him."

"Big sigh. I'll have you know, it took me an hour to get to work this morning." He lowered his voice. "And the worst part was that I had to go down the stairs from the garret on my ass. These crutches are not the glamorous conversation piece I imagined. So what else is new?"

"Ryan is going to be my partner in the toy-moving project."

"What? I thought you hated him."

"I do, but I'm desperate."

"Santa slut."

"Oh, Leo, give me a break! I'm digging deep here, trying to come up with people. It's made me rethink everything. I mean, I'm wondering if this program is really worth it." I lowered my voice. "It's certainly not earning me any brownie points at work, and it's sucking up all my free time during the Christmas season, when I need free time to hunt down someone to spend Christmas with."

I could feel Nicole listening in from the next cubicle. When I craned my neck toward her, she picked up a file and headed into Barry's office. Great. Now my personal life would be posted in the next internal office e-mail. Nicole needed to get a life so she could pull her nose out of mine.

"Listen, Bob Crachitt," Leo was saying, "we need to have a talk. Of course the toy program is worth it. Isn't that what Christmas is about? Children? Giving? Charity? Don't make me hobble over there and spank you, girl."

I sighed. "I don't know. Working with Ryan . . . ugh!"

"Maybe he'll bail out," Leo said. "Once he figures out that you're not interested."

"He's already called to confirm," I said, not sure what to hope for. "We're on for a toy delivery in the morning."

"Oh, well . . . how can I cheer you up? Listen, maybe I was a little hard on you and your skyrocketing standards for a mate. Yes, you're picky, but with good reason. Okay, Virginia? There is a Santa Claus, and the right man will fall into your lap when you least expect it. When you stop trying so hard? That's when you'll find him."

"Are you reading from a fortune cookie?" I asked him. "Or do you have that old nugget on a bumper sticker over your desk?"

Leo laughed. "Busted!"

That evening I rode the escalator to the eighth floor of Bloomingdale's, rising into the heavenly sights and sounds of Christmas. Frank would be here in a few minutes, but first, I wanted to soak up the atmosphere.

When I asked Frank to meet me on the eighth floor of Bloomingdale's, he didn't know it was a test. Call me crazy, but the test is a protocol that must be administered to any guy I date at Christmastime. If the male candidate cannot pass the test, then he is not worth the investment. And the test is quite simple. The candidate needs to meet me at Bloomie's and simply appreciate the virtual cozy Christmasland those wizards of retail create on the eighth floor. A simple "This is wonderful," is all I ask.

You'd be surprised at the candidates who fail the test. Some come so close—a borderline grade—but I have to maintain my standards.

Case in point: the Wall Street investment banker who agreed to meet me at Bloomingdale's, but once he arrived refused to get out of the company limo. When his cell called my cell and he told me to meet him in the car by the Lexington Avenue exit, I knew it was over. In my book, if you don't like Christmas, you are not a keeper. Listen, I suffered through childhood with a cheapskate father. The last thing I need in my life—or my bed—is an Ebenezer Scrooge.

Even before the escalator reached my floor, the sounds

and scents came wafting down, scents of pine and cinnamon potpourri and candles. A trio of carolers trolled their merry cheer from the tiny mezzanine. Deep breath. Big goofy grin. Can't help myself once the Christmas sentiment washes over me. I stepped carefully off the escalator in my skinny-heeled Manolo Blahniks. There is nothing like the eighth floor of Bloomingdale's at Christmastime.

It's a wonder that I don't blow a whole week's pay here, and at times I've toyed with the notion. I lift shiny glass ornaments from their bins and imagine how they would look on my tree. I peer at the delicate displays of gingerbread houses and chocolate-mint sticks. Those sticks would be the perfect gift for the host of that last-minute Christmas party. You know, the one thrown by your distant friend's friend that you get dragged along to. Once I bought a gloriously romantic box of chocolates set in a Victorian box adorned with ribbon and lace. That box would have made a spectacular host gift, if I could have managed to restrain myself from snacking on the chocolates.

I wandered over to a separate room lined with huge wooden armoires thrown open to display fat candles and a vast assortment of wreaths adorned with pinecones or fruit or glittery white snowflakes. Although my co-op association has a rule against hanging anything on the apartment door, residents blatantly ignore it. I held up a full green wreath with a fat red bow and tried to picture it against the gray of my apartment door.

"Madison?"

I glanced up and spotted Frank, looking dapper in a navy business suit with a periwinkle blue shirt. His hooded eyes seemed very official, which gave me a moment of panic. He wasn't happy here. He hated Christmas. He was going to fail the test.

I swallowed hard, trying to think of a way to coach him without breaking the rules.

"Isn't this wonderful?" I gushed. I held the wreath up to

my face, smiling at him through the center of the circle. The red ribbon dropped down into my face, and I blew it away.

"Very nice," Frank said, lifting the ribbon. I was laughing when he leaned in toward the wreath and kissed me on the lips.

Right in the Christmas department of Bloomingdale's!

"Mmm." I had to clamp my lips down on his to keep from laughing right into his mouth. His move surprised me, but I had to give him credit for his spontaneity. And there was a real drive in his kiss. Like he'd do a heck of a lot more than kiss me if we weren't on the eighth floor of Bloomingdale's on a Wednesday evening.

The kiss ended, and I took a deep breath. "Wow."

"Yeah." He smiled. "Wow."

I lowered the wreath, holding it out so he could look at it again. "I was thinking of this for the front door of my apartment. I always decorate my place. Well, usually other years more than this year, but I always have a tree-trimming party."

He nodded. "It's nice. Do you need help hanging it?"

I blinked. Was he inviting himself over? I mean, the vibe was strong between us, and I could tell he was into me. I just wasn't sure I wanted to move quite so fast. "We'll see. I haven't made a final decision yet, but you should come to my party. It's next Friday, the nineteenth." Was it too early to put that out there? I wasn't sure how much I liked Frank yet. On the other hand, would it hurt to have one more single man over thirty at my party? If I wanted to pass him on, Nicole and the other girls from the office could always hold a silent auction for him.

"Sounds good." He unbuttoned his suit jacket and put his hands in his pocket. "They do a nice job here, don't they? New Yorkers do know how to kick it up at Christmas. The whole city gets a little bit nicer."

As he spoke, my heart grew about eight sizes larger, just like the Dr. Seuss character. I was falling in love with this guy. "Are you hungry?" I asked. "I know a great little place nearby where they serve a kick-butt margarita."

He moved next to me and slid an arm around my waist, his hand cupping my hip. Surprising, these physical displays in public. But somehow Frank made it work. "Now you're talking," he said.

We held hands all the way down seven escalators. And as we ducked under the blinking lights of Bloomie's Lexington Avenue awning, I remembered how great it felt to be a woman in love in Manhattan.

Okay, maybe just a little in love. But hey, we take what we can get.

29

December 10, 2003, 6:45 P.M.

By the time we'd finished our coconut shrimp, I knew something was not right.

Although Frank was fun to talk to, he was putting the pressure on so hard, I felt as if I were hanging from the fender of a stock car as he drove us madly careening around the track.

He wanted to hold my hand while we ate. He had to sit beside me. He had to kiss me between bites. He wanted to feed me from his fork. Hey, I'm all for romance, but a concubine I am not. Besides, I hoped to come back to Cabana, one of my favorite Cuban restaurants on the East Side, and if I didn't do something drastic to make the wait staff stop giggling behind their menus, my reputation would sink lower than yesterday's black bean soup.

Disentangling my hand from his, I went on with my story. "So anyway, my friend Sugar, the one I was telling you about? She's on that morning show."

"'Scott and Todd in the Morning'?"

"No, she's not *that* lucky. She's the Sugar of 'Mornings with Cream and Sugar.' Anyway. Sugar is in the public eye all the time, and sometimes guests pop into the radio station unannounced, and though it might be someone famous like Jennifer Aniston or Tom Hanks, she absolutely does not recognize them. She once told Andre Leon Talley, the grand pooh-bah of fashion, that he was statuesque and ought to think about modeling. Then there's the time when J. Lo walked in and she asked her—"

"Wait!" Frank interrupted, blowing on his fork. "You've got to taste this salmon."

"No, no, that's okay," I said. "Anyway, she asked J. Lo to—"

"Really. Taste it!"

"No, thanks."

"You're gonna love it," he said, shoving it toward my lips.

"Frank!" I craned my neck back, trying not to make a scene by whacking his hand and sending salmon sailing across to the next table. "Would you stop trying to feed me already? I've been managing a fork since I was one, and I hate it when you shove something into my mouth when I'm in the middle of a story."

"Sorry." He pulled the fork back sheepishly. "Was I doing that? I'm not overbearing. Really! Well, don't ask my ex-wife. Damnation! I'm sorry. I didn't mean to bring her up."

He was backpedaling so hard, I didn't have a chance to tell him that he was headed for a crash. It may seem harsh, but we weren't even halfway through our entrees and already I was writing Frank off in my mind. Nice guy, but too much baggage.

Which is the dilemma a thirty-one-year-old woman faces when she is trying to pick a mate from the remainder of available men on the planet. The majority come with too much baggage—ex-wives who've been to hell and back with them, children who dance into the scene just often enough to reprise their guilt, and oddly attractive ex-girlfriends who still come around, presumably for the "oh, what the hell, we've done it before!" fuck. The guys who come without the baggage—well, they can be the worst kind, mostly because they've got the baggage and they're not even aware of it. Okay, maybe they never married, but by the age of thirty any man worth a look has been through a string of relationships. If he says nothing serious—beep, beep!—sound the alarm; this guy suffers from acute failure to commit.

"It's just that, every year at Christmas Shari corners me about what I'm getting for the kids. And every year I tell her that I'm giving them cash, because I don't know what the hell they're interested in these days. And she blows a major gasket. Calls me Scrooge, says that if I cared I'd know what my own kids want for Christmas."

I nodded. "Shari being your ex-wife?"

He rolled his eyes. "Yeah."

"And how old are your kids?"

"Twelve and fifteen."

"Ooh, ouch. Take it from an expert gift buyer, those are tough years to buy for. You are so right to give them cash. And Shari's the one who's the Scrooge here. Maybe she's bent out of shape because you forgot *her* gift last Christmas." I tossed the idea off with a laugh, but Frank seemed to find some merit in it.

"You know, you could be right. You might have something there. I wonder . . ."

As he debated the nuances of gaining his ex-wife's approval, I began to wonder if I should uninvite Frank to my tree-trimming party. When I'd agreed to a date, I'd imagined us talking about writing. After all, Frank wrote for a newspaper, and I had been putting a good amount of my time at work into writing brochures and educational materials for many of our traveling exhibits. I enjoyed writing and I was ready to take the next step—whatever that might be—and somehow I had envisioned exploring those aspirations and interests with Frank.

My mistake. Somewhere in the back of my mind I knew that most people didn't talk about their jobs in social situations. They don't want to mix work and pleasure, and many of them hate their jobs so much that they cannot contemplate them for one extra second once they step out of the office.

I finished off my chicken salad, wondering if I should break it off with Frank now or give him until dessert to perform some miraculous reversal. Then there was the matter of uninviting him to the party.

I sighed as a waiter came by and cagily eyed our hands to make sure we were behaving. Oh, hell, as my wise friend Jenna once told me, "You don't have to decide today."

Words to live by.

So, there would be no after-dinner event with Frank, who was probably going to rush back to Bloomie's to buy his ex-wife a Christmas gift, anyway. Meanwhile, I would have a whole week to decide how I really felt about him. And if worse came to worst, he would be one more "interesting" single man at my party come Friday night.

I took a deep sip of my margarita, contemplating the wisdom of my plan.

You could never have enough "interesting" single men at a party.

30

December 11, 2003

"I'm sorry," I told Ryan, hating the fact that I had to apologize, especially since it wasn't really my fault. We were in the lobby of Sugar's building, ready to take Sugar's SUV on a toy run, but the doorman had just informed me that Sugar took the car to work. "We'll have to pick the car up at the garage by the radio station," I explained to Ryan as we headed out to the curb to hail a cab. "For some reason, Sugar drove to work. She must have forgotten I needed the SUV."

"No problem," Ryan said, easygoing as ever. Sometimes, I wished the guy would show a little annoyance. Didn't anything ever bother him?

At Thirty-fourth Street, we checked in with security in the building lobby, then rode the elevator up to the well-insulated studios of the radio station. Despite the huge success of "Mornings with Cream and Sugar," the station had a very relaxed, jovial atmosphere, which had encouraged many spontaneous celebrity visits over the past two years. An energetic receptionist greeted us outside the elevator.

"I just need the keys to Sugar's car," I told her. "She's letting me borrow it for a toy drive."

She glanced up at the studio lights. "Actually, you can go on into the studio and talk to her. They're on a commercial break now."

Ryan followed me as I went down the corridor, waved at Sugar and her fellow deejay Charles Cream through the glass studio window, then cracked open the door.

"Hey, there! Don't want to interrupt. I just need the keys to your car."

Sugar waved us in. "The toy drive! I forgot! I went with a friend for sunrise brunch in New Jersey, and we had to drive straight here." She wheeled away from the console and reached into her bag. "Here's the keys. The car's in the garage." She glanced over at Ryan. "Hey, who's the hottie?"

"Come in, come in!" Cream insisted, pointing to two empty chairs. "Have a seat, guys! We're in need of a few fresh voices this morning. You don't mind sitting in, do you?"

I swallowed, not really in the mood to "share" with New York City today, but Ryan was already seated, pulling his chair up to the counter with the microphone. *No, no! Don't sit!*

I had sat in on "Cream and Sugar" before, and though it was a thrill, an appearance required a certain level of energy and honesty that I didn't possess at the moment. "We don't have a lot of time," I said, checking my watch.

"Don't worry!" Cream emphatically directed me to the empty chair. "Sit, sit, sit! We'll plug your toy drive and get you out of here pronto."

Against my better judgment, I fell into the chair and shrugged at Ryan as the sound engineer waved Cream and Sugar out of the commercial.

"We're back on the air with two surprise guests, who I'm sure will help us with some insights on today's topic: the ever-shrinking dating pool," Cream said.

"I'm sure you all remember my best friend, Madison Greenwood," Sugar said. "She's working on the toy drive we helped promote last year. And today she's here with a delicious specimen of manhood." She leaned closer to her console to face Ryan. "Don't mean to make you blush there, big guy. Madison, why don't you introduce your man?"

"This is my friend Ryan Wilkinson. We met when we were kids in San Francisco and now he's helping me with the Taft Museum Toy Drive."

"Childhood sweethearts?" Cream prodded.

"I guess you could say that," Ryan admitted, bugging the hell out of me.

"But not anymore," I added. "Now we're just friends. I mean, until this week, the last time I saw Ryan was ten years ago when he was in the Navy."

Sugar squealed. "No way! This is Vanilla Milkshake Ryan?"

Actually, I think of him as Fucking Ryan, but I know you can get fined if you say that on the air.

"She used to call him Vanilla Milkshake," Sugar quickly explained to the listeners, "because when he wore his dress whites for the Navy he looked like a long, tall, sweet concoction! Isn't that right, girlfriend?"

Ryan squinted at me, as if processing this information in a scholarly way. I could only hope he didn't take it too seriously.

"Something like that," I muttered.

Sugar giggled. "So maybe we should say, today we have Sugar and Cream and Vanilla Milkshake, too. Sorry, Madison, can't work you in unless you want to be an avenue."

Oh, hardy-har-har. How did Sugar stand this small talk every day?

"Well, this is a banner day," Cream said quickly. "Seeing Madison with a real live guy in tow. For a minute there, I thought you were going to provide evidence that the dating pool was actually growing. It's not every day that a woman walks in with such a good-looking guy at her side."

"I didn't say I couldn't find good-looking guys," Sugar

claimed. "I'm just saying that they're not date material, Cream. You know, sometimes you don't listen."

"I do listen, just not to you, Sugar," Cream teased. "Anyway, guys, we were just talking about the shrinking dating pool, which Sugar is always complaining about."

"With good reason," Sugar cut in. "Every time I look, there are fewer datable men out there, and I know Madison has the same problem. At least, I thought you did, Madison, until you walked in with Vanilla Milkshake."

"He's just a friend," I repeated, leaning into the mike. "Ryan and I have been friends forever."

"Since high school," Ryan added. "Then I went off into the Navy. Hence the nickname, Vanilla Milkshake."

"But you've changed your look," Sugar said. "What can we call you now? Banana Boy? You're looking very Banana Republic. Or is it J. Crew?"

Ryan smiled. "Maybe a little of both. But please, I'd rather not be named after a fruit."

Sugar and Cream laughed, and I blinked. Ryan was a lot more adept with the clever responses on the air than I would have expected. Okay, maybe I tended to push him back into that adolescent high school compartment, but in my mind it was where our relationship had ended.

"But back to the shrinking dating pool," Cream said. "Because if I don't keep this show on track, nobody will."

"That's for sure," Sugar teased. "Because you know I'll just go off and plug my January centerfold. Which, by the way, should be out in two weeks. I'm expecting an advance copy any day now." Yes, my good friend Sugar Plum was spreading her own brand of cheer in the pages of *Playboy* this holiday season. Initially I had tried to talk her out of it, but of course, she didn't listen, and in the long run, Sugar had loved the entire experience.

"Yes, yes, we've heard all about that, and I'm sure we'll hear more," Cream said. "So Madison, what's your take on this shrinking dating pool?"

"Cream, I would say it's not even a pool anymore. Call it a puddle of men."

"That shallow, eh?" Cream whistled. "I've only been with my partner a year and you'd think a dating millennium had passed. Is it really that bad?"

"It's ridiculous," I said. "And you are talking to two women here who really step out and give the man-tree a shake. We're active and assertive, not that it does us any good."

"Do you ever look back and worry about the one that got away? The fish that slipped off the hook?" Cream asked.

"Never," Sugar insisted.

"How about you, Madison? Worry about those missed opportunities?"

"I don't think I've walked away from 'The One,' if that's what you mean. But this Christmas I've been all over town with the toy drive we're doing at the Taft Museum, and everywhere I go I encounter ghosts of boyfriends past."

"Ghosts of boyfriends past?" Cream giggled. "I love that! And what do the ghosts say?"

"Mostly they seem to harp on me for being a single woman in my thirties," I said.

"Ugh!" Cream groaned. "Like that's a crime."

"There's so much pressure to mate," Sugar said. "I keep telling you that, Cream. The message is out there: Be part of a couple or you're not a worthwhile being."

"Now there's a depressing thought," Cream said. "Well, I'm here to say, it's not true! Single women of New York, we love you! We validate you! There is room on this planet for you, too!"

"Uh, Cream?" Sugar said. "That's very sweet of you, but you already have a significant other. It's sort of easy for you to say, when you've got a sweetie to go home to."

"Guilty," Cream admitted, "and yet I still believe in the message. You don't need a mate to be worthwhile in this world."

"Amen, brother," Sugar said.

I forced a smile, feeling like the girl who never gets asked to dance. It was nice of Cream to put the positive word out there, but it didn't make me feel any better about being single. I wanted to meet that one special person, and no amount of consolation prizes was going to dissuade me from competing in the contest.

"Now, let's talk about that toy drive you mentioned," Cream went on.

As I rattled off the information, putting in a plug for a delivery service that might want to donate its time, I started to feel sorry for myself. Cream had just advertised my lonely single status to all of New York. I was stuck moving toys with a guy I could barely stand. And during all these hours I spent away from my job, the work was piling up on my desk.

My life was the pits, and with Christmas coming and the pressure to find holiday bliss increasing, things were bound to get worse.

31

Within the hour, Ryan and I were at Times Square, backing Sugar's Volvo SUV into the loading dock. "This is an awesome car," Ryan said as the worker waved me in within what must have been inches of smashing the bumper. "I've seen the XC40 advertised, but I never rode in one. When did Sugar get it?"

"It's brand new," I muttered, breathlessly watching the signalman in my rearview mirror.

"Okay!" he shouted.

I slammed on the brake and sighed, relieved that I'd managed to maneuver it into the bay without body damage. "She put a down payment on it when she got the money from her centerfold spread." I rested my head on the wheel a second. "You know, maybe you can drive the next leg. Now that I think of it, I don't think I have a valid license anymore." I certainly didn't need one, living in Manhattan.

"No problem," Ryan said. "But what did you mean by a centerfold?"

I grinned. "Yep, Sugar Plum is Ms. January. Can you believe it?"

"Well." That seemed to stump Ryan for a moment. "She seems to have the right attributes for it, but I thought that female nudity in magazines was considered derogatory toward women."

"Sugar sure didn't seem to mind it." We piled out of the car and spoke with the head of the loading dock, who told us that we wouldn't be allowed to load the car ourselves—something about liability issues—but he'd have his workers take care of it. We were to check back with him in an hour.

"Okay, then," I said as we headed out of the garage area into a sunny but cold day. I wrapped my scarf tighter and buttoned my trench coat, a little sorry that I hadn't worn boots today. When the wind blew, it was downright nippy.

"Let's get in out of the cold," Ryan said. "How about coffee?"

We hustled across Broadway to the nearest Starbucks, shivering all the way.

"So what's our cargo today, boss?" Ryan asked as we waited for a light to change.

"Lego sets," I told him. "We need to deliver half of them to the Police Athletic League. The other half will go to the museum, since they tie in with our Ancient World collection. Can you believe they have blocks designed so you can build a pyramid with a removable mummy's tomb? Since we have a mummy and sarcophagus at the museum, Barry is thrilled to have an educational tool we can give out to supplement a child's visit to the museum."

"Sounds cool," Ryan said. "I wonder if my niece would like something like that."

"How old is she?"

"She's seven, but she's a tomboy. Loves basketball and video games." Ryan held the door to Starbucks open as I stepped in. "Maybe you can meet her. I think she and my sister are coming to stay for Christmas."

"That's nice." Notice I did not say that *would be* nice. The last thing I wanted to do was meet Ryan's family when I should be out there soaking up the remaining drops of the shrinking dating pool. This morning's topic on "Cream and

Sugar" had made me feel more driven than ever to go hunting and gathering for a mate.

While Ryan went to get our drinks, I found a table by the window, where we could watch tourists pose for photos. From here, I could see the old marquee of the Palace Theater as well as the newer theater that always seemed to be part of the downstairs lobby of the Marriott Hotel.

Last Christmas, I had seen *Aida* at the Palace Theater with Philippe Margot, who was visiting from France. A blind date via Sugar, Philippe was charming—knowledgeable about fashion and cuisine and theater—but I never really got the feeling that he liked me. Oh, I was fine as a dinner companion, but I think he was holding out for someone more haute couture. Like some *Vogue* or *Vanity Fair* editor . . . or maybe Harvey Fierstein. Of course, this is all wild speculation, as Philippe never confided in me. But trust me, after a handful of blind dates, a girl knows when she's about to be ditched for the likes of Eddie Izzard.

A few years before that, it was a revival of *Damn Yankees* in the Marriott Theater, with Sean, who had cheered for all the baseball references but was totally lost when Bebe Neuwirth tried to seduce Joe in the "Whatever Lola Wants" number. That was one of the things about Sean; not only did subtlety elude him, but he also seemed to miss many of the more obvious moments in life. A gorgeous guy, that Sean, and not bad as a love slave, but when I finally accepted the fact that he was as obtuse as a statue at MoMA, I knew it was time to let him go.

"Sugar?" Ryan called.

"Huh?" I shook my head. "No, I'm Madison. Sugar is back at the radio station."

"Do you want sugar with your coffee?" he asked as he sat two paper cups on the table. "You're a million miles away. Did you want milk?"

"Just that toxic sugar substitute," I said, shaking a little packet.

"What are you so preoccupied about?" Ryan asked as he sat down across from me.

"Just visiting with some of my old ghosts. Whenever I walk through Times Square, I think of the Broadway shows I saw. I can usually connect the theater with the show, and the person I saw it with."

"That's what you meant about ghosts of boyfriends past?" He studied me carefully. "And what about me, Madison. What category do I fit in?"

His question took me by surprise. "Well, you were definitely an old boyfriend, but since you're sitting right across from me, you can haunt me in person."

"That wasn't what I meant."

Uh-oh . . . he was pushing the old romance pitch again. "To be honest, I see you as a brother, Ryan. Always there, annoying at times, but lovable and trustworthy."

"So you do trust me?"

"Of course I trust you! You are probably the most trustworthy person in my life."

"But I'm annoying." He lifted his coffee to his lips, then paused. "In what way?"

"Because you ask so many damn questions!" I bellowed as my cell phone started to ring.

I nodded as I grabbed the phone. "This will just take a minute," I told Ryan. Although I was happy for the interruption, I hate people who talk on their cell phones while they're with someone else. It's downright rude. Even if Ryan was not my favorite person in the world, I refused to stoop to that level and breach my personal sense of etiquette.

"I heard you on the radio." It was Leo.

"What? Weren't you at work?"

"I was on my way in a cab, and I had the driver turn it up. I can't believe you brought Ryan on with you."

"It wasn't really my choice," I lamented, "and I can't talk now."

"He's with you, isn't he?"

"Yes."

"In bed?"

"No! We're waiting for a few cases of toys to be loaded into the car."

"Oh, well, I just have to say, the chemistry between you two is amazing. If we could bottle it, I'd pour it all over our romantic leads on *All Our Tomorrows.*"

"Are you kidding me?" I was miffed. On the air I had griped about how hard it was to find a guy, and Leo interpreted that as romantic chemistry?

"You two really came across."

"You've got it all wrong, Leo. Maybe you were listening to 'Scott and Todd in the Morning.' "

"Listen, Ms. Avenue, I'm your best friend and I know these things."

"Whatever. I have to go."

"You go, girl," Leo said. "We'll talk later."

I flipped my phone closed, shaking my head. "I am sorry," I told Ryan. "Sometimes I think cell phones were a cruel invention to completely isolate people in their own society."

Ryan laughed. "I like your theory."

My phone rang again, and I gritted my teeth. "If it's Leo, I'm hanging up on him. Hello?"

"Madison? It's Nicole. From the office."

"Nicole . . . hi. I'm just out this morning on a toy delivery. Is everything okay there?"

"Well, yeah. I just heard you on the radio."

Didn't anyone in this city do their jobs anymore? "Oh, no, tell me it wasn't on in the office." The last thing I needed was for Barry to think I was out promoting myself while he gave me time off to work on the toy drive.

"No, but I was listening on my Walkman while I checked proofs. Your friend Ryan sounds very nice."

"He is," I said, wishing Nicole would get to the point.

"Were you serious about just being friends with him?"

"Of course. We're friends."

"Then *I* want him!" Nicole blurted out. "When can you introduce me?"

Leaning back in my chair, I glanced at Ryan's handsome face as a wickedly clever idea gelled in my brain. Ryan and Nicole . . . Nicole and Ryan . . . it was serendipitous. I would be instrumental in bringing two people together, in ridding my life of two needy individuals.

"How about my party, next week?" I asked Nicole. "Are you coming?"

"I'll come if he's going to be there."

"Let me work on it and I'll get back to you," I said, flipping my phone shut.

"So Ryan," I said, lifting my warm paper cup. "Did I mention my tree-trimming party next Friday night?"

32

December 19, 2003

Although I will never match my mother's talent as an entertaining hostess, I pushed myself to throw the tree-trimming party each year. It was a great way to get single guys into my apartment, and as long as I kept the liquor flowing and the food trays filled, the tree got decorated in no time.

This year, party preparations had been hampered by my supercharged schedule: moving toys around town with Ryan, trying to squeeze in a few hours of quality work at the office each day, then rushing to the stores at night to take care of my Christmas shopping. Although I only needed to buy for Mom, Leo, Sugar, Wolf, and my Secret Santa at the office, the process of shopping was so much a Christmas ritual that I couldn't bear to give it up, even after I'd accumulated all the gifts on my list.

Thanks to Ralph the doorman, my tree was set up in front of the window, its branches relaxed and ready to be adorned. The beer was iced down, the wine was uncorked, and I'd mixed up a pitcher of whiskey sours. Thanks to my buddies Dean and Deluca, the quiches were warming in the oven, and the table was loaded up with salads, pumpkin-cranberry muffins, and a huge platter of salmon spread shaped like a giant fish.

Pausing in front of the mosaic-tile-framed mirror by the kitchen, I checked out my new acquisition. The classic woman's black evening tux was sexy and elegant, its black velvet vest revealing just the right amount of cleavage to take the mannish edge off. The dramatic tail of the jacket did make me feel a little like a penguin, but it was sort of fun to feel it flopping back and forth as I moved through the apartment. I was sipping a whiskey sour and setting out boxes of ornaments when Ralph buzzed to let me know that the first guests were on their way up. I slid a bunch of Christmas CDs into the carousel, pressed play, and opened the door.

Jenna was the first off the elevator, leading with her wide, ample tummy.

"Look at you, sticking out of your coat!" I ran into the hall to throw my arms around her. "You look great!"

"Thanks. Benjamin takes good care of me," she said, flashing a loving look at her husband.

"Hey, Madison." Benjamin gave me a hug, then gestured toward a tall man with dark hair and a black cashmere coat. "This is our friend and neighbor, Owen Drummond."

"Hey, there! Merry Christmas," I said, extending a hand.

Owen shook my hand firmly, peering at me through thin wire-framed glasses. Definitely the studious type, which is sometimes fun to defile. "So where's the party?" he asked.

"Jingle Bell Rock" spilled out of the apartment as I waved them in. "Help yourself. Drinks are in the kitchen, but I will wait on you, pregnant lady." The guys ducked into the kitchen. I danced Jenna around until she giggled. "What can I get you? Eggnog? Milk? Or seltzer?"

"Nothing yet," Jenna said, slipping off her coat. She wore a smart houndstooth tunic with a black velvet collar over a black skirt. Cute, but nothing could divert the eye from her huge belly.

"You are enormous," I said. "Sugar and I are determined to throw you a shower, but we can't find a date. Maybe after the holidays?"

"Oh, you don't have to," Jenna said. "Really, my neighbors and business associates have done so much—two baby showers already. We've got the crib and a roomful of baby clothes. Everything will be decorated with a Noah's Ark theme. Benjamin is going to put up the wallpaper next week."

"Sounds great," I said, though I worried that any gift I purchased would seem inappropriate now that a theme had been chosen. Did I need to buy tiny baby clothes with animals on them? Little ark-shaped booties? A lion-head cap? Jenna was entering an alien world, and I wasn't completely comfortable letting her go. I had a million questions for her. Was she still happy being married to Benjamin? Was she afraid of the pain of childbirth? Was she thinking of leaving her job in the psych ward at that Queens Children's Hospital?

But now wasn't the time for girl talk, especially since Benjamin and Owen had reappeared with drinks. Benjamin went over to admire my tree. "This looks nice and fresh," he said, tugging on a few pine needles. "Do you want me to put the lights on?"

"Benjamin is great at stringing lights," Jenna told me as she rubbed her belly. "Go on, honey. We may not be able to stay till the end, so let's get the tree started."

Meanwhile, Owen paced through the living room, examining my wall hangings as if he were visiting a gallery. "I heard you were in the art field," he said without looking at me.

"Owen teaches at Queens College," Jenna said, trying to stir up a mutual attraction between us. "He was my advisor when I did my clinicals. He teaches psych."

"Oh, really? That must be interesting," I said. "How do you find the caliber of students these days? Is it a challenge to teach them, or are standards slipping?"

"Some of them are brilliant," he said. "My wife was one

of those. A remarkable aptitude, but did she apply herself?" He shook his head. "I find that many of my students are simply lazy, fraught with a strong sense of entitlement . . ."

Did he say wife? As Owen went on I mouthed "Wife?" to Jenna.

"Owen means his ex-wife," Jenna interrupted. "He's divorced."

"The paperwork will be filed in January," Owen said. "It's sad to think that I'll become another statistic of our society—another failed marriage."

Sad is right, I thought. I stepped back, seeking escape, then grabbed a tray of cheese balls to cover the fact that I was trying to get away from Owen. In theory, I had no objection to dating a man who was divorced, but there was divorced and there was Night of the Walking Wounded.

"Cheese ball anyone?" I asked, holding out the tray.

Jenna and Benjamin helped themselves, but Owen declined. He probably had major food allergies, too. Lactose intolerance. One sniff of a nut and he would blow up like the Fuji blimp.

"Where did you get this picture?" he asked me, nodding at a print.

"I don't know, it's a fairly popular painting by Mary Cassatt. Do you know her work?"

"It looks familiar," he said. "Haunting." His eyes searched from behind his glasses, as if I had the answer he was looking for. "I find it interesting that you would choose to hang it here in your living room."

I hugged the cheese ball platter and turned away. "I like it," I said, ducking into the kitchen before he asked me to hop on the couch and tell him all about my father. Note to self: Remind Jenna not to bring any more psycho psych experts around.

Another bachelor out of the running. Disappointed, I caught a glimpse of my fabulous tux in the reflection from the toaster. I hoped this classic outfit wouldn't be wasted.

Maybe Frank could come through tonight, emerging from his former shadow and proving himself to be a strong, stand-up guy worth pursuing. Fingers crossed, I went out to answer the doorman's buzz.

The apartment quickly began to fill up with people. My boss, Barry, arrived with his partner, Upton, one of the sweetest guys I'd ever met. Mrs. Warner from next door appeared with a dish of kugel. Leo sprang off the elevator, maneuvering like a champ on his crutches. A group of women from the museum came together, a traveling cloud of perfumes barbed with manicured nails. Nicole wore a leopard-print skirt that was just a tad too tight to be tasteful, but I bit my tongue, sensing that she was nervous about meeting the man of her dreams.

"Okay, everyone, you've got to put at least three ornaments on the tree," I said. "If everyone does their part, then you'll be allowed to return to your homes with peace and goodwill!"

The women from the office gathered around the tree, commenting on Benjamin's fine job stringing the lights. I hurried over and pulled out a few ornaments I wanted to hang myself: a papier-mâché globe of the earth that I'd made for my father in Brownies, a crystal teardrop Mom had brought me from Switzerland, and the snow globe of Rockefeller Center that Leo had given me some ten years ago.

"Do you remember giving this to me?" I asked, dangling it in front of him. "That was ten years ago."

He swiped the ornament and gave it a shake. "I can't believe I still work there."

"I can't believe we're still friends," I teased.

He rolled his eyes. "You'd be lost without me, Ms. Avenue, and you know it."

"Maybe so," I said, "but just remember who introduced you to the love of your life."

"Ugh! You're never going to let that debt go," Leo growled.

"Never!" I said, taking the snow globe back to hang on the tree.

When Ryan arrived, I gave him a perfunctory introduction until we came to Nicole. I had planned to give her a major buildup, but there was one problem: I couldn't think of a positive way to sell her. I mean, she's always struck me as a nosy, spoiled brat. Last month I found out her parents paid cash for her co-op on West Twenty-fourth. Cash! That wouldn't bother me so much if she weren't so competitive at work, always reminding Barry of the work she's done, always pointing out my failings to him in her whiny, victim voice.

So anyway, I kept saying things like: "Nicole and I work very closely together." Or "We're almost cubicle mates!" Or "Nicole is a good person to know." Whatever the hell that meant.

Of course, being the polite guy that he was, Ryan stayed captive at Nicole's side, listening as she talked her nonsense about shopping for Christmas gifts and walking into a great sale at Bed, Bath and Beyond.

I was a little annoyed with Nicole, having spent the week prepping her with interesting little nuggets about Ryan. I had found out that he lived in a restored carriage house in the Village, a place he was proud of. I told her to ask about his years in the Navy. I'd tipped her off that he was an architectural engineer, and even recommended that she pick up a copy of *Architectural Digest* to get a feel for the landscape.

All this prep work, and here she was telling him about a bath boutique?

I actually felt a little sorry for Ryan as I wandered off, but then again, the guy knew nobody in New York, so even the vacant-minded Nicole would be a start.

Mission accomplished, I moved over to laugh with Leo and Jenna, who was telling a story about Benjamin's nerves over being a new father. Which put me in a position by the door when Frank arrived.

"Hey, there," he said, handing me a little gift bag. "I brought you an ornament," he said, "and something else." He stepped forward and pulled me into his arms, planting his lips on mine.

Ooh! I blinked in surprise, trying to answer the kiss without breaking into heavy petting. But then, as my warm feelings swelled with the chorus of *N Sync's "Merry Christmas, Happy Holidays," Frank thrust his hips forward and ground against me, performing a primitive dry-hump ritual for all to see.

"Excuse me?" I didn't mean to sound like a schoolteacher, but this guy was definitely going to detention. "Is that a lump of coal in your stocking, or are you happy to see me?" I grabbed his shoulders and shoved him away. "Christ, Frank. A little subtlety, please."

"Sorry." He shrugged sheepishly. "But it's good to see you, Madison."

"Do *I* get a kiss?" Sugar asked, appearing in the doorway. She looked stunning in her winter white Arden coat, trimmed in faux fur and slit up to the wazoo in the front. She squeezed Frank's arm, then patted his cheek affectionately. "I have no idea who you are, but I must admit, I like your Neanderthal style."

He grinned at me. "At least someone appreciates me."

"He's a total horndog," I told Sugar.

She shrugged. "The sign of a good party—there's something for everyone." She dropped her leather bag from her shoulder and pulled it open. "And I've brought a little Christmas surprise. My preview of January *Playboy* came today."

"No way." I draped an arm over her shoulder as she turned to the "Sugar Plum" feature. The headline, "Visions of Sugar Plum," was superimposed in dark red over a glossy photo of Sugar licking her fingers, naked, of course. The angles of creamy light over her mocha skin were exquisite, from the curve of her hips to the delicate fullness of her breasts.

"Wow! You look great! The smooth texture of your skin, and the sculpted curves. You could be one of Michelangelo's goddesses."

"Yeah," Frank moaned, leaning close. "Really nice."

Smiling, Sugar sighed. "Man, I am so happy with the way it turned out. And what a pleasure it was, doing the work."

"And the pleasure just keeps on keeping on," Frank said, devouring the photo. "Go on, turn the page."

Sugar turned the page and squealed. "Oh, man! This one turned out great!" In the photo, Sugar's legs were propped up on the console of a studio with a microphone popping up between her legs. "They got a bunch of these, with me in this pretend radio station. Isn't it hysterical? Wait till Cream sees them. He's gonna wet his pants."

Frank's eyes were bugging out. "Ouch, baby. You are one sexy thing."

Sugar squinted at him. "Who are you, anyway?"

He extended his hand, with a smug smile. "Frank Falcone, and the pleasure is all mine."

Shaking his hand, Sugar let out a full-bodied laugh. "You're a real crackup, Frank."

I patted Sugar's shoulder, warning her: "Keep an eye on him. He bites."

Frank let out a low growl, and Sugar laughed again.

I couldn't believe she was humoring the creep. I also couldn't believe I thought I might fall for him. Big sigh. I was running out of possible dates, and the party was only half over.

Now was the winter of my discontent.

33

December 22, 2003

It was through a haze of a very sour whiskey sour hangover that I had spent the weekend cleaning up my apartment and trying to remember the significant events of the party.

1. My tree was trimmed. With its colored lights and multi-generational, multicultural mishmash of ornaments, this tree had character.

2. Ryan had invited everyone at my party to his place for an open house on Christmas Eve. I couldn't remember his face, but I assume that he must have been as drunk as I was to extend such a sweeping invitation. Which reminded me, I needed to warn Ryan to expect a crowd. Knowing my friends, they'd show.

3. Everyone had celebrated Sugar's appearance in *Playboy*. I vaguely remembered extracting staples so that we didn't rip her belly button.

On Monday, at the office, Nicole was so in love with Ryan, she was chattering a mile a minute. "He lives in a carriage house. Have you seen his place? It's so charming, sort of like a country home in the middle of the city. I'm helping him decorate for the open house. You're coming, aren't you? Oh, it's going to be a wonderful party. By the way, Ryan wanted to make sure you're still on for the toy delivery today. You're supposed to call him if it's cancelled. You have his number, right? At the architectural design firm? I can't believe I'm dating an architect . . ."

I tried to ignore her as I draped gluey newspaper around the cardboard tube from a paper towel, trying to shape my creation into a mummy's sarcophagus. It was one of the crafts I was writing up for our *Ancient Arts Educational Guide,* and I never included a craft that I couldn't do myself. However, when I chose this activity, I hadn't expected to have the nearly irresistible desire to cover myself with sticky paper and curl up in a mummy's coffin for a few thousand years.

Why was I so depressed? I had just matched up two people who were bound to be infinitely more happy than J. Lo and Ben. I had just thrown one of the wildest, most festive, tree-trimming parties in my building's history (much to Ralph's dismay—he'd warned me that I'd be getting a slap on the wrist from the co-op board).

Pinching the edges of my mummy's head, I shaped a headdress, then sat it on the edge of my desk to dry. Tomorrow, I would see whether paint or markers worked best to draw the face and decorate the body. So far, the project seemed easy enough, though my hands, covered with varying layers of white, peeling glue, were beginning to resemble a decaying mummy. I was on my way to the rest room to wash my gluey hands when I nearly ran into Ryan in the reception area.

"Oh, that's right, we've got a delivery this afternoon," I said, peeling some dried glue from one thumb. Then I noticed that Ryan held a bouquet of flowers—red roses surrounded by a delicate white spray. I lifted my peeling hands toward them, feeling a little tickled that he'd brought me flowers, then annoyed that he was so persistent with this ridiculous courtship . . . then embarrassed when I realized they probably weren't for me.

"They're for Nicole," he said, confirming my suspicion. "What happened to your hands? Molting season?"

"I was doing a kid project," I said, dropping my hands to my sides. "Why don't you go on into the office? I'll be there in a second." Swiftly I turned away to make my escape. Maybe if I dunked my head in cold water my big, red face would cool down.

When I returned to the office, Ryan sat on the edge of Nicole's desk, which was beside mine, while Nicole fluttered around looking for a flower vase and gushing over how "gooagious" the flowers were.

"Did you see them, Madison?" she asked. "Aren't they beautiful? That was so sweet of you, Ryan. Flowers for no reason. Isn't he great?"

"He's amazing." I sat at my desk and shook the mouse to bring my computer to life. "If you don't mind, Ryan, I just want to update my notes before we go. We're actually not due at KayBee Toys for another hour."

"No problem," he said, swinging around toward my desk. He leaned close to my sticky project. "What's this? A model of a mummy?"

"Ten points for you," I said, clicking open the Ancient Treasures file. "It's one of the projects that will be added to our family guide for the Ancient Treasures exhibit."

"A guidebook?"

"Actually, it's a complimentary activity book that's given out to all visitors under the age of twelve." I handed him a pamphlet from our Medieval World exhibit. "It contains kid-friendly information about the exhibit, along with activities to reinforce learning at home. Places to draw pictures, crosswords, word searches, projects."

He flipped through the family guide. "You wrote this?"

I nodded. "That's my job."

"It's great. Very accessible, and I like the choice of illustration."

My fingers flew over the keyboard as I wrote in a few new sentences. "I didn't bust my butt on an MFA for nothing."

"Do you enjoy your work?"

I paused, my fingers poised over the keyboard. "Actually, I do. When I came here, the museum had nothing in the way of educational programs. Attendance was down, and when children came to visit, the docents didn't have tours that tied in with school curricula. Now, all that's changed. Not only do we have docents trained to guide school groups, but also we have the educational materials to reinforce what kids learned on their visit." I shrugged. "I feel as if I made a difference here, and it's a joy to write about art treasures from different historic periods."

He nodded. "That's what it's about, isn't it? Making a difference. Accomplishing goals that matter to you."

"Yes," I said, thoughtfully. "That's true." I hadn't thought much about my job since I'd joined the museum four years ago, but looking back, I was proud of the body of work I'd accomplished here.

"My niece would love this," he said. "Maybe she can tour the museum when she visits for Christmas."

"I'm sure we can get her in," I said, projecting ahead. Christmas was Thursday, and at the moment, aside from the open house at Ryan's place, my calendar was completely open. Hell, I could give the kid a personally guided tour.

I was that available. Scary.

A few minutes later, I yanked Ryan away from a gushing, blushing Nicole and headed off to KayBee Toys to pick up a shipment of dolls, games, and cars. Today's booty was headed for Union Hill Hospital, where the pediatrics ward was in need of some diversions for their patients. When we arrived at the hospital, we were given wheelie carts and told to bring the gifts straight to the ward, where a nurse met us with a smile.

"This is wonderful!" she said. "The children are in the dayroom, and they'll be thrilled to see you. If you'll suit up, you can go on in and give out some of the toys yourself."

I looked at Ryan. "Do you have the time?" Although we'd made nearly a dozen toy deliveries, this was the first time we were invited to meet the children.

"Sure," he said. "Just wish I'd brought my clown nose."

Suiting up meant changing into scrubs in prints of pink, bright red, purple, and turquoise. "Some of the children have compromised immune systems, so we need to keep out the street bacteria," the nurse said. She even gave us little booties to cover our shoes. Then we headed in.

"We heard you needed some new toys in here," I said as we wheeled in our stash.

"Ho, ho, ho! Merry Christmas!" Ryan bellowed, making me laugh.

A little girl with bright eyes and baby dreads looked up from her wheelchair. "You're not Santa," she said. "You're way too skinny."

"And I don't come from the North Pole, either," Ryan said, going over to squat beside her so that his face was at her level. "You're very observant. What's your name?"

I handed cars to two squealing boys who were playing with blocks on a mat. As I grabbed a few dolls, Ryan settled in with his new friend Nayasia.

She frowned at him. "Where you from?"

"Northern California," he said. "But don't hold it against me. Would you like a doll?" When she looked away, he added: "No, you look too mature for dolls. How about a game? Monopoly? Guess Who?"

"Guess Who," Nayasia said.

"Excellent choice," Ryan said, taking the game from the cart. "I never did understand why anyone would want to invent a game about American economics."

She laughed as he handed her the game and wheeled her over to a table. "You're funny."

As Ryan started a game with Nayasia, I handed out toys to the other children in the room. I got down on the mat to play with the boys, who seemed to enjoy knocking down every tower I built by driving their car into it. A few minutes later, a nurse came to take them back to their rooms, and other children came in. I made sure each child received a gift, but Ryan made sure they all had a chance to laugh. He clowned around, juggling blocks, then stacking them on his head to do a dramatic pratfall on the mat. He made a show of letting one of the baby dolls wet his shirt, then complained that the doll was leaking. The girls got a huge giggle out of that one.

By the time we left, I was feeling warm and fuzzy toward this new Ryan, a guy who could laugh at himself and reach kids on their own level. As we walked toward the lobby, I couldn't help but tease him. "What's with the comedy routine? Have you been taking lessons from Jim Carrey?"

"Those kids need a few laughs," he said.

"But from you? I mean, honestly, Ryan, I didn't think you had it in you."

"See, that's the thing about you, Madison. You've got me pigeon-holed in this pimply high school geek place. What would you say my greatest flaws were?"

"Before today?" I bit my lip. "Well, that you're corny and sort of dull and . . . persistent."

"Aha! I knew it." He pointed a finger at me as we reached the lobby. "You left out pimply."

"Not anymore." Outside, fat flakes of snow were falling. "I love snow in December." I smiled. "So fair is fair. Now you get to take a shot at me. What are my greatest flaws?"

He rolled his eyes. "That's easy. You're inflexible, resistant to change, and stubborn as a bull."

"I am not! That is so not true."

"Do you want to cancel your evening plans and have dinner with me?"

"No way."

He grinned. "Told you." He flicked a finger on my nose, then danced off into the snow, jumping up to click his heels. "I'm singin' in the snow," he sang.

I stood there in awe. Who was this man?

"Corny, maybe," he called to me. "But *dull?* Now that is completely wrong. You underestimate me."

Buttoning my coat under the hospital awning, I realized Ryan was right. I had mistaken him for the guy he was ten years ago, and he'd definitely evolved into a person with many facets and dimensions. But silliness? Who was this man, dancing and singing down the snowy avenue?

I was no longer quite sure.

34

December 22, 2003

When my cell phone rang I was on the eighth floor of Bloomingdale's, holding a delicate pink blown-glass ornament frosted at the top with sparkling white glitter. It was shaped like a tiny little sprite, an enthralled pixie holding a thin glass wand that stretched out, as if casting a spell over the world. The wand wobbled in place, but the salesclerk had checked in the back and this was the last one. I figured that was an omen, so I had to have it. Although the ornament wasn't very Christmasy, something about it had attracted me. The fairy was so ethereal and joyous that I wanted her on my tree, bringing a ray of hope into my life.

But really, how many more ornaments did I need? She was totally impractical. Which made me want her that much more.

Anyway, when my cell rang, I had to put her on the shelf beside two baskets of candy canes and dig through my bag. I flipped open the phone. "Hello?"

"It's me." Ryan. Why was I disappointed? He was supposed to meet me here in half an hour.

"I'm at Bloomingdale's already," he said. "Do you want

me to go up to the customer service office and get things going?"

"No, no, I'm here, too. Meet me up on the eighth floor and we'll go together."

"Gotcha."

I moved down the aisle, browsing through snow globes of Victorian scenes and Hanukkah candies. I was eyeing some adorable foil-wrapped chocolate dreidels when Ryan joined me.

He wore a brown leather bomber jacket and worn blue jeans—very casual, but there was something different about him. His eyes seemed sharper, shinier, and happy. Ryan looked as if he'd just won the lottery.

"Wow." He put his hands in his pockets and eyeballed the place. "Wow."

"Ready to go?" I asked. "Customer service is just around the corner."

"This is an amazing place," he said, walking over to a bin of ornaments. "The music, the decorations . . . I mean, look at these trees. What a fabulous Christmasland. Don't you just want to crawl under one of the tables and stay until New Year's?"

I clutched the edge of a fake snow-covered bin and wondered why the right things happened with the wrong person. This was the reaction I had been waiting for all these years. Finally, a man who shared my hopeless enthusiasm for Christmas, and with my screwy luck that man had to be Ryan. The fates were definitely cursing me this year.

"It's a great little Christmas boutique," I said begrudgingly. "Let me just pay for this ornament and then we'll go." I went back to the shelf with the candy canes and reached for my little pink fairy. She sat there on the shelf, but somehow her little glass wand had broken off.

"Oh, no," I frowned. "My little fairy of hope."

"Nice ornament," Ryan said.

"It's broken." Disappointment weighed me down.

He looked closely. "I see. Where did you find it? You can pick up another one."

"No, it's the last one," I said, sitting her on the shelf again. I hated to leave her behind, and I wondered how she had snapped apart. "We'd better go," I said, feeling inordinately sad about the little pink ornament. *Hormones,* I told myself as Ryan and I headed off to customer service. *Hormone imbalance coupled with Christmas frenzy. A dangerous combination.*

It turned out that our toy donation was ready, but the customer service people wanted to gift wrap them for us. "It'll just take us an hour or so," said the store representative. "Why don't you go take a walk or something and meet us at the loading dock in two hours?"

"Hungry?" Ryan asked.

I had to admit, it had been awhile since I'd eaten. "You know, there's a cute place near here, and if you liked the Christmasland, you'll love Serendipity," I said, thinking of Serendipity 3. It was one of those little fairy-tale enclaves that put on a festive, whimsical face even when it wasn't decorated for Christmas. Besides, they sold cool little toys downstairs. "Let's go grab a sandwich."

While we waited for a table at Serendipity, Ryan and I had fun playing with the little toys and sorting through the sparkly tchotchkes in the ninety million bins lining the shelves. The restaurant was draped with garland adorned with glittering white lights, just enough glitter to make you feel festive without feeling like you're in a casino.

"Check this out," he said, showing me a spinning whirly doo-hickey.

"How do you make that spin? I was working on that one for hours," I insisted.

"I'll give you lessons at the table," he said, handing me the toy. After we were seated, he showed me how to operate the complicated gizmo. It twirled so fast it made my hair blow back.

"I see. Yes, Ryan, that engineering degree has definitely paid off. Your mother would be proud to know that you can make the whirligigs at toy stores go round."

He grinned. "I always told you I had hidden talents."

"Right." I snapped open my menu, realizing I'd been unduly hard on Ryan over the years. His intentions were always kind, and underneath that dull facade he had a smart sense of humor. Yes, I'd underestimated him. Nicole would have to thank me big-time. I'd reeled in a major catch and dropped him right into her fishing basket.

"So tell me," I said, feeling a burst of seasonal generosity. "How is everything going for you here in New York? I mean, it must be kind of hard to come to a strange city and just strike out on your own."

"So far it's been great," he said. "I live in a warm house with a lot of character, and you and Todd have introduced me to some nice people. I enjoy my work." He spread his hands out expansively. "Life is good."

"Really?" I smiled. "I'm so jealous."

He laughed. "Why? From what I see you have a wonderful life, too. *It's a Wonderful Life*, George Bailey."

I winced. "Do I sound ungrateful? Because I don't mean to be. It's just that I'm not really where I had planned to be at thirty-one."

"And where might that be?"

I squirmed in my chair, a little uncomfortable at revealing so much to Ryan, but I was the one who opened this can of worms, and besides, it was Ryan, the mayor of understanding.

"You know, maybe engineering was wrong for you. Did you ever think of psychology?"

"You're dodging my question," he said. "What's so secretive about your life plan?"

"It's no secret. It's just . . . a little ordinary when you get down to it. But to answer your question, I thought I would be married by now, with one or two kids. I mean, the husband thing still is a possibility for me, but at the rate things are going, it's not likely to happen until I hit retirement age. Which would then rule out the possibility of kids."

He nodded. "And you haven't met anyone who could help you along with your dream?"

I let out a breath. "Not even close. Well, there was one guy . . . I really thought we were in love, but he turned out to be all facade. A big fake. He was married, lying to me about it all the time. Can you imagine? I felt so stupid . . . and hurt."

"But you haven't met the person who completes you? Your soul mate?"

I nearly spit my water out through my nose. "Don't tell me you believe in that soul mate theory? Think about it, Ryan. It's the stuff that romance novels and Hollywood films are made of—a big, fat load of marketing crap."

He shrugged. "Sure, the commercial world plays it up. But that doesn't mean it doesn't exist."

"Oh, please!" I stabbed a spoon into my frozen hot chocolate. "I can't believe I'm hearing this from a grown man. Do you really think there's one woman out there whom you're destined to be with?"

"I know it. And I think, subconsciously, you know it, too. That's why you haven't settled. You're waiting for the one." He seemed so confident and calm that I couldn't resist needling him a bit.

"And how in the world are you going to find her, Ryan? I mean, you're the math whiz engineer. What are the odds of every person on the planet finding their one and only soul mate? Talk about a needle in a haystack."

"The sad thing is, some people don't wait to find their soul mate. They settle for a more practical choice—a person they can share a home with. Now if that's what you're look-ing for, there are thousands of choices. Face it, Madison, there are plenty of men you could manage to live with and still find a modicum of happiness."

"Do you think?" I glanced around the restaurant. "In this restaurant? Or do you mean, in the world? Because I would love to meet one of them." I grinned. "I'm not getting any younger, you know. I need to start that mating thing. Preferably before Christmas, so," I gestured to the room, "do you see any likely mates here for me?"

"Go on, be facetious," he said. "But you've got to admit, if you held out all these years, there must be a reason. Sure, you could settle." He scraped at the top of the dessert. "I settled for practical when I married Katie. And she was a really nice person—just not my soul mate."

I shook my head. "So you let a marriage end because there were no fireworks?"

"It's about more than that. It's about connection. When you know it's out there, once you've felt it, falling back on a secondary relationship is like, well, it's like settling for second best. An admission of failure."

He seemed so genuinely moved that I realized I'd better back off on my criticisms. "It's a nice theory, Ryan, but I think you're setting your expectations awfully high."

"Maddy, don't you believe in magic anymore?"

I shrugged.

"The way I see it, a soul mate is the one magical thing left in life. To know there's a person out there who can bring total fulfillment . . . it's a miracle. The way Christmas brings magic to your life every year? That's how I feel when I'm with her."

"Wait a second. So you've met your soul mate?"

He looked at me, his eyes intensely blue. "Mm-hm."

I felt a little shiver. Nicole? Had I introduced Ryan to his soul mate? Whoa . . . big developments in the little PR offices of the Taft Museum. "Okay, then. Wow. So I guess you'd better move on that."

He smiled. "It's a work in progress."

I swallowed back a little mound of frozen chocolate. Ryan was zeroing in on Nicole, right on target. He was going to find his soul mate for a happily-ever-after. They would probably get engaged for Christmas.

And meanwhile, I hadn't even stumbled on someone to settle for from the "second-best" list. Suddenly my throat felt tight, and despite my best efforts to shut down the emotion, tears stung my eyes. I was a colossal failure at love. I was going to die alone. I didn't have a clue how to go about finding a true soul mate.

A brass quartet version of "Silent Night" was playing as I dropped my spoon and sobbed. The music amplified my feeling of being a lost soul in a snowy, cozy universe of soul mates who had found each other.

"Maddy, what is it?"

I shook my head and pressed my napkin against my eyes. If I weren't so overcome with emotion I'd have had the good grace to be embarrassed at getting all choked up in the center of Serendipity. "Nothing." My voice trilled like a nervous sparrow. "It's nothing."

But that was a lie. I'd just gotten a glimpse of the biggest failure of my life—the failure to connect with my soul mate. How had I wasted so much time looking for love when I should have been searching for sheer magic?

"We should get back to Bloomingdale's," Ryan said, checking his watch. "I mean, we don't want to hold up the guys at the loading dock."

I nodded, swallowing back tears. "Sure," I squeaked. Through the haze of sorrow I could still see the tiny glimmer of light at the end of the tunnel. Okay, maybe I would be alone this Christmas and every holiday season henceforth. But at least Ryan and I were making a difference with the toy drive.

Although it felt like a consolation prize, I had to remember that generosity was the real purpose of this season—the season of giving. It was a painful lesson, but I had to absorb the fact that Christmas wasn't about having a man to share my tree.

I dried my eyes, added a twenty to the one Ryan had put on the check, and stood up. "Okay," I told Ryan, "let's go play Santa."

35

December 24, 2003

"I'll bet tonight is the night," Nicole said as she ladled cups of wassail from the punch bowl on Ryan's dining room table. I couldn't help but notice that her nails were perfectly manicured, trimmed short, and lacquered with cherry red polish adorned with tiny holly leaves. All the better to show off the fat, sparkling diamond after Ryan slipped it on her finger.

"Well, good luck," I said, though I didn't really mean it. For the past few days in the office, Nicole had been harping on her Christmas gift from Ryan, so sure she was getting an engagement ring, so much in love with him, so grateful to me for introducing them, blah-blah, blah-blah, blah-blah. Her bliss was killing me.

I pushed Leo up the stairs and around the balcony that overlooked the wide-open living room.

"Nice place," he said, touching the mahogany newel post.

"Psst!" I tugged him into the game room, which was still empty as the party had just begun and most of the guests hadn't made it this far yet. "Was I that bad about Ian? That obnoxious? That smug?"

"Please, honey, don't compare yourself to that Pamela Anderson wannabe."

I sighed as we sank down on a buttery leather couch. "Why does that girl bother me so much?"

"Isn't that obvious?" he said.

I leaned back and let my head roll over the arm as I took in the room's exposed beams, the track lighting, the stucco walls hung with portraits in watercolors, the Oriental rug, the pool table. There was also some sort of video game setup in the corner, as well as a pinball machine beside the windows. For a Manhattan abode, Ryan's carriage house was downright decadent. "Does Nicole get under everyone's skin? Am I missing something here?"

"Only the fact that you're in love with Ryan."

I bolted upright. "What?"

"Didn't I tell you that eons ago? Granted, Nicole is an annoying little twit, but she was not a threat until she stole your man away."

"Ryan is not my man," I said in a hushed voice. "Yes, he's become a good friend, and I care about what happens to him. Maybe that's why Nicole irks me. I don't think she's good enough for him."

"Of course not. How could she be when you are his perfect match?"

"Leo, you've been watching too much of *The Bachelor.*"

"And you've been living in denial. Every time I talk to you, you've got Ryan on your lips. Something you did together, something he said, some intellectual topic the two of you have been debating."

"Can't I have a good friend without being in love?"

Leo sighed, clearly frustrated with me. "Then let me ask you this: Is this man the Ryan you expected when he turned up in the lobby of your building?"

I thought back to that morning when I'd been so annoyed to see him hanging behind the doorman. "No. He's changed."

"That'll happen to a person in ten years," Leo said. "How has he changed?" When I rolled my eyes, Leo put up a hand. "Just humor me with this little exercise."

"He's not as naive and cloying," I said. "He seems very straightforward, but he's got a nice sense of humor when it's put to the test, and he's incredibly generous with his time. He takes an interest in the world around him, in the people around him."

"Plus he's got a dynamite job and lives in one of the best properties on the isle of Manhattan," Leo added. "Face it, the guy is a great package, inside and out. Tell me, why would you want to palm him off on someone like Nicole? Isn't this man a keeper?"

Letting my head loll back again, I tried to picture myself with Ryan . . . having dinner with him, going on outings like our toy deliveries, engaged in intimate conversation . . .

The visions were so similar to the highlights of my last two weeks—the best moments of my recent life. I hadn't really thought through the fact that my times with Ryan would be coming to an end so soon.

I wasn't ready to give him up.

"Oh, Leo, you're right," I said as my spirits began to sink. "He's . . . I'm . . . I could love him," I admitted. "I really could love him, but it's too late now. He's all wrapped up in Nicole."

"Is he?"

"Didn't you just see? They're getting engaged. He brings her flowers. She's serving the punch at his party."

"They're in the planning stages. It's not too late, Madison. Go after your man! Stake your claim."

"I can't." I tossed back the rest of my wassail and sat up straight. "I just can't do that now, Leo. I may be a lousy matchmaker, but I will not wreck someone else's relationship just because . . . because I was slow to see something that was in my face all this time." I raked back my hair, feeling totally bummed. "What can I do?"

Leo lifted his glass in a toast. "My recommendation? Drink heavily."

I took Leo up on his advice. The wassail didn't seem to be a fast enough ticket, so I meandered over to the bar where Benjamin was mixing some martinis.

Wolf was there, stabbing olives from the jar with a holly-tipped skewer. "Madison! You must let Benjamin mix you a drink. Did you know he used to tend bar at the Iguana?"

"I poured my way through grad school," Benjamin said, tipping a frosted shaker over a martini glass.

Wolf popped an olive into my mouth. "Did you know, there's no hangover if you eat the olives?"

I chewed vigorously. "I'll hold you to it," I said, picking up one of the martini glasses. "Now there's a drink with my name on it." I took a sip and let out a little howl. "That is one kick-ass martini." I tossed it back, letting it burn in a steady stream down to my toes.

"You'd better watch that stuff," Benjamin said. "It sneaks up on you."

I popped the olive in my mouth and handed him the glass for a refill. "It's all right. I'm not driving."

"Okay," he said, reaching for the bottle of Tanqueray. "But don't blame me when you start seeing double."

"Benjamin, let me tell you. I have seen many things in the past few weeks. I've been visited by the ghosts of Christmas past and Christmas present. And b'lieve me, I don't want to look into the future."

He smiled. "Aw, the future's not so bad. I'm going to have a kid in the future, and I've gotta believe there's hope for this world."

You poor, poor man, clinging to hope, I thought as the room seemed to grow a tad darker, the pain a little bit lighter. I took another drink and suddenly my glass was empty again.

"Uh-oh!" I slid it closer to Benjamin. "Dry again. Is that why they call them dry martinis?" I giggled.

He refilled my glass from the shaker. "I don't know how you handle it," he said. "Two martinis and I'm ready for bed."

"'Sanks," I said as I stumbled off with my sexy, sexy drink.

36

Somewhere in my martini stupor I danced with Wolf to "Jingle Bell Rock." Ryan had moved his furniture to the side for a dance floor, and people seemed to be into it. The living room was perfect for dancing, with a grand cathedral ceiling, made even more majestic by the upstairs hall that surrounded the ground floor with a mahogany balcony. Wolf was a sharp dancer, very cool and low-key, similar to his personality, and with his new haircut, trimmed close on the sides with a few thick curls on top, he looked so damned cute. We stayed in the pack when the music switched to the Beach Boys' "Little Saint Nick," then "Rockin' Around the Christmas Tree."

At one point I spun around and found Ryan dancing behind me. He stepped up to me, laughing, but I felt a little sick, like I was flirting with someone else's guy. I broke away from the dance floor and went straight to the bar for a bottle of water.

Ryan came off the dance floor and waved at me. "Come on, there's something I want to show you," he called.

What could I do? I followed him over to the Christmas tree, where he picked up a silver embossed gift bag and handed it to me. "Merry Christmas," he said.

I clutched the bag, feeling like a total idiot. Ryan had gotten me a gift, and I had nothing for him. Once again, I had dissed the love of my life. "Ryan, you shouldn't have," I said.

"I couldn't resist," he said. "Go on, open it."

I reached into the bag. Nestled in white tissue was a shiny pink object—the pink sprite I had admired in Bloomingdale's Christmas shop. I lifted it, biting my lips as the thin glass wand twinkled in the light from the tree. "My ornament."

"I had a feeling it was special to you."

"But it was the last one in the store, and it was broken."

He shrugged. "There are other Bloomingdale's in the country. I ordered it online."

"Thank you," I said, feeling my throat grow thick as I thought of how hopeful the fairy had made me feel. She had been my symbol of hope, and now, ironically, I owned the lovely ornament, but there was no more hope. I'd missed my shot with Ryan. I'd dated just about every eligible male in Manhattan. No . . . from now on, the only hope in my life would be in my job, or maybe in the toy drive. I would have to channel my energies into my career and become the old spinster maiden of my floor, taking Mrs. Endicott's place.

"Are you okay?" Ryan asked.

"I need a drink. I think I sweated too much of the alcohol away on the dance floor." I kissed his cheek, trying not to let my fingers linger too long on his shoulder, but ooh, could I just savor the electricity of touching him one last time? And his scent—soap and cedar. I had to get away from him before I started crying. "Thanks again," I said, turning away.

I grabbed a bottle of red wine and two glasses and wandered upstairs, circling along the balcony, hoping to find a room with Madison-friendly occupants. The game room was now filled with men who seemed in the throes of competition. Who were they, and where did they come from? I peered at them from the doorway, then turned away and stood at the balcony overlooking the action below. Nicole stood by the tree with Ryan now, the two of them looking like a portrait for a yuppy Christmas card. He reached over and brushed a strand of blond hair out of her eyes, such a loving gesture, such an intimate gesture, I couldn't stand to watch.

Pushing away from the railing I moved on to the next room. It was a little library/den, and Jenna was stretched out on the sofa with her feet up. Sugar and Leo were behind her, examining book titles on the wall of shelves.

I stepped in and held up the bottle. "Greetings and libations!"

"For me?" Jenna grinned. "You can keep the glasses. I'll just guzzle from the bottle."

I curled onto the floor beside her. "Listen, sister, it won't be long until you're back in the saddle. When is opening day—March? April? You, me and a few cups of that godawful swill they call beer at Yankee Stadium."

"You are on," Jenna said. "You know, sometimes I look down at this huge belly and I wonder how I got here. I mean, two years ago, I wasn't even married."

I poured myself a glass of wine. "When it happened, it happened fast."

"Yeah, but you were a slow starter," Leo said over his shoulder. "How many years were you with Benjamin before you even had sex?"

"Shhh!" Jenna rasped. "Benjamin is a very private person."

Just then Ryan poked his head in through the open doorway. I steeled myself, hoping he would just go away, but no such luck. "Who's telling secrets here?" he teased.

"Jenna's about to spill the most intimate details of her life," Sugar said, coming around to the front of the sofa. "And I'm going to do the PowerPoint presentation."

"Ryan." Jenna put her hands together, as if praying. "Could you light a fire for us? It would be so cozy."

"No problem," he said, stepping over to the side of the

fireplace. He flicked the switch, and flames popped up over the logs. "It's gas."

"I love it!" Jenna applauded with her tiny hands.

"Okay, Madame Cho," Leo said. "We've set the stage, now spill."

Jenna glanced toward the door. "Okay, I'll tell you, but someone has to warn me if Benjamin is coming. He's such a private person; he'd die if he heard me talking about this."

"I'll stand guard," Sugar said, draping herself across the doorway.

Ryan sat quietly in a chair beside the fireplace. Realizing that he was staying, I took a deep slug of wine to dull the pain.

"Tell us, Jen," I said, wiping my mouth on my sleeve.

"Was he holding back?" Leo asked. "I mean, you two were just friends for like, ten years."

Jenna shook her head. "It was totally me. I was the one holding things up, keeping us apart, pushing Benjamin away. I was so sure that I wanted to be with a different kind of person. I also had rebellion issues with my parents, and I was determined to marry a non-Asian guy just to assert my independence and prove to them that I could defy them."

"So what happened?" I asked. "What finally made you realize that you and Benjamin belonged together?"

"It was at a party," Jenna said, leaning her head back on the couch. Her dark hair fanned out over the gold velvet sofa, and I was struck by how exquisitely beautiful she looked with her shiny black hair, her smooth, creamy skin, her strong, high cheekbones.

"A bunch of psychologists were talking, and someone was describing the components of a strong relationship. I was a little relaxed from drinking wine, and I remember looking across the room at Benjamin and laughing each time she made a point. By the time she was finished, I was totally choked up, tears streaming down my cheeks. That was when it hit me. I knew that Benjamin and I belonged together. I was in love with him, but I had buried that feeling because it didn't fit in with my parental rebellion."

"Tell us the components!" Sugar prodded. "What were the elements of love that made you recognize that you and Benjamin belonged together?"

"They were highly subjective," Jenna said. "Not really supported by clinical evidence."

"Which makes them that much juicier," Sugar insisted. "Spill, sister!"

"Well, let's see if I can remember," Jenna said. "Trust was a big issue. You need someone you can trust."

Through my wineglass I stole a glance at Ryan. He was certainly a person I could trust. In fact, he had asked me about trust.

"Of course I trust you! You are probably the most trustworthy person in my life."

"And some of the stuff seems like common sense," Jenna said. "They talked about finding a person who is considerate of your goals and feelings."

I remembered Ryan in my office, the way he'd picked up my gluey mummy statue, the way he'd admired the brochure I'd written.

"That's what it's about, isn't it? Making a difference. Accomplishing the goals that matter to you."

Another slug of wine. I needed it.

"And there was something else she mentioned," Jenna went on. "Something totally unorthodox. She talked about magic, about believing in the power of love. I know it sounds like so much magazine drivel, but she talked about finding a soul mate."

I turned away from Ryan and leaned against the couch, afraid to look at him, afraid that everyone would feel the charged electrons in the air around us as his words spun through my mind.

"A soul mate is the one magical thing left in life. To know

*there's a person out there who can bring total fulfillment . . .
it's a miracle."*

I poured myself some more wine as Leo and Sugar shot a
few more questions at Jenna. This environment was toxic for
me; I knew that. I wanted to leave the party, but I also knew
that would cause a bigger scene than I could handle in my
compromised emotional state. So I leaned back against the
couch and anesthetized myself, waiting for the night to end.

Somewhere in the haze someone mentioned that it was
after midnight.

"Merry Christmas!" Ryan said.

Everyone was laughing and wishing a Merry Christmas,
and I felt my face sinking into the couch as I realized how
lucky I was to be in a place that was safe and warm. If only
the room would stop spinning.

37

At some point I woke up and realized I was sleeping on Ryan's couch, but when I lifted my head I knew I was too dizzy to walk. I let my heavy skull drop back onto the gold velvet and relapsed into my semi-coma haunted by strange dreams of Ryan and Nicole.

In one dream, Nicole was wearing a beautiful white veil and a bridal gown made of newspaper that I had glued and sculpted for her. Ryan and Nicole were getting married in the small outdoor courtyard that the museum café used in summer months, except that in the dream version, the courtyard now featured Rodin's "Thinker," and I was sitting on one of the Thinker's thighs, watching the ceremony from on high.

Barry performed the service, and Nicole kept giggling and flicking back her blond hair. Ryan looked gorgeous at the altar, a sapphire prince who waited patiently for his bride to stop squealing with laughter.

From the back of the crowd, Leo turned and motioned for me to come down from my perch, but I ignored him. "What's wrong with Madison?" he asked my mother.

"Didn't you know?" Mom said, with a sad sigh. "Madison

has been burned by love. She was trying to hold herself back from emotional involvement, think things through. But as you can see, if you take too much time to think, you might be too late. Do you know what I mean?" Mom asked.

"I do!" Nicole squealed. "I do, I do, I do!" she shrieked, jumping up and down like a three-year-old.

I found myself worrying that she might tear the hem of the dress I'd sculpted for her out of old newspaper and glue—until I realized that she'd just said the words that would take Ryan away from me forever. The final vows. Oh, sh-sh-sugar!

I turned to the Thinker. "Can you believe this? Does my timing suck, or what?"

Hmm. He had to think about that.

Then Nicole was about to throw me the bouquet, but instead, I was showered by rice.

"Cut it out!" I yelled at her. When the pelting stopped, I noticed someone sitting across from me, on the Thinker's other knee. A thin man cloaked in a silky brown hooded gown.

"Who are you?" I asked, suspecting the worst as I picked rice out of my hair. "No, don't answer, I know. You're the ghost of Christmas Future, aren't you?"

He tipped back the hood to reveal golden highlighted, silky hair. "Actually, I'm Steven Cojocaru, here to find out what possessed you to create that paper gown. Although it's very Eurotrash-recycle-chic-meets-bedouin-bride, somehow, with her inimitable style, Nicole manages to pull it off."

"No! No, you can't be a celebrity guest!" I insisted, pounding a fist against the Thinker's thigh. "You need to be the Ghost of Christmas Future. And you have to tell me if it's really going to happen. Is Ryan really going to marry Nicole, or do I still have the power to change the future? Tell me, Spirit! Tell me!"

He crossed his arms. "Somebody needs a little anger

management. Besides, you should have worn the Manolo
Blahniks to the wedding. Those Chanel heels are so last
year's Oscars."

"I'm sorry." I slid off the Thinker's lap, down to the ce-
ment pavement. "But I love these Chanels, and I love Ryan,
too. That's why I need some answers about those two." I
dropped to my knees. "Spirit," I whispered, the toes of my
Chanel heels digging into the pavement behind me, "is this
the vision of what might be, or what will be?"

He lifted his chin and squinted at the crowd. "I'm not really sure, but I think I see Queen Latifah hiding behind that
potted palm, and it looks like she's sporting a new shade of
lipstick." He slid off the statue, landing like a cat in a fabulous pair of Yves Saint Laurent sandals. "Queen, over here!"
he yelled, pulling a microphone out of the deep sleeve of his
cloak.

I turned back toward the wedding party and they were
gone.

The furniture had been cleared away from the courtyard,
and a small pink object lay in the snow. I went over to pick it
up, but I saw that it was smashed.

My pink fairy ornament lay in a hundred pieces.

I woke up facing a block of winter white sunlight. It pow-
ered relentlessly into the shadeless window, though the
clock said it wasn't even seven yet.

Seven A.M. Christmas morning. I thought of Scrooge
waking up on Christmas Day, a transformed man in a world
of possibilities. If only I could be so lucky.

Stretching, I realized I felt surprisingly good for a person
who had consumed her body weight in alcohol the night before. Maybe Wolf was right about those olives. Someone had
put a fleece blanket over me, and as I sat up I wrapped the
blanket over my shoulders, since my sleeveless lace top wasn't
going to do much to ward off the morning chill.

I poked my head out in the hall. The house was still. Downstairs, the furniture had been slid back into place in the living room. For a place that had rocked last night, there seemed to be very little party damage.

Where was Ryan? I peeked toward the upstairs corner with the master bedroom. Oh, no! He was probably in there with Nicole! I had to get out of here. I dumped the blanket back on the couch, then dissolved into shivers. I couldn't make it in this skinny top. Inside the closet were boxes. Mostly books, but I managed to find one with workout clothes. I pulled out a gray zip-up sweatshirt and pressed it to my face. That smell—soap and cedar. With a sigh, I tugged it on.

I hurried down the stairs, anxious to flee but unable to ignore the desperate urge to pee. I ducked into the cute little downstairs powder room, took care of business, then faced myself in the mirror. My hair wasn't too awful, considering the night I'd had, but my mouth warranted a hazmats sign. I rifled through the sleek, recessed medicine cabinet and came up with a sample bottle of mouthwash. With a thorough rinse and a finger-combing of my hair, I could ride the subway without driving other passengers off to find seats in other cars.

I opened the bathroom door to the smell of coffee. Coffee? Eek! Was someone up? Sneaking a look into the kitchen, I detected an all clear, though the coffeepot was full. I swiped a half cup, black, just for good measure. Quietly placing my cup in the sink, I nearly tiptoed toward the kitchen door, hoping that my coat would be hanging in the hall closet with my wallet in the pocket.

Ryan was coming down the stairs, looking comfortable in jeans and a periwinkle cashmere sweater that brought out the blue in his eyes. His hair was damp from the shower, making me feel skunky despite my gypsy bath. "Merry Christmas," he said, continuing down the stairs as if I were a regular morning fixture in his home.

"Merry Christmas." Okay, I was busted. But that didn't

mean I had to ruin Ryan's morning. "I was just on my way out, but I didn't want to wake you . . . and Nicole."

"Nicole?" He arched an eyebrow. "She wasn't too happy with me when she left last night."

Nicole was gone? She wasn't upstairs snuggling in Ryan's big bed? I felt a devious thrill, then realized that was mean of me. "Is she mad because of me?" I asked. "Because you let me stay here? Well, you didn't exactly have much choice when I passed out on your sofa. But I'm sorry," I said. "I'm sure she's not too happy with me either, and tell her I'm sorry, okay? I . . . I just let things get out of hand last night and . . ." I pressed a hand to my forehead, raking back my hair. "Just tell her I'm sorry. I really am. And . . . there's more, but I don't want to make you late. She's probably mad enough already."

"I'm not going to Nicole's," he said, putting his mug into the sink. "Is that what you think?"

"Well . . . yeah." I blinked. Ouch, that hurt when my eyelids moved. "So," I scratched my head. "Where are you going, then?"

"I'm not sure I want to tell you. It's corny and dull and, Lord knows, it'll just prove that I'm fucking persistent. Which is a black mark in your book."

"Tell me," I said, following him out to the vestibule. "You know I'm stubborn. I won't back down until you tell me." Three large, black garbage bags leaned against the wall by the closet. They looked a little too neat to be party rubbish, but then Ryan was such an orderly guy I didn't question it until I saw a few bright green and red ribbons springing out of one.

"What's this?" I asked, peering into the bag. It was loaded with gifts—more than a dozen of them.

"Presents," Ryan said, slipping on his coat. "For kids, okay? The kids at Union Hill."

"On Christmas morning?" my voice creaked. "You're going to the hospital on Christmas morning?"

"I told them I'd be back," he said. "And what better time? It's got to suck, being stuck in the hospital on Christmas Day."

I nodded as my brain started to absorb the facts. Ryan wasn't going to see Nicole. He was playing Santa.

Could this guy be any kinder?

Could I be any stupider?

"Ryan, that's very kind," I said as tears formed in my eyes. The perfect man. Here I'd been dancing around him, avoiding him, calling him names and making jokes to my friends, and all along he was the perfect guy for me. "You're such a kind, generous person," I squeaked, trying to talk past the knot in my throat. Just when I needed it, I was losing my voice, probably from too much drinking and too little sleep.

"Oh, don't start crying," Ryan lamented, sinking at the knees. "You know I can't stand it when you cry."

"I am such an idiot."

"No, you're not." He hoisted a bag of toys over one shoulder.

"All this time I pushed you away. When you're just, like, the kindest, sweetest guy in the world. And I'm so stubborn, I wouldn't admit that I was falling in love with you. And now you're going to marry Nicole, after you spend Christmas Day playing Santa to sick kids. You're so wonderful and I'm just a big stubborn boob."

"No, you're not."

I sniffed. "Yes, I am."

"Okay, you are. But what was that you just said?"

"I'm a boob?"

He shook his head. "Before that. Something about falling in love with me?"

I slapped my hands over my cheeks. "I know, rotten timing, right? Oh, Ryan, for the rest of my life I will be sorry that I've been such a stubborn ass, but I swear, I won't mess things up for you and Nicole. I may be stubborn, but I'm not a total bitch."

Ryan put the bag of toys back on the floor. "I guess you didn't understand . . . Nicole tore out of here last night. She was angry with me, disappointed with her gift." He took a deep breath. "Maybe I misled her. She was expecting an engagement ring, but I told her that I wasn't that into her. I mean, I just met her a week ago."

"So you're not engaged?" I asked, my voice croaking like a frog.

"Not even thinking of it. At least, not with her."

I felt my jaw drop as I looked up at him. He stepped toward me and grabbed the zippered edge of the gray sweat jacket. "Now if *you* were to ask the question, I might think twice."

"I . . . me? After the way I've pushed you away, you would still . . . still love me?"

"You know me. I'm fucking persistent. Besides, when there's magic, it's worth waiting around for."

"You feel magic with me?" I dashed the tears from my cheeks to look him in the eye. "You feel it between us?"

"Don't you?" He leaned down and kissed me, nipping at my lower lip just a little. "I knew it the minute I saw you, trying to blow me off in the lobby of your building. We're soul mates. Don't you feel it?"

I closed my eyes and swayed against him. "I do. I didn't before. Honestly, ten years ago, I had no idea, but now, I do." I lifted my chin to take in his handsome face. "I feel it! I really do!"

His eyes burned with intensity as he lifted me into his arms and carried me over the threshold, into the living room.

"Ohmigosh!" I squeaked. "This is, like, right out of *An Officer and a Gentleman*!"

He swung me over a lamp, moving toward the couch. "Except that I'm not an officer anymore, and I've got to end this love scene in about ten minutes and get to the hospital."

"Ten minutes? What is this, drive-through service?"

"I was thinking of one of your expert blow jobs," he teased.

I slapped his shoulder. "I think I've perfected that move. A little more job, less blow."

"Can't wait."

"But we'll need at least twenty minutes."

"Fifteen?"

Cupping his smooth, handsome face in my hands, I smiled. "Okay, fifteen minutes. But let's make each minute count."

"Absolutely," he said as he lowered me to the couch, his blue eyes glimmering.

I pulled him down on top of me, reeling with joy. "Oh, God, can you believe it? What a difference one night can make. And to think that the spirits did it all in one night."

"I love you," he said. "But can we put Charles Dickens and the old boyfriends to rest? Send their ghosts packing?"

"They're gone," I squeaked. "Long gone."

"You're losing your voice."

"Shut up and kiss me."

THEY'VE MADE THEIR LISTS . . .

As the celeb obituary writer for the *New York Herald,* Jane Conner can sum up a person's life in three hundred words. She could sum up her love life in even less: Great sex = great time. Commitment = annoyance overload. Maybe it has something to do with being "overly critical," as her boss, the short-sighted idiot, put it. Being "discerning" has at least kept Jane from making the same relationship mistakes as her sister, Ricki, and best friend, Emma. Hasn't it? Now, with the holidays bearing down like a freight train from You Screwed Up-ville, Jane's about to get a second chance she never expected . . .

. . . CHECKED 'EM TWICE . . .

Ricki Conner has run her life on signs from the universe, and right now, she's looking for guidance about her boyfriend, Nate, a.k.a. Mr. Mixed Signals. He keeps reassuring her that his divorce will be final by Christmas. So why is there still no ring on Ricki's finger?

. . . NOW, THIS CHRISTMAS, NOTHING'S GOING ACCORDING TO PLAN

When the pregnancy test turns pink, it's a good sign . . . unless you've had wild ex-sex with your former boyfriend while the current one was out of town. This is not exactly the holiday gift Emma Dee had hoped for. It's bad enough that her career track at the bank has been derailed. Now, she gets to spend the season ladling eggnog for her friends and saying, oh, by the way, I'm pregnant with another man's baby— drink up, everybody! Oh well, at least things can't get any worse . . . . right?

Christmas. It's a time for going into debt, neuroses-gone-wild, dates from hell, seriously spiked eggnog, and maybe even a miracle or two. And for three women on the verge of what seems like certain holiday disaster, it just may be the season to toast the best times of their lives . . .

Please turn the page for an exciting sneak peek of Carly Alexander's new novel, THE EGGNOG CHRONICLES, now available wherever trade paperbacks are sold!

1

"People have died for millions of years and been put to rest without my shining obituaries," I told my boss over the phone. "I think you'll survive one day without me."

"Of course, of course, Jane," Marty responded in that hushed New York accent that reminded me of a younger, less hyper Woody Allen. "But first and foremost, I wanted to make sure you're okay. Ms. Jane Conner on a sick day! You, who never call in sick and rarely take vacation. Well, are you okay?"

"Fine." I pressed the hot teacup against my forehead, over my temple, against the throbbing cheek that wasn't plastered to the phone. My eyes burned like pearl onions and the network of pain inside my head was so tangled and intense, I just wanted escape. "I'd be perfect if I could have everything above the neck surgically removed."

"Oh, dear." Confusion and concern mixed in Marty's voice. "Well, that's not good at all, is it? We've got to get you into shape."

"I'm working on it." The teacup was scalding my cheek, but somehow that felt good. "I've got an appointment with an ear, nose and throat guy to zap this thing once and for all."

"Good. Very good." Sometimes Marty Baker spoke so softly I imagined he'd trained for the priesthood. It's amazing that a man as kind as Marty had risen to a position of power in the editorial pit of snakes, but I counted myself lucky to have him as a boss. Besides his mild manner he was cute in a nebbishy sort of way. He'd be a possibility if I didn't have steady studly Carter. "Good to see a specialist," he went on. "Well, okay, then. You rest up. The only questionable item is the Yoshiko Abe interview."

I switched the phone to my left ear and pressed the hot mug to my aching cheek as I remembered the Japanese violin prodigy I was slated to meet this afternoon. "Oh, right. Can you reschedule?" I wanted to sit with an adolescent musician like I wanted a hole in the head. On second thought, the hole in the head might assist in sinus drainage.

"She and her mother are flying to San Francisco tomorrow for the Klein competition, then back to Japan, so it's just got to be done today. But not to worry. I can put someone else on it. Genevieve will do it."

Genevieve? My nemesis.

"Not her," I objected, trying to avoid the image of Genevieve Smythe resting her pert little size six Pradas on my desk and laughing at my notes. "Can you give it to someone else?"

"Oren is on loan to Arts until after Chanukah, and Lincoln is on vacation. It's got to be Genevieve."

"I'll do it." I hated myself for saying it, hated that I'd spend the afternoon cajoling another pent-up prodigy instead of pampering myself in bath gels, but it seemed to be the only way to make the image of the diabolical, power-mongering Genevieve disappear from my scope. "Make the interview for three at Oscar's and I'll do it."

"Are you sure?" Marty sounded concerned. "It's not fair to you, really. If you're not feeling well—"

"Just reschedule it, okay?" I said, losing patience with

Marty's idealistic concerns about fairness in the workplace. Did he really believe in that myth?

"Okay, okay. Oscar's at three. And you feel better, okay? Let me know in the morning if you need more time to recover. We'll talk tomorrow, then."

Tomorrow. Closing my eyes, I imagined that by tomorrow I would feel better. Tomorrow I'd be able to breathe through my nose, wonder of wonders. In a few days I would wake up and not have to spend the first hour of my day hacking and snorting into a tissue. I would be freaking out from cigarette cravings and wanting to have sex with my boyfriend again. Order would be restored, damn it.

I hung up from Marty and went back to my number two priority after getting healthy—my novel. I tucked a strand of jet-black hair behind one ear and hitched my nightgown up so that I could sit in lotus position on the sofa with my laptop balanced on the triangle of legs. Since I had the day free—sort of—I had planned to crank on the novel, a work in progress that I had started writing in the middle, mostly owing to the fact that I understood the gravity of a killer first line and therefore had not yet been able to come up with one.

The first line.

Ignoring the pain in my face, I sucked the salt from the end of a pretzel stick and wondered what that elusive opening sentence might be.

Every book needs a great first line to hook the reader with subtle promises of texture and intrigue, engaging emotional involvement, poignant insights, pithy observations, and yeah, some of that romance crap, too.

"Sure, romance sells," my agent-friend Raphaela had told me. "But follow your muses. Do something different. God knows, we'd all like to read something fresh."

"Fresh," I said now over a mouthful of pretzel. "Right." So I'd have to trash the story of my ill-fated marriage and the subsequent steady stream of loveless relationships. Not that

I really cared. In the city that never sleeps, romance—especially bad romance—was so ten minutes ago.

I gnawed on the pretzel, savoring. Numm . . . burnt black on one side, fat crystals, crispy but not crumbly. With my sinuses clogged I could only half taste it, which made it less effective as a placebo: I still wanted a cigarette. Was it a mistake to quit smoking while I was trying to break into a new field of writing?

I had a good thirty pages under my belt, which my friend Emma Dee was reading for me. Thirty pages of smoking sex and cutting dialogue. As soon as I sold this book, which, of course, I had to write (a mere technicality!) I could quit my job at the *Herald* and stay home every day. I leaned back against the upholstery and focused on the pretzel taste, slightly diminished since my sinuses were blocked, but I wasn't going to let a sinus infection ruin my cushy morning at home. This was the life of a freelancer. Big sigh! Sleep in. Work in my nightie. Ignore the phone. I hadn't felt so free since my mother died nearly four years ago.

Which might sound like a terrible thing to say, but there you have it: having watched her suffer on a respirator during the last few months of her life, I'd been relieved . As the oldest child, and the only one in town at the time, responsibility for Alice's care had fallen on my shoulders during the short span from diagnosis to death—May to October. A smoker all her life, she wasn't surprised to hear lung cancer, though I think she'd hoped for a fighting chance of survival in the beginning. But two months after the diagnosis, she was told to get her affairs in order, and less than a month after that my mother, a former Poet Laureate at Columbia University, could barely rasp out a simple haiku. That summer had ticked off so quickly: the doctor's visits, the daily pilgrimages to the apartment I'd grown up in on the Upper West Side, the negotiations with health care workers and the addition of oxygen tanks and a fat hospital bed that faced the sliding glass windows. With my younger sister Ricki up in

Providence starting summer semester of grad school, I'd been thrust into the caretaker role, the loyal, local daughter who could do nothing more than be present to observe the process with a sense of alienation and helplessness.

If death is truly the final journey of a lifetime, shouldn't we have some say in planning the itinerary? I could accept losing my mother, but to see her slip gradually into breathlessness was an image that caused me pain for years.

I shuddered, then noticed the blank monitor mocking me. Quickly I typed:

Just because I haven't nailed down a plot doesn't mean that I won't.

Yes, the words still flowed for me, along with post-nasal drip. I was blowing my nose as the phone rang again. I snatched it and barked out a hello.

"Jane, it's me. What are you doing home?" It was Ricki, her voice backlit by strains of "Hark the Herald Angels Sing" and the jingle bells that chimed whenever the door of her shop opened.

"You sound like a Hallmark commercial," I told her as I balled up the tissue and tossed it into the pile on the coffee table.

"My life *is* a Hallmark commercial," she said merrily. After grad school Ricki had followed her heart and (in my opinion) a beef jerky of a man to the Outer Banks of North Carolina, where she'd opened up a shop that featured warm and fuzzy Christmas paraphernalia.

When I had visited her last August I'd felt a mixture of amazement and horror at my sister's skill in creating a Christmasland that featured holiday crafts and decorations, a myriad of exquisitely decorated trees, and an overwhelming potpourri of scented items. I was impressed by the functional items such as napkins and chair covers and potholders—all decorated with miniature Santas or angels or holly sprigs. With the smell of spiced cider and the chime of the bells, the shop transported sweaty tourists from the beach to a wonderland of Christmas nostalgia. "This shop is like a scene from *It's a Wonderful Life*," I'd accused my sister, and Ricki had swooned over the connection, adding: "I love that movie! I sell the DVD in 'Film Forest,' that section behind 'Santa's Workshop.'"

That was my sister, the Christmas junkie. I wasn't sure how her studies at Brown University had led her to this sentimental retail folly, but at least she seemed to enjoy what she was doing.

"I called the office and they told me you were sick," Ricki said. "What's up?"

"Another sinus infection. And this after I gave up smoking."

"Janey! You're smoke-free? Congrats! Was it going to be my Christmas present?"

"Don't get too excited. Right now I'd kill for a cigarette, though a butt just might kill me."

"Poor baby! Are you taking care of yourself?"

"I'm on it. This time, I'm not messing around with the GP. I'm going straight to a specialist. Got an appointment with an ENT in,"—I checked the clock—"soon. I'd better get out of here."

"Are we still on for the 'Singles in the City Christmas' dinner? I was just about to book my flight to New York but I wanted to make sure you're not planning to fly off for an interview in Belize or Paris or Prague."

"I write celebrity obits now," I said with the dull tone of a woman announcing the death of her career. Granted, in the beginning I'd been intrigued by the formula—encapsulating a life in three hundred words or less, but lately I'd become bored with it. *Dead Reporter Walking*. "My days of exotic assignments are over, at least for the time being." Not that I'd ever landed an international assignment, but it was useless to remind Ricki that my promotion to the Death Squad was a far cry from a Pulitzer nomination. The day I was hired by the *Herald*, Ricki called various Manhattan liquor stores until she located one that would deliver a bottle of champagne. She was my one-woman cheering squad; the quixotic optimist to my goth fatalist.

"So we're on for Christmas?" she asked. "I'm planning to come early this year. We can ride the Ferris wheel at Toys R Us and wait in line at FAO Schwarz. Ice-skating at Rockefeller Center. Lunch at Tavern on the Green. Dessert at Serendipity. I love New York at Christmastime!"

I pictured myself chain-smoking out in the cold while Ricki sought Christmas inside the Fifth Avenue department stores. I would need an entire carton to keep up with my sister the tourist. "I was thinking more along the lines of a stiff vodka at Firebird," I said, "but the answer is yes, book your flights. We'll do the holiday thing here."

"Oh, goody. Goody gumdrops."

"Ricki, I think the Christmas music is affecting your brain function. And what about Nate? Tell me he's not going to sulk for months because you're spending Christmas with me."

"Nate's going up to Providence to be with his kids. He'll be fine," she said. "You go, see your ear, nose, and throat guy. Feel better."

"Later," I honked, my head thick with congestion and pain. And already it was time to close my laptop and get dressed and seek help from the sinus guru. Hard to believe it was December already, but I was relieved that Ricki was coming for Christmas. She would make me drink spiced cider, watch a few Christmas videos, and mist over about that little girl who thinks she's found Prancer. Nothing wrong with having a good Christmas cry with your little sister at Christmas. Hey, what are holidays for?

Contemporary Romance By
Kasey Michaels